THE TE...
ARCHIVE

A Lost Treasure of the Templars Novel

JAMES BECKER

SIGNET SELECT

NEW YORK

SIGNET SELECT
Published by Berkley
An imprint of Penguin Random House LLC
375 Hudson Street, New York, New York 10014

Copyright © 2016 by Peter Smith

ISBN 9780451473967

First Edition: September 2016

Printed in the United States of America
1 3 5 7 9 10 8 6 4 2

THE TEMPLAR ARCHIVE

Prologue

"We are facing a disorganized rabble, nothing more. You cannot even dignify this motley collection of farmers and serfs by calling them a peasant army. I would prefer not to sully my blade with the blood of any one of them."

The man who'd spoken was standing with a group of his fellow knights near the center of a large open area of flat land, the site they'd chosen for their overnight camp. All around them, snowcapped mountain peaks contrasted with the pale blue of the sky, a low bank of clouds to the west threatening more snow later. The clear blue waters of Lake Ägeri shimmered just a short distance away from the edge of the camp.

The knights were fully armed and ready for combat, each wearing a linen surcoat bearing his armorial emblem, with the device repeated on his shield. These were essential means of identification in the confusion of a battlefield, where each man's face would be hidden inside his enclosed helmet. They were waiting for the orders from the leader of the army, Leopold of Austria, to mount their warhorses and ride as the vanguard of a force of more than ten thousand well-trained men-at-arms. Their task, on behalf of Frederick of Habsburg, Duke of Austria and Styria and King of Germany, was to smash their way through any opposition and by doing so open up the most direct route through the mountainous terrain in front of them and then drive on into Italy and seize this strategic swath of territory for the Habsburgs.

There was not the slightest possibility that his experienced, well-armed, and properly equipped fighting men could fail to prevail over the ragtag opposition that the fledgling confederates of Schwyz and Uri had apparently managed to assemble, and Leopold knew it. But even then, he had taken no chances.

The operation had been planned as a surprise attack, with his army advancing from the south past Lake Ägeri and then on through the Morgarten Pass, and he had expected nothing less than a total victory. The ace he was playing was that the obvious approach for his army to take had been from the west, passing near the village of Arth, where his spies had confirmed that the confederates of Unterwalden had already erected fortifications and had dug themselves in to prepare for the expected battle.

That crucial piece of intelligence was why he and his men hadn't done that but had instead approached from the south, effectively splitting the opposition forces. By the time the confederates of Unterwalden finally realized they had been outmaneuvered, it would be too late for them to regroup. Leopold's army would first destroy the men from the Schwyz and Uri confederates, then move on to mop up the confederate of Unterwalden.

Their opposition was, as the knight had just stated, a hastily assembled force of perhaps a thousand men, not militarily trained, and equipped with the simplest and most basic of weapons, and Leopold's men knew it. And that, perhaps strangely, was the reason for their disquiet. In an age where chivalry and the responsibilities of knighthood were taken very seriously, many of the men listening to him shared exactly the same sentiments. Sending a mounted and armored knight into battle against ordinary foot soldiers was not considered simply unsporting, but actually disgraceful conduct and entirely unworthy of a member of the warrior class.

"Perhaps our swords can remain sheathed, my brother," one of his companions suggested. His armorial device identified him as a member of the powerful Austrian Huenenburg family. "We have seen no sign of movement in their camp since early this morning, so possibly they took my advice."

Several of the other knights chuckled at this remark. They were all aware that the previous evening, on sighting the position where the opposing forces had established themselves for the night, Henry of Huenenburg had prepared a simple note, crept to within a few dozen yards of the enemy camp, then attached it to an arrow and fired it into the center of the encampment. The brief written communication had simply explained that Leopold's forces would be traveling through the Morgarten Pass the following day and advised the peasants that their best option would be to return home, put their primitive weapons aside, and not attempt to interfere with their passage.

"The problem, as I see it," Henry continued, "is that there may well be nobody over there who can actually read."

There were more chuckles from the other armed knights.

"But it is true that their camp appears to be deserted this morning," another knight said. "So clearly they must have gone somewhere, and faced with an army of this power and ability, all these experienced warriors"—he swung his arm in an expansive gesture to encompass not only his fellow knights but also Leopold's entire encampment, where the final preparations for moving out were just being completed—"their best option would definitely be to run away or hide somewhere."

"Perhaps," the first knight replied, injecting a note of caution, "but let us not forget that they do have legitimate claims over this land, claims that were actually agreed to and ratified in the past by our own Habsburg masters. Agreements that should never have been made and documents that should never have been signed, I agree, but agreements that definitely exist. Maybe we should not be quite so quick to dismiss them."

"But whatever the legitimacy of their cause, against us they are powerless. They can do nothing except create a nuisance," Henry of Huenenburg insisted. "We are a trained fighting force and we outnumber them by more than ten to one. They have no knights to face us, and they have no training and virtually no weapons. If they are stupid enough to offer any opposition, it will be a rout. But I am hoping that our march past the lake and through the pass will be entirely unopposed. Anyway, we'll find out soon enough."

He pointed to the center of the encampment, where Leopold and his most senior advisers were now clearly ready to leave.

Within twenty minutes, the entire army, appearing massive and unwieldy when scattered around the make-shift camp they'd occupied overnight, had metamorphosed into an organized fighting force, formed up into regular lines and columns, and begun a steady advance toward the shores of Lake Ägeri.

The knights, mounted on their heavily armored war-horses, led the way at a sedate walk, maintaining a slow but steady pace that the foot soldiers could easily match. Placing the knights at the head of the column was a deliberate tactic. They were essentially the heavy armor of medieval combat, virtually invulnerable in most battle situations, and the presence of such a large mounted force would almost guarantee, at least in Leopold's opinion, that the army would be able to continue its advance unmolested. Taking on a single knight, even for a large group of armed foot soldiers, would usually be suicidal. To take on dozens of them—because Leopold had ensured that his army was as strong as possible by recruit-ing knights from most of the noble families in Austria—would be nothing short of madness.

And it looked as if Leopold was right. Their overnight encampment had been only a short distance from the shores of Lake Ägeri, and within a few minutes the force had reached the water and passed along the shore, heading toward the Morgarten Pass, which lay a few hundred yards ahead. They neither saw nor heard the sound of any enemy soldiers. It was as if the entire area had been robbed of human presence, apart from the dull rolling thunder of the marching and steadily advancing army.

In front of them, the path began to narrow, but that was to be expected because of the mountainous terrain, and the knights had to spread out into an elongated line, riding only three or four abreast. That was a slight cause for concern, because along the more restricted path the armored and mounted men would have little room to maneuver. Then the track they were following swung around a rocky outcropping, and almost in that instant everything changed.

In the vanguard, Henry of Huenenburg pulled back on the reins of his warhorse as he stared straight ahead. Perhaps fifty or sixty yards in front of the advancing column, the path they would have to follow narrowed even more, a steep slope on one side and what was clearly a bog or marshy ground on the other.

But what particularly concerned him was that the track was very obviously blocked, a roughly constructed pile of rocks and tree trunks spanning it from one side to the other. The blockade wasn't particularly tall, and in all probability the foot soldiers would have little difficulty in clambering over it. But for the knights it was a different matter.

Their armored warhorses were unable to jump anything of that size, or indeed to jump at all, so the obstacle would need to be dismantled before they could proceed.

Henry reined his horse to a stop and scanned the slope above the path. He looked farther along the track as well but saw nothing to concern him beyond the blockage. No sign of a single enemy soldier.

"I think," he said to his companions, and glanced around him, "that they probably prepared this barricade to slow us down, perhaps so that they could regroup and summon reinforcements. Or maybe they intended to ambush us here but changed their minds when they saw how large our force was. It's obviously now deserted."

"It will have to be taken apart before we can advance," another knight said. "But that shouldn't take too long."

Henry swung his horse around and called out orders. Immediately the whole vanguard of knights came to a stop and then parted enough for some of the foot soldiers to move forward, heading toward the roughly constructed obstacle.

And then, before the men could move a single log from the barricade, they all clearly heard a single shrill whistle from somewhere above them. And then it was as if the hillside suddenly came alive.

Seemingly erupting from the very ground itself, a crowd of men appeared close to the top of the hill. Their motley array of clothing identified them as farmers, laborers, serfs, and peasants, and none appeared to be carrying any kind of weapon apart from a mere handful who had daggers attached to their rough belts. They stood and bellowed their defiance at the army of intruders who were defiling their lands.

Instinctively the mounted knights raised their shields, but no missiles—no swarm of arrows or thrown spears or even hurled rocks, the assault they had all clearly expected—materialized.

Orders were shouted back to the leading ranks of foot soldiers, and some forty archers pushed forward to stand between the mounted knights and the precipitous slope. The commanders had realized immediately that bowmen—or more accurately their arrows—were the only weapons the army possessed that could easily reach the ragtag opposition.

But before a single archer could loose his arrow, another whistle sounded from up the slope, and was followed just seconds later by an ominous crashing and rumbling sound that grew instantly louder.

And then the elegant simplicity and lethal effectiveness of the ambush became only too clear. Jumping and tumbling down the steep slope, gathering speed with every second, piles of rocks and cut lengths of tree trunk began smashing through the undergrowth, heading directly toward the vanguard of the invading army.

The knights, the most formidable element of the invading force, had nowhere to go. The barricade blocked their advance, and the press of foot soldiers on the narrow path behind them prevented their retreat. A handful turned their warhorses toward the bog that bordered the path, the only possible avenue of escape, but those that reached it quickly became mired in the soft and treacherous ground, the weight of the armor worn by both the knights and their horses causing them to begin sinking immediately.

And then, with a rumbling roar that was almost deafening, the avalanche of wood and rocks smashed into the helpless warriors. The bouncing rocks, some of them half the size of a man, wreaked appalling carnage on the almost stationary leading ranks of soldiers, while the tree trunks carried away the legs of the warhorses, fatally wounding the animals and tumbling the knights to the ground, where the falling rocks finished off the job.

Screams and howls of agony tore through the air as the pride of the Habsburg army was reduced to a disorganized rabble in a matter of just a few moments.

The surviving officers and knights shouted orders and counterorders, but there was no mistaking the mood and intentions of the Habsburg foot soldiers. They had just seen the most powerful part of their formidable fighting force destroyed in seconds, without a single enemy soldier coming anywhere near them. With one mind, the frightened warriors turned around to retrace their steps. But the numbers were so great, and the path so narrow, that even this caused chaos, soldiers being forced into the bog to die a lingering death by drowning or worse, while others were trampled underfoot by their panicking companions.

Then, from the vanguard of the army, a handful of surviving knights began forcing their way through the fleeing soldiers, trampling more of them in their wake, heading back toward the more open ground where they would be able to confront whatever other enemy forces had been assembled.

But even as they did so, other ambushes that had been prepared by the outnumbered and ill-equipped confederate forces were triggered. Further avalanches of rocks and logs were triggered above the track now choked with a mass of panicking foot soldiers and retreating mounted knights, decimating the invading army.

Before the echoes of the last falling rock had died away, there was renewed yelling from the hillside above the path, and just seconds later the confederate warriors ran down the slopes and fell upon their enemies. And many were carrying a new weapon, the halberd, a device that was cheap to manufacture and easy to use, and which inflicted terrible injuries on the Habsburg soldiers, both from the sharpened point at the end of the shaft and from the ax blade that could easily decapitate a man.

And when the surviving knights finally reached open ground and turned to face this new enemy, they discovered to their cost that the halberd was equally effective against mounted soldiers.

As four of the knights charged toward the ragged confederate line, the foot soldiers they were facing simply rammed the ends of the seven-foot shafts of their halberds into the ground behind them, then gripped the shafts so that the lethal points formed a row about six feet above the ground. And it wasn't just the halberds that they used. Several of the soldiers were carrying eighteen-foot-long pikes, each tipped with a sharp iron point, a much longer weapon than the lance carried by a knight.

When realization finally dawned, it was too late for the knights to rein in their steeds, and the helpless animals, carrying their equally helpless riders, slammed into the halberds. The horses died instantly as the points of the pikes and halberds drove through their armored breast-plates and deep into their chests, and the knights, the wind knocked out of their bodies by the impact with the ground, died soon afterward.

The entire engagement took only a matter of minutes. Seeing the mounted knights brought down and slaugh-tered, the surviving Habsburg soldiers abandoned both their weapons and all thoughts of combat and simply fled for their lives.

And then, when the result of the brief and brutal con-flict was no longer in the slightest doubt, six mounted men approached the scene of the battle along the track, from the far side of the rough barricade. Seeing them coming, a gang of confederate soldiers quickly began removing the tree trunks and rocks to open a passage wide enough to allow them to ride through.

The newcomers were fully armed and armored knights, each equipped with a dagger, a battle sword, and a shield, and three of them carried lances. But where they differed from the Habsburg knights, many of whom lay dead and dying on the ground in front of them, was in their shields and surcoats. All were pure white, and devoid of any heraldic device or emblem, nothing to identify them. The lack of such a symbol proclaimed to anyone who saw them that these men owed allegiance to no lord or master, and fought for no king. For whatever reason, they were their own men, independent and answerable to no one.

"The White Knights," one of the confederates whispered, almost reverently, moving to one side as he did so.

A confederate officer, virtually indistinguishable from his fellows, stepped forward and bowed before the knights as a mark of respect.

"It worked exactly as you predicted, my lord," he said.

The knight nodded and pointed behind the officer, where two confederate soldiers were holding down a wounded and dismounted knight while a third soldier drove a dagger into his eye socket through the slit in his helmet.

"That is not permitted," the knight said. "You may do what you wish with the rank-and-file soldiers, but the nobility are to be accorded special privileges. Their wounds are to be treated, and word sent to their families so that they may be ransomed."

The confederate officer glanced behind him, where the same three soldiers were steadily advancing toward another badly injured knight, and shrugged.

"You explained that to us before, my lord," he replied, "but we are few in number and so vulnerable, and we believe it important that our enemies receive a very clear message of our intent and determination. We are not interested in ransom. We are only interested in being left alone."

The wounded knight screamed once, long and hard,

his body bucking and kicking against the restraining hands of the confederate soldiers, as the dagger point was slowly pressed home; then he fell silent.

The White Knight nodded.

"As you wish," he said, his voice betraying something of the emotion he was feeling.

The Rule by which he and his comrades had lived for so long was absolutely specific: they were forbidden to engage in combat with other Christians, which was why they had taken no direct part in the battle that had just been fought. But at the same time, their order had suffered what many considered to be the ultimate betrayal, cast aside by those for whom they had always fought and for whom so many had died, and in those circumstances most of the precepts of this overriding Rule now seemed almost irrelevant.

"This is your country, not ours," he went on, "and no doubt you are better able than us to judge the situation. I merely wished to point out the normal rules of chivalric behavior."

"Thank you. And thank you, too, for your guidance and suggestions for the battle today. If we had met the Habsburgs in conflict on open ground, the result would have been very different, and for that we are most grateful."

The officer glanced behind him again, where roving teams of confederate soldiers were methodically working their way through the ranks of wounded and disabled soldiers, slaughtering each one as they reached him.

Over fifteen hundred Habsburg soldiers died that day, and such was the brutality shown by the confederate troops that many of the retreating infantryman walked into the lake and drowned themselves rather than face the swords and daggers of their victorious foes.

The confederate officer was quite right: they were sending a message, to the Habsburgs and to everyone else. A clear and unequivocal message.

"As I said, we owe you our thanks. Your arrival here was indeed fortunately timed. Will you now be continuing your journey?"

The obvious leader of the White Knights shook his head.

"We are not undertaking a journey in the way that you mean," he replied. "In fact, we have probably traveled as far as we need to. If you can find space for us here in your country, we would very much like to stay."

The confederate officer nodded briskly. "After what happened today, I am sure that that would not be a problem for anybody. I am also sure that there is much that you can teach us."

"There is, and not just about battlefield tactics. We have hard-won experience culled from two centuries of campaigns, assets that span the continent and even farther afield, and esoteric knowledge that has guided us in our endeavors. And we will be happy to share everything with you in exchange for a safe haven in which to live. That, my friend, is all we ask."

"Then you are indeed welcome, my lord. You and your companion White Knights."

1

Present day

Via di Sant'Alessio, Aventine Hill, Rome, Italy

Privacy costs money, and was a benefit that few could afford in Rome. The Via di Sant'Alessio was one of the most exclusive areas of the city, and in that quiet road privacy was both expensively purchased and expected. Very few of the properties located there displayed the slightest outward indication of what activity or activities were carried out inside them. One of these, a substantial detached building encircled by well-tended gardens behind high walls, offered nothing more than a house number to anyone who looked at it.

Inside this building it was always busy, because it contained some of the more private administrative facilities of a much more public organization that was located in a building facing the Lungotevere Aventino, not too far from the minor basilica of Santa Sabina.

One of the departments working within the building was a specialist intelligence and operational unit, a group of people who had virtually no contact with any of the other staff in the building because they had no need to do so. Their place of work was a small suite of air-conditioned rooms in the lowest level of the basement, accessed only through a steel-lined door that was permanently locked and only ever opened to allow the unit's staff to come and go. None of the other people working in the building, not even the most senior administrators, had any right of access to the basement at any time or for any reason. It formed the most private and deniable part of the Ordo Praedica-torum, was answerable to nobody, and had essentially unlimited funding. Provided, of course, that the long-term goals of the organization—goals that might appear sense-less to an outsider—were met.

In his private office within that suite, Silvio Vitale leaned back in his chair and stared with barely disguised hostility at the man standing in front of him. It was an obvious measure of the tone of the interview so far that his subordinate, Marco Toscanelli, was still standing rather than sitting in one of the comfortable leather chairs in front of the desk.

"How sure are you that they're both dead?" Vitale demanded.

He was a slim man who had a pencil-thin mustache and a deceptively friendly appearance. Deceptive because, as Toscanelli knew only too well, he could erupt without warning into violent rages that were characterized by calculated brutality and extreme violence directed against anyone who had offended him. As always, Vitale was wearing a black suit, the unofficial uniform of the organization of which he was the head.

Toscanelli shook his head. "I can't be certain of that, no. After we opened the chests in the cave, they both ducked down into the tunnel system that ran under the cave. We didn't even know that the tunnel existed, because the entrance that had been exposed once they'd shifted the rocks and timbers just looked like a hole in the ground. We tossed a grenade after them, but I don't know if they were caught in the blast or not. I had other things to deal with at the time."

Vitale nodded.

"Yes," he said frostily. "You had to take care of things like shooting two of your own men because they were too badly injured to be moved out of the cave. That brought your tally of men from this organization that you have personally executed out in the field to an impressive total of five. Not to mention the other man who you claim was killed by Mallory. And all of them, I would remind you, died on one single operation."

"I had no choice," Toscanelli protested, shaking his head. He had Italian movie-star good looks, tanned and regular features under curly black hair, but the anguish in his brown eyes was obvious and his unusually pale complexion was a sign of the strain he was feeling. He knew there was a better than even chance that Vitale would end the interview by ordering his execution, because failure was something the order never tolerated willingly. He shook his head and explained again what had happened.

"Their injuries were so severe that even if we could have somehow got them to a hospital, they would certainly have died from shock and blood loss. We had no clue that those two medieval chests contained booby traps. Lethally effective booby traps."

"Obviously," Vitale replied dryly. "But what I find interesting is that from what you've told me both Mallory and Jessop apparently guessed that some kind of device might have been built into the chests, because of the way they made their escape at the very instant that your two men opened the lids. I've seen the chests, obviously, but not the booby trap. How exactly did the mechanism work, the device that did the damage?"

"I can do better than explain it to you," Toscanelli replied, encouraged by what he thought was a subtle change in Vitale's tone. "I have one of the chests outside and I can show you precisely how it worked. With your permission, of course."

Vitale nodded assent.

Toscanelli turned, walked back to the office door, opened it, and issued a short command. A few moments later, a man walked into the office carrying a fairly small and obviously old wooden chest, the curved lid inlaid with an intricate pattern of wrought-iron decoration. He stepped forward, lowered the chest to the carpet where Toscanelli indicated, bowed respectfully to Vitale, and left the room.

"It's smaller than I had expected," Vitale said, "and it doesn't look like much."

"It's not what it is so much as what it does. And that's really impressive, in a brutal sort of way."

Toscanelli stepped behind the chest, leaned forward over it, grasped the front of the lid, and lifted it. With a faint creak from the pair of ornate hinges that were mounted on the back edge of the chest, the lid swung open, revealing an entirely empty interior.

"That," Toscanelli said, "was what we expected to happen when my men unlocked and opened the two chests. What we hadn't anticipated was this." He pointed inside the curved lid, where an intricate construction of metal had been concealed by whichever medieval craftsman had fabricated it. "And because of the weight of the chests we were certain they were full, and of course they were, but filled only with rocks, which we definitely hadn't expected."

He closed the chest again and pointed to a pair of small metal objects in the form of rings or circles, one on either side of the lid and each rising about an inch above the complex decoration.

"Obviously these aren't the original locking pins," he said. "I had these made up in the workshop here, once we worked out how the mechanism had been set and triggered."

He slid his right forefinger through one of the circular objects and pulled firmly. As the length of steel emerged, Vitale heard a very faint metallic click from somewhere within the chest, a sound that was repeated a couple of seconds later when Toscanelli removed the second pin.

Each piece of steel was about four inches long and roughly a quarter of an inch in diameter.

"With the pins removed, the holes are virtually invisible and appear to be just a part of the complex decoration on the lid. Which was obviously the idea, so that there would be no external indication of the mechanism inside."

"So removing the pins was like priming a hand grenade?" Vitale suggested. "A hand grenade with a fuse set for half a millennium?"

"Yes, though it was set, in fact, for eternity, because they'd only be triggered when somebody came along and opened the chests. Both mechanisms had obviously been very well lubricated to ensure that they stayed in good condition. And they were also protected by the chests being closed and locked and then buried underground, because both booby traps worked faultlessly. This is what happened when my men opened them."

Toscanelli again reached forward and grasped the front edge of the chest lid and lifted it back and toward him.

The moment the lid cleared the body of the chest, there was a metallic clatter and two polished steel blades scythed outward from it, the action like opening an enormous pair of scissors. The speed of the blades, clearly driven by powerful springs because of the way the chest itself rocked backward, was too fast for the eye to see, but the deadly intent of the booby trap was obvious.

Toscanelli raised the lid all the way, revealing the extent of the complex mechanism within, a mechanism that was now harmless because it had just been triggered.

"The blades are hinged at the base, but the whole

frame is cantilevered to give them extra reach," he said, pointing at one part of the structure. "When it's released, this whole section moves forward as the blades swing out. The arc they cover is wide enough to ensure that anyone standing or sitting in front of the chest will be severely injured. You saw the way the chest moved with the force of the blades deploying?"

Vitale nodded.

"When we found the chests, they were full of rocks, as I said. I think the people who hid them under the floor of the cave in Cyprus did that for two reasons. First, the rocks would give the impression they were stuffed full of treasure, to ensure that they'd be opened as quickly as possible by whoever discovered them, but I think the second reason was to give them enough weight to provide a firm base for these blades to do their work. When they were triggered, neither chest moved at all when the lids were opened, despite the blades cutting two of my men virtually in half."

"And you said the chests were locked as well."

"They were. But again I think that was just to convince anyone who found them that they contained something of great value, which would make them more eager to get the chests open without inspecting them too closely."

"Someone exactly like you, in fact," Vitale observed.

"Yes," Toscanelli replied shortly, his tone bitter.

"But as I said a few minutes ago, you told me that Jessop and Mallory took advantage of the confusion to dive into the tunnel under the cave and escape. That suggests they knew—or at least they guessed—that something was going to happen when you opened the chests, which raises all sorts of other questions."

"I have a theory about that."

"Do enlighten me," Vitale said, shifting his attention from the chest on the floor and back to Toscanelli himself.

"Back in Dartmouth, when I went up into Jessop's apartment to find out what had happened, I saw the most horrendous wounds on Giacomo's hands. It looked as if somebody had driven several large nails through the palm of his left hand and others into the knuckles of his right. He was unconscious and had bled a lot, though either Jessop or Mallory had secured his wrists with plastic cable ties, and these were acting as a tourniquet. Both our men had been armed, and the people they were facing were not, so to me the only thing that makes sense is that there was some device in the apartment that had caused these wounds."

"What do you mean by 'device'?"

Toscanelli shrugged. "I don't know. But we know Jessop must have found the *Ipse Dixit* parchment or scroll because of the search strings she used on the Internet, and it wouldn't have been just lying around somewhere. Logically it must have been secured in some kind of container, a box or something, and because of the mechanism we found inside the chests, I think that was probably booby-trapped as well. There was nothing I could see in the apartment that could have been the cause of the injuries I saw on Giacomo's hands, but there was a safe in the corner of the room, so maybe whatever it was had been locked away in there. Either that or presumably Mallory or Jessop took it away with them."

Vitale nodded slowly.

"That makes sense," he said. "But if you're right, why didn't Jessop also trigger the booby trap when she opened whatever this object was?"

Toscanelli shrugged. "I don't know, but I can guess. She's a woman, so I suppose she might have used some kind of tool to open the container rather than just her bare hands, and that could have protected her from injury."

"Or maybe she was a lot smarter than Giacomo and guessed the object incorporated a defensive system," Vitale suggested. "And then she managed to jam or disable it."

"Perhaps. But with any luck, we've seen the last of those two. Hopefully they're dead and buried somewhere in the tunnel system under that cave in Cyprus."

Vitale shook his head decisively.

"They're not," he snapped. "We know that they flew out of Cyprus the day after you left the island, and ended up in France. Then they flew in a private aircraft to a small airfield in Devon called Dunkeswell, near a town named Honiton, and then, according to one of the tertiaries who acts for us in the British police force, they drove to Exeter. According to the same man, they're talking to the police there at this very moment, presumably putting their side of the story. How well they tell it will no doubt affect how quickly they'll be released. But I'm sure they will be back on the streets soon because they would hardly have gone to the police unless they'd got their stories straight and had devised a sequence of events that ensured that they weren't implicated in any of your killings."

Toscanelli looked both surprised and extremely irritated by this information.

"So what do you want me to do about them?" he asked.

Vitale gave him a long look. "What I want done is exactly the same thing I wanted you to do originally. Thanks to your incompetence, they know too much about us and our quest and they're probably going to try to interfere with what we have to do next. So we—not necessarily you, but some members of the order—are going to have to find them and kill them."

2

"And that's your story, is it? You're going to stick with it? Is that it?"

The disbelief in the man's voice was both quite obvious and quite obviously intentional.

On the other side of the metal table, David Mallory stretched out his long legs and leaned back as comfortably as the hard wooden chair would allow. For a few moments he didn't respond, just stared up at the ceiling, which was painted the same depressing institutional light gray as most of the rest of the interview room. The color was relieved only by a lower band of cream paint that began about four feet up the walls and continued down to floor level. Much of the paint was faded, and in places small areas had been scraped or had cracked off to reveal whitish plaster underneath. It was not, by any stretch of the imagination, a pleasant place to be. But on the other hand, that was really the point.

"It's not a story, as you put it," he replied, dropping his gaze to stare again at the interviewing officer, "and I am going to stick with it because it happens to be the truth. You might not like it, but that's your problem, not mine. Unless you can prove I'm lying—which I'm not, so you can't—that's pretty much the end of it. You need to either charge me with something or let me go."

Inspector Paul Wilson, flanked by a bulky detective sergeant in plainclothes who had been introduced for the benefit of Mallory—and for the video feed from the camera positioned in one corner of the room and the twin tape recording device mounted at one end of the table—simply as Detective Sergeant Goddard, shook his head.

"Not yet, Mr. Mallory. You're a long way from walking out of here."

"So charge me."

"We might do that," Wilson replied, looking down at a surprisingly bulky file open on the table in front of him. "We just might do that. Let me just refresh your memory about what's happened over the last couple of weeks. When we responded to an emergency call from your girl-friend's apartment in Dartmouth, a call that you have admitted making, our officers found three dead men there, and I still don't understand how you can claim to have had nothing to do with that."

Mallory eased forward slightly. "You really haven't been listening to me, have you? To anything I've said?

I've already told you, at least six times, that Robin Jessop is not my girlfriend. The first time I met her was the same day that your people found those three bodies. I've never denied being there, and I told you I made the triple-nine call. But as I've also told you numerous times, when we left the building the three Italians were still alive. A bit battered and bent, I grant you, but undeniably still in the land of the living. And I would also remind you, when Robin and I were attacked by them, we reacted purely in self-defense. We incapacitated them, nothing else."

DI Wilson looked completely unconvinced.

"You're fairly big and you look quite fit, Mr. Mallory," he replied, "and I've no doubt that you could probably have subdued one of those men, but I don't buy the idea that you and Miss Jessop, who at best can be described as petite, could have incapacitated—as you put it—three heavily built men, all of whom you claimed were carrying pistols. I know," he continued, as Mallory opened his mouth to object, "that you told us she has some martial arts skills, but I doubt if that would be anything like enough to do what you claimed."

Mallory laughed. "I never said that Robin Jessop had 'some martial arts skills.' What I actually said was that she's a martial arts expert. There's a vast difference. She holds the equivalent of a black belt in aikido and karate, and I've never seen anyone move the way she can. But don't take my word for it. Just put her in a room by herself and then send in one of your biggest and most expendable police constables with instructions to attack her. I can guarantee that in less than two minutes he'll be lying flat on his back, with bits of him broken in all sorts of interesting and painful ways."

Wilson still looked doubtful.

"Perhaps," he said, "but even if that were true, it still doesn't explain the injuries one of the men suffered to both his hands."

"Not only do you not listen to what I say, Wilson," Mallory snapped, his patience rapidly running out, "but you also don't listen to what Robin has told you. Or if you did listen, you didn't understand. When we came back to Britain, just about the first thing we did was report to the police station here in Exeter. This police station, in fact, where I've been ever since, let me remind you. We both agreed that it was essential we told you the unvarnished truth about what happened. Neither of us wants anything like this hanging over our heads. We have our lives to get on with. So I absolutely know that Robin has already told you about the book safe, that medieval casket with a hidden antitheft device built into it. One of the intruders picked it up and opened it with a paper knife, and that triggered the release of the two sets of spikes. It was those spikes that ruined his hands, and it was that injury which gave us a chance to overcome him and the other man. We can show you the book safe if you want to inspect it. Enough of his blood is probably still on it for you to get a positive match from it."

Wilson didn't respond for a moment, just studied what looked to Mallory like a witness statement in the file in front of him. "Miss Jessop did say something along those lines, but all that proves is that you got your stories straight before you came to the police. Nothing else."

"We didn't need to get our stories straight, because we're both telling the truth, something that I doubt you'd recognize if you woke up sleeping next to it."

Mallory saw the beginnings of a grin appear on Goddard's face.

"Look," Mallory said. "I've got better things to do than sit here watching you try out all the techniques you learned in the Complete Idiot's Guide to Police Interrogations, or whatever book you used to polish your alleged skills."

Wilson's lips tightened in cold fury as he listened to Mallory.

"And there was another dead man," the detective inspector said, carrying on remorselessly, "shot through the chest at close range and his body left in a wood near Exeter. I suppose you still claim to know nothing about that, either?"

Mallory nodded. "You're absolutely right. I know nothing about that. If you think you can prove I'm lying, charge me, and then we can both watch as my barrister rips you to pieces in court. If it ever gets that far, which I doubt, unless the Crown Prosecution Service turns out to be even more incompetent than usual."

"And then there's—"

But Mallory interrupted him before he could even finish the sentence. "Look, I've told you the truth and I'm quite sure that Robin has as well. But I'll just tell you yet again. The short version. The version I've already told you about a dozen times so far. When those two men turned up in Dartmouth waving automatic pistols at us, we had no idea who they were or what they wanted. They forced us to climb up the staircase into the apartment, and then they started asking questions about some Internet searches Robin had done. Questions about an ancient piece of parchment she'd found in among a load of old books she'd bought as a job lot. We thought it was just a curiosity, a bit of text referring to something that happened nearly a thousand years ago, but for those Italians— and you've already told me you've confirmed their nationality—it was much more important. It was something their organization had been trying to find for hundreds of years. The piece of parchment was hidden inside that book safe, and they made it very clear, in my opinion, that they were going to take it and most likely kill us in the process. We both knew the only chance we had of walking out of that building was to hope that the medieval antitheft device would work. It did, and the moment those spikes slammed into the first Italian's hands, Robin knocked out the other man and we tied them up."

Wilson nodded.

"We will definitely want to examine the book safe that you claim did so much damage to this man," he said, "but why didn't you call the police right then, as soon as you'd disarmed them, and wait for us to arrive?"

"That's very simple. We wanted to live. When that first man pointed his pistol at me at the bottom of the stairs, I saw the lights flash on a Range Rover parked down the street, and one of the two men facing us gave a wave as it did so. That meant that we weren't facing two armed men, but most probably three, and we thought our best bet was to get out of the apartment and take our chances on the street, rather than hope that the police would turn up before the third man decided to join the party. The only reason we'd been able to overpower the first two was what happened when one of them opened the book safe, and that was a trick we could only use once. So yes, I made the triple-nine call. We waited for the sound of sirens and then we legged it."

"And the man outside the apartment, presumably the third man from the car, who also ended up dead. What happened to him?" Wilson demanded.

"When we opened the door to leave, he was just standing there. He was as surprised to see us as we were to see him. But Robin doesn't just move quickly; she thinks quickly as well. She just stepped up to him, threw him over her shoulder, and dislocated his arm for good measure. We tied him up as quickly as we could and then ran."

"And you'd picked up one of the pistols the Italians had been carrying? For your own protection?"

Mallory grinned at Wilson before he replied.

"I don't believe I told you in any of my statements that either Robin or I had any kind of weapon," he said. "Though it might have been quite useful if we had been armed. Somebody else, presumably another member of the gang, chased us through the streets, and we know he was carrying a pistol because he shot at us. Luckily he missed and we got to my car before he caught up with us. That's how we managed to get away."

Wilson stared at him levelly. "The forensic evidence that we've collected from Dartmouth proves that pistols were definitely fired on the streets that night. Note that I said 'pistols,' not 'pistol.' The cartridge cases we've recovered show that two weapons were used, not one."

"I have no idea how that could have happened," Mallory said, adding another blatant lie to his mental tally of untruths. But he was very well aware that unless the police could prove he had used a weapon, which they couldn't because it would have meant catching him with one in his possession, he was fireproof. "Maybe I was wrong, and there were two men with pistols chasing us. As I told you before, I only saw one."

"You do know that I don't believe you."

"What you believe is up to you, Wilson. I've told you what happened. If you can prove differently, you'd better get on with it. Anyway, the point is that we incapacitated both the men in the apartment, and the third man who was waiting outside the building, and then we ran for it. You've told me that all three of these men were then shot execution-style through the head. And I've told you they were still alive when we left. If you can prove otherwise, I suggest you do so."

Mallory leaned forward and rested his arms on the table.

"Look," he said, sounding exasperated, "Robin is an antiquarian bookseller. I'm an ex-policeman and now an IT consultant. We only got together because the parchment Robin found in that book safe was encrypted, and I've got an interest in codes and ciphers. We had no idea, no clue, that what we'd found was of anything other than academic and maybe some historical interest. We certainly didn't expect to be facing half a dozen armed Italian thugs who wanted to take it away from us and, incidentally, kill us in the process."

Wilson leaned forward as well, matching Mallory's gesture. "How do you know there were six of them?"

"I don't. I'm just guessing, and I'm quite good with basic mathematics. You know, two plus two. That kind of thing. We knew about the three in Dartmouth, because we saw them, and you told me about another man killed near Exeter. I presume he was a part of the same gang. That makes four, and we were chased by a fifth man through the streets of Dartmouth. If your forensic people are right, and there were two men with guns running around that night, then that's your half dozen."

"Very clever, Mallory," Wilson snapped, realizing that his suspect had neatly sidestepped the trap he had set. "So how did you know that they intended to kill you?"

"Again, I didn't. But I searched both the men in the apartment, and they were each carrying a suppressor as well as a loaded Beretta pistol. You could argue that the weapon was just to frighten or intimidate us, but the suppressor adds a whole new dimension to the situation. The only function of a suppressor is to muffle the sound of a shot, so logically they must have been intending to use their weapons. I think their orders were simple enough. They were supposed to recover the parchment and then kill us to make sure that their secret stayed safe."

"Orders? Orders from whom?"

"I have no idea," Mallory said. "But their identical appearance, carrying identical weapons, suggests to me that they were a team, acting on behalf of somebody else, or maybe some organization. But I've no clue who or what."

Mallory leaned back, then pointed at Wilson.

"You know as well as I do," he said, "that you're looking for means, motive, and opportunity. I grant you that we had the opportunity to kill those three men in Robin's apartment, and if we'd taken one of the pistols, we had the means as well. But what possible motive would we have had? We'd already incapacitated all three of them. If we were going to kill them, why didn't we just do that instead of taking the time to tie them up? It's a lot quicker to shoot somebody than tie their wrists and ankles together.

"As I told you, we'd never seen these people before, and at first we had no idea what they wanted. But do you really think that we would have made a call to the police, a call that would immediately be traced to Robin's apartment, if we'd already decided to shoot them? Why would anybody call the police and then commit murder? That makes no sense whatsoever to me, and I think that any reasonably competent barrister could quite easily convince an averagely dense jury of our peers that it makes no possible sense to anyone else, either."

Wilson looked back at the file.

"You claim that all three men were armed," he said, and Mallory nodded, knowing exactly what was coming. "When we searched the bodies, one of the men inside the apartment had an unloaded pistol in his pocket, while the other one had a magazine and bullets. The man outside had no weapon, though a loaded pistol was found on the ground at the bottom of the staircase."

"I already told you what happened. Once she'd disarmed the third man, Robin kicked his pistol off the balcony and down to the ground. That seemed like a good idea, to separate the bad guy from his weapon."

"You did tell me that, and maybe that is what happened," Wilson said. "At least that bit of your story does make sense. So who disarmed one of the two men inside the apartment? Who took the second pistol?"

"There are two answers to that, Wilson. Me, and I have no idea of his name. I've already told you, several times now, that once we'd incapacitated the two Italians we searched them. Each was carrying a pistol, a suppressor, and loaded magazines. We didn't know who they were, though by that stage we thought we knew what they wanted, and I guessed that the easiest way to stop them coming after us was to give the British police force a cast-iron reason to hold them. That's why I put an unloaded pistol in the pocket of one man and the magazine and bullets in the other man's jacket. I left the other weapon on the desk, well out of their reach. I guessed that having those objects in their possession would result in their arrest as soon as the police arrived.

"But what happened after that, I didn't know until we ran into that Italian in the cave in Cyprus. He actually admitted to us, as you've already heard in the recording I made on my mobile phone, that he climbed up to the apartment, found the men unconscious, two of them with incapacitating injuries, and executed them himself because he already knew that the first police car was only seconds away from the apartment. He had no time to get them out, and he obviously didn't want the men to be in any position to explain what they'd been doing."

Mallory spread his hands in a kind of "I told you so" gesture.

"That's it," he said. "That's my story, and that's the truth. What you need, and what you haven't got, is the slightest shred of proof, or any kind of evidence at all, to link us to any of these murders, or the slightest hint of a motive. Even you need at least one of those."

Wilson shook his head. "But that's not everything," he said. "There's also the matter of Miss Jessop failing to report to the police after she knew that the bodies had been found, although she definitely knew that we wanted to interview her. The telephone call she made to her shop was recorded by us, and she was told then. That could be considered a serious and deliberate obstruction of a police investigation."

"Now you're just clutching at straws, Wilson. In fact, she wanted to come in and talk to you, but I convinced her that it would be a really bad idea, so if you want to go that route I'm the one you should be charging."

"And why did you stop her?"

"Because I knew exactly what would happen if she did. I know precisely what 'assisting the police with their inquiries' actually means in police-speak. She'd have been arrested on suspicion of murder and shoved into a cell somewhere while you lot buggered about trying to find enough circumstantial evidence to justify taking the case to the CPS. There are quite enough innocent people locked up in British prisons without adding Robin Jessop to the list."

"That's a very serious accusation, Mallory."

Mallory noticed that the "Mr." had been dropped, a sure sign that he was getting under Wilson's skin. "It's not an accusation. It's a statement of fact. The British police have a long history of fitting up people for crimes they didn't commit, just so they can close cases and go down to the pub for a celebratory pint. You know that I was a copper, so I know exactly how the system works. And the reason I left the force was that I was on the receiving end of a serious and organized attempt to fit me up for something I didn't do. So don't even think about preaching to me about British justice, because I know it's just a joke."

Wilson looked slightly stunned by the vehemence in Mallory's tone. "We could still charge her with obstruction."

"Good idea. Why don't you go for it? She'll get a slap on the wrist and you'll look like an idiot, though that'll just be a confirmation of what most people probably already think."

"Then there was the matter of the aircraft you stole."

Mallory shook his head. "We didn't steal it. We just borrowed it. And when we'd finished with it we returned it to the airfield, as you already know. We even topped up the fuel tanks. Has the owner lodged a complaint?"

"Not as far as I know."

"Then what's the problem? If he's happy, where's your case? And before you go any further, remember that I know all about PACE, the Police and Criminal Evidence

Act, and that means I know exactly what you can and can't do. Your time's up, so what you can't do is hold either of us any longer unless you can dream up a halfway-convincing charge. If you could do that, you'd have done it already. The bottom line here is that you've got nothing to hold either of us on, and you know it."

Mallory leaned back again and shook his head. "But what you do now know, because I've told you, several times, is exactly who shot those three Italians, or four Italians if you count the one you said you found in the wood. I gave you the photograph I took of the killer in the cave on Cyprus, and the audio recording I made on my phone at the same time. Robin also made a recording, so you've got two separate copies. He was holding a gun on us, as the photograph clearly shows, so there was no coercion by us, and he freely admitted what he did. He's the killer and he's the man who should be sitting in this seat, not me."

"I don't dispute that for a moment," Wilson said, exasperation evident in every syllable. "But trying to identify him from that image is virtually impossible. We've run a check through Interpol, but he's not on any of their databases, and the Italian authorities simply aren't talking to us. Either they genuinely have no idea who he is and don't want to admit it, or their bureaucracy is even more chaotic than usual."

"There could be another reason," Mallory suggested.

"What?"

"I think they could know exactly who he is and who he works for, but because his employer is a powerful organization, the authorities may not wish to reveal this information, to you or to Interpol or anyone else. Just think about the timeline for a moment. Robin ran those searches on the Internet when she recovered the parchment, and within a matter of a few hours six—or however many it really was—Italian thugs turned up and started roaming the streets of Dartmouth carrying pistols and suppressors and looking for her. All three of the men who were killed at Dartmouth were holding diplomatic passports, according to you, so that in itself lifts this crime out of the usual league.

"And all that implies—or at least it does to me—that some group in Italy is running sophisticated Internet analysis software, and is then able to dispatch a group of professional killers, probably in a private aircraft, to another country to recover the relic. This wasn't some off-the-shelf operation run by a handful of amateurs. This was a professional operation, run by a professional group with very deep pockets. And that means your chances of finding them are pretty much nil."

"Then we're screwed," Wilson said bitterly.

"In a nutshell," Mallory agreed, "but I'm pleased to say that it's your problem, not mine." He stood up. "Now, unless you can think of some other reason to waste my time, I'm walking out of here."

3

Toscanelli nodded.

"I'll be very happy to take care of them," he said, relishing the thought of finally eliminating the irritating English couple. "I'll get a flight organized, unless you've already booked something for me?"

"Not yet," Vitale said. "As I said, I do want them dead, but not necessarily immediately, not necessarily killed by you, and also not necessarily in Britain. We've had our experts looking at the chests ever since you brought them back from Cyprus, and none of them have so far found any clue or indication about where we should be looking next. It is just possible that if our people fail to solve this riddle, Jessop and Mallory might do the job for us. They've proved themselves to be quite resourceful so far, so it's possible that they'll see some marking or pattern in the design of the metalwork or elsewhere that has eluded us. And if they do, we have to be able to follow them and take whatever they find."

"But we have the chests," Toscanelli objected, "and they don't."

Vitale shook his head. "I almost wish they were working for me, because I'm quite sure I wouldn't have to explain every single thing to them, the way I do with you. Don't you remember something that happened in that cave when your men opened the chests? You even mentioned it in your report, though clearly you didn't realize its significance."

Toscanelli looked blank, and then his face cleared.

"The flash of light? Do you mean that?" he ventured.

"Of course I mean the flash of light. What did you think it was? Some kind of incendiary device the Templars left there over half a millennium ago? Something like that? Eh? Work it out."

Toscanelli looked confused.

"It was the flash from a camera, obviously," Vitale snapped, losing patience. "Nothing else makes sense. One of them, maybe both of them, had either a camera or a camera phone, and I'm certain they would have been taking photographs of the entire process, from the moment they uncovered the chests at the bottom of that hole. Don't forget that Jessop is an antiquarian bookseller. With her academic background and in that profession, she would appreciate the importance of documenting what they'd found, step by step."

"So you think they've got photographs of the chests, of the patterns in the metalwork?"

"Of course they have. It's obvious. That's not quite as good as having the chests themselves, but it's the next best thing. Make no mistake, Toscanelli, those two are still in the race, and they will have to be taken out eventually. But right now it's more important to work out where the trail leads us next, and it's just possible that they might help us. Unwittingly, of course. I've ordered surveillance to be started on the girl, because I think she's the key, with her background."

As Vitale finished speaking, there was a knock on the door and moments later a junior member of the order walked in, carrying a sheet of paper on which was a photographic image and a block of text. He handed it to Vitale, bowed deeply and respectfully, and then withdrew.

Vitale glanced at the picture, looked up at Toscanelli, still standing in front of his desk, and then read the text.

"I will still want Jessop and Mallory dead," he said after about a minute, "but it almost certainly won't be you who kills them. Or not if they stay in Britain, at least."

He turned the paper round so that Toscanelli could see it. "I think that proves the truth of what I said about them earlier."

Toscanelli peered at the paper, his attention drawn to the photograph on the page. With a start of surprise, he realized he was looking at a picture of his own face, and the unmistakable background was the wall of the cave on Cyprus in which the abortive quest had come to an end.

And in that instant he decided that, no matter what Vitale wanted, Mallory and Jessop were as good as dead. He was quite certain that the order's experts would be more than capable of working out where they should now be looking for the treasure of the Templars, the relic that had been lost for the better part of one millennium. There was no way, in his opinion, that anyone could reach the right conclusion from just looking at photographs. The clue was hidden somewhere in or on the chests. The order had them, and that was all that mattered. Toscanelli had contacts, and if Vitale wouldn't send him to do the job himself, he would make his own arrangements.

"Not only did the two of them certainly take photographs of the chests," Vitale continued, "but one of them also managed to snap a picture of you in the cave, presumably at the precise moment when you ordered your two men—or to be absolutely accurate, *my* two men—to open the chests."

He tapped the sheet of paper. "This has been sent to us by one of our supporters, one of our tertiaries, who is a senior officer in the British police force covering the county of Devon in England. Obviously Mallory and Jessop released this image to the police, and according to this statement you are wanted for questioning about the murders of three Italian businessmen in Dartmouth and another one near Exeter. Apparently the British police have not only your photograph, but a confession to the first three of those killings *in your own words*, secretly recorded by Mallory while you were in the cave, holding him and Jessop at gunpoint and presumably gloating over your own cleverness. Misplaced cleverness, obviously."

Vitale stared at Toscanelli, the hostility in his gaze unmistakable. "The only thing—quite literally the one single grain of comfort—that you can salvage from this is the fact that the British police still don't know your name. Though frankly I'm very tempted to put you on an aircraft to London, then tell them who you are and get rid of you permanently that way."

Vitale held Toscanelli's gaze until the younger man finally looked away.

"The only thing that's keeping you alive, Toscanelli, is the fact that you've had more contact with these two people than anyone else, so we can at least expect you to recognize them if you see them again. The men who survived the encounter in the cave on Cyprus saw them, obviously, but none of them saw them clearly enough to guarantee that they could identify them in the future. Perhaps," Vitale finished coldly, "they were somewhat distracted by the sight of their comrades being cut in half by the booby traps hidden in those two chests. Booby traps that you weren't smart enough to guess were there."

Vitale gave a dismissive gesture, then pointed at the open chest on the floor in front of his desk.

"Get out," he snapped, "and take that lethal box with you. And just make sure our archivists and researchers find whatever clue is hidden in it or on it."

"And if they can't?"

"Don't tempt me, Toscanelli. If this search stalls, then I don't have much further use for you. I might just get you to open that chest again, but this time I'll have you sitting in front of it with a video camera running. As an example to anyone else in the order who offends me or proves to be as incompetent as you apparently are."

4

Just over two hours later, Mallory braked his Porsche Cayman to a standstill in an open-air parking lot, purchased a ticket for an hour at the machine near the entrance, placed it on the dashboard where it would be clearly visible, and then strode away down the street. It was lined with shops of various kinds, charity shops being in the majority, as was the case with so many British high streets after the recession, but he ignored them all. He knew exactly where he was going.

On a corner about a quarter of a mile away and fairly close to the city center, he pushed open the door of a café, glanced around, and then walked over to a table by the back wall where a slim, pretty girl with short dark hair was studying something on the screen of a small tablet computer, an empty coffee cup and a small plate in front of her, a scattering of crumbs on it.

He put his computer bag down beside the table, retraced his steps, and bought two coffees at the counter, then pulled out the chair opposite her and sat down.

"You certainly took your time," she said, lowering the tablet and nodding her thanks for the fresh cup.

"It was Wilson," Mallory replied. "He's like a bloody terrier, just wouldn't let go. He kept on digging and probing, looking out for inconsistencies. I really thought he was going to hold me on suspicion of something, just because he's got four unsolved murders on his hands, and no halfway believable suspects anywhere in the frame apart from the two of us. In the end, I started insulting him, trying to make him angry, because I thought that might make him a bit less critical of what I was saying."

"You mean he might miss some of the lies you were telling?" Robin Jessop inquired sweetly.

Mallory grinned at her, and lowered his voice.

"Technically," he said, "I wasn't actually telling lies, just not telling the entire truth, which isn't the same thing at all. The only actual lie I trotted out during that entire final interview was when he asked me what I knew about a dead Italian lying in a wood near Exeter, and I said I knew nothing at all about it. Obviously we both know what happened because we were there when he died, but apart from that our stories have stuck pretty closely to the truth all the way through."

"Well, it worked, because you walked. And here you are." A sudden thought struck her. "What about your car? It is still in the police pound?"

"No. It's in the car park just down the street. As far as

I can tell, that Italian thug didn't damage it while he was driving it, and I even got back the original key, so I guess he just dumped it in some back street after we'd got away from him, and probably left the key in the ignition."

Robin nodded and smiled. "If he did, you were really lucky that the woodentops found it before some local tea leaf got his hands on it. Unattended cars with the keys in the ignition have a really short life around here. Porsches especially, I would have thought."

"I know. But the Italian did leave me a kind of present."

Robin looked quizzically at him, but didn't respond, and Mallory looked around cautiously before he said anything else, again ensuring that his words could not be overheard by any of the other patrons of the café or the man behind the counter.

"Tucked away neatly under the driver's seat," he said, "was one of the Beretta pistols that all those Italians seemed to be carrying, along with three spare magazines, all fully loaded. That was probably the weapon he used to kill the three men in your flat. He probably left the pistol in the car in the hope that the police would find it and that would provide a definite link between me and the murdered men. A link I'd find very difficult to disprove."

"But why didn't they find it? Don't the police search stolen cars that they recover?"

Mallory shook his head. "That's a slightly gray area. Strictly speaking, in order to search the vehicle they need either permission from the owner or a search warrant. With stolen and recovered vehicles they sometimes get around that by claiming to be looking for clues to the identity of the person who nicked it. And if, during that search, they find some marijuana or crack cocaine or anything else that's interesting from a legal—or rather an illegal—point of view, they'll happily charge the owner of the vehicle with whatever offense they think they can make stick.

"If the plods had found the pistol, then I would certainly be sitting in a cell right now, and quite probably so would you. The only favor that Italian did me was to tuck the weapon well out of sight so that it was invisible to anyone looking into the car, or even driving it, but making sure that anything more than the most casual inspection of the vehicle would find it. And obviously nobody did carry out a check."

"I'm amazed that Wilson didn't order the car to be searched."

Mallory smiled again. "That's the thing, you see. Traffic officers are the lowest of the low. Even other police officers call them 'black rats.' The detectives are at the other end of the scale, and officers who specialize in murder investigations are another few levels above that, right at the top of the tree. Most detectives won't sully their reputations by actually talking to traffic officers, and the reverse is also true. There really can be that much of a lack of communication between the different sections. And there's another factor as well that would have muddied the waters."

"What?"

"The Porsche isn't actually registered in my name," Mallory pointed out. "Just like you, I have an accountant, and when I told him that I was going to buy a fairly expensive car he explained that there were a couple of helpful tax breaks I could use if I bought it in the name of my company, rather than personally. So that's what I did. If by any chance Wilson had decided to take a look at the list of vehicles held by the Exeter nick, my name wouldn't have appeared anywhere, only the name of a small and obscure IT outfit down in Cornwall. So I'm pretty certain that he would have had no idea my Porsche was sitting in the police pound while he was trying to persuade me to confess to a bunch of crimes that I genuinely hadn't committed. Because if he had, I'm absolutely convinced that men with latex gloves and wearing white overalls would have been scrambling all over it, just in case they managed to find something to put me in the frame."

"What have you done with the pistol? Not left it in the car, I hope."

Mallory shook his head. "Right now it's in a left-luggage locker at Exeter Airport, wrapped up in a track suit and inside a sports bag I found in a charity shop. I'll collect it later and find a better place to hide it."

"Should we just dump it somewhere? Get rid of it completely?"

"Not yet, because I don't think this is anything like over. I like the idea of having a weapon or two available, just in case the Italians decide to pay us a return visit to try to finish off what they started. And we've still got that other Beretta stashed away, the one we brought back from France in the Cessna you kind of borrowed from your pal Justin when he wasn't looking."

"I hadn't forgotten. And you're probably right. Being

armed is no bad thing, bearing in mind what we've been through already. So what next?"

"That all depends," Mallory replied, "on whether we can work out the next clue Tibauld de Gaudin or Jacques De Molay left for us. If we can't do that, then we're going nowhere."

Robin nodded and turned her tablet computer round so that he could see the screen. On it was a detailed image of an ornate piece of metalwork overlying obviously old wood, the metal formed into swirls and curves and intricate shapes. "The good news is that the pictures we took of the lids of the two chests we found in Cyprus are surprisingly good quality, bearing in mind we were only using the cameras in our mobile phones. But the bad news is that the patterns just look like decoration—complex and intricate decoration, granted, but just decoration—to me. I simply don't see anything that could be a clue to help us decipher the next section of the manuscript."

Mallory used his finger and thumb to alter the size of the image on the screen, zooming in to examine particular sections of it, and then widening the field of view to look at the entire image.

"I've been going boss-eyed looking at those pictures ever since the rozzers let me walk out of the station," Robin said, "and I can't see anything useful in them."

"But there has to be something," Mallory insisted. "Nothing else makes sense. The trail led us to that cave on Cyprus, and apart from the chests there was nothing else in there. No markings or signs of any sort. Which makes sense, because if there had been carvings or something, that might well have prompted other people to start exploring it years earlier. As it was, we only discovered the chests because you spotted that pile of weathered stones inside the cave. Stones that shouldn't have been there. Most people—including me—would probably never have seen what you saw. The chests were so well hidden that if there really was a clue to the next part of the quest anywhere in that cave, it had to be either on or in those two wooden boxes."

"Luckily, or perhaps unluckily, we never got to see inside them," Robin said. "But suppose the clue, whatever it was, was inside the chests? That would make sense, because the Templar knights who set the trap could then be sure that whoever found the chests would have to bypass the booby trap, those lethal blades, and get the chests open before they could decipher the clue or clues. It would be one more test that would have to be passed."

Mallory nodded slowly.

"Maybe," he agreed, "but there could be another way of looking at it. We know the chests were filled with rocks, and perhaps that means there probably wouldn't be a carving or something on the inside of them, because the sheer bulk and weight of the rocks might damage it and make it unreadable. And I still believe whoever started this quest or whatever you want to call it intended that the trail should endure. He would have been hoping that the Templar order would somehow be revived, emerge from the darkness and disgrace forced on it by Philip the Fair, and resume its former power and authority. So perhaps he planned that a Templar who discovered the chests would have assumed they contained some kind of trap or device, and wouldn't have risked trying to open them. And in that case, the clue—whatever it is—would have to be visible on the outside. Well hidden, obviously, but certainly visible, which means it would have to be somewhere in the scrollwork."

Robin looked completely unconvinced.

"I suppose you could be right," she said, the tone of her voice making it clear she thought this a most unlikely possibility. "And if you are, then the only way we're going to find it is if we look at these images on a full-size computer screen, not this microscopic tablet. The only bit of good news, I suppose, is that we both took several photographs of the chests when we found them, so if there is some hidden meaning lurking in the metalwork, there's a fighting chance we'll be able to see it on at least one of the pictures."

Mallory finished his coffee and glanced at Robin, who nodded. She slipped the tablet computer into a leather case and put that in her handbag. Then they both stood up and walked out.

5

As they left the café, a man who'd been sitting at a table against the opposite wall lowered his copy of the *Daily Mail* newspaper and looked thoughtfully at their retreating backs. He was in every way average, and that was, strangely enough, his strength, his edge. Average height, average build, average and unmemorable features, his clothes carefully chosen so as not to stand out in any way in a crowd.

He was a member of one of the smallest professions in the United Kingdom: a private inquiry agent. Unlike America, where according to some reports you could find the office of a "private dick," a PI, on almost every street corner, in Britain they were comparatively rare. Those who did exist tended to work either in the commercial sector, checking for an insurance company that one of their policyholders who claimed to have broken his back at work wasn't in fact playing tennis every afternoon, that kind of thing, or out gathering evidence for suspicious wives that their husbands' excessive overtime was being spent in hotel rooms with secretaries rather than analyzing and reviewing important balance sheets, which was what these errant males frequently claimed. Or occasionally vice versa, when husbands started to suspect that their wives were enjoying entirely different kinds of ball games with their tennis coach than might be expected.

Gary Marsh—that was his real name, though it wasn't the name printed on the business cards tucked inside his wallet—was rather more of a specialist than that. He didn't usually get involved in matrimonial matters, because these usually ended in either screaming matches or violent recriminations, or sometimes both, and he much preferred the quiet life. And he found the commercial field—sitting for hours in a parked car staring through the viewfinder of a high-spec camera waiting for the person he was investigating to finally appear and do something that he shouldn't—too utterly boring to bother with, despite the fact that it usually paid well.

Marsh was both more and less of a specialist. He'd realized at a fairly early age that his appearance was a considerable asset. He was so nondescript that he could almost literally spend an evening at a party talking to a dozen or so people, and at the end of the evening not one of them would be able to provide anything like a useful or usable description of him. His specialty was nonmatrimonial close-quarters surveillance. Specifically following people to see where they went, who they met, and, where possible, what they did, and ideally obtaining both photographic and audio evidence of whatever deeds or misdeeds they got up to. It was the kind of work often commissioned by companies that were worried they had become the victims of industrial espionage, and which usually suspected one of their employees to be the person playing both sides against the middle.

This job was turning out to be rather different. He'd been contacted the previous day by phone, given the outline of the job, and offered a fee that was substantial enough to dispel any hesitation he might have had about accepting it. The first tranche of the money had appeared in his bank account less than half an hour later. Half a dozen photographs of a pretty dark-haired girl had been sent to his professional e-mail account at virtually the same time. These had clearly been taken from some kind of surveillance camera. That in itself was not unusual, but on two of the pictures the background clearly showed that the footage had been taken inside a police station, inside an interview room, in fact, and that was a first, even for him.

Marsh knew perfectly well that access to audio and video recordings of suspects being interviewed was very carefully regulated. That suggested that his unidentified client—his initial and, so far, single subsequent contact had been by mobile phone with no names being mentioned—most likely worked for the police force and was, in all probability, a police officer.

And that conclusion rather forced the question: why was a police officer employing a private investigator to follow a person who was presumably a suspect in some kind of crime? Wasn't that what the police themselves were supposed to do?

Marsh had contacts with people in dozens of different organizations, including the police force, a network of paid helpers who could be relied upon to supply information that he needed when he wanted it, and doing a back check on the mobile phone number used to contact him was easy enough. Unfortunately it was also a dead end. The pay-as-you-go phone had been bought with cash in a shop in Exeter the previous day, and the SIM card had been loaded with fifty pounds' worth of credit by the purchaser as part of the transaction. In the parlance of the time, the phone was a burner: a cheap, virtually obsolete model that could be dumped at any moment, and with no way for the police or anyone else to link the mobile to the man who'd actually used it.

As well as the photographs, Marsh had been given a name—Robin Jessop—and an address in Dartmouth, which turned out to be a bookshop owned by Jessop. That name rang a bell, and a few minutes' work on the Internet produced some information that had served only to confuse Marsh even more. According to the newspaper reports he found, Jessop had been wanted for questioning by the police over the murders of three men in her apartment. It wasn't usual for even the British police force to let murder suspects out to roam the streets. Usually they were required to occupy alternative accommodation characterized by substantial steel doors, barred windows, and a marked lack of entertainment facilities.

That afternoon, he'd received a third call on his mobile that had confirmed his suspicion about the probable occupation his client followed. He'd been told that Jessop would be leaving a specific police station in Exeter, and at approximately what time. That information had made everything that followed remarkably easy.

He'd chosen a position on a public bench on the street from which he could see the front of the station, taken out his newspaper and opened it, and then fixed his eyes on the entrance door. He wasn't ideally placed, because the main door was some distance away, but the bench offered a kind of concealment: people didn't usually lean against a wall to read a newspaper—his only other option—but many sat in parks and elsewhere to do so. There'd been a couple of false alarms, but finally a young woman who was quite clearly Robin Jessop—he'd transferred the photographs to his mobile phone and checked the images to make absolutely certain of his identification—had walked out of the station. She barely even glanced in his direction, but instead had walked briskly down the street, heading, as it turned out, straight for the coffee shop.

Marsh had quickly caught up with her, matched her speed along the pavement, and then stepped into the café a few minutes after her. He'd taken a seat at a table from which he could observe her covertly, a task not made any easier because the café was clearly not the most popular establishment along that particular street, and was virtually empty. It was always much easier to be covert in a crowd. In fact, when Jessop and Marsh walked in, they had precisely doubled the number of customers, the only other occupants being an elderly man sitting in one corner perusing the sports page of a tabloid newspaper and muttering to himself, and a teenage girl on the opposite side of the room talking earnestly into her smartphone, her side of the conversation consisting almost entirely of the phrases "yeah," "you know," "like," "right," "know what I mean?" and "whatever."

All Jessop had done since that moment was study something on a small tablet computer, drink two cups of coffee, both quite slowly, and consume a cake that looked to Marsh like some breed of muffin. After she'd walked over to the counter and purchased her second cup of coffee and the cake, Marsh had quickly used the lavatory at the back of the café—he didn't want to be caught short, not knowing how long his target would remain in the café, or where she would be likely to go next—and had purchased another café Americano when he returned.

Then Marsh had had a stroke of luck, precisely because the café was not a popular rendezvous. In technological terms, he was highly proficient, more or less a necessity because of the nature of his employment, and was very well aware that the intelligent use of cutting-edge technology would provide him with a significant edge in many situations. In particular, he knew only too well that a single man trying to provide surveillance of a single target was at a very considerable disadvantage. To do that kind of job successfully would normally take at least half a dozen people. Despite his fortunately nondescript appearance, it really would only ever be a matter of time before any target he was allocated realized he or she was being followed. Even the most relaxed and unobservant of people would eventually be bound to spot him and start wondering.

But technology, and particularly Bluetooth technology, could provide an answer. Originally considered to be essentially a solution looking for a problem, Bluetooth had come of age with the introduction of smartphones, which relied heavily on this particular piece of electronic wizardry. Virtually everyone who owned a smartphone had Bluetooth almost permanently enabled on it, so that the device could be linked to printers, hands-free car systems, and other peripherals, and Bluetooth was designed to be as easy as possible to use, which was both its strength and—from the point of view of people like Gary Marsh—also its weakness.

The theory was that before one Bluetooth device could link to another Bluetooth device, there had to be an exchange of data between the two pieces of equipment, and as a part of this a password would be sent between them. The weakness of the system was that in most cases the password was incredibly simple, precisely so that connection would be as easy as possible. In many cases, the password was "0000," "1234," or "4321," which hardly required much in the way of decryption.

Gary Marsh owned a smartphone, an uncommon model that was significantly more bulky than the majority and with a rather larger screen, and on it he had what amounted to a surveillance tool kit, one part of which was a tracker.

The obvious problem with most tracking systems was that a transmitter of some sort had to be attached to the target vehicle or placed somewhere on the person being followed, but both these methods offered the obvious and severe disadvantage that if the car was parked and the target proceeded somewhere on foot, the mobile tracker immediately became useless, and people tended to change their clothes, so even if a tracker could be attached to a particular garment, it would cease to be useful as soon as the target put on something different. Even women periodically tended to swap their handbags.

But the one thing almost everybody had with them at all times was their mobile phone, and that was the genius of the software that Marsh had built into his smartphone. The system was based on Bluetooth, and in order to set up a tracker, he only had to be within a reasonable range—a few dozen feet at the most—of the target phone. The only difficulty was that it was nondiscriminatory. Unless he knew the telephone number of the target mobile, he could not guarantee he was placing the tracking software on the right mobile.

He didn't know the number of Jessop's phone, of course, but once the teenage girl had finished her pointless conversation and left the café, he seized the opportunity. The old man in the corner didn't look as if he would even know what a mobile was, and the burly man behind the counter had made only two telephone calls while Marsh was in the establishment, and had used the wall-mounted landline phone both times. The probability was that the only smartphone within range was the one sitting in Robin Jessop's handbag. And he was quite sure that she would have one.

Marsh placed his smartphone on the table in front of him, but shielded by his newspaper, accessed the tracking program, and initiated a search for any Bluetooth devices within range. As he had hoped, the scan produced only a single result. His Bluetooth software connected with the other phone and requested permission to load the tracker. As usual, the recipient phone generated a request for a password before pairing could take place. His software automatically accepted the six-digit random number her phone generated, and then the clever part of his program kicked in. Normally she would have had to press the "OK" option on her phone, so that both parties were aware of the link, but Marsh's software used the partial Bluetooth link to force her mobile to accept the pairing without her intervention or knowledge. And then, in confirmation that the installation and initiation of the tracker had been successful, the phone in Jessop's handbag emitted a single muted beep.

Throbs, beeps, and other noises from smartphones were not exactly unknown, and as Marsh had expected, Robin Jessop did precisely what most people would do. She opened up her handbag, took out her phone, pressed a button on the side of it, and then swiped her fingertip across the screen to wake it up. For a few seconds, she looked at the display, but apparently saw nothing to account for what she had just heard, the tracker being entirely covert in operation. She shrugged, put the phone back in her handbag, and turned her attention once again to her tablet computer.

A few minutes later, the man had appeared and bought

two coffees. He and Jessop had talked together, and perhaps ten minutes after that both Jessop and the new arrival had left the establishment.

The moment the door closed behind them, Marsh stood up, folded his newspaper neatly, and slipped it into the side pocket of his coat. Then he, too, left the café and took up station about fifty yards behind them, easily matching their speed.

Although he already knew that the tracker was working, and that he could access the mobile phone network through his software and locate Jessop—or at least her mobile phone—to within a matter of yards as long as it was switched on and she was in an urban environment, he was curious enough about his assignment to rely upon his normal surveillance skills and simply see where they were going, if possible hear what they were talking about, and watch what they ended up doing.

6

Exeter, Devon

"What about the Italians?" Robin asked. "Do you think they've given up?"

Mallory shook his head in a decisive manner. "Not a chance, in my opinion. They were quite prepared to kill both of us in your apartment at Dartmouth—I'm quite sure of that—and then they did their best to finish us off with that grenade in the cave on Cyprus. They obviously still haven't found what they're looking for, so there's no doubt that they'll still be on the hunt. The only good thing, I suppose, is that they might think we're both dead and buried in the rubble under the cave, and so they might not give us any more trouble here in Britain. But sooner or later I think we'll come face-to-face with them again."

"I guessed that would be what you'd think, and you're probably right. So what's your plan now? Have you got a plan, even?"

"I thought you knew me a bit better than that, despite our short acquaintance. Of course I haven't got a plan. That's not the way I work. I more kind of make things up as I go along."

"Funnily enough, I expected that as well. So let me tell you what I think. What we have to do is try to crack whatever code is incorporated in the pattern of metalwork on those two chests. And if we can do that, then we can decide what to do next. Stay flexible. Think on our feet, that kind of thing."

Mallory nodded again. "Exactly. Just like I said. We'll make it up as we go along."

"And if we can't crack the code? Or even find it? What then?"

"I suppose we give up, because the only thing we've got is those photographs of the metalwork on the chests. If we can't work out the next clue from them, that's pretty much it. There's nowhere else we can look, and nothing else we can do."

Robin slowed her pace slightly and glanced sideways at Mallory.

"There's something else we need to talk about," she said.

"There is?" Mallory sounded puzzled.

"Yes, obviously. I mean you and me. You only got involved in this because I asked for your help in solving a riddle, to decode a piece of enciphered Latin text. You've got your own business to run in Cornwall, and I should really be heading back to Dartmouth to see what's happening in the shop. Can either of us really afford the time to go off on what might turn out to be another wild-goose chase? Following another set of clues that could very easily lead us to another couple of empty chests or whatever?"

Mallory suspected that there might be more to Robin's question than was at first apparent. He'd had enough girlfriends to know perfectly well that the female of the species would often ask one question when she was actually expecting an answer to something completely different, something that she no doubt felt was implied in what she'd just said. And he also knew that most men were too stupid or out of touch to realize this.

What he was quite certain about was that Robin Jessop's antiquarian bookshop could probably manage quite happily without any interference from the owner. Betty, the lady who actually ran the place on a daily basis, was more than capable of doing everything herself, especially as Robin would almost always be available on her mobile phone to field any questions that Betty couldn't answer. And as Mallory had already explained to her a couple of times, his IT consultancy work required him to be contactable by phone, and to have high-speed Internet access when necessary to sort out any problems for his clients, but not necessarily to be actually on-site.

So he listened to the question that Robin had just asked, but gave her two answers: the obvious response to the question she'd actually asked, and then the answer to what he hoped she was really asking.

"I think both of our businesses can more or less take care of themselves, Robin," he said. "We've got something more important going on here. I think we need to continue the search as quickly as possible. Otherwise we might find that we're beaten to the prize by whoever those Italians are working for. That's the practical solution, in my opinion. And the other thing is that I think we make a pretty good team, so the last thing I want to do is walk away from you now, irrespective of what the next chapter of this peculiar quest might bring. I want to know more about you, and to spend a lot more time with you. So if you're okay with that, then I'll be here, standing right beside you, until the bitter end."

"So you think we're heading for disaster, do you? Why did you say the 'bitter end'? There might be a happy ending to all this lot. You never know."

Her voice was light, almost flirtatious, but Mallory sensed the emotion behind the words.

He stopped in the middle of the pavement, put his hand on Robin's shoulder to turn her to face him, and then kissed her, long and hard, on the lips.

For a couple of seconds, Robin didn't respond; then her arms snaked around Mallory's shoulders and the back of his head and she pulled him firmly into a close embrace. Then she released him and took a half step back.

"Thank you," she said, a smile dimpling her cheeks. "I needed that."

"I think we both needed it," Mallory said. "Seriously, I'm here for you for as long as you want me."

As they continued walking down the street, Robin's hand sought out Mallory's, and he responded with a firm squeeze of her palm.

A few minutes later, Mallory opened the passenger

door of his Porsche for Robin, then walked around to the driver's seat and started the engine. He waited for a couple of minutes until the oil temperature began to rise, then engaged first gear and steered the Cayman out of the car park.

Gary Marsh, their faithful but unseen shadow, stepped out from behind a parked van as the car drove away, the throaty exhaust note of the Porsche hinting at the power of the engine. There was no way that he could follow them, obviously. He had a car, but it was tucked away in a corner of a car park the better part of two miles distant, and his briefing had been to observe the woman and follow her on foot.

His mobile phone was in his hand, and on the screen was a very clear image of the rear three-quarters of the Porsche, showing the number plate with pinpoint clarity. He made a mental note of the letters and numbers, then dialed his contact's mobile number from memory. The phone was answered almost immediately.

"Yes?"

"They've just driven away in a Porsche Cayman," he began, "and I'm not mobile, so there's nothing else I can do right now. Do you want the plate number? You can probably track it through the traffic camera system."

The man he'd called didn't reply for a few moments, and when he did his tone was distinctly frosty. "How do you think I can do that?"

"I'm not stupid," Marsh said. "I've spent a lot of my working life analyzing data and making connections, and working out that you're a copper wasn't what you might call difficult. The only way you could have known when the female target was going to leave the station was if you were in there at the same time."

"That doesn't mean I'm a policeman," the man responded. "I could be a civilian support worker."

"And I could be Elvis Presley. Civilian support workers don't have access to surveillance footage taken in interview rooms, and two of the pictures you sent me were definitely taken from a video of an interrogation. So you're a copper, and probably hold a fairly senior rank. The kind of rank that can instruct somebody to prepare still images from an interview video without anybody being able to ask any awkward questions. Now you listen to me. I don't care who you are or what you are or even what you want, but it makes things a hell of a lot easier to sort out if you're straight with me, because I'll always be straight with you. That's how I work. Deal?"

There was another short silence, and then Marsh heard a long sigh before the man replied, "Deal. Give me the registration details."

Marsh relayed the information, then asked the obvious question. "So, what do you want me to do now? I can do moving target surveillance, obviously, but I need a definite starting point. A home address or some other confirmed location. And do you want me to continue following the woman, or do you want both of them to be tracked? I have a colleague who can work with me if they split up. But I think they're an item."

"What do you mean?"

Marsh explained what he'd seen on the street after the two people had walked away from the coffee shop, and some parts of the conversation that he had overheard. In fact, he hadn't just overheard it: he'd also recorded much of it. In one of the inside pockets of his jacket was a small digital recorder, and running down his right sleeve was a thin cable that terminated in a miniaturized directional microphone, the mike fitted with a simple slider switch that would turn the recorder on and off as required. It was a much more discreet piece of equipment than other directional recorders, and although most people might look slightly askance at someone pointing their hand directly at them, Marsh had found that simply carrying a newspaper in his right hand, with his arm bent at the elbow, looked entirely natural and worked very well, allowing him to point the microphone unobtrusively at his desired target. It was another very valuable part of his surveillance armory.

"Do you know the identity of the man she was with?" he asked.

"It was almost certainly a guy called David Mallory. He's also in the frame for this investigation, but we've had to let them both walk because we don't have enough evidence to hold them or charge them. We still think that the woman is the prime suspect, or at least the more important half of the couple. But I'll send you pictures of Mallory as well, just in case she was with somebody else that we don't know about."

"You don't need to bother," Marsh replied. "I've got

half a dozen shots of him, in the street and in the car. I'll pick the best two or three and send them to your mobile as soon as we finish this call. You can ident him for me."

"Thanks. That'll speed things up. Right, I'll get back to you with new instructions once we've located either the suspects or that car. Can you be prepared to go mobile at very short notice?"

"Of course. I'll grab a taxi and go to pick up my vehicle. I'll be ready within a maximum of thirty minutes."

7

Dartmouth, Devon

"Are you sure this is a good idea?" Robin asked. "That Porsche is powerful enough to get us away from any trouble we might meet."

"I agree," Mallory replied. "But unfortunately it's also distinctive enough to get us into trouble in the first place. It's a very difficult car to hide, and for the moment I think anonymity is a lot more important than speed."

A few minutes later, Mallory reversed the Cayman into the single parking place at the back of Robin's antiquarian bookshop. She had started her Golf and parked it a few yards away down the street to allow him to occupy the space. Mallory transferred their bags to the smaller vehicle, locked the Porsche, and walked over to the Volkswagen, carrying a small black bag in his hand.

"Do you think we're going to need that?" Robin asked, pointing at it.

"I hope not, but having a loaded pistol with us still seems to me like a good idea, until we find out what's happening with those bloody Italian thugs."

"Are you sure we couldn't stay in my apartment?" Robin asked, pointing at the level above the bookshop. "We are here now, after all."

"I really don't think that's a good idea, just in case we are being watched. We should try to be as unpredictable as possible and just pick a hotel somewhere at random. I prefer the idea of staying somewhere where there's more than one way in and out."

"That's okay with me, if that's what you want."

As Mallory approached her, Robin walked around the car to the passenger door and opened it.

"You drive," she said. "I'm going to look at the pictures on my laptop again, just in case anything leaps out at me."

"That's fine with me," Mallory said, buckling his seat belt and starting the Golf. "Any preference where you'd like to stay?"

"No, not really, but I think I'd prefer country rather than town. Just surprise me. You've done that once today already."

Mallory smiled at the memory but didn't respond.

Beside him, Robin opened her laptop and pressed the space bar to wake it up. She had a copy of the photographs they'd taken in the cave on Cyprus on the computer as well as her tablet, and hoped that the laptop, with its larger screen, would make it easier to identify the code or pattern that they believed had to be concealed within the ornate metalwork that covered the lids of the two medi-eval chests. Assuming it was there, of course.

They had both taken a number of pictures of the chests with their mobile phones in the indifferent lighting of the cave, some using the flash and some without, and despite these unfavorable conditions the quality of the pictures was actually quite good. Certainly she could see a considerable amount of detail, even down to the tiny patterns, little more than groups of etched lines, that decorated almost all of the complex pattern of metal that encased the old wood.

She began by looking at the overall pattern on the pho-tograph of one of the chests, tracing the intricately curved lines of metal with her eyes as she tried to identify any kind of symbol or shape that might be significant. Then she switched her attention to a photograph of the second chest and did the same thing before reducing the size of the two images, loading them onto the screen at the same time, and studying them as a pair rather than as individual objects.

"Any luck?" Mallory asked as he steered the car out of Dartmouth and pointed them in a generally westerly direction, mainly because there weren't any roads going north, which was the direction he actually wanted to go.

"Not really," Robin replied. "All I can tell you is pretty much the same as we already knew. Which is, basically, that the lids of these two chests are covered in a pattern of metalwork that is almost certainly too elaborate to simply be decoration, especially bearing in mind the cir-cumstances in which they were buried. And, as we saw when we uncovered them in the first place, the patterns are different, which again suggests that there's some kind of hidden message in the scrollwork."

"What about the etchings and marks on the metal itself? Could there be a clue hidden in those tiny marks?"

"I'd feel a whole lot better if we had the actual chests in front of us and could examine them properly," Robin replied, "because it's always possible that there's something the cameras didn't pick up. But, as far as I can tell from studying the pictures, those small marks are really just decorative. There are a few places where some of the marks do seem to form letters, but I really can't be sure that I'm not seeing something that actually isn't there. I mean, I'm looking at three straight lines, say, and if I apply a bit of poetic license I can almost make them form the shape of a letter *N*, and I can turn two lines into a *V* or four lines into a *W*. But if you looked you probably wouldn't see the same association at all. I think I'm just seeing letters because that's what I'm hoping to see, and the bottom line is that even if I am right and on one of the curved bits of metal there is a letter *N*, for example, that doesn't really help us because it's just one letter by itself. We're looking for a phrase or at least two or three words, not individual letters."

Mallory was silent for a few moments, mulling over what Robin just told him. What she said hadn't come as a surprise. Although they hadn't discussed it in detail, they had already come to more or less the same conclusion.

"What about the differences between the two patterns?" he asked. "We already knew the metalwork wasn't the same on the two lids, but what actually is the difference? Are the two patterns completely dissimilar, or are we looking at just fairly minor changes from one to the other?"

Robin glanced down at the computer resting on her lap before she replied. She studied the two images on the screen, the side-by-side photographs of the lids of the two chests, and then shook her head.

"They are sort of similar," she admitted, "but different enough that you would never mistake one for the other, if you see what I mean. I can see shapes in one that aren't there in the pattern of the second chest, and vice versa. But what I don't see are any shapes that could be letters or anything of that sort, and unless we've got it completely wrong, we need another piece of plaintext or a code word that we can use to translate that final section of encrypted text on the parchment. Is that what you think as well?"

"Pretty much, yes," Mallory said, nodding and glancing over at Robin. "That really is the obvious way forward."

A few minutes later, he turned the Golf right at the Halwell T-junction to head north up the A381 toward Totnes.

"Where are we going?" Robin asked, a few minutes later. "Not Exeter again, I hope. I had about enough of that particular city the last time we were there. No good memories, except that we did manage to walk away."

"No, not Exeter," Mallory agreed. "I still haven't got anywhere definite in mind, so I was generally heading up toward Okehampton. We should be able to find a quiet hotel somewhere up there on the edge of Bodmin Moor."

"Sounds good to me."

Robin closed the lid of her laptop with a decisive *click* and slid it back into her leather computer case.

"If I look at those pictures any more, I will definitely go boss-eyed," she said. "We'll have a proper look—both of us—once we get to the hotel, where it's quiet and we can concentrate."

A little over an hour after they'd driven away from Robin's bookshop in Dartmouth, a nondescript Ford saloon drew to a halt a few yards down the road and an entirely unmemorable man stared across at the parked Porsche. He didn't need to check the registration number because he had already memorized it. In his business, a good memory for numbers, information, and especially faces was a definite asset.

He made sure his car was legally parked, because coming to the attention of any of the British authorities for any reason was something he always tried to avoid, then walked away from the vehicle and approached the antiquarian bookshop's street door. Inside, he held a very brief conversation with the slightly plump lady behind the counter, then stepped out again and returned to his vehicle.

Marsh took out his mobile phone and dialed the number of his temporary and still-unidentified employer.

"The good news," he began, "is that I've found the address in Dartmouth and I've also found the Porsche. The bad news is that neither of the targets is here. According to the woman in the shop, they drove down from Exeter about an hour and a half ago, parked the car, and then left almost immediately in Jessop's vehicle. And for that I don't have a make or model, though the woman I talked to thinks it might be silver or gray, and fairly small, maybe a hatchback."

"That's not a problem. I can get those details to you in a few minutes. Did this woman have any idea where they were going?"

"No. All that Jessop apparently told her was that she and Mallory were involved in some kind of project, and they were going off to do some research. I did manage to get Jessop's mobile number, so you should be able to triangulate their location fairly easily, as long as she leaves the phone on, of course. That bit wasn't difficult. She has it printed on her business card."

What Marsh was not prepared to do was admit that he could also triangulate the location of Jessop's mobile phone. That particular ability and that software were both entirely illegal under British law for anyone outside the police force or the security services.

"Good. I'll set the wheels in motion. There's no point in you staying in Dartmouth, because the one place they're not going to be is back down there, so I suggest you return to Exeter and wait for me to contact you again."

Marsh told him Robin Jessop's mobile number and then ended the call. But for a few minutes he did nothing else except use his eyes and the rearview mirrors on his car.

One of the obvious characteristics of people involved in his profession was the ability to be constantly alert, to observe rather than simply to see. And what he was observing was giving him pause for thought.

A dark blue Ford sedan with two men inside it, one

driving and the other in the front passenger seat, had just made two circuits of the small block of buildings that included Robin Jessop's antiquarian bookshop. Of course, the driver might just have been looking for somewhere to park, a task that was notoriously difficult anywhere in Dartmouth, but Marsh didn't think he was. Apart from anything else, it was the fact that on each occasion as the Ford had driven past the rear of the shop, the vehicle had slowed down considerably, and both men had very obviously been staring up at the second-floor apartment, rather than at the Porsche, which was a more unusual sight in the town.

And on their third circuit, their intentions became clear. The car stopped at the side of the street on a single yellow line, where parking was not permitted, and the passenger stepped out of the vehicle, the driver remaining where he was, the engine of the car still running.

The passenger looked both ways up and down the street, but in a manner that seemed to suggest he was possibly looking for any potential witnesses rather than checking for oncoming cars, then crossed over to the rear of the shop and swiftly ascended the spiral staircase that gave access to Robin Jessop's apartment. When he reached the metal landing, he walked over to the apartment door and rapped on it sharply.

There was no response that Gary Marsh could see, which was entirely unsurprising, as he knew for a fact that both Jessop and Mallory had left Dartmouth together some time earlier. As he watched the unknown stranger standing by the apartment door, Marsh sank a little lower in the seat of his car and at the same time took a powerful compact digital camera from his jacket pocket. He aimed at the man, used the telephoto lens to zoom in on his face, and took about a dozen images. For good measure, he also took a handful of pictures of the illegally parked car, making sure that the registration plate was clearly visible.

The man on the landing turned and looked around him, then reached inside his loose jacket and took out an object that glinted metallically in the early-afternoon sun. As Marsh switched his camera to video mode and started filming, the man extended the object, which Marsh could then identify as a collapsible jemmy, stuck the point into the space between the door and the jamb, and gave a sharp push.

The crack as the door gave way was clearly audible even from where Marsh was sitting inside his car. Immediately the intruder vanished from sight into the apartment.

"Interesting," Marsh murmured to himself, and continued both watching and recording.

It was perfectly obvious to him that the apartment had to be fairly small, simply because of the dimensions of the building, and so he wasn't surprised when the unidentified man stepped back out of the door less than two minutes later, again glanced around him, and then descended the spiral staircase. At the bottom, he glanced over toward his companion in the parked Ford, shook his head, and headed through the alleyway that led to the main street and the front of Jessop's shop.

Marsh briefly contemplated following him, but just as quickly rejected the idea. The most obvious reason for the man walking down the alley was for him to go into the bookshop, exactly as Marsh himself had done only a few minutes earlier, to try to find out where Robin Jessop had gone.

This time, the man was out of sight for rather longer, but not by much. About three minutes after he had disappeared into the alley, he stepped out again and strode briskly across to the parked car. Again Marsh filmed him, the telephoto lens on his camera bringing his face and figure sharply into focus.

Almost as soon as the man sat down in the passenger seat, the driver of the Ford indicated and the vehicle drove swiftly away down the street.

Marsh watched it depart, but his attention was concentrated not on the car, but on the video images he had just recorded. Something had struck him about the man as he had walked back to the car, and he scanned through the digital images, looking for the relevant frames.

Then he saw it. The unexpected bulge in the fabric of the stranger's jacket and then the briefest of glimpses of the object that was causing it as he walked across the street.

For a few moments, Marsh studied the images, making sure that he wasn't mistaken. Then he took his mobile and dialed his contact, the man who was his temporary employer.

"I've got a question for you," he said, when his call was answered.

"What?"

"Am I working this gig solo or have you got another team in play?"

His question produced a brief silence at the other end.

When his contact finally replied, his voice was hesitant, almost uncertain.

"No, it's just you. Nobody else. Why?"

"I'm still in Dartmouth, and I've just watched a two-man team break into Jessop's flat and, probably, check out her shop as well."

"That's nothing to do with me. Did you get pictures?"

"Obviously," Marsh replied. "I always record everything. That's what I do. I'll send a copy of the stills and video to your e-mail as soon as I get back. But there's something else you need to know. One guy stayed in the car while his partner did the breaking and entering, and unless I'm seeing things that aren't there, the B and E player was tooled up. A shoulder holster and what looked to me like an automatic pistol rather than a revolver. And that does kind of add an extra dimension to this surveillance operation."

There was another brief silence before the other man replied, "Are you sure? That he was armed, I mean."

"Pretty certain, yes. When you see the footage, you'll know what I mean."

"Are you still in?"

This time Marsh didn't reply immediately, choosing his words carefully. "For the moment, yes. But if and when the shooting starts, you won't see me for dust."

8

Via di Sant'Alessio, Aventine Hill, Rome, Italy

Vitale was a long way from being pleased. The order employed experts in a number of different disciplines, but primarily archaeologists—or, to be exact, people who specialized in the interpretation of archaeological information, which wasn't quite the same thing—and linguists who had impressive skills in understanding and translating texts written in the numerous dead languages of the world, particularly Latin, ancient Greek, and Aramaic. But they could not call on experts in code breaking, because only very rarely did they encounter ciphers of any sort, and when they did, these were usually fairly simple letter substitution codes, such as Atbash, which were generally quite straightforward to unscramble. Roman Benelli, the man in the organization who knew most about encryption systems, actually specialized in the translation of Aramaic and related languages into Italian. For him, codes and ciphers were definitely of secondary importance.

The problem the order was currently facing was trying to work out whatever message or other piece of information had been incorporated within the ornate metalwork adorning the lids of the two medieval chests they had recovered from the cave in Cyprus. And the main difficulty didn't stem from any kind of decryption that might be necessary, but from a far more basic and fundamental question.

"So, are you telling me that there *is* a code or something built into that scrollwork or not?" Vitale demanded. "Are we looking at just a pretty piece of metalwork or is it something else?"

The man standing in front of his desk—late-middle-aged, short, plump, wearing a suit so tight that it looked as if it had been painted on him, and with an impressive five o'clock shadow, given that it was still early afternoon—shook his head. "At this stage we still don't know. We've been over the chests with magnifying glasses, several times, and as far as we can tell none of the marks on the metalwork represent letters in any known language. They appear to be nothing more than decorative. Having said that, I'll add that there are a number of markings that could perhaps be interpreted as letters in the Roman alphabet, but these are always isolated and it is difficult to see how they could possibly form part of a code word or key. By definition, any code word has to possess a reasonable number of letters. Otherwise it simply will not work."

"What about the insides of the chests? Did you find anything there?"

Benelli shook his head.

"Again," he said, "we examined them with the most powerful magnifying glasses we possess, and the insides of both chests are completely unmarked. We have even removed that hideously effective antitheft device from the inside of the lid of each box, just in case anything had been painted or carved onto the wood before it was assembled. But there is nothing. There are no marks of any sort inside the chests. If there is a clue to be found—and I'm by no means certain that that is the case—then whatever it is has to have been incorporated within that exterior scrollwork."

Vitale glared at his subordinate for a few seconds, and then dismissed him. The man was, he knew, doing his best, but it was beginning to look as if the man who had ordered the chests to be constructed—definitely either Jacques de Molay, the last grand master of the Knights Templar order, or his immediate predecessor, Tibauld de Gaudin—had somehow managed to encode the vital information needed to decipher the last clue to the puzzle in a way that would defeat any later analysis.

Or perhaps, he thought as another possibility struck him, there was no clue built into the chests. Maybe the chests were just a kind of lethal farewell gesture left on Cyprus by the last of the Knights Templar before they returned to France.

But that really didn't make sense. Vitale knew as well as anyone that the enormous treasure of the Knights

Templar had never been found. When the mass arrests were performed by the soldiers of Philip the Fair, the treasure vaults in the commanderies and preceptories throughout France were largely empty. The vast wealth of the Templars had somehow been spirited away and vanished from the historical record, and the only possible clue that could give even a hint as to the whereabouts of this hoard was in the form of the elaborate metalwork pattern incorporated in the lids of the two wooden chests now under the control of the order.

Even more pertinently, the Ipse Dixit parchment, the translation of which had led Toscanelli and his men to the cave near the castle of Saint Hilarion in Cyprus, a place they had become aware of only because they had been following Jessop and Mallory, was the only clue to the possible location of the treasure that had surfaced in well over half a millennium. And the clues in that parchment had resulted in the discovery of the chests. So, logically, and despite the lack of any hint as to what clue the chests might contain, the information they needed to obtain had to be encoded in them somehow. The chests simply had to be the next step in the path, because there was nothing else.

And the sheer fact that they had been so well concealed, buried under layers of heavy wooden planking in the floor of that remote cave on Cyprus and then covered with tons of stone, simply confirmed that. Nobody would have gone to that much trouble to hide the chests unless they either contained something of immense value—which they hadn't, simply being full of rocks—or were vitally important in some other way. Although they couldn't see it right then, the metalwork had to be hiding the clue that the order was so desperately seeking.

That set him thinking about the English couple who had so effectively outwitted Toscanelli, both in England and on Cyprus. The interview he'd just conducted had reinforced his own doubts, and the mission on which the order was engaged was too important, far too important, to be allowed to fail.

He had considered ordering the elimination of Jessop and Mallory in Britain as soon as he'd found out that they had survived and returned to their homeland. That was why he had ordered the tertiary, the senior British police officer who acted for the order, to organize a surveillance operation against them. At the very least, he needed to know where they were and what they were doing.

But perhaps, as he'd suggested to Toscanelli earlier, just perhaps the English couple could still be useful. They had photographs of the metalwork on the chests, he was sure about that, and they had already proven to be both knowledgeable and resourceful. That was why they had beaten Toscanelli to Cyprus, obviously. Maybe his best tactic would be to give them a bit more rope. Let them work on decoding whatever clue was built in to the decoration on the chests.

Yes, the two of them could become a second string to his bow. He would delay ordering their execution for a little while longer.

Decision made, Vitale reached for the phone and dialed a U.K. mobile to issue his new instructions.

9

Outskirts of Okehampton, Devon

It was almost two hours after they had settled themselves down in the large double room on the fourth floor of the hotel, a room from which they had distant views of the bleak heathland of Bodmin Moor, before either Jessop or Mallory saw anything useful in the photographs they were studying. And even then, it seemed more accidental or coincidental than deliberate. It also didn't seem, at least at first glance, to be particularly helpful.

Robin was sitting in front of her laptop, using the scroll button to zoom in and out on various parts of the photograph on the screen. Mallory had just made two more cups of instant coffee—he claimed the caffeine helped his concentration—at the small table behind her, and was walking back carrying the drinks. He glanced at the screen as he did so, and saw something that both of them had missed.

"Hang on," he said. "Don't alter the picture for a moment."

He put the cups down and leaned closer to the screen, but almost immediately muttered a curse. "It's gone. I can't see it now."

Robin looked at him in irritation.

"You can't see what now?" she demanded.

"I saw a kind of shape in the photograph."

"What sort of shape? You mean like a letter, or a word? Or what?"

Mallory shook his head. "No. It was more like a figure. The shape of a person, I mean. Or at least a face."

Robin stared at the image on the screen.

"I don't see anything like that," she said.

"Nor do I, now," Mallory admitted. "It was just an impression, like the outline of something familiar, the kind of shape that your memory or imagination or whatever fills in for you. You know, like those drawings of a cat's face, where all you have are two lines showing the shape of the pointed ears and the bottom of the head. It doesn't look much like a cat, really, but at the same time that's quite unmistakably what it is."

Robin looked back at him with an expression of dawning interest on her face. "As long as you're not trying to tell me that you've seen the face of a cat in this scrollwork, I'll buy it. What shape do you think you saw?"

"It looked like a woman, though that really doesn't make any sense."

Mallory sat down beside Robin and began manipulating the photograph, trying to recapture what he thought he'd seen. Then he stopped altering the magnification, and instead began to rotate the image on the screen. He turned it through ninety degrees, so that they were looking at the picture of the chest as if it was standing on one end, and then he pointed toward the top of the pattern in the metalwork.

"There," he said. "That curve looks like one side of a female face. Those two marks could be one eye and an eyebrow, and that line below them would be her chin."

Robin shook her head, then stopped and nodded slowly.

"I think I can see what you mean," she said. "But even if you're right, I don't see how this is going to help us. What we need is a code word to decipher the last part of the text on that parchment, and I don't see what relevance a female figure could possibly have to that. And I'm still not certain that you're not seeing something that really isn't there." Gathering her thoughts, she paused for a moment, then continued. "What we need are some photographs, printed photographs, that we can use to trace the outline of that figure. At least that way we should be able to confirm whether this is just a figment of your imagination."

She selected two of the clearest photographs showing the metalwork pattern for both of the chests and copied them onto a memory stick. "You stay here and see if you can identify anything else. I'll just nip downstairs and ask the girl at reception if she can run me off two or three copies of each of these pictures on the printer she uses."

She walked back into the room a few minutes later holding a sheaf of paper. "I've got half a dozen copies of each photograph, so we can really play about with them. Now," she added, "grab a pencil and show me where you think this figure is."

Mallory selected one of the printed photographs, rotated the page, and then drew a single curving line near the top of the image.

"That's what I was trying to show you before," he said. "That looks to me like one side of her face, which means her neck would be here"—he sketched a couple of short vertical lines to indicate that bodily feature—"her shoulders about here, and on down to her feet near the edge of the scrollwork."

Robin took the paper from him and studied it for a few moments.

"I do see what you mean," she said. "This is a bit like one of those images that used to be printed in the newspapers. The ones that looked like just a mass of dots or something, but which actually contained a clear and identifiable image."

"I remember those," Mallory agreed. "You could spend ages just staring at the thing and seeing absolutely nothing, and then it would suddenly click and you'd wonder why you hadn't seen it right from the start."

"And the reason why this is so obscure, I think, is that what looks like at least half of the image of the figure is missing. It looks to me as if whoever prepared this design first etched or carved the image of the figure onto a metal plate, and then cut out large sections of it so that the coherence of the shape was completely destroyed. So unless you knew that you were looking for the image of a woman, you'd probably never see it."

"That makes sense, but it still leaves us with the bigger question, which is how the concealed image of a female figure is going to help us identify the code word we need to use to decrypt that last section of the parchment text."

Robin nodded.

"True enough," she agreed, "but it's all we've got to go on, so ultimately whatever that shape is supposed to represent, somehow it has to make sense."

10

Exeter, Devon

Gary Marsh was facing something of a crisis of conscience. On the one hand, he was being paid well—paid extremely well, in fact—to follow and monitor Robin Jessop. On the other, he now knew beyond doubt that a second team of at least two men was also in the game, because he'd seen them, and those men obviously had a very different agenda from his.

Nobody in Britain carried a firearm unless they intended to use it, because private ownership of handguns had been made illegal years earlier, and to be caught in possession of such a weapon invariably led to a mandatory prison sentence. That legislation had been the result of a knee-jerk reaction by the British government and had resulted, predictably enough, in an overall *increase* in gun crime since the move passed into law. Criminals intent on robbery, for example, knew that they faced prison if caught. But they also knew that carrying a weapon would give them enough of an edge over the usually unarmed British police officers that their chances of getting away were significantly increased. So why wouldn't they go tooled up? It would be stupid of them not to.

At least one of the two men who were obviously following Robin Jessop had been carrying a pistol, and it seemed unlikely that robbery was his motive. That, to Marsh, raised a much darker possibility. Was she on somebody's hit list? He didn't know her, but he had found out quite a lot about her as part of his research, and unless she had a really well-hidden criminal past that had attracted somebody's unwelcome attention, he didn't think she deserved to die.

Then there was the matter of his fee. Put simply, he'd been paid well over the odds, something like twice what he would normally have charged, for the job he'd been given. And that didn't really make sense. Or, rather, it made sense in only one context: the senior police officer—and Marsh still had no doubt at all that the anonymous voice on his mobile belonged to such a man—had been desperate for him to drop everything else and take the job. Which was, of course, exactly what he'd done.

Marsh didn't know whether to believe his employer's protestations of ignorance about the other two men. He could easily have employed another group to dog Marsh's footsteps, relying on his expertise in surveillance to locate their quarry, and have told them to terminate Jessop as soon as they got the chance. He could be using Marsh as a kind of stalking horse, and if that were the case, he might well have also issued orders to the other men to kill him at the same time, to snip off a potential loose end.

The other scenario, that the police officer was telling the truth and the other men were working on behalf of somebody else entirely, differed only in the details.

In either case, Marsh was acutely aware that he was inevitably in the firing line, and that was a position that he didn't like at all.

He leaned back in his chair at the corner table in the small café where he'd stopped for a drink and a sandwich before returning to his rented apartment in the city, and stared out of the slightly grimy window. He really didn't know what to do for the best. Terminating his services might possibly be the safest move, but the downside to that was that if he dumped his employer and walked away, he might well find that his name suddenly popped up on somebody's hit list, because he was without doubt a loose end, and loose ends could cause problems.

Without really even being aware of it, Gary Marsh shook his head, having come to a decision. He would stay in play, carry on doing whatever his anonymous employer tasked him with. But he would definitely keep his eyes and ears open, even more so than usual, just in case.

He picked up his mobile from the table in front of him and dialed his employer's number from memory.

"I'm back in Exeter," he said when his call was answered.

"Okay. Good. Stay put. Just be ready to move as soon as we've triangulated Jessop's location. That shouldn't take too long."

Marsh ended the call with a slight smile on his face.

The other man didn't know it yet, but he had a feeling that tracking down Robin Jessop was just about to get a whole lot harder.

He took a notebook out of his pocket, flicked through it until he found the page he needed, read a mobile phone number from it, and dialed.

11

As Mallory turned his attention back to the printed photographs, Robin's phone rang. She glanced at the mobile before answering it.

"It's a private number," she said, then swiped her finger across the screen. "Hullo?"

She listened for a few seconds, the expression on her face changing; then she interrupted the caller. "Wait. I'm putting you on speaker. He's right here with me."

Mallory gave her a quizzical glance as she placed her finger over the microphone. "Who is it?"

"I don't know and I don't recognize his voice. But he says he knows who we are, and he's got something important to tell us."

Robin selected the speaker option, took her finger off the microphone, and nodded. "Right, you're on speaker and we're listening. First of all, what's your name?"

The caller gave a short chuckle before he replied, "My name really isn't of the slightest importance, but you can call me John. What matters is the message, not the messenger."

"Okay, *John*," Robin replied, her voice emphasizing the obviously false name he had given. "So what's the message?"

"It's not so much a message as a warning. As I said, you don't need to know who I am, but you do need to know what I do. My job is surveillance, and at this precise moment that actually means surveillance of you two. Somebody hired me to keep an eye on you, Robin. I don't know who the man is and I don't know his reason for wanting you followed, because that's not the way this business works. I don't need to know. I'm just a watcher. That's what I do."

The anonymous caller's frank admission came as a surprise to both Robin and Mallory.

"So you're not a part of the police force or one of the security services?" Mallory asked.

"No chance. I'm strictly freelance. It pays better and there's an almost total absence of bullshit and form filling. But all that's irrelevant. The important thing is that I picked up your trail in Exeter, where I thought you might have done rather better than the café that you chose, and then I trundled down to Dartmouth after you. Swapping cars was probably a good idea, because that Porsche really does stand out. Now, have I got your attention?"

Robin's face was clouded with fury, and she opened her mouth with the apparent intention of telling the caller precisely what she thought of him and his job, but Mallory held up a restraining hand and then replied.

"Okay," he said. "You've convinced me that you've been following us, but what I still don't understand is why you're talking to us. I presume you haven't just called us to gloat about how clever you are."

"No. I'm calling you because of something that happened while I was at Dartmouth. I'd already called my employer to tell him that you'd left the town, but before I left the place myself I saw someone break into your flat, Robin, using a jemmy to force the door. At the very least you're going to need someone to go round and secure it. Otherwise I have no doubt any valuables you keep in there will vanish."

If anything, Robin looked even more irritated than she had a few seconds earlier, but again Mallory replied before she had the chance.

"That's very public-spirited of you," he said. "Leaving aside the possibility that it was actually you who forced the door of Robin's apartment—assuming that that really did happen and you're not just making all this up—I still don't understand why you're talking to us."

"I called you because I'm reasonably certain that the man who broke into the flat was carrying a pistol, and you both seem like quite decent people, despite the interest that the local woodentops appear to be taking in you. So really, this is just a heads-up, a warning that you appear to have at least one armed man following you around, and I doubt very much if those two people—whoever they are—have your best interests at heart."

"Whereas you do, I suppose?" Robin snapped.

"I don't know you. All I'm doing is telling you what I saw. What you do about it is entirely up to you."

"Can you prove what you're telling us?" Mallory asked.

"I already have, actually. When Robin calms down a bit, why don't you ask her to check her messages? I filmed the entire event and I've sent a copy to her business e-mail account."

"I suppose you didn't think about doing anything other than filming it?" Robin demanded. "Like trying to stop them? Or calling the police? Anything helpful like that?"

"I don't mess about with people carrying weapons. I live my life in the shadows, and I'm really happy to keep it that way. By the way, don't bother trying to trace the e-mail. I used a VPN and bounced it through a bunch of proxies, so it's as totally anonymous as makes no difference. But if you send a reply to the same address, I will get it."

Mallory glanced at Robin, who was already checking the messages on her laptop.

"Well, thanks," Mallory said. "Is there anything else you've got to tell us?"

"Only a piece of advice," "John" replied. "I'm sure Okehampton is a pretty good place to stay for a few days. On the edge of the moor, quiet and peaceful, all that kind of thing. But if I were you I wouldn't hang around. If I can triangulate your location based on the phone that you're listening to me on right now, I don't think it's too big a leap to guess that maybe the bad guys can do the same thing. My advice is to dump that phone, or at least pull out the battery, buy yourselves a couple of burners, and get yourselves somewhere else real quick."

"Oh, shit," Robin said.

"I think that covers it," Mallory replied. "Thanks, John. Whoever you are."

12

Devon

The sound of the mobile phone ringing filled the interior of the parked car. The passenger hadn't been expecting it, and he fumbled in his pocket to pull out the phone.

"What does he want now?" the driver muttered.

The passenger glanced at the screen of the mobile, shrugged, and answered the call, putting the phone on speaker as he did so. Only one other person had the number of the phone, so neither man was in any doubt about the identity of the caller.

"Yup?" he said.

"Where are you?"

"Where you told us to be. Outside the hotel, with eyes on the target car. Sitting and waiting."

"Good. Listen. There's been a development. A few minutes ago the woman's phone was switched off completely and we lost triangulation on it. The most likely explanation is that the battery went flat, and it'll come back online once she's connected the charger."

"Yeah," the passenger said. "Or just maybe she's finally realized that having it switched on is like waving a big red flag and saying 'Here I am' to everyone. So is it still a go or does this change something?"

"I've heard nothing new from Italy, so it's still on. This call was a heads-up, just in case she does something unexpected. Let me know when it's done."

The passenger checked that the call had ended, then glanced at the driver.

"Interesting," he said. "I thought he was the principal, but from the sound of it he's taking orders from somebody else. Someone in Italy, no less. Maybe we're working for the bloody Mafia now."

The driver nodded. "He's probably just a cutout, so the back trail stops with him. But as long as he makes the payment to us when we've done the job, I don't care who he's working for."

Ten minutes later Mallory was standing just outside the main door of the hotel, bags in both hands, carefully scrutinizing the parking lot and the street outside the building for any sign of the Ford sedan that had appeared so clearly in the digital video "John" had sent to Robin's business e-mail account. Robin was inside at reception, checking out of the hotel and pleading a family emergency as the reason for their unexpectedly quick departure.

As far as Mallory could tell, it was all clear, and after a few moments he strode over toward Robin's Golf, pressing the remote control to unlock it as he approached the vehicle. He opened the hatchback, took another look around him, put the bags inside, and then closed the hatch. Then he walked around the car, opened the passenger-side door, took a fairly heavy black package from his jacket pocket, and slid it under the front of the passenger seat.

Seconds later Robin walked out of the hotel, quickly glanced all around her, and then walked briskly over to the car. The strap of her handbag was over her shoulder, and inside the bag were the pieces of her smartphone: the body, battery, back, and SIM card. Mallory had reduced the mobile to its component parts within seconds of ending the unexpected call from "John."

"I'll drive," she said briskly, "just in case we meet any opposition, because I'm a whole lot faster than you. I hope you've got the weapon somewhere convenient. There may not be time to stop the car and dig around in our luggage for it."

Mallory tossed her the keys.

"Just what I was going to suggest," he said. "You driving, I mean. And yes, the pistol's tucked under the passenger seat. Out of sight, obviously, but ready to hand if we need it."

"Which way?" Robin asked, pulling her seat belt tight and turning the key to start the engine of the Volkswagen.

"Head east to Exeter," Mallory said without hesitation. "That's not where I want to end up, but that's the fastest road out of Okehampton and we just need to put some distance between us and this place."

"Right."

Robin put the car in gear and steered it out of the car park and onto the street. There was a sat nav on the dashboard, but there was no need for her to use it because there was a clear direction sign visible just a few tens of yards ahead. She drove up to the junction, checked the crossing traffic, indicated, and swung the car onto the eastbound carriageway.

Less than ten seconds after Robin had made the turn, a black BMW repeated the maneuver and began following the Golf, matching its speed and staying about one hundred yards behind. The two men inside the car had been frustrated at the hotel, precisely because it was a hotel, because their orders were to complete their task out of the public eye. They'd hoped that their quarry would go for a walk or at least leave the building at some point, which would have allowed them to do their job. But when they'd seen the man Mallory carry the bags out of the building, they'd realized that their best opportunity had just presented itself.

The car was one of three they used on a regular basis. They'd decided not to use the Ford after they got back from Dartmouth, just in case somebody had seen them there and noted the number, and the BMW was a faster vehicle, which they'd guessed might be important if they ended up chasing their targets across Devon.

The car was street legal in every respect but two. The registration plate was a fake, bearing the number of a virtually identical BMW that they'd identified weeks earlier. That meant they could ignore speed cameras and the like because the subsequent ticket would be sent to the owner of that other vehicle.

The second modification was far from obvious. Fitted within the engine compartment was a two-tone siren and concealed behind the front grille and built into the rear lamp clusters were high-intensity flashing lamps fitted with blue bulbs. Both pieces of equipment were controlled by hidden switches in the car, and were exactly the same specification as the devices installed on unmarked police vehicles and that, of course, was precisely the point. On anything except the most detailed inspection, the car appeared to be a standard BMW, but once on the road activating the lights and the siren gave the sedan the unmistakable appearance of a police vehicle.

"Bit of luck, this," the passenger said, his eyes fixed on the target vehicle.

"Been better if they'd taken a walk," the driver replied. "Could have wrapped it all up back in the town if they had."

"This'll do. Just wait for them to stop for a drink or fuel or something, and then we'll take them. And if they don't stop, we'll stop them ourselves," he added.

The passenger slid his hand inside his jacket and pulled out a Browning Hi-Power semiautomatic pistol. He released the magazine from the butt and used his thumb to strip each round from the top of the magazine, the ammunition forming a small golden pile in his lap, the brass cartridge cases and the copper-jacketed bullets looking deceptively innocent. Then he fed the rounds back into the magazine one at a time, reloading it, and reinserted it in the pistol.

"I don't know why you bother doing that," the driver remarked, his attention still focused on the road ahead.

"It's supposed to reduce the chances of a jam. By unloading it you release the spring in the magazine and make sure that each round can feed freely. I've always done it before a job. It's just one of the things I do."

"I know, but I still don't know why you bother. My pistol never jams on me, and all I ever do is pull the trigger."

The passenger pulled back the slide of the pistol, ejecting the round that was already in the chamber, then let it run forward again, loading a new round and cocking the weapon. Finally he set the safety catch, removed the magazine once more, added the ejected round to it, and replaced it in the butt of the Browning before sliding the pistol back into his shoulder holster.

"I know this road," the driver said, "and there are a couple of parking areas coming up, and the traffic is pretty light. We can use the blues and twos and get them off the road that way."

His companion nodded and once again checked his pistol.

"That works for me," he said. "Let's get this done."

13

Devon

About eighty yards ahead, Robin again glanced at the rearview mirror. They were in light traffic, and keeping up with the flow of vehicles wasn't difficult.

"We may have got company," she said. "There's a black BMW four cars behind us, and he's been there, matching our speed, ever since we left Okehampton."

Mallory glanced at the speedometer before he replied.

"We're all traveling at about the same speed," he pointed out, "and that's pretty close to the legal limit on this road. Maybe he's just a law-abiding citizen, in no particular hurry."

Robin laughed shortly.

"In my experience," she said, "most BMWs in Britain are driven by aggressive, barely competent dickheads who think the ideal place to overtake somebody is on the brow of a hill or around a blind corner. Obeying traffic rules and driving considerately are just not a part of their genetic makeup. You know that as well as I do."

"You've got a point," Mallory conceded. "So what do you think?"

"Like I said, I think we might have company, and that probably means we could be talking to a man with a pronounced Italian accent in the next few minutes. A man who might well be waving a gun with every intention of using it. So I suggest that you unwrap that Beretta pistol and make sure it's loaded, just in case."

As Mallory pulled out the black package from under his seat and unzipped it to reveal the blued steel of a compact automatic pistol, she again glanced at the mirror.

"Or there could of course be an entirely different explanation," she said. "He's just pulled out and overtaken the cars directly behind us, all of which moved out of his way, no doubt because of the flashing blue lights he's now displaying. He's forty yards back and closing, so it's obviously an unmarked cop car with a couple of woodentops inside. It might be a really good idea to tuck that pistol out of sight somewhere."

Mallory looked back as the driver of the BMW positioned his vehicle right behind them, then flashed his lights and blasted his horn, gesturing for Robin to pull over.

He slid the pistol into the waistband of his trousers, making sure that his jacket covered it, but at the same time ensuring that it was within easy reach.

"Can you ignore him and outrun him?" Mallory asked.

Robin glanced at him in some surprise. "On this road, probably not. I don't have the top speed that that BMW's got. On narrow country roads, maybe. But do you think that's a good idea? Running from the cops usually ends up only one way—badly."

"But that," Mallory said, "presupposes that that really is a cop car behind us, and I have my doubts about it."

Robin was already slowing down, steering the Volkswagen toward the entrance of a large turnout on the left-hand side of the road

"Explain," she snapped, taking her time decelerating.

"Unmarked cop cars normally have at least some of the usual equipment fitted, things like dash cams and other stuff on top of the dashboard, and that car behind us hasn't got anything that I can see. That's one thing. The other is that the crews of unmarked cars almost always wear police uniforms, so that when they do stop somebody on the road, there's no doubt about who they are. The two people in that BMW are wearing civilian clothes and they both look pretty scruffy to me."

"You know more about that than I do," Robin said. "So what do you want me to do?"

"What you're doing right now. Then we'll see what happens once you've stopped."

"Easy peasy," the passenger in the BMW said. "Nothing else in the turnout. We should be out of here in less than a minute."

"Don't forget," the driver said, stopping a few yards behind the target car. "You need to do both of them."

The passenger opened the door, straightened his jacket to make sure that the pistol was invisible, and then strode over toward the stationary Volkswagen, heading for the driver's-side door. When he was about ten feet away, he took a suppressor from his left-hand pocket and at the same time reached into his jacket with his right hand to take out the pistol.

He was casually confident in what he was doing. Two shots to each target to ensure that they were dead, the suppressor reducing the sounds of the shots to dull thuds that would be barely audible a few yards away, especially in the open air. Usually that would be one shot to the chest and the second to the head, but because one of the conditions of this killing was that the dead bodies had to be identifiable, he would fire both bullets into the chests of the victims. Then he would use the digital camera in his pocket to confirm the completion of the contract, and after those images had been sent to the principal who'd ordered the hits, they'd get paid.

It was the kind of job he'd done at least a dozen times before, and expected to do again in the future. Easy work, and very well paid, though not for the squeamish.

But at that instant, something totally unexpected happened.

The passenger door of the Volkswagen opened, and before the approaching assassin could draw and aim his own weapon he found himself staring down the barrel of an automatic pistol, the weapon pointed straight at him.

The man holding it looked entirely comfortable with the pistol, and quite prepared to use it.

14

Devon

"Stop right there," Mallory barked. "Drop the suppressor on the ground and then take out your weapon with your left hand, finger and thumb only."

He was already aware that the chances of the unidentified man doing what he was told were extremely slim. He was also acutely aware that he couldn't cover both the driver and the passenger of the BMW at the same time, and if one of them was armed, the chances were that the other one was as well. That meant two targets and two pistols. He was outnumbered and outgunned.

And even as that unpleasant realization crossed his mind, with his peripheral vision he saw the driver's door of the BMW start to open, and knew he had to act at once if he and Robin were going to live through it.

The man in front of him suddenly dived to his right, the pistol now in his hand and swinging around toward him.

But Mallory still had him in his sights, and squeezed the trigger without hesitation. The bullet slammed into the moving target and the man howled in pain as he tumbled to the ground, firing his Browning as he did so.

At virtually the same instant, the driver of the BMW stepped out of the car and brought his own weapon to bear, firing two rapid shots toward Mallory. He was a few feet farther away, and the extra distance meant that one bullet missed him entirely, while the other one slammed through the rear window of the Volkswagen and passed between the open passenger door and the door pillar. Mallory almost thought he felt the wind of its passage, which meant it was far too close.

Even before the shots rang out, Mallory had already started to turn, switching his aim toward the new target.

As the driver fired a third and a fourth round, both of which sounded as if they'd hit somewhere on the Golf, Mallory ducked down to offer a smaller target. He was also trying to draw the man's aim away from the car. He was keenly aware that Robin was still inside the vehicle, and that the thin steel of the car's bodywork would offer virtually no protection against a pistol bullet fired at short range.

He braced his arms as firmly as he could, and fired twice, aiming not at the man but at the door behind which his body was largely concealed. The pistol bucked and kicked in his hands, but his steady grip kept the weapon exactly on aim.

The two bullets hit the door less than a foot apart, tearing through the metal and into the body of the BMW driver, at the same moment as the man fired again. The bullet hit the ground just inches to Mallory's left.

But his own shots did the job. The driver grunted and fell backward, his pistol falling to the ground. Mallory could clearly see the weapon in the gap under the door. Then the man appeared to lie completely still. He could be dead or badly wounded. Or he could be waiting for Mallory to turn his back so that he could grab his pistol and fire a kill shot.

Mallory's first priority was Robin, but he could attend to her only when he was sure that he'd eliminated the threat to both of them from their unidentified attackers.

He stood up and turned round, his pistol extended in front of him, aiming it at the man who'd walked toward their car. Then he sighed with relief and dropped his aim, pointing the weapon at the ground, because it was no longer needed.

Robin hadn't stayed in the driving seat of the car, as he'd expected, but had obviously stepped out of the vehicle a few seconds earlier, and was standing over the passenger from the BMW, his pistol in her hand, the weapon pointed down at the wounded man. He was curled into a fetal ball, moaning loudly.

"Check the driver," she said crisply. "This one isn't going anywhere."

Mallory nodded and swung his pistol back toward the BMW and the man lying beside it. The man's own weapon was still visible, but there was sign of movement from him. Nevertheless, Mallory stepped forward cautiously, the Beretta pointing ahead to cover the fallen man.

As soon as Mallory got a clear look at him, he lowered the pistol. Both of his two shots through the door of the car had taken the man in the chest, and at least one of them must have torn through his heart, judging by the lack of blood on the body. He would have died at the instant his heart stopped beating.

"He's dead," he said, turning back to Robin.

"You're not a bad shot," she said. "Certainly better than that comedian behind you. So who the hell are these two? Not undercover cops, I bloody well hope."

Mallory shook his head. "There's a lot I don't like about the British police force, but one thing that's drummed into firearms officers is that they always make a lot of noise. They're told to shout 'armed police' whenever they approach a suspect or enter a premises where criminals are likely to be found. And they never, ever use suppressors. As soon as I saw him take one out of his pocket, I knew absolutely that they were bad guys."

The man lying in front of Robin moaned again. Mallory switched his attention to him and noticed that his right hand was bleeding, as well as the bullet wound in his torso.

"What happened to his hand?" he asked.

"He was grabbing for the pistol, so I kind of stepped on his fingers to stop him," Robin said.

"Good." Mallory bent down beside the wounded man. "Who sent you after us?" he asked.

"Go screw yourself." The words were forced out with an obviously painful gasp, the man still curled up and hugging his stomach.

"That's not very polite," Mallory said mildly. He looked more closely at the wounded gunman. "I've heard that stomach wounds hurt more than any other," he went on, "but they're not always fatal. If I call for an ambulance right now, I reckon you've got a better than even chance of walking out of whatever hospital they take you to. But if you want me to do that, then you need to tell us what we want to know. Otherwise we'll just push off and leave you to it. And I might just decide to pop a bullet through one of your knees as well. That would take your mind off the hole in your stomach, believe me. So who sent you?"

The man turned an agonized glance up at Mallory's face. He evidently didn't like what he saw, because he gave an almost imperceptible nod and then started talking.

"I don't know who hired us. It was just a contract. Two quick and clean terminations. We were given your details and told the timescale. Nobody told us you'd be carrying." He broke off and emitted a low wail of absolute agony. "That's the truth," he added. "The only thing I know for sure is that the man we thought was the principal was only a cutout. I don't know who the principal was, and we only found out today that he was an Italian. Or at least he was somewhere in Italy."

Mallory glanced at Robin, who nodded.

"Not exactly a surprise," Mallory said. "Okay. Just hang in there. I'll make the call."

He took a handkerchief from his pocket and carefully wiped every part of the Beretta pistol he'd used and then dropped the weapon on the ground far enough away from the wounded man to ensure that he wouldn't be able to easily crawl to reach it.

"That'll confuse the ballistics a bit," he said to Robin. "We'll leave that and take his Browning. I prefer it to the Beretta anyway."

He walked back to the wounded man.

"Where's your phone?" he asked.

"In the car. Quick, mate, please."

Mallory walked swiftly over to the BMW, opened the passenger door, using his handkerchief on the handle, reached inside, and picked up a mobile from the dashboard, again covering his hand with the fabric to avoid leaving prints. He dialed triple nine, waited until the operator answered, and just said, "Help me. I've been shot." Then he replaced the phone on the dashboard, leaving the line open so the location of the mobile could be triangulated, and walked away.

"Let's get out of here," he said, walking back to where Robin was standing.

The Golf was a mess. The rear window had been blown out by the second shot fired by the dead driver, and two other bullets had hit the rear of the car, leaving ugly holes with jagged edges in the metal.

"We're lucky neither hit the fuel tank," Mallory said, peering under the vehicle to check for dripping petrol. "At least it should still be drivable."

Robin got back in the driver's seat and started the engine, which sounded entirely normal.

"I'll tell you one thing," she said, releasing the clutch

pedal as Mallory sat down beside her. "This has compre-hensively buggered up my no-claim bonus."

He grinned at her for a moment, then shook his head.

"I didn't think we'd be in this state quite so quickly," he said. "Obviously the bloody Italians are still after us, even if they are outsourcing the work."

"That's a nice way of putting it. I presume you know more about this kind of thing than I do, but even I can guess that the 'principal' is the person who ordered us to be killed, but what did that man mean by a 'cutout'?"

"Ordering somebody to be killed is a big deal, and nobody who wants a murder committed is ever going to openly make a contract with a couple of assassins for hire. If at all possible, he'll use a third party, maybe more than one in a chain, to hide his identity. That's a cutout. I sup-pose," he added thoughtfully, "it might have been a good idea to take the mobile, just in case we could have tracked and identified the cutout at least." Then he shook his head. "Too late, anyway, and I suppose whoever it was will have screened his number so it would be difficult or impossible to identify him, at least with the resources we have."

Robin had brought the Golf up to speed on the now virtually empty road, and was trying to use as little throt-tle as possible to avoid exhaust fumes being sucked into the car through the destroyed rear window.

Mallory glanced back and looked at the rear tailgate. Bits of safety glass were still clinging to the window seal around the edges of the hatchback, but virtually all the glass had been blown into the vehicle.

"We've got to decide what to do about this," he said.

"What, the car or the Italians?"

"Both, though I was really thinking short-term, about the car. Getting the rear window replaced will be easy enough, but those two bullet holes are going to be a bit more difficult to hide. We can't take the car to a garage in this state, because absolutely the first thing they'd do would be to call the rozzers. And we can't really claim the car was stolen, because that would raise an immediate red flag in front of Inspector bloody Wilson. He's just itching to find something—anything—that he can pin on us."

"So what do we do?"

"I think we need to do a bit of modification to the back of it, to hide the bullet holes. If you can find a quiet parking area somewhere well off the road, I'll see what I can do."

Fifteen minutes later Robin steered the car off the road and onto a disused track, not a paved turnout, that offered some cover from the road, and she and Mallory hopped out to inspect the damage.

The two holes were fairly close together, one in the tailgate itself and the other one a short distance below it, and it was perfectly obvious what had caused them. Bullet holes in thin metal left unmistakable damage.

"I think," Mallory said, "that we need a slight rear-end shunt to conceal these."

He looked around, then pointed a short distance farther down the track at a rocky outcrop. "That might do it. Let me just do a bit of creative panel beating first."

He picked up a heavy stone about the size of a grapefruit, one side of it a jagged point, and rammed the sharp edge hard against the lower hole. The fairly thin metal bent and tore, and after repeating the treatment five times, the telltale hole was so torn and distorted that it was impossible to tell what had caused the damage.

Then Mallory lay flat on his back and looked under the vehicle, checking to see if the bullet had lodged somewhere in the chassis.

"There's a dent and a scar on a part of the rear subframe," he said, "but the bullet is nowhere in sight."

"The tailgate is going to be more difficult," Robin said, "because it's double-skinned."

While Mallory scrambled to his feet, she opened the tailgate and peered into the open trunk of the vehicle.

"You're not going to like this," she said.

"What?"

"The bullet stayed inside the trunk. What stopped it plowing through and into the car—and potentially into my back—was your computer bag. And, unless I'm mistaken, your computer."

Mallory's expression darkened. His computer was his life, and his main source of income.

"There's a hole on this side, but no hole on the other," Robin continued, lifting out the leather bag.

Mallory almost snatched it from her and opened it to pull out his laptop. He looked at both sides of the computer but could see no immediate sign of damage

"It looks untouched," he said, his tone puzzled. "So what . . ."

"I think this is what you're looking for," Robin said,

reaching into the bag herself and pulling out a distorted and bent oblong black metal object, from the side of which about half of a copper-jacketed nine-millimeter bullet protruded. "It's one of your backup hard disks. Hard, in this case, being the most important part of the description."

Mallory took it from her, an expression of profound relief on his face. "I always said backups were vital, but until this moment I didn't know just how important they could be."

"Look at the angle," Robin said. "I think that probably saved my life. If that bag had been lying flat instead of standing upright, the bullet would have gone right through the back of the driver's seat."

Mallory took the ruined disk from her and looked at it. Then he wrapped his arms around Robin.

"Thank God for that," he murmured, kissing the top of her head.

"Enough of that. Later," Robin said, disengaging herself. "We've got stuff to do."

Mallory picked up the hard drive and seized the end of the bullet, but it was stuck fast in the metal of the hard disk. He took out a folding multitool from his bag, opened it to expose the jaws of the pliers, and prepared to grasp the missile once again, but Robin stopped him with a gesture.

"I'd like that as a souvenir," she said. "With the bullet in place, obviously. It'll be the first time a computer's ever saved my life, rather than tried to drive me to suicide. I think I'll get it mounted."

"You're welcome to it. It's all yours," Mallory said, handing it over. "Now let's see what we can do with this bullet hole."

He used the rock again to distort the point of impact and conceal the cause of the damage. When he was satisfied that nobody would be able to prove that a bullet had hit the vehicle, he started the car, drove it a few yards along the track to the rocky outcrop, turned the vehicle, and then backed it hard into the rock. Then he got out again and checked the damage.

"That should do it," he said. "It just looks like a bit of really clumsy reversing, which I know you wouldn't do, not with your driving skills. But that's the best we can do. Now we can book it into a garage somewhere and get the damage fixed without some eagle-eyed mechanic calling the cops."

They checked that all the rear lights still worked, then got back on the road.

"Exeter, I suppose?" Robin asked.

"That's as good as anywhere. All we need is a garage where we can leave the car to be fixed. Then we'll hire something else so we can stay mobile."

Robin was silent for a few moments, then glanced across at Mallory.

"And do what?" she asked softly. "I don't know about you, but this really isn't what I signed up for. Facing those armed Italians here in Devon and then in the cave on Cyprus was one thing. We were both hunting for the relic, obviously, and I suppose you could say it was inevitable that we'd end up in some kind of fight with them because of that. But unless I've completely misunderstood, those two men had just been ordered to kill us. Not find out what we knew or what we were going to do, or anything like that, but just to shoot us down in cold blood. And that's a whole different ball game."

Mallory nodded. "You're absolutely right, but I do think it was a predictable reaction, just because of what happened. Think about it. We managed to escape those Italians in Cyprus, and once we came back to the U.K. we passed over what we'd discovered about their identities to the police, including that video of the leader of the group telling us how clever they'd been, and admitting that he'd killed the three men in your apartment in Dartmouth. He only told us that because he knew we were about to die. But because we escaped, he's now a wanted man here in the U.K., and that's entirely down to us. So trying to kill us does make sense from his point of view. It's simple revenge. Nothing more, nothing less. And he would have had to outsource the job because his face will now be on a watch list at all British airports and other points of entry to the country. Or it should be, if Wilson has any brains at all."

"So are you saying that he'll try again once he's found out that his first attempt didn't work?"

Mallory spread out his hands. "I have no idea. Possibly. Maybe even probably. And that really leaves us with two choices. We can hide, go to ground, and hope that who-ever he sends after us next time can't track us down. Or we do the other thing."

"Which is?"

"We carry on with the quest. We try to identify the next clue and see where that takes us."

Robin nodded. "That's what I guessed you'd say. But are you sure we'd be safer if we carry on?"

Mallory shook his head. "I really don't know. I suppose my logic is that if we do follow the trail and find whatever the Templars hid all those centuries ago, then the quest will be over. We'll have won, and that would finally knock the Italians out of the race."

"But they might still come after us," Robin pointed out.

"They might," Mallory admitted, "but there's not a lot we can do about that, apart from trying not to get killed when they show up."

"That's not a hell of an attractive plan, if you don't mind me saying so: try not to get killed. Is that the best you can do?"

"It's worked for us so far," Mallory said, a smile briefly appearing on his face. "But," he added, "I still think that going on, following the trail and trying to identify and decipher the next clue, is potentially the safer option of the two. Being active, I mean, rather than passive, just hanging about and waiting for something to happen."

"Okay. Actually I think you're right. Finding whatever the Templars hid might not just be the best way of getting these Italian comedians off our backs—it might be the *only* way to get rid of them. So we'll crack on, agreed?"

"Agreed."

Mallory used his mobile to locate a Volkswagen dealer on an industrial estate on the outskirts of Exeter. He was very keen not to drive through the city, because he was certain the damage to the car would be visible on traffic cameras, and that could provide a tenuous link between them and the shooting, a link that he knew Wilson would definitely exploit if he got to hear about it. But the garage he'd picked was far enough out for that not to be a problem. He hoped.

Robin followed his directions to the dealership and handed over the Golf for repair. The workshop was pretty well backed up with cars awaiting servicing or repair, and the best estimate the workshop reception could provide was about two weeks before the car would be ready for collection. They would have preferred a rather shorter timescale, but right then they were out of other options.

They took a taxi to a car hire company and rented a rather dull and ordinary Renault, which Mallory hoped would be relatively anonymous.

"Do we find a hotel here, or do you want to go somewhere else?" Robin asked.

"We'll head toward London and find somewhere en route," Mallory said. "I'd like to put a bit of distance between us and Okehampton, because of what happened there. By now there'll be a heavy police presence in the area, and being somewhere else seems like a pretty good plan to me, even though there'll be nothing to connect us directly to the shooting."

"The passenger might spill the beans about what happened."

"I doubt it, actually. If he is stupid enough to tell the rozzers that he had a contract to kill us, what they'll do is add a charge of attempted murder to the murder rap he'll already be facing, because bullets from that Beretta pistol killed the driver. So telling them what really happened will make his own situation worse, not better."

"But he didn't fire the weapon," Robin pointed out.

"No, but he did fire the Browning, so a routine paraffin test on his hands will show that he'd used a firearm. The lack of his fingerprints on the murder weapon is bound to be an oddity that will puzzle the cops, but I doubt if that would stop a prosecution. They'll just assume he wiped the pistol before he dropped it. The bigger anomaly will be the bullet that hit him in the stomach, which was the first one I fired from the Beretta. I don't know how they'll explain that one away, but knowing the British police they'll think of something. Maybe they'll decide he had an argument and shot the driver, then stumbled and accidentally pulled the trigger while the muzzle of the weapon was pointing at his stomach. Something like that."

15

Yeovil, Somerset

They didn't drive that far, turning off the A303 near the Royal Naval Air Station at Yeovilton in Somerset and heading south to the market town of Yeovil and picking a small hotel on the northern outskirts. Once they were settled in their room, they started work again.

Working on the photographs, Mallory spent almost an hour trying to identify every mark on the metalwork that could possibly be a part of the shadowy female figure. It wasn't easy, but knowing where her face was, and a part of one of her feet, meant that at least he knew where he should be looking. When he'd finished, he sat back, scrutinized what he had done, made a handful of tiny changes, and then showed the result to Robin.

"That's as good as I can get it," he said, "and at least I think I found enough marks on the metal to confirm that it's not just a figment of my imagination. There really is a drawing of a female figure concealed within that pattern."

Robin took the page from him and looked at it intently.

"I believe you," she said. "I really thought you were wrong on this, but I can see enough of a correlation between what you've drawn and the marks on the metalwork to confirm it. And that means that we know what we have to do next."

"Yes. Go through the same process on the metalwork from the second chest. Maybe the second symbol or shape—and I'm sure there is one—will give us a pointer as to where we should be looking."

It didn't seem that difficult a job. After all, they had managed to identify and then re-create the image hidden in one part of the ornamental scrollwork, but trying to identify anything at all in the photograph of the top of the other chest proved to be much more difficult.

"I don't know if it's just me," Mallory said, nearly two hours later, "but I'm not seeing anything in these pictures."

"Nor me," Robin agreed. "The only possible mark I have found is near the top of the pattern, and I think it might show a circle, something like that."

"Let me see," Mallory said, leaning over to look at the page Robin was holding.

"There are two marks, here and here," Robin said, pointing near the top of the picture, "and another one much lower down, just here. If you connected those lines together, they would form a circle or a sphere, something like that."

Mallory nodded.

"I missed that," he admitted. "I've been trying to find anything that looked like a human figure, but actually I was probably wasting my time. There's no reason why the other symbol would have to be another figure. In fact, that's probably quite unlikely."

"Why?" Robin asked.

"Because the only purpose of these hidden images has to be to provide a clue to a name that we can use as a code word to decipher the last piece of that text, or to send us somewhere where we'll find the code word. To me, nothing else really makes sense."

"And as all we have so far is the outline of an anonymous woman, with no idea what historical figure the image is meant to represent, I suppose you think we will have to visit some significant location? Mind you, I still don't think that's necessarily right. I mean, why couldn't they simply have incorporated the code word directly into the metalwork pattern?"

Mallory shrugged. "I don't know. Don't forget that we're dealing with a cunning medieval mind, and what might seem sensible and logical to you and me might not have even occurred to whoever ordered that scrollwork to be fabricated. Or perhaps this kind of round-the-houses approach was intended to provide an extra layer of security."

"Well, it's certainly done that," Robin said, "because we're no further forward now than we were when we started."

"That's not quite true. We've managed to identify the outline of a female figure built into the metalwork, so that at least means that we're not looking for the name of a man. So whatever code word or other information is encoded into a decoration on those chests, we can be certain that it's not the name of Jacques de Molay or any other Templar knight. Women were not part of the order, don't forget. When knights joined the Templars, they were required to be single, and they were also forbidden from any and all contact with females while they wore the *croix pattée*. So while I don't know who this woman is supposed to be, realistically there can't be that many contenders."

"So what you're saying is that if this figure was meant to represent Mary Magdalene or one of the French queens or somebody, then the name of that person might well be the clue to deciphering the encrypted text?"

"Possibly, yes," Mallory replied, "but if it was the Magdalene, and I guess that's the most likely contender, then I would expect at the very least the figure to have a halo, or for there to be some other reference or object that would confirm her identity."

As he spoke, Robin picked up the photograph again and began looking carefully at the area above the figure's head. After a few moments, she muttered an exclamation and pointed at two lines she had just spotted.

"Unless I'm guilty of wishful thinking," she said, her voice high with excitement, "that could well be a circle behind her head. Not the kind of ring of light that's characteristic of paintings done after the late medieval period, but the solid white object that was used to indicate divinity in those early days. So if I'm right and I'm not seeing things, this could well be Mary Magdalene."

Mallory looked carefully at the marks she was indicating.

"You may be right, you may be wrong," he said, "but Mary was one of the very few women who fulfilled any kind of role in the early Christian church, and so if the Templars were looking for a female figure who could be identified later and who might be associated in any way with the order, she would be a pretty good choice. It's certainly worth a try," he added.

He took a sheet of paper from his computer case on which he had transcribed the final and so far undeciphered section of the parchment Robin had discovered what seemed like months ago locked inside the medieval book safe. Then he took a fresh sheet of paper and wrote out "Mary Magdalene" in a variety of different forms, including the spelling in Latin, in modern and ancient French, in Occitan, and any other language that the Knights Templars might have used at the beginning of the fourteenth century.

And then they began a process of trial and error, using the name of the Magdalene as they applied Atbash decryption—the oldest and simplest possible letter substitution encryption method—to the text.

But absolutely all they succeeded in doing was repeatedly turning one piece of gibberish into another, equally unintelligible, piece of gibberish.

"That's not it," Mallory said at last, throwing down his pencil in frustration. "And I suppose when you think about it, it's not that likely a code word anyway, because even the English version contains the letter *M* twice, *A* three times, and *E* twice, which would make a code word of only thirteen letters pretty much unusable. Any code word where only three letters represent over half of the possible letters really isn't going to work, because there'd be so much repetition. That figure may be Mary Magdalene—I suppose she is the most likely candidate— but what we're looking for definitely isn't just her name. We're missing something here, and I don't mind telling you I have no idea what it is."

"Nor have I," Robin said, "but what I do know is that there simply must be something on the other chest. Something hidden within the scrollwork that would make sense of the image. So all we have to do is find it."

"It sounds easy if you say it quickly," Mallory said, "but absolutely the only thing you found was that circle. If it is a circle, of course. But you're right. The rest of the clue has to be there somewhere, so we need to take another look at it."

For the next few minutes, they sat side by side at the small desk, both concentrating on the printed copies of the photographs in front of them. And then, at almost the same moment, they each found something that might possibly help clarify what they were looking for.

"You go first," Mallory said.

"I've found a couple of marks that might be the shape of a box," Robin said, almost doubtfully. "These two sort of small letter L shapes could be the bottom corners of it, though the corresponding marks of the top aren't anything like as sharp, almost as if there's something on top of the lid, or maybe the box is supposed to be open and those shapes are objects that are sticking out of it."

They both stared at the marks she'd found. They were faint, and definitely subject to interpretation—and of course misinterpretation—but what convinced Mallory she was on the right track was the fact that the two small marks she'd found lined up precisely, one with the other. He still had no idea what it could be representing, but at least the marks appeared to him to be deliberate rather than accidental. And that was good news.

"What have you spotted?" Robin asked.

"It's this circle shape," Mallory began, a smile spreading across his face. "It's not a lot, but I've found what looked like the marks of several other circles inside the outer one that you spotted first."

Robin looked at him suspiciously.

"And that means something to you, does it?" she demanded.

Mallory nodded slowly. "Actually I think it does. The figure of a woman, most likely Mary Magdalene, and a drawing of what looks like a large number of concentric circles? Oh yes, that very definitely means something to me." He glanced at his watch. "It's too late to head off today, but we should get back on the road first thing tomorrow morning. We've got a trip to make, and if my hunch is right, we might be able to read the plaintext of that parchment by tomorrow night."

16

One of the more unusual aspects of the organization based on the Aventine Hill was that although it was a very secure unit, particularly the intelligence section located in the windowless basement, there was almost nothing in the building—apart from the computers and associated equipment—that would attract even the most sophisticated thief or burglar.

There were a lot of old and even ancient books stored in the basement, books written in Latin, Hebrew, and Aramaic, and even more stored as collections of scanned pages on the massive hard drives of the secure local area network, which was both physically and electronically secure because no part of it was connected to the Internet. But none of these volumes, actual or virtual, had any particular value on the open market. The only people likely to be interested in them were academics working in various somewhat obscure fields, and in any event the contents of most of the books were already out there in the public domain.

But despite this, security was extremely tight, which was why Marco Toscanelli never even attempted to take his unregistered personal mobile phone into the building: the portal scanners would have detected it the moment he tried to gain entrance. Instead he carried only his "official" mobile, the one issued to him by the organization, and left the other mobile locked securely in the glove box of his car.

Ever since he'd made the call to one of his contacts in Britain, he'd been expecting a text confirming that his orders had been carried out, and had made a point of leaving the building for lunch every day and checking his phone on his way to or from the restaurant of his choice.

That day, when he checked his mobile, there was a text message, but the content wasn't what he had expected to read. Instead of a brief "Job done" or something similar, the text was an equally terse two-word message: "Call me."

Toscanelli checked his watch. He had time to call the man before he needed to return to the building, so he called another unregistered mobile, this one with a British number.

"You asked me to ring you," he said, without preamble.

"Yes, I did. There's been a problem."

"What kind of problem?"

"Terminal, really," the other man replied. "The team we contracted to do the job failed. One of them didn't make it, and the other one is in custody."

Toscanelli muttered a particularly foul Italian oath.

"What about the targets?" he asked.

"As far as I know they walked away, or rather they drove away, after the contact."

Toscanelli repeated the oath with even greater emphasis. "Where are they now?"

"I don't know. I haven't been able to talk to the member of the team who was wounded, because he's still in intensive care at the hospital. He may not even survive. Contact took place at a parking area on a road in Devon, and by triangulating the main target's mobile we'd established that she was in a hotel in Okehampton, a few miles west, earlier that day. Presumably she and the man then left, the team followed them and forced them to stop on the road, and then it all went wrong. I've no idea if the targets' car was damaged or if they were injured, or where they went."

"Can you find out?" Toscanelli demanded.

"I'm trying, but right now I have almost no sources of information I can use. The woman's mobile is still off the network, and so far I've not been told her car has been spotted by any traffic cameras. That information takes a long time to collate unless it's a high-priority investigation, and because I'm not officially involved I have to tread carefully. I can't show too much interest in an investigation that I'm not a part of."

"So what you're telling me," Toscanelli said, "is that until she surfaces, both of them are off the grid?"

"Exactly. Until then, there's nothing more I can do."

Toscanelli was briefly silent, considering his options, then issued another request.

"Can you do that?" he asked.

"Yes, but it will have to be low priority, which means I might not get the information until a day or so later."

"That will have to do. Put it in place."

Toscanelli ended the call a few moments later. His mood, when he walked back into the building, was dark.

17

Chartres, France

"Are you absolutely certain about this?" Robin asked, for at least the fourth time since they'd caught a morning flight out of Gatwick Airport.

They'd flown to Paris, experienced virtually no delays at the arrival airport because they were each carrying only a cabin bag, and Mallory had quickly hired a car. They'd cleared Paris and picked up the A10 autoroute, L'Acquitaine, at Palaiseau on the southwestern outskirts of the city and headed straight for Chartres. At Ponthévrard the autoroute had divided, L'Acquitaine turning south for Orléans, while they continued southwest on the A11, L'Océane.

Mallory didn't reply for a few moments, just pointed ahead through the windshield of the hire car at the green copper roof of the cathedral, which was then clearly visible.

"The short answer," he said, "is no. I'm not sure, but

the only thing that made sense to me from trying to interpret those two pieces of carved metal was that the female figure most probably was Mary Magdalene, and the cathedral at Chartres is dedicated to Notre Dame, to Mary. Obviously there are lots of other cathedrals and churches dedicated to or named after the same person, but it was the circles that clinched it for me."

"You still haven't explained what you think that is," Robin complained.

"Actually I thought you would have guessed it by now. As far as I know, there's only one church anywhere in the world where there's a pattern of concentric circles. Quite a famous pattern, in fact."

Robin's face clouded as Mallory glanced at her. Then she suddenly brightened and snapped her fingers as realization dawned. "You mean the Labyrinth?"

"Exactly. It's one of the most famous features of that cathedral, and both the building and the Labyrinth predate the purging of the Knights Templar order by about a hundred years, so the man who manufactured the scrollwork would almost certainly have known about both."

Mallory steered the hired Citroën off the autoroute and stopped at the tollbooth to pay the fee. Then he drove on toward the center of the city, passing the Aérodrome de Chartres-Métropole on his right. Flying directly to Chartres would have been more convenient, but the flight times simply hadn't worked out.

He drove in toward the city center, the sat nav built into his smartphone navigating him perfectly competently. They were both keeping their eyes open for a convenient parking place, and when they turned down the Boulevard du Maréchal Foch Mallory spotted at least half a dozen spaces on the opposite side of the street by the bank of the river L'Eure. He waited for a gap in the traffic coming toward him, then swung the car across the road into an unoccupied space.

"And I suppose now you're going to tell me that that was the easy bit," Robin said as they climbed out and Mallory locked the doors. "Just getting here, I mean."

He nodded.

"It probably was," he said. "We've got the obvious problem of discovering precisely where we should be looking. I'm pretty certain we're in the right place, because of those two carvings, Mary Magdalene or Notre Dame, and a simple outline of the Labyrinth. It's the next step that's going to prove the tricky one, trying to find out exactly which bits of carved text or whatever we are supposed to be looking at."

The vast bulk of the cathedral loomed in front of them as they made their way toward it.

"It's a big place," Robin said, "and I suppose right now you don't have any idea where we should start looking."

"You're absolutely right," Mallory replied. "I haven't. I've never been here before, and to me the obvious way to tackle this is to have a wander around the entire building, inside and out, and just see if anything strikes us. Then hopefully we can try to narrow down the search area."

Robin nodded agreement and walked on a few steps before she slowed to a halt to look up at the vast bulk of the cathedral.

"What?" Mallory asked.

"I was just thinking," she replied. "This building's been here for a long time, right?"

"Yes. I think it's tenth century or thereabouts."

"So whoever prepared that clue to be incorporated on the lids of the chests would have known about the building. That's obvious. And he would also have known, I presume, that in a place of this size there are going to be dozens, perhaps even hundreds or thousands, of carved inscriptions decorating the walls, the tombs, and no doubt all sorts of other bits."

She glanced at Mallory, who nodded agreement. What she was saying exactly mirrored his own opinion.

"And your point is?" Mallory asked.

"My point is that if that anonymous Knight Templar who started this hare running knew all that, he must surely also have known that he would need to provide more information or better directions to show anyone following the trail where they should be looking."

"That makes sense. So?"

"So I think that outline of a box or whatever it was in that scrollwork must be significant. That must be the final clue. The outline of the woman, Mary Magdalene, told you the name of the place you should be looking, and the drawing of the Labyrinth confirmed the precise location, the cathedral of Notre Dame at Chartres. The image of the box must mean something, and we need to work out exactly what so that we don't waste time looking in the wrong places."

"Good thinking. But I still think it would be helpful

to take a look around the cathedral before we do anything else, just to get a feel for the place."

"Absolutely. I agree. We need to do a quick visual survey, and pick up a decent guidebook written in English, then find a hotel for the night because it's already late afternoon. Then we should do our best to work out which bits of the place we ought to be looking at when we come back here, bright-eyed and bushy-tailed, first thing tomorrow morning."

"I do like a woman with a plan," Mallory said, grabbed Robin's hand, and led her toward the entrance of the imposing cathedral.

It was already late afternoon, but despite that the building was still crowded, groups of tourists being shepherded from one area to another under the watchful eyes of their tour guides and the various uniformed security guards stationed at intervals throughout the echoing interior of the cathedral. Notre Dame had always attracted a wide variety of visitors from around the world. The Japanese tourists were unmistakable, festooned with cameras that they were using at every opportunity, and chattering away excitedly as each new feature was pointed out to them. A party of uniformed schoolchildren, possibly Dutch, walked past Robin and Mallory in an orderly crocodile, one teacher holding a flag as she led them across the stone floor while another teacher followed behind, presumably checking for stragglers and strays. And as they began their own survey of the building, Mallory heard four American tourists conversing in subdued whispers, clearly somewhat overawed by both the immense size of the structure and its very obvious age.

Robin and Mallory didn't make the slightest attempt to study any part of the building, just concentrated on identifying the principal features so that when they began looking at the guidebook—which they hadn't yet bought—they would have a much better idea of what was being described in it.

Their quick walk-around over, they spent some minutes looking at the publications on offer in the shop before settling on two different large-format books, both containing a text written in English and both illustrated with what they hoped were accurate plans and diagrams of the building and numerous photographs.

By the time they stepped out of the building, the afternoon was virtually over, so as soon as they got back to the hire car, Mallory used the sat nav system on his smartphone to identify the hotels in the area.

"That's handy," he said. "If this is right, then there's a hotel pretty much just around the next corner. That should put us about the same distance from the cathedral as we are now."

"Can we walk it?" Robin asked. "We've only got our two carry-on bags to handle."

"We probably could, yes," Mallory agreed, "but there are plenty of vacant parking places along this stretch, so if the hotel doesn't have parking we can always come back here. But I think we might as well drive there first of all."

Less than five minutes later, he pulled the Citroën to a stop outside a hotel belonging to a chain that covered much of Europe, a hotel that offered underground parking as something of a bonus, as well as air-conditioning and Wi-Fi in all rooms. They took a double room on the second floor, sorted out the stuff they would need to use overnight, and then they both began what Mallory had mentally referred to as their "homework," reading through the guidebooks to try to learn as much as they could about the Notre Dame Cathedral in the shortest time possible.

They broke for dinner just after half past seven, and were back in their room an hour later. By ten, Mallory had gone through most of the chapters in his particular guidebook and had also looked carefully at all the illustrations, both photographs and diagrams. He closed the book with a brisk snap, then leaned back against the pillow.

"Anything?" Robin asked.

"Well, I now know a hell of a lot more about Chartres Cathedral than I knew before, and probably more than I ever wanted to know. But if you mean 'have I worked out where we should be looking yet,' then the answer's no. It is an enormous building, and it could take us days or weeks to cover every part of it. And you were right in what you said earlier. There are inscriptions everywhere, so what we absolutely have to do is try to work out which one we should be looking at before we even set foot in the building again. Have you got anything?"

Robin shook her head.

"Pretty much the same as you, really," she replied. "I now know an awful lot about the history and building of the cathedral, but as far as I can see none of it is in any way relevant to what we're looking for."

"So we definitely need to work out the meaning of that other image on the photograph of the scroll?"

"Absolutely. That really is the only way forward, as far as I can see."

They studied the image together, and Mallory tentatively added a line between the two lower *L* shapes that Robin had discovered, then extended two vertical lines upward from those shapes toward the rather less distinct markings that she believed might show either the contents of the open box—if that was what it was—or the shape of the lid. That part of the photograph was crisscrossed by almost half a dozen lengths of metal, all part of the pattern on the lid of the chest, and each bore a number of markings that might, or equally well might not, form a part of the hidden image.

"That shape there," Robin said, pointing at one particular part of the image, "looks almost like a small face. I think I can see eyes, maybe a mouth, and almost certainly a nose. But I don't think that can be right, because on the bit of metal just to the right of it, behind the face, as it were, I think I can see a part of a wing."

"You mean a bird's wing?" Mallory asked.

"Maybe, yes. Or at least, there are lines etched into the design that look to me more like feathers than anything else."

Mallory looked carefully at the area she was indicating. "Yes, I see what you mean, I think, though that really doesn't make any sense to me. I was wondering if what you found was a diagram of a tomb, although the shape would be a bit odd if it is meant to be the grave of some

knight or local lord. But I don't think feathers were ever
the kind of decoration that you would expect to find on
the tomb of an aristocrat. Swords, yes. Chain mail definitely, but feathers probably not."

"Maybe I'm looking at it all wrong," Robin said bitterly. "Right, that's it. My head's spinning with all the
reading I've done, and my eyes are starting to ache
because of these photographs. I'm going to sleep on it
and hope one of us has some kind of brain wave before
we go back to the cathedral tomorrow morning."

They each spent some time in the bathroom, taking a
shower and performing the usual ablutions, then climbed
into the generous double bed. Neither of them fell asleep
for quite a while, but that was nothing to do with trying
to solve the riddle of the chests, and much more to do
with getting to know each other a whole lot better.

18

"There's been a shooting," Silvio Vitale said as Toscanelli walked into his office.

"What? Where? Here in Rome?"

Vitale shook his head. "Probably, but that's not what I'm talking about. It was in England. In Devon, to be exact."

Vitale looked closely at his subordinate.

"Do you know anything about it?" he asked.

"Me? No. Why should I?"

"I'm just asking, because the watchers I tasked with following Jessop and Mallory have lost contact with them."

"Were they involving in this shooting?" Toscanelli asked.

"Not as far as I know. But I don't like coincidences, and for those two to vanish from sight at the same time as there's a shooting in exactly the same area seems remarkably coincidental. Shootings in Devon are quite rare, especially using handguns, which were apparently the weapons used in this incident."

Vitale's gaze never wavered.

"I know you have issues with those two," he went on, "but I specifically ordered you not to touch them because of this quest. If I find out that you were involved in this, you will live—at least for a short time—to regret it."

"But how do you know this killing was anything to do with them?" Toscanelli protested, feeling a chill run down his back as he digested the implications of what Vitale had just said.

"I didn't say it was a killing," Vitale said. "Only that there'd been a shooting."

"I just assumed that was what you meant," Toscanelli said quickly, immediately aware of his slip.

"Maybe. Assumptions can be dangerous. Sometimes they can even be fatal. Anyway, my watchers are on their trail, and they should relocate them quickly. Sooner or later one of them will use a credit card or do some other kind of transaction that will identify them so we can pick up the trail again."

"You still think they could be useful to us?"

Vitale stared at Toscanelli for several seconds, as if considering his response. Then he nodded. "Possibly. At this stage, I don't know. But what I do know is that somehow they managed to decipher the first clues in the Templar trail before anyone here was able to do so, despite the number of alleged experts we employ and the resources we can command here. However you look at it, that was an impressive feat, bearing mind that Jessop is only a bookseller—"

"An antiquarian bookseller," Toscanelli pointed out.

"She sells old books, yes, but as far as we've been able to discover, she has no knowledge or experience of cracking ancient ciphers."

"But Mallory apparently has. We know that he responded very quickly to her first e-mail and solved the Atbash cipher she discovered on the parchment. And I said right from the start, as soon as we first encountered him, that there was more to him than at first appeared. He might not be a computer expert, but we do know that he was previously a police officer, and he can handle himself in a fight."

"I understood it was Jessop who did most of the damage to your men. And she's only a woman, and a small one at that."

Toscanelli nodded, a grim smile on his face. "She may be small, and she's easy to dismiss as a threat, but she's extraordinarily competent in martial arts, and we've since discovered that she has a competition driving license, which means she's a qualified racing driver. She also has a private pilot's license. As a pair, they do pose a potential threat, and in my opinion they should be eliminated."

"But not in mine, Toscanelli. They beat you to Cyprus, and in fact you ended up following them because we hadn't managed to crack the code in that manuscript. If they hadn't got involved, we wouldn't even have discovered those two chests in the cave. So for the moment at least we don't touch them, just in case we can't work out where we should be looking next, but they do."

19

Chartres, France

The following morning, Mallory woke early and slid out of bed without disturbing Robin. He sat down at the small table where he'd left his laptop, logged on to the Internet, and began searching, looking for any ancient relic, any object from antiquity that could possibly fit the vague shape they seemed to have identified: a tallish oblong box with a raised lid that might be decorated with an image of either a small face or the wing of a bird. Or maybe both.

And whatever it was, assuming they were looking in the right place—the cathedral of Notre Dame—it also had to be an object that they could identify at Chartres, either in the cathedral itself or possibly very close to it; otherwise the clue didn't make sense. Mallory assumed that he was most probably looking for an unusual memorial, or some part of the fabric of the building itself, such as the outline of one part of the ancient cathedral, or maybe a gravestone. Something of that nature. Or, and despite what he had said to Robin the day before, just possibly it could be the end of one of the raised stone tombs that were popular in the medieval period.

It seemed like a fruitless task. They'd both spent the previous evening staring at dozens of photographs, sketches, and plans of the building, and neither of them had seen anything that even vaguely resembled the shadowy outline they thought they'd identified within the metal scrollwork. And the Internet, almost invariably everyone's first port of call when they had a question that needed answering, to the extent that a new verb—"to Google" something—was now an established part of the English language, was for once not producing anything that seemed particularly helpful.

There were pages and pages of Web sites that contained information about the cathedral, including the history and construction of the building, its importance as a center of worship, scholarly architectural analyses of the design and construction of the cathedral, and the inevitable sites produced by the lunatic fringe making a wide variety of astonishingly unlikely claims about hidden purposes and hidden meanings relating to the place, most of which made no sense whatsoever.

Quite apart from its obvious importance as a Roman Catholic place of worship, and one of the most important such buildings not just in France, but anywhere in the Western world, Mallory also found a large number of sites dedicated to the Labyrinth. In the main, these consisted either of serious studies covering the origin, meaning, and construction of this well-known feature of the cathedral, or far more speculative Web sites that concentrated on the *real* reason for its construction. Unfortunately none of the sites agreed as to exactly what this real reason might be, and many of the suggestions would have stretched the credulity of most people to well beyond breaking point.

He was just about to give up completely when a sleepy voice interrupted his concentration.

"What are you doing?" Robin asked. "Not looking at porn sites while I'm asleep, I hope."

"With you around the place," Mallory replied with a grin, "the very last thing I need to look at is any porn. No, I was just doing a quick cruise around the Web, looking for anything that might fit that other shape you found in the scrollwork."

"I believe you, but most women probably wouldn't. Any luck?"

"Not yet, no. In fact, if there was anything, any object or feature that looked anything like that shape, I would have thought there would at least have been a hint about it in one of the guidebooks. After all, they do cover the entire building in considerable detail. In fact, the only positive suggestion I have is that we go and check all the gravestones."

"You mean the ones inside the building?" Robin asked. "I saw a number incorporated in the floor of the cathedral, and there are probably quite a few built into the walls as well."

Mallory shook his head.

"We can check those, of course," he said, "but I was actually thinking about regular gravestones, the kind you find in most churchyards. Think about it. The shape we sketched out is an oblong that's almost square, with a straight base and straight sides, just like the sides of the box, in fact. But that shape could also be a gravestone, the base sunk into the ground with straight sides, and the suggestion of a face and a wing at the top of the object could well be a depiction of an angel. Or something of that sort."

Robin sat up in bed and nodded enthusiastically.

"You're absolutely right," she said. "We could very well be looking at the shape of a gravestone, and the other obvious thing about a gravestone is that there will invariably be words carved onto it. Even if it's only the name of the person buried there and the dates that he or she was born and died."

"And realistically," Mallory agreed, "the person who compiled that parchment could have used any combination of letters—proper names or an epitaph or anything else—as a code word, so I really do think we could be on the right track."

French breakfasts tend to be heavy on coffee and light on almost everything else, and ten minutes after they'd each consumed a couple of croissants and a small *pain au raisin*, washed down by large cups of strong black coffee, Mallory and Robin strode out of the hotel and made their way through the streets, covering the short distance to the cathedral. Mallory had somewhat reluctantly left his laptop locked up in the hotel room—as he had frequently admitted to Robin, he was paranoid about losing the computer and it went almost everywhere with him—and he was carrying a digital camera plus a spare battery and printed copies of the photographs they had been working from. Robin was toting quite a large handbag that contained her camera, plus her tablet computer.

And, as she pointed out to Mallory as they walked toward the cathedral, she had also brought along her brain, which was by far the most important component the two of them possessed.

"If what we're looking for is anywhere here," she assured him, "then I promise you I'll spot it."

There were a lot of gravestones in the vicinity of the cathedral, and they immediately decided to split up, to search independently, simply because that would speed things up.

"Are you happy about the date range?" Mallory asked.

"I think so, yes. We don't know exactly when that parchment was written, but it has to be after 1307, because that date is actually encoded within the text, and my guess is that it was probably written a few years after that, so say after 1320. So if we take that as the cutoff date, we're looking for gravestones of any year prior to—well, let's say 1330, just to give us a bit more of a margin."

"Got it," Mallory said. "I'll start over there," he added, pointing to the far side of the graveyard.

What quickly became apparent was that there was no sort of order or plan to the timing of the burials. In some cases the occupants of adjacent plots of land had died as much as five hundred years apart, and the appearance of the gravestones was a far from infallible indicator of their age, some of the comparatively newer stones looking much more ancient than many of the much older grave markers. That meant checking the dates listed on every stone was an essential first step. And sometimes even that proved difficult, when patches of lichen, moss, and other greenery obscured the relevant parts of the inscriptions. So both Mallory and Robin inevitably spent time simply clearing vegetation from some of the older stones before they could confirm the date of the burial.

And although they found plenty of tombstones that had been erected before the end of the thirteenth century, almost all of them were plain and simple grave markers, devoid of any form of decoration apart from occasional random shapes carved by long-dead stonemasons to frame or separate the information on the gravestone in the case of multiple burials in the same plot.

A little over two hours after they'd started, they met again at the entrance to the graveyard, both hot—it was a very warm day—sweating, and irritated.

"Anything?" Mallory asked.

"Oh yes," Robin said brightly. "I now know almost all the popular family names of people who died in this area eight hundred years ago. And I also know that almost every man and woman seemed to have preferred the simplest possible memorials. Usually just their name, date of death, and some kind of French or Latin one-liner if they were feeling particularly elaborate, usually something along the lines of the contemporary equivalent of 'rest in peace.' But if you're asking me if I've found a roughly oblong gravestone decorated by the face of an angel flapping its wings, then the answer is no."

"I thought so," Mallory said. "Let's go and get a drink or something."

They took their combined irritation to a small bar a few streets away and fairly close to the river. Strong alcohol seemed like a bad idea, bearing in mind the comparatively early hour, the heat of the day, and the fact that they still had to find what they were looking for, so they both opted for glasses of lager.

"There are still a few gravestones we haven't looked at," Mallory said, lowering his half-empty glass to the table in front of him. "We might get lucky. There's still a chance."

Robin shook her head. "Frankly I doubt it. If it had been the local habit to decorate tombstones with carvings, then I think we would have found far more evidence of this in the graveyard. As it is, about the only embellishments I found on any of the stones from the right period were just straight lines or occasionally curved marks to function as a kind of border to the epitaph or whatever was carved on it. What I didn't see, anywhere, was anything as frivolous as an angel. Mind you," she added, "there were a lot of tombstones with that kind of decoration from the post-medieval period, and especially moving right up toward the present day. But almost all of the early stones were largely undecorated, very plain and austere."

Mallory took another sip of his drink.

"So, do you think we're wasting our time?" he asked.

"I'm sorry, but I do. When you came up with the idea of checking gravestones, I really thought that might be the answer, because it fitted so well with that vague shape we detected. But now I definitely believe we're looking in the wrong place for the wrong thing. We need to go back to the drawing board and start again."

Mallory pulled out the photographs and put them on the table between them.

"I still think we got the shape right," he said. "More or less oblong, like a box, and with this angel or something decorating the lid."

They both bent forward over the printed image, struggling to see any other marks that would indicate what they should be looking for.

"What about that?" Robin asked, pointing. "Could that be another wing? I think I can see what look like feathers etched into the metal."

"Possibly," Mallory agreed. "If you're right, it's on the opposite side of the box, so it can't really be an extension of the same wing. So are we looking at two angels?"

Then a sudden thought struck him, and it was almost as if a surge of excitement passed through his body as his mind struggled to come to terms with the possibility that had just presented itself.

The sudden change in his mood communicated itself to Robin, and she looked at him quizzically. "What? What is it?"

Mallory didn't reply for a moment, but instead stared with total concentration at the photograph.

"I really don't believe it," he said, his voice trembling with excitement, "but just look here. And here."

He pointed at the photograph, roughly two-thirds of the way up from the base of the oblong shape.

"Do you see that?" he asked.

Robin stared at the mark he was indicating.

"I see a small vertical line," she said. "Nothing more."

"Exactly. There's one line here, on this piece of metal, and there's another one just here, matching it."

He had already drawn pencil lines on the photograph to indicate the base and sides of the object depicted there. He now took a pen from his pocket and drew a line that extended well beyond the box shape and passed through the two short vertical marks that he had identified. Then he turned the paper round so that Robin could see it in what he believed to be the correct orientation.

"What do you see?" he asked softly.

"I see what might be a box with a line drawn across it," she said. "Obviously."

"Just imagine for a moment," Mallory said, "that those two vertical marks are rings on the side of a box, and that the line I just drew represents a pole that's been passed through them. Now what do you see?"

"A box that can be lifted and carried about the place, I suppose," Robin said. "But I still don't—"

"There is one particular box," Mallory interrupted, "that the Knights Templar would certainly have known all about. In fact, there is a body of opinion and possibly even some circumstantial evidence that they didn't simply know about it, but possessed it. That they found it when they were doing their excavations underneath the Temple Mount in Jerusalem. And two of the most important characteristics of that box were the rings on each side, which allowed wooden poles to be inserted so that it could be carried, and the decoration on the lid. And that decoration was not angels with wings, but two cherubim, facing each other on the top of the lid."

Robin looked at him, a mixture of dawning comprehension and blatant disbelief clouding her features. "You're not talking about the Ark of the Covenant, are you?"

"That's exactly what I'm talking about," Mallory stated.

20

Via di Sant'Alessio, Aventine Hill, Rome, Italy

Realistically there hadn't been too much of a trail to follow, but Mallory and Jessop had inevitably left a series of electronic footprints behind them, and given the right access and connections—which the intelligence section run by the Dominican Order possessed in most European countries—working out where they had gone wasn't difficult. The biggest problem the order faced was the inevitable delay in obtaining the information they needed to track them. Details of some electronic transactions could be available within a few hours, but sometimes the information could take days to be collated and disseminated.

As a result, Silvio Vitale knew the two targets had booked a flight to Paris out of Gatwick within five hours of the scheduled takeoff time, though he had no idea how they had reached the British airport. The information that Mallory had hired a car in Exeter only arrived sometime after that, and was by then irrelevant, as the two people were already in France.

He guessed that they'd either hired another vehicle in Paris, or possibly bought tickets for a train, unless wherever they were going and whatever they were looking for was actually in the French capital. The thought that they might simply be spending a few days in Paris on holiday never even crossed his mind: he had never met either of them, but he assumed that they were as keen to continue the Templar quest as he was.

As soon as the destination of the Gatwick flight had been confirmed, Vitale briefed four of his men to fly to Paris, book into a hotel, and await orders. Toscanelli wasn't one of them. Vitale was still uncertain about his subordinate: the shooting in Devon still bothered him and although he had no proof that Toscanelli had been involved in organizing it in some way, he certainly had his suspicions. And there was a practical reason as well for not sending him. Although Toscanelli would obviously be able to recognize the targets, the reverse was also true—they would recognize him—and that was something Vitale wasn't prepared to risk. He wanted the two of them watched, not spooked.

His men had already been in the air before another point in the electronic trail was reported to him. The targets had booked a room in a hotel in Chartres the previous afternoon. He still had no idea why they were in the ancient religious center, but at least his surveillance team now had a definite starting point for their search.

Vitale quickly prepared an encrypted e-mail and sent

it to the leader of the group he had sent. As soon as they landed, they would also travel to the cathedral city and there hopefully observe Mallory and Jessop at close quarters. The men were unarmed—they had been briefed to carry out surveillance, nothing more—and also had a range of electronic devices with them that would help record what the two targets said to each other, as well as bugs they could conceal in their hotel room, if they could gain access to it. Their diplomatic passports ensured that their luggage would be exempt from searching.

Soon, Vitale guessed, he would know a lot more about both the targets themselves and, more important, what clue or clues they had managed to identify and decipher. And then, very probably, he would be able to send in additional men and order their executions, as soon as their usefulness to the order was at an end.

21

"Listen," Mallory said, "before you decide I've fallen off the trolley or had some kind of brainstorm, let me tell you what I mean."

"I'm listening," Robin said, but the tone of her voice implied that whatever he had in mind, she would take some convincing that it made any kind of sense.

"I'm not suggesting for a moment that the Ark of the Covenant is lurking somewhere at Chartres Cathedral. If—and it's a big if—it had been taken there at some point in the distant past, it was definitely moved and hidden elsewhere at a later date, because otherwise it would already have been found."

"If it even existed in the first place," Robin pointed out.

"Absolutely. Personally I believe virtually nothing that's written in the Bible," Mallory said, "because none of it's even approximately contemporary with what it's supposed to be describing and it's arguably the most heavily edited book ever written. By which I mean that what's included in the Bible is only what the early Church decided supported their own version of the story of Jesus Christ, and they excluded every other piece of text that contradicted it, which predictably enough meant that they dumped most of it. At least in the New Testament.

"But the Ark is one of the few things that does seem to have actually existed. The descriptions of it are fairly consistent and specific, and references to it aren't found just in the Bible, but also in the Koran. Though it's also fair to say that a lot of the Koran was lifted wholesale from the text of the Old Testament, so that's not the best possible supporting evidence. But assuming the Ark was real, it's possible to trace most of its movements over the centuries, or at least until it vanished from the historical record."

"Which was when?"

"About 586 BC. That was when the First Temple in Jerusalem was destroyed by the Babylonians, led by Nebuchadnezzar. But the reality is that that's a long way from being definite. As I said, as a historical document, the Bible is startlingly unreliable, and full of all sorts of fundamental errors that are incredibly easy to identify."

"Like what?" Robin asked.

"Oh, like the battle of Jericho, for example. Joshua was supposed to march around the town blowing trumpets, and eventually the walls fell down. All complete nonsense, of course. Assuming that Joshua was a real person, which is by no means certain, when he was supposed to have achieved this impressive military victory, Jericho had already been abandoned for well over a century. In reality, there were no walls to fall down."

"And the Ark?" Robin prodded gently.

"The sequence of events is simple enough. Until about 586 BC, the Ark received a number of name checks in the Bible. Then Nebuchadnezzar and his army appeared and basically destroyed Jerusalem, and after that there are no more mentions of it. The obvious assumptions are that it was either destroyed during the fighting or seized as a prize by the Babylonians and carried off as a part of the spoils of war. But if they had grabbed it, then logically there might have been some later reference to it being seen in Nebuchadnezzar's palace or somewhere else in Babylonia. Because there aren't, the other possible fate that's been suggested is that the Ark might have been secreted in a cave or tunnel underneath the Temple Mount by the Jewish priests before the Babylonian attack began."

"But surely, if that were the case," Robin objected, "once the conflict had ended and peace had eventually been restored in Jerusalem, wouldn't the priests have recovered the Ark and put it back in the temple?"

"Possibly, but not necessarily. If the Ark had been hidden and not discovered during the looting, then the hiding place must have been pretty good. The corollary to that argument is that if the Ark had been secreted away, the only people who might have known where it was would have been the priests who hid it, and if they didn't survive the fighting, which is quite likely, the knowledge of its resting place would have died at the same time as they did. And that is certainly conceivable. The other variant of this story is that the priests didn't hide the Ark, but instead sent it away for safekeeping, and many of the people who believe that think it went first to Egypt but that it's now in Ethiopia, hidden away in the Orthodox Church at a place called Axum behind locked doors and guarded by a single priest. His job is to protect the Ark, and he remains in the church as the sole resident until he dies. The Ark never leaves the church, so it certainly could be there, or alternatively the priest might just be guarding an empty room in an empty building. Nobody knows, and there is no obvious way of finding out.

"Another story is that it ended up in Zimbabwe, but that's quite a difficult scenario to believe. A less likely, and certainly less believable, suggestion is that it's still in Jerusalem. In 1989 a man digging in the vicinity of Calvary claims to have found a chamber within which he saw and photographed the Ark. Unfortunately, or quite possibly deliberately, the pictures he released were so blurred as to be useless, and for various unlikely reasons nobody has been able to get into the chamber since then, so that was probably a hoax. Other suggested locations include the Languedoc area of France, where it was apparently transported by knights returning from the Crusades, and even Warwickshire in England, where it was supposed to have been taken by a Templar knight named Ralph de Sudeley in the eleven eighties. The short, snappy answer is that nobody really has any idea what happened to the Ark."

Robin nodded. "I've heard some of those stories before, though not the one about the Templar knight and the Ark being hidden in Warwickshire. But I still have no idea what the relevance of any of this is to our search."

"The relevance," Mallory said, "is that somewhere in Chartres Cathedral there are some carvings or sculptures that are supposed to depict the Ark being transported; I think it's in a cart or wagon or something of that sort. I read something about that ages ago, and I only remembered it when I realized that the shape you identified could be a representation of the Ark."

"So you're not expecting to find the Ark itself, obviously?"

"We should be so lucky. No, of course not. But those carvings, wherever they are, are inside the building where they'd be safe from the elements, and would have been done well before the arrest of the Templars, so the date would fit. What I can't remember is whether there's any writing or inscriptions associated with the carvings."

Robin finished her drink and looked across at Mallory.

"There's only one way to find out," she said. "Let's go."

Mallory paid the bill, and they left.

Identifying the carving didn't take as long as either of them had expected, not least because they now had some idea what they were looking for, and a couple of the guidebooks pointed them in the right direction.

"According to this," Mallory said, "the North Portal of the cathedral dates from the first quarter of the thirteenth century and is dedicated to the Virgin Mary. It's decorated with apocryphal scenes from her life, as well as illustrations derived from the text of the Old Testament. And that's where I think we need to start looking."

Mallory and Robin climbed the steps that gave access to the portal, checking everything they saw around them as they did so. It quickly became apparent that there were a lot of carvings to inspect, most of these apparently depicting events and characters mainly from the Old Testament. They saw angels, prophets, priests, Jesus, and Mary herself. On one panel the patriarch Abraham stared upward, his hand holding the knife with which he planned to sacrifice his son Isaac on Mount Moriah. Moses, his robes flowing behind him, stood as the centerpiece of one sculpture, holding one of the two stone tablets of the Covenant in his left hand.

"This place is like the Bible carved in stone," Robin said, staring up at the carvings, her words echoing around the chamber.

"You got that right," Mallory agreed. Then he pointed to his right. "That could be what we're looking for."

Robin looked up. Carved into two pillars, side by side, was a complex battle scene, marked by soldiers carrying lances, and one very clearly clad in chain mail.

"It is?" she said. "You could have fooled me. What's it supposed to represent?"

Mallory consulted his guidebook before he answered.

"According to this, it's a representation of the Battle of Aphek," he said. "It comes from the First Book of Samuel and it shows the Philistines stealing the Ark of the Covenant. The Ark was supposed to be guarded by two men named Hophni and Phinehas, the sons of Eli, but they were killed in the battle, the Ark was seized and carried off to Ashdod, but that wasn't the end of the story.

The Philistines didn't have a good time at all with the Ark. Apparently they placed it in a temple dedicated to the god Dagon, but when they returned to the building the following day they found that the idol had fallen forward onto its face, almost as if it was praying to the Ark. They restored the idol to its correct position, but the next day it was again found lying prostrate before the Ark and broken into several pieces. That's what this particular sculpture is supposed to be depicting."

Mallory pointed out a part of the carving before turning his attention back to the guidebook.

"This bit's rather sweet, actually," he said, "though not, obviously, for the Philistines. The Ark is then credited with inflicting a plague of hemorrhoids on them, followed by a plague of mice and then a plague of boils. Not too surprisingly, the Philistines only put up with this for about seven months before they agreed to return the Ark to the Israelites. And, by way of atonement, they also presented them with five solid gold images of the hemorrhoids and a further five solid gold images of the mice."

Robin looked at him askance.

"I can fairly easily picture what a solid gold mouse would look like," she said. "And that would be rather sweet, but I'm having real trouble trying to work out how any sculptor could produce a copy of someone's hemorrhoids. In fact," she added, "I'd be prepared to pay money to see that particular sculpture. I mean, did it include the bum as well, or just the—how can I put this delicately?—relevant area?"

"I have no idea," Mallory said, with a smile, "and maybe we'd better move on. Though if you look quite carefully at that sculpture, there is actually a small mouse carved into it. But no sign of the hemorrhoids, which is probably a good thing. You can see the Ark," he went on. "Just up there. There's a carving of the Ark on a cart that's being pulled by cows or oxen and guided by an angel. It actually looks rather more like a chest, but according to the guidebook there's no doubt about what it is because of a carving just to the right of that scene. That depicts an open box that contains the three things that the Ark was initially believed to hold: the Covenant, the stone tablets, obviously, but also the pot of manna and Aaron's rod."

"And there are a couple of inscriptions directly underneath the carvings," Robin pointed out. "Are those what we should be looking for?"

"Until we try to use them to decrypt the text on the parchment," Mallory replied, "I have no idea. But my guess is that those words, or a combination of the two inscriptions, are what we need."

Robin raised her camera and used the telephoto lens to zoom in on each of the inscriptions in turn, taking several photographs of each, just to ensure that she had good-quality images.

Below the left-hand cylinder, because both sculptures were carved into circular pillars, they read the words:

ARCHA CEDERIS

while under the second cylinder was a rather longer inscription that contained the same two words as part of a longer phrase:

HIC AMITITUR ARCHA CEDERIS

"That's interesting," Robin said.

"What is?"

"My Latin is a bit rusty," she admitted, "and that does look like Latin to me. But as far as I know the word *amititur* doesn't exist in that language. On the other hand, I'm pretty sure that the word *amittitur*, spelled with a double *T*, genuinely is Latin. I'd need to check a dictionary to be certain, but I think it's derived from the noun *amitto*, which basically means to release or to lose."

Mallory looked at where she was pointing.

"Are you sure you're reading it right?" he asked. "That fourth letter of the word looks to me to be more like a *C* than a *T*. If it is a single letter *T* it's very stylized, almost like a *T* and a *C* being combined into one. I suppose it couldn't be a sort of shorthand for indicating a double *T*?"

"Maybe. I really don't know, though that idea does seem a bit unlikely, because in fact there would have been plenty of room to have carved two letter *T*s if that had been the correct spelling of the verb."

"That makes sense. So perhaps it really is meant to be a letter *C*. What about *amicitur*? Is that a Latin verb you recognize?"

"Recognize, no," she said, "but that doesn't mean it's wrong. It looks like a future participle of something, but I really need to sit down with my laptop and an online Latin dictionary to confirm that. Mind you, it's quite possible that it doesn't matter what the inscription actually says. If all we're doing is using it as a code word to translate that encrypted text, we just need the letters. The meaning of the Latin is actually completely irrelevant."

Mallory repeated her action with his own camera, taking several pictures of the two inscriptions below the sculptures, and photographs of the sculptures themselves as well.

"There's only one way to find out if we are on the right track," he said. "Let's get back to the hotel and see if it works."

22

"As I said before," Robin murmured about forty minutes later, leaning back in her chair, her laptop open on the desk in front of her, "this *is* interesting. According to most of the references I've been able to find online, the Ark of the Covenant seemed to be consistently referred to, at least in the Latin Vulgate Bible, as the *Arca Foederis*, not the *Archa Cederis*. But you were right about the objects that the Ark was supposed to contain, and all of them are very clearly represented in that sculpture, so despite the two different words, I guess that both the expressions have to be referring to the same thing, though they have quite different meanings in Latin."

"They do?" Mallory asked.

"Yes. *Arca* translates as an ark or a box, and *foederis* means a contract or a promise, so *Arca Foederis* is a very clear reference to the Ark of the Covenant. But *archa* translates as an archangel, not an ark, and I'm still trying to work out the meaning of *cederis*. The word appears to be derived from the Latin verb *ceder*, which means to go, to make way, or to take the place of, but I really am not sure how that fits.

"I've done a bit more digging around on the Internet, and one reference suggests that *archa cederis* translates as 'you are to work through the Ark,' and that the whole expression *hic amititur archa cederis* means 'here things take their course, and you are to work through the Ark.' I'm not sure I agree with that, mainly because unless all the dictionaries I've looked at are wrong, I was right and the word *amititur* with a single *T* as the fourth letter never actually existed in Latin. The same word spelled with two letter *T*s could be translated as meaning to yield, in which case the sentence might translate as 'here is the Ark, let it go,' or something like that."

"I thought Latin was supposed to be a precise language," Mallory pointed out. "Do you think the mason who carved those inscriptions simply got the words wrong, or is there more to it than that?"

"I suppose it's just conceivable that a mistake could have been made and *arca* became *archa*, but I think that's unlikely as well because the word is repeated, and I can't believe that the mason wouldn't have been supervised by a priest or somebody else who would know precisely what the inscription was supposed to be. And *cederis* is so completely different from *foederis* that the spelling simply has to be deliberate. Even an illiterate and unsupervised mason—and he would have been a very rare animal indeed in this period, especially working on a cathedral of this importance—couldn't possibly mistake the two words. And you're right: Latin is, at least usually, a very exact language, so personally I believe that that inscription reads precisely the way it was intended to be read, but perhaps the usage and meanings of these words has altered in the better part of a millennium since the carving was made."

She slid her finger across the touch pad and opened up another of the tabs in her browser.

"I did find an alternative translation of the inscription that is quite interesting," she said. "In fact, it's more than interesting. It's potentially explosive."

"Well, don't keep me in suspense," Mallory said. "Tell me what you found."

"If we assume that the first letter *T* in *amititur* is actually supposed to be a letter *C*, that changes the sense of the verb entirely, and the meaning of the whole sentence. If that assumption is correct, and if we agree that the words *archa cederis* do refer to the Ark, then *hic amicitur archa cederis* can be translated as 'here is hidden the Ark of the Covenant,' because the Latin verb *amicitur* means hidden or covered up, something like that."

Whatever Mallory had been expecting, that wasn't it, and for a few moments he simply stared at Robin. Then he shook his head. "Do you really think that means that the Ark of the Covenant, arguably the most famous and important lost treasure from antiquity, could be lying hidden in a vault or crypt underneath the floor of the cathedral, about a quarter of a mile from where we're sitting right now?"

Robin smiled at him before she replied.

"I'm just telling you what one translation of those words carved in the stone might mean," she pointed out. "Personally I'm a long way from being convinced, because of the potential ambiguities and different possible translations of the expression. You have to ask the question why the carving uses the word *archa* instead of *arca*, and why it's *cederis* and not *foederis*, though the carving above the inscription does fairly clearly seem to be related to the historic Ark. And as I said, it is just one possible translation. Or an interpretation of a translation, in fact."

"But actually," Mallory said, "you could muster an impressive argument, based on circumstantial evidence, that the Ark did actually end up here in France, and at Chartres. If you go back to the earliest days of the order, and the digging they did below what is now the Al Aqsa Mosque on the Temple Mount, maybe they did find this ancient relic. And if they did, that does help explain several inconsistencies in what happened a few years later. Nine knights were involved when the Templars formed, and contemporary accounts suggests that they remained in their quarters on the Temple Mount, presumably digging away underneath it, for nine years. At the end of that time, they were still only nine in number, and apparently didn't possess any significant assets at all.

"But despite that, the pope recognized the order remarkably quickly and soon afterward he published the papal bull, which exempted them from the payment of taxes, allowed them to cross any border unmolested, and confirmed that they owed allegiance to one person only, the pope himself. All that was achieved with suspicious speed, and several researchers have speculated that one possible reason might have been a form of medieval blackmail. Because if the Knights Templar had turned up at the Vatican and confirmed that they were in possession of the genuine Ark of the Covenant, then the pope would immediately be aware of two things. First, he would know beyond doubt that the Jews, far from simply being seen as the killers of Jesus Christ, which was a popular medieval view, were in actuality God's chosen people and that by definition the Catholic Church and Christianity had no believable spiritual or religious authority at all. That would probably have been enough to terrify the pope and everybody else at the Vatican, and would have been something that they would never, ever have wished to be made public under any circumstances.

"The second and perhaps even more frightening possibility for the occupant of the Throne of Saint Peter would have been that the Ark of the Covenant was essentially believed to be a machine for talking to God, and any group that possessed the Ark really did have the ultimate weapon of the age. So in that circumstance, it would be entirely unsurprising if the pope had acceded to any demands or requests made by the Templars."

"That makes sense," Robin said, "as long as you believe that the Ark is real, of course, and that it still exists, at least three or four millennia after it was supposed to have been fabricated, and two and a half millennia after it vanished from the historic record."

"There is that. But if you assume for a minute that that

was the case, and the Templars had recovered it, then it's quite likely that it could have ended up somewhere in France. That was where the founders of the Templar movement came from, and it was where the order held many of its most important assets. According to the guidebook I read, the Templars were probably responsible for providing much of the funding for the construction of Chartres Cathedral, and were almost certainly directly associated with it during the building process. So the idea that the Ark might still lay hidden away in some forgotten corner of the building isn't quite as mad as it might at first appear."

"I grant you all that," Robin said, "but whether or not it's still here today is probably quite doubtful. That carving was probably done in the first quarter of the thirteenth century, approaching one millennium ago, and while it might have been an entirely true and accurate statement of account when it was carved, it's entirely possible that a year or a decade or a century later the Ark could have been removed from its hiding place in the cathedral and taken somewhere entirely different. Perhaps to another religious building, or maybe even to a different country. The carving obviously wasn't amended, because that was never done, and so even if the Ark had been hidden in Chartres Cathedral at that time, we have absolutely no idea where it was taken to later, and no clue that we could start to follow to try to find it."

"Unless," Mallory suggested, "the section of text on the parchment we've been trying to decipher tells us exactly where we should start looking."

"You mean you think it's possible that the trail we've

been following is going to lead us to the Ark of the Covenant? Are you serious?"

"I have no idea. I was expecting that this kind of strange treasure hunt might lead us in the end to something of considerable value, but I never for a moment thought it would be something like the lost Ark. And I still don't, really, but it is an intriguing possibility. Anyway, in the real world," Mallory went on, "none of that actually matters. Maybe in the future the location of the Ark is another trail that we could think about following, but for the moment I'm much more interested in trying to crack the encrypted text that's been bugging us ever since we started this. So let's do it."

"So which bit of the inscription do you think we should be using as the code word?" Robin asked. "We saw the words *archa cederis* on the left-hand cylinder, and that's repeated within the expression on the one on the right-hand side."

"Trial and error," Mallory replied. "In my opinion, it's not likely to just be *archa cederis*, because that's too short, not to mention having four repeated letters—*A*, *C*, *E*, and *R*. My gut feeling is that because both of the sculptures are concerned with the fate of the Ark of the Covenant, the compiler of this code probably used both of the inscriptions, so first of all we'll try *archa cederis hic amititur archa cederis*, which gives us a total of thirty-five letters. I know there are also a lot of duplicates in that, but the sheer number of letters makes it feasible to use the entire expression as a code word to use in the Atbash cipher. Anyway, let's give it a try."

He wrote down the letters on a sheet of paper, leaving the same spaces between them so that they merged into a single combined word, then wrote out the standard full Latin alphabet, reversed, underneath it. When he reached the twenty-sixth letter, he started again until a letter of the alphabet was directly underneath each of the letters in the expression they had found.

"You reversed it," Robin pointed out.

"Only because our expression also starts with the letter *A*," he replied. "It just seemed to me that the medieval compiler of this message probably wouldn't have wanted the first letter in the code to be represented by the same letter in the plaintext. If it's wrong, if the decryption makes no sense, then we'll try it the other way round. And there's one other thing I want to do."

Quickly he added the letter *C* above the above the first letter *T* in *amititur*.

"Just in case that is the correct spelling," he explained.

Robin opened up one of the Word files on her laptop and scrolled down until she reached the transliteration of the encrypted text. Then she read it out, letter by letter, while Mallory referred to the table of letters he had already prepared and jotted down what he hoped would be the plaintext equivalent. Because of the number of duplicates in the putative code word, in many cases there was inevitably more than one possible letter, and when this happened he wrote all of the possible alternatives in a short vertical line in the correct place in his transcription. It was boring and repetitive, but because they had done it when they succeeded in transcribing the larger section of text on the parchment, they knew what they were doing, and the operation didn't take long.

When they reached the end, Mallory showed Robin the plaintext that he had produced, and she nodded thoughtfully.

"That might actually have worked," she said. "Quite a lot of those words do look like Latin to me already. While I go through it, why don't you nip downstairs and see if you can buy a sandwich or something? Because I'm starting to get hungry."

As Mallory left the room, she took the piece of paper and spent about ten minutes checking it over, deleting some of the suggested letters and accepting others, and inserting spaces between words that she thought made sense. The original text had no breaks in it, a basic precaution to make deciphering it that bit more difficult. When she'd finished, she took a fresh sheet of paper, copied out a final version of the Latin text, and then again used an online Latin-to-English dictionary to render the text into the language they both spoke. Then she looked up as Mallory opened the door and stepped back into the room, carrying a paper bag from the end of which poked two baguettes.

"The one thing I can tell you, right now," she said, shaking her head, "is that we guessed correctly about the code word needed to decipher that piece of text. And, just as an aside, I suppose, it's worth saying that the translation only works if the second word is spelled *amicitur*, not *amititur*. The other thing I can tell you is that I'm quite sure we're not on the trail of the Ark of the Covenant, but something very different."

23

Chartres, France

"So, where are they?" the thickset man wearing a dark suit asked. He was using the work name Paolo.

His companion—work name Mario—didn't bother replying to what was clearly a rhetorical question. They'd been watching the hotel where their targets had booked a room, according to the information supplied by Silvio Vitale, and had been doing so for the last couple of hours.

They had identified the building within minutes of arriving in Chartres in the two cars they'd hired at the airport in Paris. They'd taken two cars because that provided them with a backup vehicle in the event of one breaking down or being involved in a traffic accident or any other unforeseen problem. They'd then decided to separate, two of them going to a café on the opposite side of the street that offered a clear view—traffic permitting, obviously—of the hotel, while the second pair took seats at a table outside a bar just a few yards from the main entrance to the hotel. They'd decided to stay as two pairs, because a single man sitting alone and clearly watching a particular building was always likely to attract attention, whereas two men sitting at a table opposite each other and talking together looked completely innocent. They could just be friends meeting for a drink, or two business-men discussing a job or a contract.

But whether they blended in to the pedestrian traffic of the street scene was of secondary importance to all four of them. What was giving them all cause for concern, to a greater or lesser degree, was the complete absence of any sign of the people they were supposed to be mount-ing surveillance on.

"I hope to hell that we haven't missed them," Paolo added. "I mean, it must at least be possible that they came here, found what they were looking for, and then got back in their car or on a train and left the city. They could be halfway to Paris, or halfway to almost anywhere, by now."

"You could be right," Mario said, somewhat testily, because it wasn't the first time his companion had explored that subject since they arrived in Chartres. "You could also be completely wrong, and sitting here speculat-ing isn't going to answer the question one way or the other. So why don't you just shut up and keep your eyes on the hotel? If they've not appeared by the time it gets dark, we'll have to think again. Then we'll need to ring Vitale or the duty officer and tell him the situation. But right now I don't want to talk to him and I doubt very much if you do, either. He's got a nasty temper at the best

of times, and telling him we haven't even seen these people despite sitting out here for most of the afternoon
would be a really good way of annoying him."

"We'll have to check in with him sometime today."

Something across the street attracted Mario's attention, and he didn't respond, just picked up his smartphone
and swiped the screen to wake it up, then stared intently
at the display, where a picture of a male face was visible.

"That looks like him," he said quietly, inclining his
head slightly in the direction of the hotel. "I'm pretty
sure that's Mallory."

A few yards down the street, a well-built man with an
obvious healed scar on one side of his face had walked out
of the hotel entrance and was heading down the street.
Seconds later, he entered a boulangerie. By the time he
emerged, a paper bag in his hand, Mario was already
talking to Silvio Vitale.

"He's just bought a couple of sandwiches, by the looks
of it," he reported in Italian, "but there's no sign of the
woman, so she's probably in their room at the hotel. This
is a confirmed sighting," he added, as Paolo—who had
been closely studying both the target and the two full-face
photographs the order had uncovered of David Mallory—
nodded to him.

"Good," Vitale said. "Now we know where they are.
They'll have to come out sooner or later, and when they
do you have to get close enough to them to see what
they're doing and where they're going. Plant a bug on
them if you can. If you can't, try to overhear what they're
saying. You all speak good enough English to do that."

"Understood."

Mario ended the call, and the two of them watched as Mallory reentered the hotel and disappeared from view.

As soon as he was out of sight, Mario waved to the other two men and they crossed the street to join them. Now that they'd established a definite location for the targets, they needed to prepare for whatever came next. They didn't know if Mallory and Jessop had traveled down to Chartres on a train or by car, and that was something they needed to find out.

"Let's make this easy," Paolo suggested. "We know he's in that hotel, and it looks like he's just bought a late lunch for him and Jessop, so presumably they'll be in there for at least another hour or so. We're going to need somewhere to stay tonight, so why don't I go and book a couple of rooms in the same place? That'll give two of us access to the building, and we might be able to find out their room number."

"And us?"

Mario glanced at the speaker. "There's another hotel just across the road. You both take rooms there, and make sure one of the rooms faces the street, because that will give you eyes on the target hotel, just in case they slip out without us noticing."

That seemed to work as a tactical plan, and there was an unexpected bonus: when he and Paolo had checked in and put their overnight bags in their rooms, Mario took the lift down to the underground parking garage. There were hire cars in three of the spaces, and he noted their makes, models, and registration numbers before returning to his room to call Vitale.

That meant a trace could be run by tertiaries of the order in France to identify which vehicle—if any of them—had been rented by the targets and that, in turn, would allow the surveillance team to attach a tracker to the vehicle. Vitale promised that he would get the information within a couple of hours, and until then there was nothing the four men could do apart from make sure that if one or both of the targets left the hotel, at least two of the team would be right behind them.

24

Chartres, France

"Like what?" Mallory asked, then took a bite from the end of his torpedo-shaped ham and salad baguette.

"Ah, well, right now I don't exactly know," Robin replied. "If this encrypted text had referred to an ark or a box or a chest, anything like that, then it would certainly be a lot more exciting. As it is, there are very few direct references to whatever the trail is leading toward. In fact, there are only three nouns used that give any indication of what has been hidden. And those three words translate as 'deeds,' 'titles,' and 'archive.' In fact, the last noun—it's *tablinum* in Latin—has three possible meanings, including a terrace or a gallery, but in the context 'archive' seems to be the most accurate translation."

Mallory nodded as he took in the implications of what Robin just said.

"I think I know what that means," he said. "More

important, does the translated text indicate where this archive or repository can be found?"

"Not directly, no. There's a reference to a valley that includes some detail that might be a help if you knew exactly where the valley was, and the next sentence of the text refers to some kind of local organization, a *cofraternitas*, which translates as brotherhood. I think it probably means a union of villages or towns. Something like a league, perhaps."

"Could it possibly translate as 'confederation'?" Mallory asked.

Robin glanced back at the online dictionary that was still open on the screen of her laptop, typed in the Latin word, and then pressed the ENTER key to see the translation.

"That's not one of the options that's coming up in this dictionary," she said, "but the meaning is pretty much the same as most of the nouns listed here. Hang on a moment."

She selected a different dictionary and input the word *cofraternitas* again.

"Yes," she said, "or at least this dictionary suggests that 'confederation' is a possible alternative meaning." She looked at him keenly for a few seconds, then glanced back at the transcribed Latin text. "This means something to you, doesn't it?" she asked.

Mallory nodded. "Yes, it does. It most probably means that we're on the trail of a rather different kind of Templar treasure. We're not talking about gold or silver bullion, jewelry or precious stones, nothing like that. I think what this is referring to is probably the most valuable part of the entire Templar treasury, the Archive. Remember that one of the ways in which the order became so wealthy so quickly was that the Knights Templar essentially invented modern banking and, just like today, many of the assets that they held on behalf of third parties didn't consist of portable goods. In probably thousands of cases, the Templars provided loans or capital advances secured against real properties of various sorts, including houses, farms, estates, and even castles. But before they would advance any money to an applicant, they would as a matter of routine take his title deeds or other proof of ownership of the asset from him as a form of security."

"Exactly like banks do today, only they call it a mortgage," Robin said. "I didn't realize it had been going on for so long."

"And there were a couple of other things that the Templars did that also resulted in them holding title deeds or other documents relating to property ownership. When a knight applied to join the order, he was supposed to join for life, and so the usual routine was for him to hand over all the assets in his possession, and these were often lands or houses that generated rent, as well as having an obvious capital value. So the bigger the order grew, the more properties it had control of. And the second thing was that, just like the Church today, the Templars also relied on donations, on people handing over assets in return for spiritual favors."

"That was also true in the Crusades," Robin said, "if I remember rightly. Going on a crusade was a moral duty in the eyes of the Christian Church, and anyone who embarked on such a campaign automatically had all their sins annulled and were guaranteed a place in heaven when they died."

"Precisely. And the other refinement that the Templars took advantage of—they may even have introduced it for all I know—was that by handing over significant assets to the order, a donor would be guaranteed a place in heaven because of his support of the Warriors of God. In the medieval period, you have to remember that heaven and hell were both thought to be absolutely real, and when anyone died his soul would be carried off in one of two different directions, either up to heaven or down to hell. A soul condemned to an eternity in purgatory or in the depths of hell was truly damned. It was a terrifying prospect that people would do almost anything to avoid."

Robin nodded. "So you think that we could be on the hunt for the Templar Archive, do you? If so, isn't that just a waste of time? I mean, even if we managed to follow the trail wherever it happens to lead and open up a chest or whatever containing the archives, all we're going to find is presumably a bunch of medieval property deeds written in Latin. That will be a find of enormous importance for historians, but unless I'm missing the point, I don't see that it will have any value today."

"Not necessarily," Mallory said. "It's quite possible that the archive—assuming it still exists, of course, and that the documents are still readable—could be both valuable and dangerous. Valuable because it could show that some very expensive real estate in Europe isn't actually owned by the people who are living on it, and danger-ous for precisely the same reason. I'm not quite sure how the law would view a document that, for example, proved conclusively that a few thousand acres of prime French real estate had actually been given in perpetuity to the Knights Templar in the middle of the thirteenth century. That would mean that anyone who occupied it after that date would be a squatter, with no legal right whatsoever to the land. It would be a very interesting legal squabble to see how that would be resolved."

Robin laughed shortly.

"Perhaps it would," she said, "but it probably wouldn't come to that, possession being nine-tenths of the law, and with the Templars having been permanently disestablished in the early part of the fourteenth century. I mean, these days would anybody care?"

"They might," Mallory said. "I saw a very interesting television program a few years ago. It proved conclusively that the British royal family, the House of Windsor, are usurpers to the throne, because of a break in succession that took place two or three hundred years ago. The researchers for that program did the genealogical research needed to prove their case, but, more important, at the same time they tracked down the genuine heir to the British Crown. If my memory serves me correctly, he was something like a sheep farmer working in the Australian Outback. They interviewed him, and asked him if he'd be prepared to mount a claim for the throne, but he wasn't interested. But in law, he would have had an extremely good case, because the genealogical records proved his succession absolutely. There was no gray area. The present members of the British royal family have no legal right to occupy the throne, and he absolutely possessed that same right. Now, if the Templar Archive contained information anything like that, recovering it could be explosive."

"Maybe," Robin said, sounding anything but convinced, "but I have my doubts. I mean, would we just be wasting our time trying to track down a bunch of medieval land deeds?"

"Until we find it," Mallory replied, "we have no idea what it contains. But there's another factor we need to remember. We're following a trail here. The first leg of the search took us from Dartmouth, strangely enough, though it should probably have started in Scotland, from what you told me about the origin of the parchment and the book safe, and then all the way to Cyprus. The second leg seems to be taking us in search of the Templar Archive, but if we don't find it, then we obviously also won't find the information we need to follow the third leg. If you remember from the text on the parchment we translated earlier, the author referred to three trials, or three trails, that had to be followed, and by implication followed in the correct sequence. If we want to reach the end of this search, then we have to follow it through."

"Right," Robin said. "I don't disagree with any of that, because it makes obvious sense. When I said that the Latin word I was looking at could translate as something like 'league,' you asked if it could possibly mean a confederation. So does that mean that you know where we should be looking next?"

"Maybe, yes. There's an interesting story about the high mountain regions of Switzerland that dates right back to the same decade in which the Templars were purged. At the end of 1315, a motley band of poorly armed and hopelessly outnumbered peasants took on the might of the Austrian Habsburg army not far from the present Saint Gotthard Pass and completely defeated it. That in itself would be unusual enough, because in that battle uneducated and untrained farmers were facing a huge army of well-equipped and properly trained soldiers led by a large cadre of knights, and the result should never have been in the slightest doubt. To put it into modern terms, that's rather like a guerrilla army equipped only with rifles and pistols taking on a proper national war machine with aircraft, tanks, and artillery, and then coming out on top. It shouldn't happen, and it almost never does happen, but just occasionally you find something like the Vietnam War that breaks all the rules."

"So how did they manage to do it?" Robin asked.

"Well, that's the point, isn't it? Military tactics in those days were firmly established, and in general worked quite well. The heavy armor of the medieval army was of course the mounted knight, a highly trained warrior clad in steel plate armor and sitting astride a massive horse, also clad in protective steel armor and trained to be almost as aggressive as the man sitting on its back. The bulk of the army was made up of rank-and-file soldiers armed with swords, daggers, and spears or other thrusting weapons, while arguably the most lethal members of the force were the bowmen, the archers, typically using longbows or the equivalent, though some armies preferred the more powerful and more accurate crossbow, although these had a much slower rate of fire than a longbow.

"You could argue that battle in those days was formalized. The tendency was for the opposing forces to face each other across open ground, where the battle would finally take place. The opposing forces would typically remain in that position for some days, preparing to fight, while at the same time negotiations might be carried out between the two leaders to see if some kind of agreement could be reached without the necessity of doing battle. When all those possible avenues had been exhausted, then battle would commence. The outcome tended to be predictable, the larger and better-equipped force normally prevailing over the opposition. And in Switzerland, if the peasant farmers from the fledgling confederation had faced the Habsburg army in straight combat, there's no doubt at all that they would have been annihilated. So they didn't. They resorted to guerrilla tactics, blocking the path the Habsburgs had to take and then taking advantage of the hilly terrain to rain down boulders and tree trunks on the enemy forces essentially trapped below them.

"Militarily speaking, it was both brilliant in terms of tactics and completely successful, the Austrian army being routed and with enormous loss of life. But the point really is that it is extremely unlikely that any group of people with no established background in combat or battlefield tactics could have come up with such an unusual and effective strategy. Unless, of course, they had help. And that's what most of the stories about that conflict imply.

There's a persistent legend that a small group of White Knights—meaning knights who were their own men, who owed no allegiance to any lord or master—were in the area before the battle and devised the tactics that were used to overcome the Habsburgs.

"Of course," Mallory went on, "that doesn't mean that those knights, assuming that the legend is true, were Templars, but it's difficult to suggest who else they might have been. By 1315, the Templar order had been purged and the last grand master had died in the flames of his execution pyre in Paris. But only a mere handful of Templars had actually been arrested, and remarkably few of them were the highly trained knights who formed the core of the order's military machine. Those knights who escaped the cull would almost certainly still have been in Europe, and most probably would have been looking for some safe haven where they could live without fear of persecution by the French king. The lawless mountains and high passes of Switzerland would have been a fairly obvious choice, and it's more than possible that some Templars did end up there, exchanging their extensive knowledge and experience of combat for the right to stay. They could easily have devised the plan that more than leveled the battlefield in favor of the peasant farmers when the Austrian army approached, and that would certainly explain the overwhelming defeat that the Habsburgs suffered."

"I hear what you say," Robin said, "but there could be other explanations. The Swiss peasants must have known the terrain where the conflict was going to take place really well. So maybe they could have come up with a suitable battle plan all on their own. Or perhaps there were just a few unattached knights, White Knights, as you call them, and they were persuaded to lend a hand in preparing the ambush. What I mean is, the ambush didn't have to involve the Templars at all."

Mallory nodded.

"You're absolutely right, of course," he said. "And after this passage of time, there's no proof, or even a lack of proof, one way or the other. But there are another couple of pieces of what you could call circumstantial evidence that are worth considering. We've already talked about the way the Knights Templar basically introduced the modern concept of banking into medieval Europe. In almost all important respects, the systems invented by the Templars are exactly the same as the systems we use today. You can trace the origin of the bank account, the check, charging interest, bank fees, security charges, cash advances, conversion of assets, and even bearer bonds all the way back to the financial acumen of the Templars. And what is perfectly obvious is that if you ask anyone today what Switzerland is famous for, a very high proportion of people you question are probably going to mention banking. The gnomes of Zürich and all that. The point is that a very short time after the serfs and peasant farmers of the high cantons defeated the Austrians, a banking system that was virtually identical to that used by the Templars began to be operated in that same area, apparently by those same peasant farmers and serfs.

"Now, as I see it, there are only two possibilities here. Either the Knights Templar, or at least some members of the order, did settle in Switzerland and simply introduced their tried-and-tested banking system once they were established in the area. That seems to me to be the simplest explanation for what took place, and makes logical sense in view of what had happened to the order. The Templars had been dissolved at the instigation of the King of France and on the orders of the pope, but destroying the order obviously would not have eliminated the people who were a part of it. They would have retained the knowledge and abilities that they had learned while members of this group of warrior monks, and they would have had to set up home for themselves somewhere, and ideally in a country over which neither the French ruling house nor the Vatican would have any particular authority. And this area of high mountain passes virtually in the center of Europe would have fitted that bill admirably.

"The alternative is that the Templars had nothing whatsoever to do with the emerging nation of Switzerland and somehow this collection of uneducated laborers and peasant farmers came up with a banking system virtually identical to that used by the Templars entirely on their own. That is, of course, also possible, but in my opinion it's extremely unlikely."

"And the second piece of circumstantial evidence?" Robin asked.

Mallory grinned at her. "That's the very visible symbol that everybody knows about, but which very few people manage to connect with the order. The Templars went into battle wearing the bloodred *croix pattée* on their white surcoats, a design that is nothing more than a cross with arms of equal length, the ends of which are splayed outward. Remove the ends of the arms, and what you're looking at is the flag of Switzerland."

For a few moments, Robin didn't respond. Then she smiled at Mallory.

"You know," she said, "I genuinely never thought of that, but you're absolutely right. I suppose it could be a coincidence, but in things like this, the simplest explanation is very often the right one."

"Well, it makes sense to me," Mallory said. "At the time of that conflict with the Habsburgs, Switzerland didn't exist as a country. In fact, technically it still doesn't. The country we call Switzerland is actually a confederation of separate cantons, not a unified nation at all, though for all practical purposes that doesn't matter. But at the beginning of the fourteenth century, the Austrian forces were opposed by the people of three cantons that had banded together. They were the cantons of Schwyz, Uri, and Unterwalden and in those days they were called confederates, rather than cantons, which is why I asked if that Latin word could mean a confederation."

As he spoke, Robin picked up the page on which she had written the Latin text and began scanning it.

"I thought so," she said. "There's a word here that wasn't in any of the Latin dictionaries, and which I guessed might be a proper name. It's probably not exactly the same spelling, but it's really close to Schwyz."

She paused for a moment, then looked at something else on the sheet.

"What is it?" Mallory asked.

"What was the name of the Austrian king, or whoever it was who was in charge of the Habsburg army when they clashed with the Swiss peasants?"

"Leopold, if I remember rightly."

"You probably do remember rightly, as you put it. There's another phrase here that might help confirm the story. It talks about the *eversio* of a ruler named Leopold, and that does seem to me to be a fairly definite reference to what happened, because that Latin word means 'destruction' or 'expulsion,' something catastrophic like that. So unless Leopold's forces were in the habit of being destroyed on a regular basis, that probably does mean the battle you've just described."

"His troops weren't, as far as I know."

Robin nodded and looked at Mallory. "So I suppose this means that now we have to go to Switzerland?"

Mallory nodded again. "Yes. That works for me."

25

France

"You still think it's best if we keep moving?" Robin asked as Mallory steered the hire car northeast along the autoroute that would take them back to Paris. "I wouldn't have minded spending another night in that hotel. Chartres looked like a really interesting place to explore."

"It probably is, but the answer is yes. I think our safety does depend on being mobile. Don't forget, we've been leaving a clear electronic trail all the way from England. The hire car in Exeter, the plane tickets at Gatwick, and this hire car and the Chartres hotel. We had no real option but to pay for those with credit cards, and if those Italians have access to records of electronic transactions—which I think they definitely do—they will be able to follow our movements from one country to another. The only saving grace is that there should be a delay of at least a few hours between one of us using a credit card and them getting access to the information."

"So they should always be playing catch-up?"

"I certainly hope so," Mallory replied, "but right now I'm not sure that they haven't moved a lot quicker than I expected."

"What do you mean?"

"I mean we seem to have picked up a tail. Or two tails, to be exact. When we drove away from the hotel, we had to stop at the traffic lights a short distance down the street. I was keeping a close eye on the mirrors and I noticed a car pull out of the parking garage about two minutes later, and it turned in the same direction as we were heading."

"That could be a coincidence," Robin suggested.

"It could well be, but it's still behind us now, seventy or eighty yards back. There's another car keeping pace with it, and every few minutes they swap places with each other. That's a basic surveillance technique to avoid the target seeing the same car in his rearview mirrors all the time. I've deliberately been varying our speed, just to see what they'd do, and each time I've slowed down or sped up, they've done the same. It looks like deliberate surveillance to me."

"You know more about this than I do," Robin said, turning in her seat to look out of the rear window of the hire car, "so I'm sure you're right. And I see the two cars you mean. But there's not a lot they can do to us here, is there? With all this traffic? Unless we pull off the auto-route into a service area, and even then there'd be a lot of people around."

"I can't be certain," Mallory said, indicating left and pulling out to overtake a group of three articulated lorries all traveling at the same speed in the right-hand lane, "but I don't think the men in those cars have any immediate hostile intent. They've been behind us ever since we left Chartres, and there were several places where they could have tried to force us off the road if they'd wanted to, well before we even reached the autoroute, but they just kept their distance. The drivers seemed to be more concerned about keeping us in sight than in getting close enough to stop us. I think we're just being watched."

Robin nodded thoughtfully. "So, do you think those two cars are full of Italians, trained killers from the Dominican Order? Or have we just somehow come to the attention of the French police, and those are a couple of unmarked Frog police cars?"

"I don't know too much about the French police force, but to the best of my knowledge they don't use unmarked cars the way the British cops do, so I think that's pretty unlikely. And in any case we've done nothing over here that would interest the police. My best guess is that those are Dominicans, but I still think they're just watching us, not planning to kill us. At least, not yet. And that does suggest something fairly obvious."

"You mean they're not just playing catch-up in following us, but trying to identify and interpret the clues we're following?"

Mallory nodded. "Remember what happened on Cyprus. They had no idea where they should be looking because they hadn't cracked the clues that we'd solved, and the only reason they turned up in that cave was that they'd been following us. Maybe this time it's the same situation. We've worked out the next clue from our photographs of the metalwork on those two chests we found, but perhaps the Dominicans haven't seen what we saw, despite the fact that they have the actual chests themselves."

"So to make sure that they stay in the race, they're following us again to see where we go and what we do. That's what you mean, isn't it?" Robin asked.

"Exactly. So I don't think they're going to attack us at the moment, because we're still following the trail, but I'm pretty certain they'll turn up to spoil the party once we find whatever lies at the end of this quest. And we're going to have to work out what to do about that."

"I think they've spotted us," Paolo said, staring through the windshield at the Citroën sedan they were following. "The driver keeps on altering his speed and he's traveling a lot slower than almost every other car on the road."

"He could just be a really bad driver," Mario suggested.

"I doubt it. According to Vitale, the man Mallory was a trained police driver, and the girl holds a competition racing license. They're not altering their speed because they're not competent, but because they're trying to flush us out. Or that's what I think, at least."

"So what do we do?"

"We don't do anything. Vitale's instructions were just to follow them, and keep him updated with their movements. So that's what we'll do. In fact, you can give him a call right now and tell him we think they're heading for Paris, probably back to the airport."

"Why the airport?"

"It's a guess," Paolo admitted, "but think it through. Vitale told us they hired a car in that town in Devon, drove to the London Gatwick Airport, and then flew to Paris. From there, they hired another car, drove to Chartres, and spent the night in a hotel, and now they're heading back toward Paris. The simplest explanation for that is that they found some information in England that pointed them to Chartres. They went there, found whatever new information they were looking for, or perhaps even discovered some object, and now they're either on the way back home again or heading to wherever the new clue has pointed them."

"Yes, that does make sense," Mario agreed. "I'll call Vitale."

The head of the order listened intently to what Mario told him, then fell silent for a few seconds. Then he obviously made a decision.

"You've got a tracker on their car?" he asked, his voice clear enough on the speaker of the Italian's smartphone. "And a good link?"

"Yes," Mario said. "We have a clear signal from it on our mobiles."

"Good. That means they can't get away. Leave the other car to keep following them," Vitale ordered, "but you can overtake them and get to the airport before they do."

"Which airport? You told us that they flew in to Charles de Gaulle, but the closest airport to us now is Orly. That's on the south side of Paris."

"A moment." Vitale was silent for a few seconds, making a decision. "Go to Orly," he said, "but don't leave the car until you're certain that's where they're heading. If they carry on past that airport, get to Charles De Gaulle as quickly as you can."

"Understood."

"Then you leave the car and wait in the departures hall until they appear. When they do, get close enough to find out what flight they're booking and then take the same flight if you can, or the next flight to the same destination if that's not possible. Keep me informed. At the very least, call me when you know where they're going, before you board your flight, and again when you reach whatever destination they've chosen."

"You heard the man," Mario said, ending the call, then dialed the mobile number of their colleagues in the car behind them to explain the change of plan.

Paolo checked his mirrors, then pulled out into the overtaking lane and steadily accelerated. As they passed the target car, neither man so much as glanced at it, keeping their gaze straight ahead.

"Maybe I was wrong," Mallory said, watching the other car steadily disappear into the distance on the arrow-straight autoroute in from of them. "Maybe the driver just wasn't in any hurry before and now he is. But the other one is still there, a distant shadow a long way behind us," he added, glancing in the interior mirror.

"Or maybe you were right and he's getting in front of us for some other reason. Now we've possibly got one car in front of us with a couple of the opposition in it and another one behind us, and I'm not too keen on that idea. It might be worth getting off this autoroute when we're a bit closer to Paris."

That seemed to Mallory like a good plan, and when they approached Paris, he took the exit just beyond Saint-Jean-de-Beauregard onto the N118 signposted to Orsay. He took his time slowing down, waiting for the suspect car to pass them, which it did, staying on the autoroute and continuing toward the French capital.

"I think I must be getting paranoid," he said as the other vehicle passed them.

"I know it's a cliché," Robin said, "but just because you're paranoid, it doesn't mean they're not out to get you. And one thing we do know about these bloody Italians is that they're definitely out to get us. Anyway, whether or not that was a false alarm, that vehicle is no longer behind us, and that's what matters."

Mallory headed almost due north up the N118, but when they got close to Saclay he turned east toward Palaiseau, effectively driving around two sides of a triangle. They'd flown from Gatwick to Charles De Gaulle Airport the previous day, because there were no afternoon flights to Orly, but for the trip to Switzerland, Orly was the ideal departure airport. Mallory had already checked the flight schedules in the hotel in Chartres, but hadn't booked their tickets because they hadn't been sure what time they'd arrive at the airport.

To minimize any chance of encountering either of the two cars again, Mallory stuck to the minor roads all the way to the airport. Handing back the hire car took longer than he'd expected, just because the desk was really busy, but after about twenty minutes they were able to join the queue at the easyJet ticket counter.

"They're definitely going to Orly," the passenger in the second car confirmed to Mario on his mobile phone, looking carefully at the tracker application on the driver's phone. The display showed the target car moving steadily east along the N118, heading for the southern approach road to the airport. His vehicle was about half a mile behind the target car, having come off the A10 just north of Palaiseau. They had parked there to watch where the other vehicle went using the tracking system after they had lost visual contact with it.

"If they'd been going back to Charles De Gaulle," he continued, "they'd have carried on around to the west of the city, or maybe headed for the center to pick up the Périphérique. I think they drove off the autoroute to try to flush us out. I still have a good contact with them. That's now confirmed," he finished. "The car has just turned north onto the N7, and about the only place that road goes to from here is the center of Orly Airport."

"Good," Mario said. "I'm already out of the car outside the terminal building. Paolo will leave it at the rental desk, and we should get to the departure hall well before the two targets arrive. I'll call Vitale and update him. We'll see you both in the departure hall in about twenty minutes."

26

Lucerne, Switzerland

"The biggest problem we have, I guess," Robin said, "is knowing where the hell we should start looking. I mean, Switzerland isn't a huge country, but it's certainly big enough to hide any number of wooden chests or whatever the Templars used as a repository for their archive."

"That's going to be the problem," Mallory said, "because the clues we found in that translation of the last section of the text on the parchment seem to me to be pretty vague."

It was late morning the following day, and they were sitting at an outside table in a pavement café near the center of Lucerne, virtually on the banks of the lake, trying to plan their next move.

They'd bought their tickets at Orly the previous evening, and both had maintained full awareness of their surroundings all the time they were at the airport. That hadn't been easy, because the departures hall was heaving, full of people and with queues almost everywhere and for everything. Even getting a couple of cups of bad French coffee and some snacks had taken Mallory over a quarter of an hour. But they'd seen nobody who looked like the men in the car that had followed them, and not one of the horde of people had seemed to be paying them the slightest attention. Not even, in fact, the clerk who sold them their tickets, who was casual to the point of indifference.

They'd taken the evening easyJet flight from Paris Orly to Geneva entirely without incident. It had landed on time just before ten, and then Mallory had hired a car to drive them into the heart of the country, where they hoped to find what they were looking for. They'd stayed off the fast roads and instead had followed the west bank of Lac Leman, stopping after driving only about four miles in a town called Versoix, because it was getting late. They'd taken a room in a small motel rather than a hotel and had had a fairly comfortable night, reasonably certain that nobody had managed to follow them.

That morning, they'd continued driving northeast toward the center of Switzerland. They didn't know if they were in precisely the right area in Lucerne, but they did know that the canton of Schwyz lay on the eastern side of Lake Lucerne. And if, as they both now believed, the peasants of that region had been helped by members of the Knights Templar order in the fourteenth century, it was at least possible that the Templar Archive— assuming it still existed—might well have been concealed somewhere in that canton. In any case, it was arguably the best place to start looking, to try to follow the sparse and cryptic clues they'd managed to decode.

"In fact," Mallory added, "just remind me exactly what the translation said about the location we need to find."

Robin pulled a sheet of paper out of her laptop bag and unfolded it.

"As you said," she began, "what it tells us is a long way from being specific, and it will only make sense, in my opinion, once we've identified the correct location. Finding the right valley isn't going to be easy, and identifying the actual hiding place will probably be a whole lot more difficult. Right, these are the clues, such as they are. The first sentence says 'seek where the serpent roars, his mouth agape.' Then the second sentence states 'beyond the moving wall, the door awaits,' and the last phrase is much shorter. That just translates as 'the guardian beckons.'"

"That's all as clear as mud," Mallory said. "They certainly haven't made it easy, have they? I know I asked you before, but are you happy with the translations? There aren't any ambiguities or alternative meanings for the Latin words?"

"Not really, no. I've got no doubt that the man who wrote this was being deliberately obtuse, just so he could provide an extra layer of protection for the archive. Deciphering the encrypted text was obviously just the first stage. He was then expecting whoever did that to have to use their brains to work out what those three clues meant. But the reference to the confederate of Schwyz earlier in the text is clear enough, so we do have some kind of starting point. Well, perhaps less a starting point than a starting area, because the present canton is quite big."

"I agree," Mallory said. "That name wouldn't have been mentioned unless it was a direct reference. And you still think that if we can find the right approximate area, we can make some kind of sense out of those clues?"

Robin nodded. "I certainly hope so, but I think so, yes. I've got a couple of ideas about the first one, anyway, and I also think that we shouldn't necessarily try to follow them in the order they appeared in the text. It seems to me as if the last clue, the one about the guardian, is more than likely telling us where we should start looking, the general area, I mean, rather than anything else. Though I might be wrong, obviously."

"So, where exactly do we start?"

Robin didn't reply for a moment, just opened the side pocket of her computer bag once again and took out a map of Switzerland. While Mallory moved the coffee cups and plates to one side to clear a space, she unfolded the map, laid it flat, and then pointed at the western end of Lake Lucerne.

"We're here," she said, "pretty much on the western shore of the lake. Schwyz is over here, at the eastern end of the same body of water. Looking at the detail on the map, it's obvious that the area we're interested in is very mountainous. The contour lines are very close together over most of the canton, which means steep slopes, high peaks, and deep valleys. There are lots of these straight lines marked on the map, and each one of those is a ski lift of some sort, running up the mountains from the lower areas and base stations to the top of the ski runs. And a lot of the roads just zigzag up the hills and then sort of stop, presumably in the car parks used by skiers in the winter and walkers in the summer. We're lucky that it's summer at the moment, because I think this search would be impossible in the winter, with the whole area covered in snow.

"So I think we should just drive around the lake, get ourselves into the Schwyz canton, and find a hotel for a couple of nights. Once we're settled, we should try to find a better map than this one, a proper topographical chart covering the whole area that we're interested in, and see if we can identify any of the features that those obtuse clues seem to me to be suggesting. If we manage that, then we can get out there and start checking on the valleys that seem most likely."

"You definitely think it will be hidden in a valley, then?" Mallory asked.

"In my opinion. That's probably the most likely. In a valley there are likely to be caves and gullies carved out by the waterfalls. I haven't looked at the geology of this part of the world, the way you did with the mountains of Cyprus, but I have a strong suspicion that the most likely location for the archive is hidden in a cave somewhere. Where it won't be is in the strong room of some castle or building, because that would have been too obvious a hiding place, and over the seven hundred years or so since the archive was hidden, someone would almost certainly have stumbled across it.

"The chests we found on Cyprus had been hidden in a cave, and that location worked well enough for the

Knights Templar there. So I think they probably did the
same thing all over again here in the mountains: they
found a natural hiding place underground somewhere,
probably modified it so it was big enough to hold everything they needed to conceal, and then made pretty certain that nobody would ever find it by accident. Just like
on Cyprus, even when we find the right specific location—
assuming that we manage to do that—it won't be a matter of just walking into a cave and picking up a few
wooden boxes. They'll be far from obvious, and we might
well have to dig them out of the ground or pull down a
rock wall to get access to them."

Mallory nodded.

"Right. Well, we're certainly not going to achieve anything by sitting here looking at the view," he said, "so
let's saddle up and get out of here."

There was obviously no direct route over to the east,
because the lake was in the way, and although it probably
wasn't the fastest way to reach their destination, Mallory
and Robin decided to follow the road that ran along the
northern shore of the lake, at least for the first part of the
journey. They drove over the bridge by the railway station,
then swung right onto Haldenstrasse, paralleling the
Nationalquai and the lakeshore as they headed east. Mallory
stayed on the same road, which changed its name to the
Seeburgstrasse when it turned southeast. In the vicinity of
Meggen, the road continued northeast, again following the
shore of the Luzernersee, but rather than stay beside the
water, at Küssnacht Mallory continued straight on to pick
up the faster A4 at Immensee. This road took them along

the southern shore of the Zugersee, another large lake, past Oberath and Goldau, and then on to Schwyz itself.

They found a hotel that suited their purposes fairly near the center of the small town, booked a room, and then set out to explore their surroundings and, more important, to find a map. That took rather longer than either of them had expected, because almost every book-shop they went into only had a stock of modern tourist maps, colorful folded pages that listed restaurants, bars, hotels, car parks, ski lifts, and local attractions, the kind of information that would be invaluable to a tourist but completely useless and irrelevant as far as they were con-cerned. But they did eventually track down a topograph-ical chart that covered the entire canton, as well as sections of the neighboring divisions.

"It's not quite as good as a British ordnance survey map," Mallory said as they stepped out of the shop, "but hopefully it'll have enough detail on it for what we need."

They walked a few paces down the road, and then he suddenly stopped.

"What is it?" Robin asked.

"Something I noticed in the window," Mallory said, and retraced his steps.

They stood outside the shop, looking at the books on display, and after a moment he pointed at a slim volume on one side of the window.

"I don't speak German," he said, "but that looks inter-esting. The one with the picture of a mounted knight on the cover. I wonder if that's just a novel or something about the Templars, or something else."

"It's not a novel, and it's not about the Templars, or not specifically about them," Robin said firmly. "The title is 'The Legend of the White Knights' and according to the subtitle it tells the true story of the Battle of Morgarten. It's written by some German author named Fritz Gruber that I've never heard of. He's probably a local and that book's most likely the result of his hobby and personal research, because it has that unmistakable look of a self-published volume."

"You speak German?" Mallory sounded astonished.

"Not exactly. As a part of my spent—as opposed to misspent—youth, I studied French, Spanish, and German, but I frankly can't really pretend to be able to speak any of them well enough to be understood unless it's just a matter of booking a room or ordering a meal in a hotel or restaurant. But I remember enough of the vocabulary of all three languages to be able to read a bit in each one of them."

"I'll buy the book, then," Mallory said.

"Do you really think you'll find a clue to the location of the Templar Archive in a cheap book some local amateur historian has knocked up?" Robin sounded scornful. "You'll probably find all that's in it is just a slightly modified rehash of the entry for the battle in Wikipedia."

"You could be right, but I still think it's worth getting. I've done a lot of genealogical research, as I told you, and I've found local histories of particular districts, usually written by somebody who's lived in the place their entire life, really helpful. They know the area far better than any stranger coming in can hope to match, and often they've got a passionate interest in what they're talking about. And books like that always end up being privately printed because the only people who buy them are tourists or locals with a bit of an interest in the subject matter. No commercial publisher would ever contemplate releasing a book like that because it would have such a limited potential market."

A couple of minutes later, Mallory walked out of the bookshop, tucking his new purchase into the bag that already held the map.

"You won't even have to flex your German reading muscles," he said. "There were three versions of the book in the shop. The original was written in German, but the author has also produced versions in French and English. How good the translation is, I've got no idea, but it'll be easier to read even a bad translation than to try understanding the original German text."

"I hear what you say," Robin said, "but I'm still not sure it'll be too much help. After all, we already know when and where the battle took place and what happened when the opposing sides met. What we're really interested in is what probably took place a few years later, once the Knights Templar—assuming that the story is true and that the local peasants were helped by a handful of White Knights—had established themselves in the area. Anyway, all information is valuable, so let's hope the author discusses more in the book than just the battle itself."

On their way back to the hotel they passed a street sign pointing toward the Kantonsbibliothek Schwyz, and again Mallory paused.

"That must be the local library," he said. "Before we

get too deeply involved in anything else, it might be a good idea to see if they have any ancient records there that might help us."

Fortunately the librarian spoke reasonable English, but when Mallory explained that they were looking for any information that might be relevant to events that took place in the canton in the first couple of decades of the fourteenth century, and particularly to the Battle of Morgarten, she shook her head emphatically.

"I think I can save you some time there, Herr Mallory," she said. "We do have quite extensive records here, but not that many relevant to that period. But there is a shortcut. One of our local residents has always been interested in the early history of the canton, and he did a lot of research, most of it in the archives of this very building. And then he wrote a book about the battle, which you can find in almost any of the bookshops in town."

"Do you mean this book?" Mallory asked, reaching into his bag and pulling out the slim volume he had just purchased. "By Herr Gruber?"

The librarian looked slightly surprised. "So you have it already?"

"Yes, but I haven't had a chance to read it yet. But you're saying that this is quite authoritative?"

"In my opinion, yes. It was the product of three years of hard work by Herr Gruber. It will give you a good overview of the event."

When Mallory and Robin had left the building, the librarian checked a record on her desk, then unlocked the top drawer and took out a folded sheet of paper. She read the text, noted the telephone number printed underneath the block of writing, took out her mobile, and dialed it.

When her call was answered, she passed a brief message and then hung up, replaced the paper, and relocked the drawer. It would probably come to nothing, but the request made so many years earlier still carried weight, simply because of the identity of the people who had made it.

"As well as buying something in that last bookshop," the watcher reported, "they've also just come out of the library. It looks to me as if they're still doing research, so we've probably got enough time to assemble a full team here."

"Copied," Mario said. "Keep your eyes on the targets and make sure Paolo and Nico know where they go next, so one of us always has them in view. I'll be off-line, bringing Vitale up-to-date."

The watcher, the fourth member of the team Vitale had sent to follow Mallory and Robin, was apparently studying the menu posted outside a restaurant on the opposite side of the road from the library. The other three men were loitering in nearby streets, linked together in a conference call, and listening to his commentary on their mobiles, each using a Bluetooth hands-free earpiece.

All four of them had been on the flight out of Orly the previous evening, and in the crowds at Geneva Airport it had been a fairly simple matter to keep their targets in view as they cleared passport control and immigration. And when Mallory had been given the keys to a Renault hire car, Mario was at the head of the queue of the adjacent booth, completing the rental documentation for an Opel sedan.

When the targets drove away from the airport, Mario and Paolo had easily been able to follow them to Versoix, the headlights of their car just another set of lights in the darkness. Once they'd stopped, Paolo had put another tracker on the Renault and then they, too, had found a local hotel for the night. The last two members of the team, using the work names Nico and Carlo, had waited at the airport until Mallory started the hire car to ensure that they had confirmed the vehicle make, model, and registration number. Then they had also hired a car and driven to Versoix.

The tracker had worked precisely as the Italians had hoped, and the two surveillance vehicles had been able to follow the Renault from Versoix, on to Lucerne, and then farther east to Schwyz without ever having sighted the car once it had left the motel. And following the targets on foot around the town was proving to be just as easy. Obviously the English couple had no idea that they were being observed.

"Three years' hard work it might have been," Mallory said, nearly four hours later, "but as far as I can see there's nothing in this book that's of any use to us."

They'd returned to the hotel, and while Robin had spent her time studying the topographical map and identifying places that looked interesting and that she thought they ought to search, Mallory very quickly read the English version of the book he had purchased.

"All he does is explain what happened immediately before and just after the battle, and covers the fighting itself in some detail. But there's almost nothing about the aftermath, about what, if anything, the White Knights did once the surviving Habsburgs ran away from the battlefield."

"I did say that to you at the time," Robin said, "so far be it from me to say I told you so. But, actually, I did tell you so. Is there nothing at all that's relevant?"

"Not really, apart from a couple of maps, one showing the site of the battle, up by Lake Ägeri, which is almost certainly not what we want, and another one that just indicates where the local settlements were located at the time of the conflict. But neither of them is particularly detailed, mainly because they're hand-drawn, so I don't think they're going to be any help."

He closed the book and tossed it on the bed. "How about you? Any luck?"

Robin shook her head.

"Not really," she replied. "I've basically been looking for valleys that could contain caves, but the terrain around here means that there are probably dozens of them, maybe hundreds, that might fit the bill. I think what we have to do is get out there and start looking, and I've picked out half a dozen places where we could start. Once we've had a good look at the countryside, maybe that will give us a kind of feel for the sort of terrain we need to study."

"That works for me," Mallory said. "How about we go down and get dinner now? Then we'll come back and both look at the map. If we make an early start tomorrow morning, we can cover a good deal of the canton pretty quickly, with any luck."

The short telephone message left by the librarian had produced immediate results. The number she had called was constantly monitored, though never answered, every message being listened to within a few minutes of its receipt. The librarian had provided two names—David Mallory and Robin Jessop—because the English couple had completed visitor forms when they visited the building.

Those names provided a starting point, and a comprehensive Internet search generated a surprising amount of information about them. In particular, a couple of local British newspaper reports linked the name of the woman to the alleged discovery of an ancient parchment and, more significantly, with the murders of a number of unidentified Italians in the small town of Dartmouth in Devon. That raised red flags for two different reasons.

The man tasked with monitoring the telephone number considered the appropriate response for a few more minutes, as he again studied the newspaper reports he had unearthed. Then he nodded, reached for his mobile phone, and dialed one of the six numbers recorded on it.

"We might have a problem," he said in German when his call was answered.

27

Canton of Schwyz, Switzerland

A little after two o'clock the following afternoon, Mallory pulled the Renault hire car to a halt in the parking area of a roadside restaurant not far from the base station of a ski lift. For a minute or so, neither of them moved, just sat there hearing the faint noises as the car's engine started to cool down, staring through the windshield. They had left the hotel almost seven hours earlier, and since then had hardly stopped, driving from one location to another, hoping to find some landmark or geographical feature that might in some way tie up with the cryptic clues they had decoded from the text on the parchment. And until that point, they had seen absolutely nothing useful.

"Well, that was a bit of a busted flush," Mallory said.

"Yes," Robin replied shortly. "We can't keep doing

this, this kind of scattergun approach, driving into a valley and just looking out of the car windows and hoping to see something that might fit the bill."

"So what can we do?"

"What we should probably have done in the first place," she replied. "We take a bit of a time-out and go back to the clues on the parchment. We need to work out what at least one of them actually means, and then try to find a location that fits the clue, rather than trying to do it the other way round and just hoping for inspiration to strike when we see a bit of countryside."

"We'll give it a go," Mallory said. "Anything's better than this pretty much aimless driving around. Let's grab a bite of lunch here, and see if we can work out exactly what we should be looking for."

Strangely enough, cracking one of the clues didn't take anything like as long as either of them had feared. Inspiration struck Robin almost as soon as she reread the transcription from the Latin as they lingered over coffee in the restaurant.

"I can't believe I missed this," she said.

"What did you miss?" Mallory asked.

Robin shook her head. "Just hang on a minute. First, I need to look at the map again."

She stared at one particular section of the map for a few minutes, tracing lines on it with the end of an elegant red-painted fingernail. Then she tapped one part of the map and nodded to herself.

"As I see it," she said, "there are three possibilities here. Three locations, I mean, that might be right."

"What have you found?" Mallory asked, sounding impatient.

"I'm not going to tell you, because if I'm wrong I'll look like a complete idiot," she replied.

"I'm getting to know you quite well now, and I doubt very much if you could ever look like an idiot, complete or otherwise. Right, if you won't tell me what you think you've spotted, at least give me a clue."

Robin thought for a moment, then nodded. "Here's a clue. When is a snake not a snake?"

Mallory looked blank. "I have no idea, but I'll bet you're just aching to tell me."

"I'm not aching to tell you, but I am quite keen to show you," she said. "Let's go. You drive. I'll navigate."

She directed him away from the area where they had searched before, giving him terse directions as she related the markings on the map to the display on the sat nav and the countryside around them. The roads they were traveling along became progressively narrower and obviously less used, though the surfaces remained good. The Swiss were nothing if not organized.

"I said there were three possible locations," Robin said, "but I've actually found four. We just have to try them all until we find what we're looking for."

"I don't know if this is good news or bad news," Mallory said, "but this road stops a couple of hundred yards ahead of us in a car park. Can I assume that that is not what you're looking for?"

"Not a car park, no. But what I am interested in is the valley that you should see just to the east of us right now."

Mallory locked the car and they strode off together, in the direction that Robin was indicating.

At first glance, the valley didn't look significantly different from the others that they had explored during the morning. It had steep grassy sides dotted with stunted bushes and a handful of trees—Mallory thought they were pines or firs, but as he was no authority on any aspect of botany, he had no idea which, or even if either guess was correct—while at the end of the valley, perhaps a quarter of a mile in front of them, he could see the flashing silver of a mountain stream tumbling down from some unseen spring or hidden lake.

Robin strode ahead of him and stopped when she reached a clear area where the entire valley was visible in front of her. Then she lifted a pair of compact binoculars to her eyes—she had removed them from the depths of her handbag before they had left the car—and for about half a minute she just stared through the instrument at the far end of the valley.

Then she turned to Mallory and shook her head briskly.

"It's not this one," she said. "The shape is wrong."

"The shape of what?" Mallory asked, sounding more irritated than curious. "The valley itself?"

"No. Keep guessing."

"What are they doing now?" Vitale asked.

"The same as they've been doing all morning, ever since they left the hotel," Mario replied, looking at the tracking application on his smartphone and talking through the Bluetooth earpiece. "They're just driving around the mountains and valleys."

"Have they been stopping?"

"Yes, but usually only for a few seconds or a few minutes—no more than a quarter of an hour—at the most. Apart from lunch, of course. That took them almost an hour, but they're now back on the road."

"They're obviously looking for something," Vitale said, "and it's equally obvious that they haven't found it yet. Keep watching, and close in on them the moment it looks as if they are staying in one place for a significant amount of time. Don't interfere with them, and don't let them see you, but find out exactly where they go. I'm sending out another two men, and they'll be bringing weapons for you all, because I think we're probably getting close to the endgame."

Mallory asked her again as they walked back to the car, but she refused to elaborate. Sitting in the passenger seat, she gave him directions to the next blind-ended valley that she wanted to investigate. It wasn't far away. In fact, Mallory guessed it was probably the next valley to the east of the one they had just looked at. This time there was no convenient car park, and the road simply petered out at the edge of a patch of woodland. Tire tracks on the ground suggested that vehicles did either park there, or at the very least turn around, and there was room for him to park the car without blocking either the road or the turning area.

They repeated the investigation process, Robin leading the way, her binoculars at the ready, while Mallory stumbled along behind, still trying to work out exactly what she was looking for. Just as in the previous location, as soon as they reached an area from which they could see most of the valley in front of her, Robin stopped and studied the far end with her binoculars. And, again as before, she then shook her head and led the way back to where they parked the car.

"A clue might be helpful here," Mallory said. "I still have no idea what you're looking for, but if you told me that I might spot something that you miss, it would make sense."

"It might make sense," she replied, "but I've already given you a clue, and you've seen all the same information that I have. So I'm just wondering how long it'll take you to catch up."

"You said something about a snake, and one of the clues mentions a serpent, but I still don't see the connection. Are you trying to tell me you're looking for a snake?"

"In a manner of speaking, yes," Robin replied. "Or, to be absolutely accurate, I'm looking for something that looks like a snake, but which isn't actually a serpent."

"Oh, right," Mallory muttered, "that makes everything really clear."

Robin took pity on him as he unlocked the car using the remote control.

"If the next place we look at doesn't fit the bill," she said, "then I promise I'll tell you what that first clue refers to. Or rather, what I *think* it refers to. Anyway, let's get back on the road. Maybe it'll be third time lucky."

Mallory was entirely unsurprised when she directed him to drive into another narrow blind-ended valley. It was slightly wider than both of the places they had visited so far, and like the first, there was a small car park at the end of the road, already occupied by about half a dozen vehicles, parked in the neat and orderly fashion that they had come to expect, even after such a short time in Switzerland. Mallory slid the hire car into a space between a German-registered BMW saloon and a Mercedes SUV with Geneva plates.

"Maybe this is a popular walking or hiking area," Mallory suggested as they made their way along a narrow track that wound its way through a stand of trees that grew in the space between the car park and the start of the valley.

"Perhaps," Robin agreed. "It is spectacular countryside; you have to admit that."

This time, they didn't have as far to walk to get a good view of the entire expanse of the valley. Almost as soon as they'd cleared the last of the trees, they were rewarded with the sight of the valley opening up in front of them. Robin stopped and took in the sight. What she didn't do, Mallory noticed, was use the binoculars. Instead she glanced at him and then pointed in front of her toward the mountain that blocked off the end of the valley.

"Now do you see it?" she asked.

Mallory looked where she was pointing, but as far as he could tell the valley they were then standing in was virtually identical to every single one of those that they had already looked at.

"I don't—" he began, but Robin interrupted him.

"Snake," she said. "Think snake and then look again."

Mallory did so, uncomprehendingly.

"I see trees and grass and a stream," he said, shaking his head.

And then suddenly he saw exactly what she meant. There had been a stream at the end of the previous two valleys. In fact, Mallory guessed that there was probably a stream in almost every valley in Switzerland, and that most likely the majority of them had been formed by the action of water over the millennia. But whereas the previous two streams had bounced and danced their way almost straight down the rocky bed they had carved out, the stream he was then looking at had followed a rather different course.

Instead of tracking straight down toward the lowest level, water always taking the easiest possible path when it flowed, for some reason possibly associated with the geology of that particular part of the mountain, the stream they were looking at flowed in a fairly regular pattern from side to side, taking a curved path that was actually very reminiscent of the shape, the classic sinuous shape, of a snake on the ground.

"I see what you mean," Mallory said. "Was that what you were looking for?"

Robin nodded.

"It suddenly came to me," she said. "I kept puzzling over the expression about a snake that roared. That didn't seem to me to make any sense at all, because the most that the average snake can manage is a hiss. I was actually thinking about what could make a roaring noise and could be found in the mountains of Switzerland when I guessed the author of that clue might have meant the noise of a waterfall. That almost always sounds like a roar, and once I made that connection I also realized that if you had a stream that kind of meandered its way down the side of a hill making lots of curves and ended in a waterfall, that could very well be considered to be a snake that roared."

"Simple enough when you explain it," Mallory said. "Let's check it out."

They set off at a brisk walk, and within only a few minutes they could both clearly hear the sound of the water tumbling down the rocks at the far end of the valley, first as a muted growl, but becoming louder with almost every step that they took. And when they finally came to a stop, perhaps seventy yards from the base of the falls, the only possible word they could use to describe the sound was a roar. Standing so close, they couldn't appreciate the full shape of the stream as it made its way down the mountainside, but they had seen it very clearly as they'd approached that spot. In fact, Robin had taken several pictures of the stream with her digital camera already.

"I think that's pretty clearly the answer to that first cryptic clue," Robin said, "so the obvious question now is, what do we do next? Where do we have to go to find the answers to the second and third clues?"

"You said you thought that the third clue, the one that mentions the guardian, might be intended to point us in the right direction, to lead us to the right bit of some valley," Mallory said. "But if we've actually come straight to the right place, maybe you were wrong. Maybe that clue is only relevant when we find ourselves inside the cave or wherever this trail leads us."

"And the other problem, as I see it," Robin said, "is that we seem to be looking at three separate clues, with no obvious link or progression between them. We're standing here right now beside what seems to me to be almost certainly the landmark that the author of that text meant us to find."

"I'm quite certain you're right about that. And if we take that as a given, then we must also logically be in the vicinity of what we're looking for. In fact," he added with a grin, "I'm slightly surprised you haven't made the connection yet."

Then it was Robin's term to look irritated. She reached into the hip pocket of her jeans and took out the sheet of paper on which they'd written the transcribed clues, and read them again. Then she looked at Mallory.

"If you're right in what you're thinking," she said, "then we're going to need umbrellas at the very least. That is what you meant, isn't it?" she added.

"Exactly. About the only thing that could possibly be interpreted as a moving wall is the wall of water, in my opinion, at least. I think we have to walk up to the waterfall and see what's behind the water coming down the mountain. But there is something I want to do first, just as the kind of basic check that we're not barking up completely the wrong tree, or try to walk through the wrong waterfall."

"What's that?" Robin asked.

"You'll see," Mallory said, and started walking toward the waterfall, stopping to pick up a golf-ball-sized rock as he did so.

He stopped right at the edge of the pool of water that had formed at the base of the waterfall, and which was itself drained into a fast-flowing river that ran down the center of the valley.

He braced himself, then took careful aim and threw one of the rocks he'd picked up as hard as he could at the waterfall. They heard no sound above the roar of the tumbling water, but the result was obvious. The rock disappeared into the foaming water about six feet above the base of the waterfall and vanished.

Mallory gestured to Robin and they walked far enough away from the waterfall so that they could hear each other.

"You saw what happened?" Mallory asked.

"Yes. There has to be a cavity of some sort behind the waterfall, which is pretty much what we expected. So that's where we should be looking, but right now we really aren't dressed for it."

28

The following day, they both had a large breakfast in the hotel's dining room because they weren't certain when they'd next be able to eat, and then set off to do some essential shopping.

"I really don't think an umbrella is likely to be much use to us," Robin said as they walked down the street looking for a shop that might sell what they wanted. "That water is coming down the mountainside at a hell of a rate. I think if you put an umbrella up and stood underneath it, it would last about three seconds. What we need are proper waterproof capes with attached hoods. That way we can walk through the waterfall and at least our clothes should hopefully still be almost dry when we step into the cave or whatever it is behind the water."

That made sense, and about a quarter of an hour later they walked out the door of an outdoor and camping shop where they'd found exactly what they wanted. They'd bought a pair of heavy-duty capes large enough to provide almost complete protection. In Mallory's case the garment covered him from the top of his head to just below his knees, while for Robin it almost reached the ground. They also bought flashlights and a decent supply of spare batteries and, from the tools section of the shop, a crowbar, two large heavy-duty screwdrivers, and a couple of collapsible trenching tools that combined the functions of a pickax and a shovel. And a pair of sturdy rucksacks to put everything in.

"If we're right and we are on the correct trail," Mallory said, "we'll probably need a lot more than this stuff. But hopefully these tools will let us get inside the cave and have a proper look around. Then we can decide what else, what other equipment, we're going to need to buy to complete the job."

They walked back to the hotel, put all the bits and pieces they'd bought in the car, and then set off for the valley, pausing only at a small general store on the way out of the town to buy a couple of large bottles of water and half a dozen alleged energy bars that they hoped would keep them going throughout most of the day.

Less than an hour after they'd driven away from the hotel, they were standing at the end of the valley and looking again at the roaring waterfall in front of them. This time, they'd seen no cars in the car park, and there was no sign of anyone else in the valley around them.

"Let me go first," Mallory suggested. "I'll do a quick check and just see if there's anything there. If I don't come back, it means I've found something, or at least that I think the place is worth exploring."

Robin nodded her agreement and watched as Mallory took the cape out of his rucksack, then slung the pack back over his shoulder before pulling the cape on over his head. The bulk of the rucksack made it look as if he had an impressive hunchback, and the cape rode much higher on his body than before, but it would still offer adequate protection for his clothes.

Mallory gave Robin a quick peck on the lips, then turned away toward the waterfall. He stopped when he heard the unmistakable sound of suppressed laughter from behind him, and turned back to look at his companion.

Robin was giggling almost uncontrollably.

"What?" Mallory asked.

"Forget the Hunchback of Notre Dame," Robin said. "What you remind me of is a kind of giant snail, with that thing on your back. Anyway, don't just stand there. Get on with it."

Mallory walked the last few feet to the waterfall around the edge of the pond, and when he reached the rock face he just stood there for a few moments, trying to see if there was anything visible behind the tumbling water.

There wasn't. There also wasn't any easy or obvious way of stepping behind the waterfall. The rock beside him was a sheer cliff, with no visible hand- or toeholds, and was in any case soaking wet with the spray from the waterfall and appeared treacherously slippery. It looked as if the only way to achieve his objective was to literally go against the flow: to go from the pond to the waterfall and climb up into the falling water. That wasn't going to be easy, and he knew immediately he was going to get very wet, but as far as he could see there was no other way.

He was wearing jeans and a pair of trainers with socks underneath the cape, and for a moment he contemplated taking them all off and stowing them in the rucksack, in the hope that they would end the journey through the waterfall in a relatively dry state. That did make sense, and so he lifted off the cape, lowered the rucksack to the ground, and unlaced his trainers.

"Probably a good idea," Robin said, watching him then take off his socks, "but my advice is you wear your trainers when you walk into that pool, because we've got no idea what's on the bottom, and the last thing you want is to tear your foot open on a piece of broken glass or a sharp rock."

"I was going to," Mallory said, undoing the belt on his jeans and slipping them off. "I feel like a bit of a lemon, dressed like this," he admitted, glancing down at his underpants, "but it's probably the best option. What we should have done, with hindsight, was to have scoped out the access on this side yesterday, and maybe picked up a couple of wet suits or something."

With his jeans and socks in the rucksack, and the trainers back on his feet, he again pulled on the cape and then stepped into the water at the edge of the pond.

"Jesus Christ, that's cold," he said.

He started wading the short distance toward the waterfall, the water getting deeper all the time, albeit very gradually. When he stepped close enough to the falling torrent to reach out and touch it, the water was only just over his knees.

Mallory had no idea what to expect, so he glanced back over at where Robin was standing watching him, gave her a thumbs-up, then took a deep breath and stepped forward.

It felt as if he had stepped into the worst rainstorm in the history of the world. The water crashed down on his head and his shoulders in a never-ending torrent, the flow given impetus by the hundreds of feet it had fallen from the spring or lake high up on the mountainside that provided its source. That was one thing. The other was that he could see nothing in front of him, nothing apart from the falling curtains of blue-black water. He took another cautious half step forward, which changed nothing. He did it again, and this time he clearly felt the force of the water lessen significantly, and he knew he was almost clear of the waterfall.

Another half step, and the pressure on his head and shoulders ceased completely, though his rucksack was still dragging on its straps as the rear of it remained inside the waterfall itself.

The other thing that struck him immediately was that it was very dark. For a moment, he wondered if he was actually looking at a stone wall, just inches in front of him, but when he stretched out his hands he felt nothing at all. Just empty space. He realized that the wall of water behind him was simply filtering out virtually all the light, and that the only way to see where he was and where he should go was to use one of his flashlights.

He had taken the precaution of putting one in the

pocket of his jacket, though the other flashlight and spare batteries were all in his rucksack. He reached under the cape, took out the flashlight, and switched it on.

Paolo pulled the hire car to a halt in the car park, stopping only a few feet away from the target car.

Sitting in the passenger seat, Mario stared intently toward the path that wound away from the car park and deeper into the valley but saw no sign of the two people he was following.

"Change the tracker," he instructed, "while I check the valley."

The tracker had long-life rechargeable batteries, but these only gave it a total useful life of three or four days, so replacing the unit while they could was a sensible precaution.

Both men were wearing casual hiking clothes to blend in with the people they might expect to meet in the mountains, clothing that was nothing like their normal dark suits, and Mario was carrying a pair of compact binoculars to complete the outfit.

He walked quickly along the narrow path that led into the valley, keenly aware that the targets had stopped their car over fifteen minutes earlier, and that they could have covered a considerable distance in that time. Vitale would be unimpressed—at best—if he failed to find out where they'd gone.

Once he cleared the edge of the vegetation, he could see the whole of the valley in front of him. More important, he could see a single figure in the distance, standing beside a pool that had formed at the base of an impressive waterfall. He stopped, lifted the binoculars up to his eyes, and focused on the distant image.

It wasn't Mallory, as he had expected, but the woman Jessop, and she appeared to be getting undressed, which was not at all what he had expected. As he watched, she slid out of her jeans or trousers, then sat down on a rock and pulled on a pair of shoes—they looked like trainers or hiking boots—before placing her discarded clothing in a rucksack. She hoisted the rucksack onto her shoulders, pulled a cape on over that, and then walked toward the end of the pool nearest the waterfall and stepped into the water.

As Mario watched, she actually walked into the waterfall itself, and then seemed to step right through it. In an instant, she completely vanished from sight, as if she had never been there.

Mario waited for a few seconds, staring through the binoculars at the waterfall in case she suddenly reappeared, but he saw nothing. Still keeping his attention directed toward the far end of the valley, he lowered the binoculars, took out his mobile phone, and used the speed dial to ring Silvio Vitale in Rome.

He explained exactly where he was and what he had just seen.

"I assume that Mallory went through the waterfall first," he said, still watching the end of the valley, "and that the woman then followed him."

"Interesting," Vitale said. "At least we now know what they're looking for. Or where they're looking for it, at any rate, which is almost as important. Stay where you are and watch what happens when they come out again, and especially check to see if they're carrying anything. And make a note of the time that they're in there."

The blackness vanished instantly, and Mallory found himself looking at a wide cleft in the rock, rather than into the cave that he had been expecting. The top of the opening appeared to be about fifteen feet above his head, and the opening gradually widened until the floor of the cleft was perhaps eight or nine feet in width, the floor rocky and uneven.

Mallory reached out and rested the flashlight on the rocks, leaving it switched on, and then used his arms and legs to lever himself up out of the icy water and into the opening. Then he removed the cape yet again, swung the rucksack off his shoulders, and lowered it to the ground.

He picked up the flashlight and shone the beam all around him to see if anything looked unnatural—manmade rather than created by the geology of the mountains—but saw nothing. However, it was immediately apparent that the cleft ran deep into the rock, and that was obviously the place where he would now have to explore.

"Have you found anything?"

The voice was loud in his ear, clearly audible over the noise of the waterfall. He jumped involuntarily and then span round.

Robin stood in front of him, her cape and rucksack on the ground beside her, and her bare legs wet from wading through the pond outside.

"I decide to follow you straightaway," she said, pressing

her mouth close to his ear so that he could hear her. "I was only about thirty seconds behind you. Bloody noisy in here, isn't it?"

"You got that right," Mallory said. He had heard nothing over the thunderous roar of the waterfall until Robin had spoken. "And no, I haven't seen anything yet, because I haven't even started looking."

Mallory bent down, opened the top of his rucksack, and took out a towel, which he handed to Robin. She quickly dried her legs with it, then passed it back to Mallory, who copied her action.

"We don't know how long this is going to take," Robin said, pulling her crumpled jeans out of her rucksack, "and I don't know about you, but I'm quite cold, so I'm getting dressed again."

"That's probably sensible," Mallory said. "Exploring a dark cave full of sharp rocks and slippery boulders when you're half-naked doesn't seem to me like a good idea."

They left their capes near the waterfall, but hoisted the rucksacks onto their backs. Then they both shone their flashlights around the walls of the cavity they had discovered, checking for anything that seemed out of place. Something gleamed whitely on one side of the cavern, and Mallory strode over the tumbled rocks to look at it.

"It's a skull," he said, shining the beam of his flashlight directly at the object.

"You don't mean human, I hope?" Robin asked.

"Definitely not. It looks like a big rat. The rest of the body is here as well, just fur and bones, really."

Satisfied that there was nothing in the cavern entrance

that could be what they were looking for, they made their way deeper into the cave, Mallory leading with Robin a few feet behind him.

"It's bigger than it looks," Robin said as the cleft narrowed significantly and then opened up almost immediately into a much wider cave.

They both shone their flashlights around the walls, the bright white beams dispelling the blackness. The floor of the wider part of the cavern was more or less level, but virtually covered in boulders and lumps of rock, which had presumably fallen from the roof of the cave as a result of geological movements, or possibly caused by nothing more than the action of water. Certainly, in about half a dozen places within the cave, trickles of water ran down the walls, and in one location a fairly steady stream, somewhat reminiscent of a weak shower, emerged from the roof and splashed into a shallow depression on the floor. It was a remarkably bare and depressing cave, the stone a dull and dark uniform color, and with none of the different shades caused by minerals and ore in the rocks, or any sign of the stalactites and stalagmites that characterized other caves they had both visited in the past.

"Do you see anything?" Mallory asked.

"I see lots of things," Robin replied. "But if you're asking if I can see some kind of doorway that might have been constructed by the Knights Templar, the answer is no. Do you?"

"No," Mallory said shortly. "What I see is a fairly small cavern, without any entrances or exits apart from the one we've just walked through, and with no sign that any human being has ever set foot in here before us. At any period of time. I can't see any signs of modern debris, like empty cans or bottles, food wrappers or cigarette ends, nothing like that. But what I also don't see are things like burn marks on the walls where medieval explorers might have placed candles or firebrands so that they could see what they were doing. And more than that, obviously, I don't see anything that could possibly be considered to be a door. Do you know what I think?"

"I think I can guess, yes. You think we're in the wrong place, and I think you're right. And quite apart from anything else," Robin added, "and thinking about the practicalities of it, getting into this cave wasn't the easiest maneuver I've ever attempted, and that was just carrying a small rucksack. If the Templar Archive occupies a large number of chests, which is what you would expect, the logistics of getting them into a place like this, bearing in mind that they would need to be kept absolutely dry because water and parchment or paper don't readily mix, would be extremely difficult."

Robin's conclusion was both irritating and depressing but, they both acknowledged, was almost certainly right. It looked as if they had jumped to a conclusion, and although the location they had identified seemed to fit the description in the encrypted text, it was now clear that either they had misinterpreted it or, and perhaps this was more likely, there was more than one location in the hills and valleys of the Schwyz canton that matched the clue as they had deciphered it.

Mallory took one final glance around the cavern,

allowing the beam of his flashlight to play over the solid
rocks that surrounded them. Then he made a complete
circuit of the perimeter, not an easy task because of the
tumbled rocks on the floor of the cave, making one final
check that they hadn't missed anything.

"There's nothing here," he said bitterly. "There's no
hiding place in here big enough to conceal a shoe box,
far less several wooden chests. We need to take another
look at that clue to make sure we were reading it right
and then, if we were, we need to study the map again and
find another location that matches this one."

When he saw the figure emerge from the curtain of water
that tumbled down into the pool, Mario shrank back into
the tree line, though he was fairly sure he was much too
far away to be noticed, and his clothes were a discreet
blend of greens and browns that would make him effectively invisible against the vegetation at that distance.

He watched through the binoculars as first the man,
and then the woman, reappeared and made their way to
the edge of the pool. What he was particularly looking
for was any sign that either of them was carrying anything, but as far as he could tell they weren't. As they
both stepped onto the ground beside the pool and began
toweling themselves dry, he checked his watch and called
Vitale again.

"There were in the hidden cave for just under half an
hour," he reported, "and they weren't carrying anything
when they came out."

"That probably means they were in the wrong place,"

Vitale said. "Either that or they might have found what they were looking for, but they've worked out that they need other tools or equipment to get access to it. You've done well on this job, and I won't forget it. Now, keep watching them, and make sure that they don't see you. And keep me fully informed."

Mario waited until the two targets began walking back toward him, then slipped silently back into the patch of woodland that separated the valley from the parking area. A couple of minutes later he walked over to where Paolo was standing waiting beside their hire car.

"You've replaced the tracker?" he asked.

"Yes, with the fully charged batteries it should be good for at least three days. What did you see?"

"They walked through a waterfall into what I assume was a cave. I've told Vitale, and his best guess is that they're following a definite clue, and that whatever they're looking for is hidden in a cave somewhere in Switzerland. So our orders are to keep following them and keep watching where they go and what they do. Now get us out of here before they walk out of the wood."

The return journey through the waterfall was quicker, but just as wet, especially for Mallory, because as he was walking away across the pond his left foot plunged into some kind of hole in the bottom of the pond and he tumbled in up to his waist before he regained his balance. That soaked his underwear and most of his shirt, and he wasn't in the best of tempers when he finally made it to dry land again.

"Right," he said, squelching his way back toward the car in his sodden trainers, "I'm not doing anything else until I've got some dry clothes on."

On their way back to the hotel, Robin studied the clues again and then suggested something, almost tentatively.

"This first clue," she said, "we translated it as 'seek where the serpent roars, his mouth agape,' and I still think that the serpent has pretty much got to be a stream of water working its way down the side of a mountain, and the roaring has to mean a waterfall. And I freely admit I kind of ignored the phrase about the serpent's mouth gaping open. I just assumed that meant the waterfall where the stream drained into a pond or whatever. But there's an alternative meaning that would actually fit rather better than that."

"Try me," Mallory said.

"Suppose that the gaping mouth means exactly that. Not just a waterfall, as I thought, but two waterfalls, the stream coming down the mountain but then being split by a rock or something at the bottom, so that it actually looks like the open jaws of a snake. I can see it in my mind's eye."

"Seeing it mentally is one thing," Mallory said, slightly grumpily, "but actually finding it might be another matter altogether. You're going to have to look really carefully at the map, but I think the biggest problem is going to be that the map probably won't show you what any of the waterfalls look like. So we'll have to get back on the road again and start checking every valley that looks like a possibility."

At the hotel, they went up to their room and both of them showered and changed into dry clothes before going down to the coffee shop on the ground floor. They felt in need of hot drinks rather than alcohol, and Mallory ordered a couple of coffees to both warm and revive them.

"I read somewhere," Robin said, "that the idea that the caffeine in coffee acts as a stimulant is a bit of a myth. But the article did say the people could become addicted to the drink, though getting unaddicted is apparently quite easy. Just pointing that out," she added, watching Mallory take a mouthful of the hot drink.

"Actually," he said, reaching out for one of the ham sandwiches that he'd ordered along with the drinks, "I don't really care. I just like the taste. Now that I feel a bit more human, let's take a look at the map."

Robin spread out the topographical map on the table-top, and they both studied it in silence for some minutes. Then Robin stabbed her finger at one particular point on it.

"That could very well be what we're looking for," she said.

The point she was indicating was at the head of a valley—the curved contour lines made that perfectly clear—and Mallory could see the blue line, indicating a stream or a river, running down those same lines.

"Why there in particular?" he asked.

"Because of this label," Robin replied. "The German word is *Stimmgabel*, and I'm reasonably certain that *Gabel* means a fork. I don't know what the combined word *Stimmgabel* translates as, but it's obviously some kind of fork or a split, presumably in that stream."

"Hang on," Mallory said, taking out his smartphone. "This coffee shop has a Wi-Fi system. I'll look it up."

He input the code that was displayed on the wall of the room, opened up an Internet browser, and used the search engine to find a German-English dictionary.

"You're right," he said, looking at the result of the translation. "A *Stimmgabel* is a tuning fork."

"That would fit well," Robin said, "if you think about it. The shape of a tuning fork is a single handle that splits into two separate arms. If that stream does divide into two like that, you can absolutely see why it might have become known as 'the tuning fork.' That name is marked on the map right at the bottom of that stream, so it pretty much has to be referring to either the waterfall or the pond. I can't think of any way that a pool of water could end up being described as a forked stick. A river, maybe. So that just leaves the waterfall."

Mallory nodded slowly, put the last piece of the ham sandwich into his mouth, and then wiped his lips with a napkin.

"That does make sense to me," he conceded. "How far away is it?"

Robin studied the map for a moment before she replied.

"Probably about five miles as the crow flies, but because of the roads we'll have to take, my guess is between about ten and fifteen miles."

"Good enough. Let's go."

29

Canton of Schwyz, Switzerland

There wasn't a proper parking area at the end of the valley, just a number of open spaces on both sides of the place where the road petered out, each surrounded by trees, shrubs, and undergrowth, where a car or van could be left, virtually out of sight. As far as they could see when they drove up, there were no other vehicles there.

Mallory picked the spot that offered the most seclusion, then locked the car. They walked through a broad stand of trees into the valley itself, and when they reached the other side there was no doubt that they had located a place that almost exactly matched the deciphered clue.

In front of them, a stream curved and twisted its way down the blind end of the valley, but before the water tumbled into a large and almost circular pond, the flow split, the water being forced to run on either side of a massive outcropping of obviously hard rock that jutted out from the hillside. From a distance, the resemblance to an enormous snake with its mouth open was unmistakable. Even the movement of the water down the hillside, the shimmering and flickering light that it produced, was remarkably like the sinuous movement of a giant serpent.

"What do you think?" Robin asked.

Mallory glanced at her and smiled.

"It fits," he said. "It certainly fits, which is actually a slight surprise."

"Why?"

"Because the description we deciphered must have been written over half a millennium ago, and I would have expected the landscape here to have changed to a certain extent during that period of time. Though, to be fair, I suppose changes to the terrain, especially changes caused by something like water or wind, would only become apparent fairly gradually, so maybe I shouldn't be surprised at all."

"Whatever," Robin said. "Anyway, it definitely matches the description, so let's see what we can find behind those two waterfalls."

Carrying their rucksacks, they strode up the valley, following the course of the stream, which drained the pond at the bottom of the waterfalls. The closer they got to it, the louder the noise of the falling water became, until it was quite difficult to hear each other speak.

As he had done before, Mallory picked up a couple of rocks when they got close to the pond and threw them, one after the other, at the two waterfalls. Both rocks flew through the tumbling water and vanished from sight.

"It looks like there's a cavity behind each of them," Mallory almost shouted to Robin, making sure that she could hear him. "In fact, there's not too much distance between the two falls, so maybe there's just one large cave that runs behind them both. Let's go and find out."

He walked around the pond to the edge of the left-hand waterfall. As with the previous waterfall they had examined, there was no obvious way to get behind the torrent of water flowing down the hillside except by doing the same thing all over again: climbing into the pond, walking through the torrent, and then clambering up into whatever cavity was hidden in the rock behind it.

"Let's try the other side," Mallory suggested. "Maybe that'll be a bit easier."

It was, but not by very much. At the very edge of the waterfall was a boulder, soaked in spray and looking potentially extremely slippery, but which might possibly allow them to step from it and straight through the falling water, rather than having to gain access by wading through the pond. That assumed, of course, that their feet didn't just shoot from underneath them the moment they tried to climb onto the boulder.

"I think that's worth a try," Mallory said, pointing at the glistening black surface of the rock. "The worst-case scenario is that I'll slip off it and fall into the pond."

"Possibly breaking your neck or your back as you do so," Robin suggested brightly. "So just be careful, okay?"

Once again, Mallory removed his trainers and stripped off his socks and jeans, placing them in the relative safety of his rucksack.

"I hope this is the last time I'll have to do this," he said, pulling on the cape.

He walked to the rock, lifted his leg, and placed the sole of his trainer experimentally on the surface of the stone. To his surprise, he felt no obvious sensation of slipping. Presumably the pattern of the sole of the shoes worked well on that particular surface, despite the amount of water on it.

"Here goes nothing," he said, and clambered up onto the top of the boulder, where he stood for a few moments looking carefully at the wall of water tumbling down the hillside in front of him. Then he extended his left leg into the torrent, pressing downward and feeling for any kind of hard surface behind the water. The sole of his trainer touched something solid, and that, Mallory decided, was enough. He wriggled his shoe to try to ensure that he had a good grip on whatever unseen ledge was lurking behind the waterfall, then simply stepped forward with his right leg and passed straight through falling water and into the blackness beyond.

"It's very similar to the place they explored yesterday," Mario said from his vantage point at the much wider and open end of the valley. He was sitting on the trunk of a fallen tree at the edge of a patch of woodland, watching the scene at the end of the valley through his binoculars and talking to Silvio Vitale on his mobile. He was using a Bluetooth headset and was keeping his voice low, though there was nobody else anywhere near him.

He had already used the camera in the phone to

capture an image of the far end of the valley and sent that
to Vitale, so that the head of the order could more easily
understand what he was describing.

"The biggest difference is the shape of the mountain
stream," he went on. "This one is split into two by a rocky
outcrop, so there are two separate waterfalls feeding into
the pool." He broke off for a few seconds, concentrating
on the two figures he was studying through his binoculars. "The man—Mallory—has just stepped through the
water on the right-hand side of the waterfall."

"Are you sure it was the man?"

"Yes, I can still see the woman quite clearly. She's getting undressed ready to follow him."

"Undressed?" Vitale asked.

"Yes. Not completely, obviously. They both have capes
that cover their upper bodies, but to avoid their trousers
getting soaked when they step through the waterfall, they
take them off as well as their socks and put them in their
rucksacks. Then they put their shoes or boots back on to
protect their feet. It's probably a good idea."

He broke off again as he watched Robin Jessop preparing to step through the waterfall and follow Mallory.

"And now the woman is getting ready to follow the
man," Mario said.

"Do the same as before," Vitale ordered. "Keep a note
of the length of time they're in that hidden cave, and pay
especial care when they come out. If either of them is
carrying anything, I need to know about it, just in case
we can end this today."

"We still aren't armed," Mario reminded him. "The two other men you're sending haven't arrived yet."

"Nor are the targets armed, and there are four of you and only two of them, so I'm sure you'll be able to mange to take them out. If I do order that before you get your pistols, tell your men to watch the woman, because she's the more dangerous of the two in close combat."

On the hillside above the patch of woodland two men lay side by side, one studying the lone female figure by the waterfall through binoculars, while the other had his attention focused on the man in the wood. They were both wearing professional camouflage clothing, ghillie suits, that broke up their outlines and made them virtually invisible at any distance greater than a few feet. Beside one of the men lay an Accuracy International L115A3 sniper rifle chambered for the .338 Lapua Magnum round, fitted with a bipod, a Schmidt & Bender 3-12x50 PM II telescopic sight, and a slim but efficient suppressor on the end of the barrel. Long-distance snipers didn't usually employ suppressors, because the noise of the shot often wouldn't reach as far as their target, and would in any case arrive sometime after the bullet itself, but they were useful for work performed at closer quarters, allowing selected targets to be eliminated without any of their surviving companions knowing precisely where the killing shot had come from.

An almost identical weapon, in the hands of a British Corporal of Horse, a soldier in the Household Cavalry, had been responsible for one of the longest-ever recorded sniper kills, at over twenty-seven hundred yards, in excess of a mile and a half, in Afghanistan in November 2000. It was a serious long-distance weapon, though really over-kill in the present circumstances and at the distances they would encounter in the valley below them. If the order came through to take out one or both of the targets, the sniper would hardly even need to use the telescopic sight. Anything less than about five hundred yards, with that rifle, was effectively point-blank range.

The other man—the spotter—was using a tripod-mounted telescope to study the man lurking at the edge of the patch of woodland.

They were freelance operators, working as a team and selling their expertise in long-distance killing to the highest bidder, and the contract they were at present employed on had been negotiated and agreed at very short notice, with only the simplest and most sketchy of briefings.

They were talking quietly together in German as each man watched his respective target.

"Who is that man in the wood?" the sniper studying Robin Jessop asked.

"I have no idea. He's obviously watching the same targets that we've been given, but he's not wearing proper camouflage clothing, just casual hiking gear. It looks to me as if he's been told to mount surveillance on them, nothing more. There's no indication that he's carrying a weapon. My guess is that his backup, or whoever the other man is that we saw when we walked in here, is still waiting in the car they're using."

"You'd better call it in. We weren't expecting to encounter a second team on this operation, and we need to know what to do about it."

His companion nodded and slid a mobile phone out of his pocket. There was only one number programed into it, and his call was answered almost immediately.

"We have a possible complication," he began, then explained what they were looking at in the valley below. "We have no idea who either man is," he finished, "the driver or the observer, but the man who's watching from the wood is obviously focused on the same two people we were given as targets."

"I also don't know who they are," the man he'd called replied, "but I'll see what I can find out. Use your camera and try to get some pictures of both of them, because that will help with identification. And get the registration number of the car they're using."

"Understood."

"In the meantime, just observe the targets and await further instructions."

To Robin, standing about ten feet away, it was as if Mallory had simply vanished. One moment he was there, and the next moment he wasn't. She nodded to herself and sat down to unlace her trainers, determined to follow him inside immediately.

In the darkness on the other side of the waterfall, Mallory shook the cape and then pulled it off over his head before reaching into his jacket pocket for a flashlight. He switched it on and quickly ran the beam around the chamber that, somewhat irritatingly, looked quite similar to the one they been standing in only a couple of hours earlier. It was marked by the same dark rock and in a number of places he could see water trickling or falling from vents and cracks in the ceiling above him. Then he turned back toward the waterfall to wait for Robin to appear, as he was quite certain she was going to.

Just a few seconds later he saw a dim shadow on the other side of the waterfall, and then Robin stepped through the torrent and straight into his arms.

"I can usually manage that kind of thing by myself," she said, "but thank you for being there, all the same. Now, what have we got this time?"

Mallory turned the beam of his flashlight in the opposite direction to illuminate the chamber in which they were standing.

"Disappointingly," he said, "it looks to me very much like the other one, at least at first glance."

Robin muttered a most unladylike expletive under her breath, then dried her legs, pulled her jeans out of the rucksack, and swiftly put them on.

"I'd hate to think we've come all this way for nothing," she said, "so let's see what we can find. I can't believe we're not in the right place this time."

Together, they shone the beams of their flashlights around the cavern, which was definitely larger than the previous cave, though the stone walls and tumbled boulders looked almost identical.

"Obviously the geology of this cave is the same as the other one," Robin said, "but at least it's bigger and getting into it was a lot easier. At least that might suggest it's a more likely location for the Templars to have concealed their archive."

"Yes, but I still don't see any sign of anything man-made in here, so if this was where they hid it, where is it?"

"I have no idea." Robin played the beam of her flash-light over the walls of the cave. "I think we can forget the floor. It looks to me like solid rock, not like the earth and soft stone of that cave we found in Cyprus. I doubt if even the Templars would have been able to dig out a hiding place in this stuff," she added, tapping her foot on the stone floor for emphasis. "You'd need a jackhammer or a pneumatic drill to get through it."

"That just leaves the walls," Mallory said. "Maybe there's some concealed cavity or opening into another space."

"Exactly. So we're looking for a hidden door or some-thing of that sort."

They walked side by side toward the back of the cave, checking both the walls for any unusual marks and the floor so that they didn't lose their footing on any of the loose stones and rocks that littered it.

"Anything?" Mallory asked when they came to a stop by the rear wall.

"No."

They swung their flashlights to both sides, checking the walls and the rock ceiling above them, but saw noth-ing. Nothing except ancient stone, anyway.

Then Mallory spotted something. Or he thought he did. He shone the flashlight beam into one corner of the cave and held it steady.

"What is it?"

"I don't know. There's movement there, I think."

"You mean an animal?" Robin asked, putting her hand on his arm.

"No, not something alive. I didn't mean that. I think it's water flowing."

"There's water flowing everywhere in this place," she pointed out, then fell silent as she looked more closely at the area that Mallory was indicating. "I see what you mean."

Together, they walked over to the spot where he had focused the beam of light. From a height of about seven feet, a virtual curtain of water, a kind of mini waterfall, emerged from a virtually straight horizontal crack in the rock and fell smoothly to the floor of the cavern, where it vanished into a deep gully.

"The second clue," Robin said, her voice barely audible over the sound of the torrent behind them. "It said 'beyond the moving wall, the door awaits.' Even without poetic license, this looks to me pretty much like a moving wall. A wall of water." She fell silent and glanced at Mallory. "So, what do we do now?" she asked. "Just step through it?"

Mallory shook his head in the darkness.

"I think that would be a really bad idea," he said. "The one thing we do know about this Templar treasure trail, or whatever you like to call it, is that not taking the proper precautions can be extremely hazardous to your health. Remember the booby trap concealed inside that book safe, the object that kick-started this little adventure, and those lethal blades hidden in the chests we found under the floor of the cave in Cyprus. Opening the book safe in the obvious way would have crippled you, but the mechanism hidden in the chests would have cut you in half. So what we definitely don't do is just walk straight through that opening."

He looked carefully at the moving curtain of water in front of him, from where it emerged from the rock above their heads down to the gully where it vanished.

"In fact," he added, "at the moment, we don't even know if there is an opening on the other side of this kind of elongated shower. So that has to be the first thing we should check out."

He shone his flashlight directly at the falling water, trying to see through it at whatever structure was on the other side.

"I don't know if your eyes are any better than mine," he said, after a few seconds, "but all I can see is blackness. That could be a solid wall of rock, or the entrance to another cave."

"That's what I see, too," Robin agreed. "I think it's time to try something physical."

There were hundreds of rocks of different sizes lying on the floor of the cavern, and Mallory bent down and picked up a handful of them. Then he motioned Robin to stand back, and lobbed the first stone toward the moving water.

It passed through, but immediately there was a faint but clearly audible click, the sound of stone hitting stone, and the rock bounced back toward them.

"I didn't expect that," Mallory said. "Maybe we've got it wrong, and what we're looking at is just an unusual waterfall."

He threw another stone toward the water, with the same result, and then a third, which also bounced back. Then he changed his aim slightly and tossed the next rock toward the right-hand side of the curtain of water. That one simply disappeared from view.

"That's different," he said. "Maybe we're looking at only a really narrow opening."

He gathered a few more stones and threw them, one after another, toward the right-hand side, aiming the first one near the ceiling of the cave and working his way down to floor level. Some bounced back, but most of the rocks simply disappeared from sight into some cavity. By the time he'd finished, Mallory reckoned he had a reasonable idea of what lay beyond.

"It looks to me like there's a tall but fairly narrow opening on the right-hand side," he said. "It's probably wide enough for one person to step through, but whether it would have been wide enough to allow a couple of Templars to carry a chest through it is another matter entirely."

"So we put on those blasted capes again," Robin suggested, "and carry on?"

"Not quite yet," Mallory cautioned. "We now know that there is an opening behind the water, but we still don't know if it's protected by some kind of medieval mantrap. Before we step through it, I want to try something else."

He shone the flashlight around the floor of the cave, looking for some object that he could use as a probe. Over to one side, he spotted a darkly sinuous shape, apparently the root of a long-dead tree that had somehow penetrated into the cave from above. The root wasn't as long as he would have liked, nor as thick as he wanted, but it was all he could see, so it would have to do.

Mallory picked up the end of the root and twisted it to free the upper end, then carried it over to where Robin was standing, framed against the wall of water.

"We have got the crowbar, don't forget," she said.

"I think this length of root will be safer, just in case there is some mechanism guarding the entrance that could knock it out of my hands. A length of root flying around could give you a bruise if it hit you, but a flying crowbar could take your eye out or even kill you."

He stepped up beside the falling water and thrust the end of the root into it at a little over head height. Nothing happened, as far as either of them could tell, except that the end of the root had clearly entered some kind of opening in the rock. Mallory pushed it as far as he could, without actually letting his hands enter the water.

"There's definitely a cavity there," he said. "Let's see if we can work out the rough shape before we go any farther."

He moved the length of root downward, keeping it over to the right-hand side as he tried to trace the outline of the opening. It appeared to be almost a vertical line, though with a number of protuberances that suggested it was probably a natural formation in the rock, rather than something cut out with hammers and chisels.

Mallory pulled out the root and then thrust it again into the water near the top. He repeated the process by pressing it against the left-hand side of the opening. Again, the line he traced was almost vertical, and this time it appeared to be much straighter.

"That could be manufactured, rather than natural," he suggested.

"Only one way to find out," Robin said.

"A couple more things I want to try first."

He ran the length of root all the way to the bottom of the hidden opening, then rammed it down hard against the rock, repeating his action half a dozen times.

"You're worried about a trip wire or something like that," Robin said. "This would make a pretty hostile environment for a mechanism like that. With all this water around, iron or even steel would rust quite quickly, I would have thought."

"You're absolutely right," Mallory agreed, "but there could be other kinds of traps, maybe using falling rocks or possibly excavating a cavity in the floor of the cave and covering it with something that would break under the weight of a man. And that sort of thing could still be able to function even after all this time, because the only mechanism needed would be gravity, and that's a pretty reliable force."

Having achieved nothing, Mallory tossed the length of root to one side and looked at Robin.

"I'll go first," he said, "and I'll talk to you all the time, to tell you what I'm seeing. What we don't want to do is just blunder in, in case we have missed something that could kill us."

He walked across the cave, picked up his cape, and put it on. Then he opened his rucksack and took out the crowbar, which he tucked under the belt of his jeans. He took out a spare set of batteries for his flashlight, then stepped back to the wall of water.

"If I don't see anything dangerous," he said, "I'll tell you, but for the moment I'd rather you stay out here, just in case I get trapped or injured by something on the other side of this. At least then you'd be able to call for help."

He gave her a quick grin, checked he had everything that he thought he would need, pulled the cape over his head, and then cautiously thrust his face into the wall of falling water so that he could see what lay beyond.

"Most of it, most of the rock behind the waterfall," Mallory said, raising his voice so that Robin could hear him, "is completely solid. Over on the right-hand side, as we worked out, there's an opening that's wide enough— easily wide enough—for a person to step through. The right side of the opening looks completely natural, but the wall on the left is suspiciously straight, so that could well have been hacked about in the distant past to widen the access, though I can't see any chisel marks or anything like that on it. The floor of the opening looks to me like solid rock, with no sign of any booby traps, or the like. And I'm not sure how long a medieval booby trap could keep operational if it was constantly being drenched in fast-flowing water."

"All understood," Robin said, from behind him.

Mallory took a cautious step forward to move completely behind the curtain of falling water and into the opening. Before he committed himself, he stamped his foot hard against the rock over which he was going to have to advance, just in case there was some trap there that he couldn't see. But the stone appeared and felt completely solid.

"I can't see any sign of a problem," he said, "so I'm going to walk through the opening. I can't see anything significant at the moment using my flashlight," he added. "All the beam seems to show is more rock in front of me. I'm just doing a final check."

He removed the crowbar from his belt and slammed the curved end into the rock floor in front of him, putting most of his strength behind it, but was rewarded only by the unmistakable sound of steel hitting rock. He did that half a dozen times, with exactly the same result—or perhaps lack of result—on each occasion.

He used his flashlight to examine the sides of the opening before he moved forward, but again saw nothing that gave him cause for concern. It looked like a cleft in the rock. Nothing more, nothing less.

"I'm walking through now," Mallory announced.

"Just be careful," Robin said, her voice sounding much closer behind Mallory than before. He turned to glance behind him, and saw that she was now standing on the inner side of the waterfall, only about three feet behind him.

He nodded, then turned his attention back to the narrow cleft in the rock in front of him. He shone the flashlight down at the floor, making sure that there were no natural hazards waiting to trip him up, as well as no obvious traps left by the Templars nearly one millennium earlier.

Then he stepped forward.

30

On the hillside, the spotter had slid backward from his observation position and made his way slowly and carefully along the top of the hill, ensuring that he remained beneath the skyline and so invisible to anyone on the ground below, until he reached a position from which he could see the end of the road below him. From his vantage point he could see three vehicles.

One—a somewhat old and battered but well-equipped four-by-four that was tucked almost out of sight behind what looked like a wall of shrubs and young trees—was the farthest away, about a hundred meters down the valley, and he could ignore it completely, because that was the vehicle in which he and his companion had arrived about half an hour earlier. Of the other two vehicles, one was tucked into a secluded parking space as far away from the hill as possible, barely visible behind the vegetation.

It was very obviously empty, and was by inference the hire car being used by the two primary targets.

The other car was much closer to the spotter, and much less carefully parked. The driver's window was wound down and the arm of the man in the driving seat dangled outside, a thin gray plume of smoke from a cigarette held in his hand rising almost straight up into the air.

That was obviously the car in which the unidentified watcher had arrived, and was still in the same position that it had been when he and the sniper had parked some distance down the road and then made their way up through the bushes and undergrowth, keeping out of sight the whole distance. Reading the number plate of the car through the powerful zoom lens on his camera was the work of a few seconds, and he took three pictures to ensure that he had recorded it clearly. Once he'd done that he waited for a few moments, deciding what to do next.

Their employer had requested a photograph of the two men as well, and that wouldn't be as easy. The face of the man in the car—indeed, all of his upper body apart from his left arm and hand, still holding the cigarette—was invisible, and there was no obvious way for the observer to get himself into a position from which he would be able to photograph him in his present position. The only option, realistically, was to get him to move, to have him step out of the car.

Sometimes, it's the simplest and most obvious things that work best. The observer placed his camera on the ground behind a tussock of grass. Then he stood up, picked up a couple of stones from the ground, each of them about half the size of a golf ball, and flung them with all his strength toward the parked car. Then he dropped flat and took hold of his camera.

The distance was perhaps fifty yards. A long throw, but achievable in part because the observer was higher up on the hill, which gave him a bit more distance, and he was fit and strong. One of the stones missed the car entirely, but the other one bounced off the roof, the metallic clunk of its impact clearly audible.

Immediately the man in the car dropped his cigarette and stepped out of the vehicle, peering all around him for whatever had caused the sound that had roused him. He obviously saw nothing, because there was nothing to see, but while he was outside the vehicle and looking around, the spotter took almost a dozen pictures of him, the high-specification digital camera entirely silent in operation.

After a minute or so, the man in the car shrugged and got back into the vehicle. The spotter waited until he was certain the man wasn't going to get out again, then eased back out of sight, slowly and cautiously. He climbed the hill and vanished from the skyline, then made his way back to where his partner was silently watching and waiting.

"Okay?" the sniper asked quietly.

"Yes. No problem."

The spotter lay down to the left of his companion. Getting pictures of the second man was easier because he was already in the open, but complicated by the vegetation that surrounded him. Nevertheless, over a period of about five minutes the spotter got three or four reasonably clear pictures of his head and face. Hopefully they would be good enough to compare with the images obtained from the surveillance cameras at the airports, assuming that the man had arrived in the country by air. If he'd driven to Switzerland by car, that obviously wouldn't work, but the Swiss registration plate on the parked vehicle suggested it was probably a rental, which in turn implied that he'd most likely flown in.

Mallory began making his way forward, moving cautiously and testing the ground every step of the way, and at the same time checking the stone walls on either side for anything that looked out of place.

The passageway curved to the left, the width of the opening and the rocks that formed it appearing essentially unchanged. Now that he was fairly confident that at least the entrance to the hidden cavern in front of him had not been booby-trapped, Mallory was able to examine the walls more carefully, and with a frisson of excitement he realized that he could see the unmistakable marks of chisels on both sides. More than anything else, that convinced him that they really were in the right place.

"Both sides of this opening are either completely manmade," Mallory said, "or at least modified by men with hammers and chisels."

Then he took another step forward, out of the curved confines of the entrance passage, and into what immediately felt like a large chamber, much bigger than the one behind the waterfall. He shone his flashlight all around him, checking for any obvious sign of danger, then turned his head and called out, "It seems to be okay. You can come through."

Just seconds later, Robin stood beside him, shining her flashlight around the chamber as her eyes started to explore the space she had just entered.

"This is quite a bit bigger than the outer cave," she said, "though that entrance is fairly narrow."

"It's probably about three feet wide at its narrowest point," Mallory said, "and that would be wide enough for quite a big wooden chest to be carried through it."

Robin nodded.

"True enough," she said, "and I suppose tactically having a narrow entrance would have provided them with an extra measure of security. If they were attacked, one or two knights could hold that entrance against an unlimited number of attackers, simply because it is so constricted."

"There might be something else," Mallory said. "I've been thinking about it ever since I saw that narrow entrance. The Templars were consummate military strategists, the best-trained fighting men of their period, and I don't believe that they would have chosen a location for one of their most precious assets that didn't have at least two entrances. I think we might've kind of come in through the back door, and there's another entrance, probably a whole lot wider, somewhere else."

"In that case," Robin asked, "why didn't the clues take us to the other entrance?"

"Assuming for the moment that I'm right," Mallory said, "which is by no means certain, I wonder if this supposed other entrance might be really well hidden, with no distinctive landscape features anywhere near it that could be used to show its location to somebody following the trail. Maybe they found this cave by accident or while they were looking for a secure location, and then discovered this inner chamber, which they then used as a storeroom. But they also realized that the only way it could ever be found again, except by the wildest of accidents, was if they left a clue or clues pointing to the entrance we came through."

Mallory looked at Robin, before turning his attention back to the space in front of them. "There are a lot of assumptions in that, I know, but to me it does make sense, because I'm certain we are in the right place. Those two clues that we followed up were too specific to be accidental or for there to be another cave like this one. So I think this almost certainly was the Templar storehouse, though obviously that certainly doesn't mean the archive is still here."

While Mallory had been talking, both he and Robin had been sweeping the beams of their flashlight around the chamber, looking for any sign of the objects they were seeking. But as far as they could tell on this first inspection, the cupboard was bare. It was also conspicuously damp, trickles of water running down a number of sections of the walls, and in a couple of places actually dribbling out of cracks in the ceiling.

"I don't know about you," Mallory said, "but this isn't the kind of place I would choose as a long-term repository for important documents. I reckon that any kind of paper or parchment that was left in here would rot away within a few years at most. It certainly wouldn't have lasted for centuries."

"What about the third clue?" Robin said suddenly. "There were three clues that we deciphered in that piece of parchment, and so far we've only been able to find locations that correspond to two of them. What about that phrase 'the guardian beckons'? How does that fit in here?"

"I have no idea." Mallory sounded quite dispirited. "Anyway, let's take a look around and just see if there is anything here to find."

As they had done before, in the outer cave, they walked around the irregular perimeter of the cavern, checking the floor and the ceiling and the walls constantly as they did so. For some reason, there were more loose boulders and large stones in this cave than in the smaller one, and in a couple of places these heavy stones were piled up almost from the floor to the roof of the cavern.

"There could be something behind one of these heaps of stones," Robin suggested. "I know they look natural, as if they had just been formed from a landslide or by a part of the roof collapsing, but they could also have been put there deliberately to conceal an entrance to another chamber."

Mallory played his flashlight beam over the groups of stones that she was indicating.

"That's possible," he conceded, "but we could spend a couple of days shifting one of those piles, by the looks of it, and there's no guarantee that we'd find anything at all behind it, apart from another solid rock wall."

They completed their inspection of the chamber, and for a few seconds just stood side by side, looking for any kind of clue to tell them where—or even if—the archive was, or had ever been, hidden in there.

"I hate to say it," Mallory said flatly, "but I don't think there's anything here to find. Maybe this cave was used as a temporary hiding place for the Templar Archive, but it was later removed, because I don't see any sign here that there's anything left. The ground is solid rock, so there's not even the chance of seeing the outline where a bunch of cases might have been stacked."

Robin nodded slowly.

"I don't see anything, either," she admitted, "but this really doesn't make sense. We already know that the encrypted text on the parchment I found wasn't written at the same time as the Templars were purged but some years afterward. We also know that the first set of clues we deciphered led us to that cave on Cyprus and the two chests. Granted, they didn't contain treasure, but we think we worked out why. So the author of the text obviously knew what he was talking about, and I can't believe that he would have planted the clues that led us here, only to find an entirely empty chamber. We must be missing something."

"You're probably right," Mallory said, "but as far as I can see, there's not much more we can do here, though it's probably worth taking a bunch of photographs of this place so that we can look at them later. You never know; something might show up on a digital image that we simply can't see with the naked eye."

Suiting his action to his words, Mallory removed his digital camera from the rucksack and set about systematically photographing every single section of the cavern, the light from the automatic flash bouncing off the dark walls.

"That'll do," he said, a few minutes later. "Let's go."

"They're coming out," the sniper murmured, staring at the waterfall at the end of the valley, where a dark figure had suddenly come into view. "Keep watching the man below. See what he does."

The man watching from the cover of the patch of woodland below stiffened as the two distant figures reappeared, and he immediately lifted his binoculars again to study them. Clearly all his attention was directed toward them, as the spotter could tell from the man's body language: if any confirmation had been needed of the man's purpose in being there, that provided it.

"Now he's moving," the spotter said. "He's making his way back toward where the car is parked."

"As we expected," the sniper said. "He's moving away because the two targets are heading back down the valley. You'd better call it in."

Again the spotter dialed the contact number they had been instructed to use and explained what was happening.

"Do you have any further orders?" he asked. "The targets are well within range right now, but they'll be back at their car in a few minutes."

"No further order at this time. Do not, I repeat, do not engage the targets. Remain in position until they have left the area. Then exfil yourselves and await further instructions. Ensure that your mobile is kept fully charged and is switched on."

Back at the hotel, Robin took a long shower while Mallory transferred the photographs they had taken onto his laptop, where they would be able to examine the images more easily. He replaced the computer in his bag, and then they both went down to the coffee shop. With the drinks on the table in front of them, Mallory made room to open up his laptop, and together they began studying the pictures that he had taken with his digital camera. They were, at a first glance, and in fact even at a second glance, uniformly disappointing. All they seemed to show was the featureless and slightly damp walls of the cavern, but they didn't appear to reveal anything that they hadn't already seen for themselves with their own eyes.

Until, that was, they looked at one single photograph, a picture taken by Mallory of one of the piles of stones stacked up against the side wall of the cave.

"Is that a mark on the rock, just there?" Robin asked, pointing at the wall to one side of the pile.

Mallory looked to the area she was indicating, shrugged, and then centered and enlarged that part of the image. The flash from the camera had caused some flares of light on the rock, but above and below these areas of brightness they could both see what looked like very faint lines.

"That's barely visible," Mallory said, "but that does look to me like a straight line, maybe carved there by someone using a hammer and chisel."

"And there, below it," Robin said, "that looks like another horizontal line, but quite a lot longer than the other one. Have you got any other pictures of that part of the cave?"

When Mallory took the series of photographs, he had deliberately allowed a considerable amount of overlap between them, and in response to Robin's question, he pulled up another half dozen images, one after another. Fortunately that precise area of rock was visible on three of them. Even more fortunately, because of the changing angle of each photograph, the flare from the flash was different in each picture.

"There's definitely something there," Robin said, looking at the pictures in sequence, "but all I can make out is those two lines. Even if they are man-made, I'm not sure how that could possibly help us."

"Let me just try something," Mallory suggested.

He loaded the best of the pictures into a piece of photo-manipulation software, enlarged the relevant area until it occupied most of the screen display on his laptop, then began tweaking it.

"The original image is a color photograph, obviously," he said, "though pretty much everything in that cave was black. Let's see what it's like if we view the image in different ways, like black-and-white, sepia, and all the rest of it. Then we can try fiddling about with the brightness and contrast, just see what comes out of that."

The successive manipulations he did only seemed to make the horizontal lines either more or less pronounced, but didn't apparently reveal any further details. Then he had another thought. He converted the image to black-and-white, and then inverted it, so that it was like looking at a photographic negative.

And that was when the image suddenly came to life. Directly below the longer of the two horizontal lines, they could see, very faintly, another line running almost parallel. Almost, but not quite, because on the right-hand side of the image the two lines met at what appeared to be a blunted point, while an equally faint vertical line was visible on the left-hand side, making the shape look like an extraordinarily elongated letter *T*, lying on its side.

"That's a bit like the Shroud of Turin," Robin said, staring at the image. "You can only really see the image on that if you view it as a negative, rather than a positive. But what is it? What is that shape?"

"I have an idea," Mallory replied, "but I'm more interested in these lines here," he added, pointing close to the top of the image.

On the artificially produced negative image, the shorter horizontal line was clearly visible, as were two vertical lines descending from either end of it, and between them, virtually framed by those three lines, was the faint outline of what looked like another horizontal line, shorter and thicker.

"I can see more of it now, thanks to your manipulation," Robin said, "but I still don't really see what that is supposed to represent."

"We really need to get back into that cave and take another look at it," Mallory said, "but I already think I know what that is. When the Templars rode into battle, they invariably wore helmets, and probably the classic shape for the helmet of a Templar knight was one with a flattened top, vertical sides, and with a horizontal slot cut out of the metal to allow the wearer to see out of it. I think those few lines are just a simple representation of the helmeted head of a Templar knight."

"It is a definite shape," Robin conceded, staring intently at the image on the screen of the laptop. "But I hope we're not just seeing what we want to see. If you *are* right, then the shape below it has pretty much got to be a Templar battle sword, and the tip of the blade is fairly clearly pointing toward that corner of the cave. So what we could be looking at here is the 'guardian' from the third clue."

"I hope so, but the bad news is that if that shape *is* the guardian, and he *is* beckoning, he's very clearly indicating that massive pile of stones and rocks. That probably means there's another chamber off the one we explored, and the only way we can get inside it is if we move every one of those boulders. That's going to be bloody hard work, and it could easily take us one or two days just to shift them."

Robin smiled at him.

"We never thought this was going to be easy," she said, "but the other piece of good news is that the rocks are still in place. If somebody else had come along centuries ago and beaten us to it, those boulders would have been scattered all around the floor of the cave, and the opening into whatever other chamber is there would have been clearly visible. So we can at least be reasonably sure that the Templar Archive is still hidden in there, and waiting for us."

Mallory nodded. "Well, it's going have to wait at least another twelve hours. It's too late to go back there today, and in any case we're going to need leather gloves, probably another crowbar or two, and a heavy hammer at the very least, plus a couple of decent battery-powered lanterns because we'll need good light in that cave to see what we're doing. So tomorrow morning we'll go shopping, and when we've done that we'll see what lies on the other side of that rock pile."

31

Canton of Schwyz, Switzerland

"They're still in the hardware store," Paolo reported, "and I can't see what they're doing. Do you want me to go inside after them?"

"No," Mario said decisively. "Don't take the risk of them noticing you. Pick them up again when they come out and keep following them. But if you can, try to see what they bought in the shop."

"Understood."

"Carlo, Nico. Make sure you stay off the street where that store is located and out of sight. Wait for Paolo to tell you which way the targets are headed. Then the one of you who's closest to them will take over the surveillance. And keep the commentary going. We need to know everything they do and everywhere they go."

Once again the Italian enforcers were using the conference call facilities on their mobile phones to remain in touch. It was a simple but extremely effective tool for the task at hand, allowing all four of them to keep in constant contact with one another.

"They've just walked out of the shop," Paolo reported. "The man Mallory is carrying a canvas work bag that looks quite heavy. I presume he's bought tools of some sort, but I can't tell what. They've turned left and are heading down the street toward Nico."

"I've got them," Nico said.

And as Mallory and Robin made their way back through the streets, the loose group of four Italians moved and shifted around them, one of them always keeping the English couple in view. When they reached the hotel and went inside, the group assembled outside the building, out of view from the windows at the front, but in a location from which they could see the main entrance, and waited.

"I'm beginning to think," Mallory said as he lowered the canvas bag of assorted tools to the carpeted floor of the bedroom, "that we've got company—again."

"Not those bloody Dominicans?" Robin demanded.

"I really don't know. I'm reasonably observant, and I seem to have noticed either the same man, or two men who look and dress remarkably alike, in the streets of this town. In fact, it's not just one man, but two or three different men who seem to be taking something of an interest in what we're doing."

"You mean they're people you've seen before?"

"Not as far as I know. And it might well be a coincidence, and we've just run into a few locals who happen to have been in the same area as us at the same time, but with what's happened to us in the past I'm inclined to be cautious."

"Definitely. Do you want to just walk away? To get out while we can?"

Mallory shook his head. "I don't want to quit any more than you do, and I may well be jumping at shadows. But I do have the distinct feeling that we're being watched, that kind of prickling sensation. And even if we have picked up a tail, I still think our best option is to keep going, to try to follow the clues and get to the archive before anybody else can."

"I feel it," Robin said. "I feel we're now so close. We'll carry on, just keep our eyes open, make sure we're not being followed, and try to make sure nobody knows where we're going. With a bit of luck, we could get inside that hidden chamber today or tomorrow, and that could be the end of the quest."

As Mallory and Robin talked together, their words were relayed from a voice-activated audio bug concealed inside a power socket in their hotel room to a digital recorder mounted in the glove box of a black Mercedes sedan parked in the adjacent street.

The bug had been installed that morning, shortly after they had left their room, by a technician who had presented unarguable credentials to the hotel manager, credentials that had been provided by the same people who were employing the sniper team. The hotel manager had supplied

him with a master key for the room the targets were occu-
pying, and the insertion of the device had taken him less
than ten minutes, including testing the chosen location for
sensitivity and clarity of reception.

As well as the recording equipment, their conversation
was also being monitored in real time by the two men
sitting in the parked car.

When Robin mentioned the Dominicans, they glanced
at each other and one gave a barely perceptible nod.

"As we guessed," one of the men murmured.

"It really had to be them," the other responded. "After
all these years, who else would have the slightest interest
in chasing down a couple of treasure hunters on the trail
of the Templars?"

"So what do we do about them? The Dominicans, I
mean."

"They are not our concern. If they get in the way, we'll
take them out, but our only real problem is this English
couple. Judging by what the woman said, it is just possible that they really have found the lost Templar Archive,
or at least they think they have. We'll have to make a
judgment about what to do with them once they've
explored whatever chamber they think they've found."

"It's a shame we can't bug them as well, but at least
we'll know where they go, thanks to the tracker the technician fitted to their car. You know he found another
device already installed on it?"

"Yes. I saw his report. At least that explained how the
Dominicans—or whoever those people are—were able to
track the English couple without driving along right

behind them. And I think we did the right thing in leaving their tracker in place. Removing it would have tipped our hand. This way, if we follow the English pair, we'll know more or less where the Dominicans are as well."

The other man nodded. "With any luck, we'll be able to eliminate all of them, the Italians and the English, at the same time as we destroy the archive."

"You still think we need to do that? The documents could have significant historical importance."

"I don't doubt it, but the contents are too dangerous to be allowed to survive. We have to totally destroy them. There is no other option."

In fact, shifting the rocks didn't take quite as long as Mallory had feared, for one very simple reason: what they had assumed, in the light from their flashlights, to be a massive pile of boulders was in fact nothing of the sort.

When he and Robin returned to the cavern that morning, they set their two new lanterns on the lowest available illumination, which was quite bright enough for their purposes in the otherwise total darkness, and would maximize battery life, pulled on the heavy-duty work gloves they had purchased, and started shifting stones. Prudence dictated that they start as near to the top of the pile as possible, because Mallory was concerned that removing rocks near the base might trigger an avalanche of boulders, which would almost certainly be injurious to their health.

He clambered up the rocks until he could reach the boulders at the very top of the pile, and passed each one down to Robin as he freed it from its resting place. When he removed the third one, he paused and stared into the cavity that his action had created. Then he handed her that stone and waited until she'd lowered it to the ground.

"There's something that looks a bit odd here," he said. "Can you pass me my flashlight, please?"

"Define 'odd,'" Robin said as she handed it up to him.

"Give me a second."

Mallory shone the beam of light into the space where the stone had been, then glanced down at Robin.

"What?" she demanded.

"A bit of déjà vu," Mallory said. "Obviously once the Knights Templar found a technique that worked, they kept on using it. Remember the cave in Cyprus?"

"I'm not likely to forget it," Robin interjected.

"Nor me. Anyway, the chests were hidden in a cavity in the floor of the cave. Then they'd covered the opening with heavy wooden planks and put stones on top. Well, it looks like they've done exactly the same thing here. Behind that stone I've just taken out, I can see the tops of some pretty substantial lengths of timber."

He climbed down from his perch on the rock pile and stood beside Robin. Both of them stared at the rocks, trying to work out where the timbers must be positioned.

"I think they leaned a sort of platform of really thick wooden beams—they're much thicker than planks— against the wall of the cave, and then just covered them with a couple of layers of rocks," Mallory suggested.

"In which case we don't need to take it down stone by stone from the top," Robin said. "As long as we stand far enough clear of the path the falling stones will take, we can just lever out some of the rocks near the bottom and then just let gravity do the rest."

"That works for me."

Mallory picked up one of the other tools they'd bought that morning, an extendable steel pry bar, essentially a long crowbar, and slid the end of it down the right-hand side of a substantial stone located about two feet above the floor of the cave. He motioned Robin to stand behind him, well out of the path the stone would take when he levered it out of the pile, and then began to apply increasing force to the other end of the bar.

Nothing happened. He changed his grip and slightly altered the position of the bar, then began pushing again, but again without result.

"That one's obviously jammed in pretty tight," Robin said.

Mallory nodded, pulled out the bar, and repositioned it to one side and behind a slightly smaller stone located above the one he had first tried to move. This time, almost as soon as he applied pressure to the end of the bar, there was a cracking sound and the boulder immediately began to move.

"Watch out," he said, then gave a final hard push on the steel bar.

With a sudden loud crack, the stone leaped free from the pile. The steel bar clattered to the ground as Mallory lost his grip on it, and, with a cracking and roaring sound that was almost deafening in the confined space, the boulders above it began to tumble out of position, bouncing off other stones as the force of gravity pulled them inexorably downward. One of the smaller rocks from the top of the pile bounced toward Mallory and Robin, then struck a much larger stone and shattered harmlessly into half a dozen pieces.

"Are you okay?" Mallory asked when the last stone had bounced and crashed and rolled to a standstill.

"Of course," Robin said, stepping out from behind him. "As you might have noticed, I was using you as a shield."

Perhaps surprisingly, there wasn't much dust, presumably because of the general dampness within the cavern. It didn't take them long to move the fallen stones that were impeding their progress, so that they could see exactly what had been hidden behind the pile of rocks.

"Those are really substantial timbers," Mallory said, looking at the lengths of wood running almost all the way up to the roof of the cave and leaning at an angle against the wall in front of them. "And they still look to me as if they're in pretty good condition."

"They obviously knew, or at least they guessed, that wood wasn't likely to survive the millennia unless it was dry and properly seasoned to start with, and also pretty massive," Robin agreed.

Shifting the wood was somewhat similar to moving the stones. Picking up and carrying the individual timbers was not really possible, because of their bulk and weight. But on the other hand, by hooking the end of the crowbar over the top of each length of timber and then pulling, that allowed the wood to topple away from the wall and crash down onto the piles of stone that now covered the floor of the cave. It was a noisy, but fairly quick, way of exposing whatever lay behind them.

And once Mallory had shifted a couple of lengths, he was able to slide through the gap that he had opened up and push the timbers from behind, which was actually an easier way of moving them. Only when the last length of wood had thudded down onto the rocky floor of the cave did Mallory and Robin turn their attention to the gap in the wall that their work had revealed.

It was a high and wide opening, shaped roughly like an arch with fairly straight sides and easily big enough for two people to walk through side by side.

"That must be about nine feet tall at the highest point," Mallory suggested, "and it's at least six or seven feet wide."

"You can see chisel marks on the sides, quite clearly," Robin said, shining the beam of her flashlight to show the obviously worked stone on both sides of the opening. "There was probably a fissure here already, and they just opened it up wide enough to make access easier for them."

Beyond them, the blackness of the inner chamber beckoned.

"Shall we?" Mallory asked, and then led the way through the opening, Robin right behind him, their dancing flashlight beams illuminating the way.

Marco Toscanelli stood beside Mario at the edge of the stand of trees that blocked the wider end of the valley and stared at the twin waterfalls that tumbled down into the wide pool below.

He and another of the Dominican enforcers—a man using the work name Salvatori—had flown in to Geneva late the previous evening and had arrived in Schwyz that morning. In his luggage, protected from customs inspection and scrutiny by his diplomatic passport, were six new and unregistered automatic pistols and four boxes of nine-millimeter Parabellum ammunition, plus half a dozen switchblade knives, so all members of the group were now armed.

"You saw them enter the cave before?" Toscanelli asked.

"Yes," Mario replied. "As I told you, since they arrived in Switzerland we've followed them to a number of different locations, but all the places they visited had one common feature: they were all blind-ended valleys. Then something seemed to happen—maybe they discovered some new piece of information or for some other reason they changed their strategy slightly—and the next locations were still valleys, but each one also had a stream running into it."

Toscanelli nodded. "And presumably the first valleys they visited didn't?"

"Some did, some didn't, but the last few have all contained streams or rivers. More important," Mario added, "on the last two they visited, both of them climbed through the waterfall at the end of the valley, so it's fairly clear that they're looking for something that's hidden in a cave that's concealed by the water."

"And this is the one they visited yesterday?"

"Exactly. After they left here they went straight back to their hotel. But this morning they went out into the town and bought some tools. We don't know exactly what, because I didn't want to send one of the men into the shop in case either of the targets recognized him from the surveillance we've been mounting."

"And now they're back," Toscanelli mused, "so they must believe that they've found something, something of importance, in that cave."

"Haven't our experts in Rome deciphered whatever clues were hidden in those chests?"

"If they have," Toscanelli replied somewhat sourly, "they haven't told me yet."

"So how come these two English amateurs"—Mario almost spat the word—"have apparently succeeded where our order has obviously failed, despite all our knowledge and resources?"

"I have no idea. Maybe they're just lucky."

"Bearing in mind they led you to that cave in Cyprus, I think it's rather more than just luck. We're still following their trail, dogging their footsteps, and that suggests to me that they're a lot better at this kind of thing than we are."

"Perhaps," Toscanelli said dismissively, "but it won't matter because we'll be eliminating them once we're certain they really have discovered what we seek. I'm looking forward to doing that personally."

Mario glanced at his watch.

"They've been inside for nearly an hour already," he said. "When do you want to do it?"

"This is as good a time as any. Leave one man in the car, and another here in the trees as a watcher. The rest of us will go in now and end this."

32

"Stop," Robin said, grabbing Mallory's arm.

He halted in midstride.

"What is it?" he asked.

"There's something wrong here. Something that doesn't fit."

Mallory looked around the passageway that they were standing in. The stones that formed the walls and ceiling around them were black and very obviously solid, and glistened damply in the light from their flashlight. The floor was more or less level and dotted with occasional puddles, clearly caused by the water trickling down some of the rocks. It all looked normal—or as normal as any hidden underground passageway abandoned for centuries could look—and completely nonthreatening.

Robin peered all around them, the beam of her flash-light tracing a slow path up and down the passageway.

"What is it?" Mallory asked again.

"I was just thinking about the booby traps we've encountered," she said. "The spikes hidden inside the book safe and then the sword blades in those chests we found in Cyprus. But here we're just walking down a corridor with no sign of even a door to unlock. We know that the Templars protected their property, and this is just too easy. They must have built in some kind of defense system, and it worries me that we can't see it."

Mallory nodded and, like Robin, scanned every part of the passageway cut through the rock.

"The only place I can see where they could have created a defensive mechanism," he said, after a few seconds, "is the ground, the floor of this passage."

"Now that you mention it," Robin said, "we've been splashing through these shallow pools of water, but just in front of us is a much bigger puddle that covers almost the entire width of the passage. Maybe that's it."

They stepped forward cautiously and halted at the edge of the water. They both looked down, their flashlights shining on the still surface.

"It only looks about half an inch deep," Mallory said, "and I can see the rock under the water quite clearly. Maybe this puddle is just a puddle."

Robin continued staring down at the water, trying to see any sign of danger. Then she grabbed Mallory's arm and pointed.

"Look down there," she said. "That looks like a crack in the rock, running almost from one side of the puddle to the other."

She traced the line she was looking at with the narrow beam of her flashlight, the reflection from the water lighting up the roof of the tunnel.

"It could be a natural feature," Mallory said, "only a fissure in the rock, but I don't feel confident enough that it is to just step on it. We could well be looking at some kind of concealed mantrap."

"Can we jump over it?" Robin asked, mentally gauging the distance to the far side of it.

"Possibly, but we have to think about getting back as well. If the Templar Archive is hidden somewhere at the end of this passageway, we'll have to return the same way, and we certainly couldn't jump over it carrying a chest between us. I think we need to build ourselves a bridge."

"The timbers we moved?" Robin suggested.

"Exactly. If we bring a couple of those from the cave, they'll easily span that puddle of water and we'll just be able to walk across to the other side."

They quickly retraced their steps to the larger cavern, selected two of the broadest timbers, and between them carried them, one at a time, along the passageway to the shallow pool of water. There, they manhandled them to position the wood more or less over the center of the water. Each piece of wood was eight or nine inches wide, and by pushing them together they formed a wide enough platform to walk over easily.

When they reached the other side, Mallory turned and looked back at the pool of still water.

"I think," he began, then paused. "Look, this might just be paranoia striking again, but I'd be happier if we lifted those planks of wood off the ground and stacked them on this side of the puddle."

"You still think somebody's following us?" Robin asked.

"I don't know, but I've had a sneaking feeling that we've attracted attention since we arrived here, and not all of it has been idle curiosity. And if those Italians are on our trail, shifting those timbers might give us a bit of protection, because they'll have to either step through the puddle and maybe trigger whatever mechanism is hidden there—if we're right—or do what we did and build a bridge over it."

"You probably are paranoid," Robin agreed, "but that doesn't mean you're wrong. Let's do it."

They pulled and lifted the lengths of wood and carried them a short distance down the passageway and stacked them on one side, where they were virtually out of sight of anyone approaching from the cave.

"Right," Mallory said. "That might not be the only obstacle we face, so keep your eyes open and shout out if you see anything you don't like the look of."

Toscanelli led the way down the valley, the three men following him in a loose group a few feet behind, all of them watching the double waterfall in case their targets suddenly and unexpectedly reappeared.

When they reached the pool, they stood over to one side and prepared to enter the cave. Having watched Mallory and Jessop step through the waterfall the previous day, Mario had sent Nico out to buy waterproof outfits that would fit over their normal clothes. He had come back with half a dozen pairs of rubberized overtrousers with rubber booties and braces attached, and six water-proof jackets with integral hoods. Nico opened the bulky bag he was carrying, pulled out the packets of protective clothing, and handed them round.

Within a couple of minutes, all four men were ready to go, their spare ammunition put away safely in the pockets of their clothes, along with the compact and powerful flashlights that Nico had also purchased, their outfits protected by the waterproof garments. Each man was holding his pistol, just in case they needed to use the weapons as soon as they stepped into the cave. The brief immersion as they stepped through the waterfall would have no effect upon the efficiency and operation of the weapons.

"Let's do this," Toscanelli said. "How did they get inside?"

Mario pointed at the large boulder sticking out of the pool and close to the curtain of falling and tumbling water.

"They climbed onto that rock and then stepped straight through the waterfall," he said.

"It could be slippery," Toscanelli said, "so all of you be careful. I'll go first. The rest of you follow as quickly as you can."

He cautiously tested the grip his rubberized booties provided on the wet rock, but they were surprisingly good and didn't slip, and he carefully stood erect. He checked that his pistol was cocked and loaded, with the safety catch on, and grabbed his flashlight with his other hand.

Then he took a single stride forward, through the falling water.

The first thing Toscanelli was aware of was the utter blackness within the cavern. Although some light did penetrate the waterfall, because the valley was largely north facing, this did little to dispel the gloom.

With his pistol held at arm's length, his thumb resting on the safety catch, ready for immediate use, he snapped on his flashlight and shone the beam in a complete circle around him.

Then Mario stepped into the cave through the falling water and the other two men followed him within a couple of minutes, each stepping from the rock and into the hidden chamber.

"It just looks like an empty cave," Toscanelli said, his voice echoing in the confined space as he again shone the beam of his flashlight around the damp rock walls. Now that the other men were beside him, he placed his pistol on the ground and began to strip off his waterproofs.

"There's obviously an exit somewhere in here," Mario said. "We all watched the two of them step inside here this morning, well over an hour ago, and they haven't come out since then."

"Check all around the walls," Toscanelli instructed, "and the floor as well. Look out for any traces of them."

All four of the men moved to different parts of the walls of the cavern and began searching.

"There's something over here," Nico called out, and the other three men walked quickly across the floor of the cavern to join him.

"What have you found?" Mario demanded.

"There's this kind of internal waterfall here," Nico said. "I thought it was just water running down the wall, but there seems to be an opening behind it."

He picked up an old gnarled root—actually the same object that Mallory had used the previous day to check what lay behind the curtain of water—and thrust it through the flow and into the hidden cavern. The root slid through without meeting any resistance.

"That must be it," Toscanelli said. "We've got them."

The narrow passage wound deeper into the mountain, twisting and turning every few feet. They made their way along it in single file because there wasn't really room to walk abreast, Mallory leading the way. After a few yards, he paused and touched the rocks that formed one wall of the passage.

"That might be a good sign," he said, turning back to face Robin. "The walls in that cave behind us were wet, or at least damp, but the rocks here are bone-dry. That's another sign that this could have been—and hopefully might still be—the last repository of the Templar Archive. They would have needed somewhere with a cool and dry atmosphere so that the parchment wouldn't just rot away."

"That's a good point. And this has to be natural," Robin said, shining her flashlight at the rocks around them. "It would have taken years to hack this out of the living rock. You can see the hammer and chisel marks on some of the stones, but I think that's just evidence of the Templars knocking off projecting bits and doing their best to straighten and widen the passage so that walking up and down it was a bit easier for them."

"You're right," Mallory agreed, "and I think that they probably used some of the rock they chipped off to form the floor of this passage, because it's remarkably flat and level."

He shone his flashlight down at their feet to emphasize what he was saying. Then he shone the light in front of him again, where the passage narrowed slightly.

Mallory slowed as they neared the natural choke point, alert for any medieval booby traps or other hazards, shining the beam of his flashlight mainly at the ground, because that was the logical place for any trip wire or trigger to be positioned. But he saw nothing.

"Maybe they didn't bother building any other defenses in here," he suggested. "Perhaps they thought that the chances of anybody stumbling on this place by accident were virtually nil."

"Well, we certainly wouldn't have found it without having deciphered those clues," Robin said, "so you may well be right. Having to walk through two different waterfalls and then shifting a couple of tons of rock and timber would be a pretty good defense."

Mallory stopped walking and just shone his flashlight at the passage in front of them.

That narrow section of the tunnel was very short, perhaps only eight or ten feet in length, and they'd just reached the end of it. And in the flashlight beam they could see that beyond it the natural cave opened up again, the walls widening abruptly, and the roof above their heads climbing precipitously, almost vertically. The path they had been following virtually vanished, the floor of the cave flattening out into a level expanse before them. The new and wider section of the cave was like a cathedral compared to the narrow passage they'd just walked along.

Robin went to move forward, to explore what they'd found, but Mallory put his hand out to stop her.

"Not yet," he said. "This is exactly where I would put a booby trap if there was something precious here I wanted to protect."

He shone his flashlight at the ground, looking for evidence of a concealed pit or some other manufactured hazard, then shifted the beam to cover the roof and walls. He saw nothing but still didn't move.

"What is it?" Robin asked.

"I don't know, but as you said back in that first tunnel, this just seems too easy. We know the Templars were paranoid about protecting their assets, so why didn't they construct some kind of defense here? It's the obvious place for a mantrap or something. Or, if they did, why can't we see it?"

Mallory carefully inspected the walls and floor again, then dropped to his hands and knees and began carefully feeling the ground directly in front of them.

"If there is some kind of trigger here," he said, "it more or less has to be on the ground. A trip wire would probably have disintegrated centuries ago."

The floor of the passage was, like the rest of it, covered in a layer of small stones, almost like gravel, and he was able to brush some of them away with his hand. Then he used the tips of his fingers to try to trace any obstruction or unnatural feature that might be hidden just below this top layer.

After a minute or so he stopped, then changed the direction of his search, running his fingertips from left to right rather than in the circular motion he'd used previously.

"Anything?"

"Yes, there is," Mallory replied. "I don't know what it is, or what the mechanism is, but I can feel straight lines, like the edges of wooden planks, just below this layer of stones. We're lucky we didn't go any farther."

"So how do get across whatever booby trap that is?"

"I don't know, but there must be a way. Even on that book safe you bought, the device that started all this, if the right size and shape dagger blade was inserted, the mechanism was locked so that the safe could be opened. There must be something like that here."

Mallory stood up and shifted the flashlight beam to examine the solid rock walls on both sides of them.

"What are you looking for?"

"I don't know. Anything that would take a key or locking bar or something of that sort. Perhaps a hole or a slit in the rock, that kind of thing."

They both studied the area around them, but it was Robin who saw what they'd both missed up to that point.

"Could this be it?" she asked.

She pointed at a natural-looking hole in the rock to their right, at about head height and partially concealed by a projecting ledge.

"Could be," Mallory said, shining his flashlight toward

it. "I can't see down into it. Can I lift you up so that you can check it out?"

Mallory slipped his flashlight into his pocket and grabbed Robin around the hips, lifting her almost straight up.

"Stop," she said. "Right. Now I can see down into it. It's quite deep, and seems to run almost straight down into the rock. The opening is rough and quite wide, and looks natural, but the hole itself is much narrower, maybe two inches wide or so, and is very straight. And it looks like it was drilled out, somehow."

"Do you see any sign of wood in the hole? Splinters or anything like that?"

"Yes, actually. There are a couple of small pieces just inside the entrance to the hole. Yes, I see where you're going with that. You're thinking that's the keyhole, and the key or whatever you want to call it was a length of stout wood that was shoved down into it."

"Exactly," Mallory said, lowering Robin to the floor again.

"So what do we do? How do we lock it?"

"How deep did you think it was?"

"Not very. Maybe seven or eight inches or so."

"Then I think the crowbar should do it."

Mallory dropped his rucksack to the ground, opened it, and took out the tool, then reached up and slid the straight end of the bar down into the hole, making sure it went all the way to the end.

"Will that do it?" Robin asked.

"I hope so, but we won't just blunder on and hope for the best."

He motioned Robin to stand a few feet behind him, then carefully rested his right foot on the edge of what he had assumed were planks of wood hidden beneath the gravel on the floor.

"They feel a little loose," he said, slowly increasing the pressure. "There's some give in them."

Then they both heard a faint click and the end of the crowbar moved very slightly as some concealed mechanism began to operate.

Mallory immediately stepped back, away from the hidden planks, but nothing else happened, except that there was another click. He reached up and grabbed the end of the crowbar, almost expecting it to be jammed in place, but the tool was loose in the hole in the rock and moved freely. It looked as if the concealed mechanism was triggered by weight or pressure on the planks, but when that pressure was released it reset itself.

He repeated the process, stepping on the planks and hearing the click, then the second faint click, which proved to him that the hidden mechanism was working, and that the end of the crowbar had successfully jammed it.

"Okay," he said. "I think we can carry on. Slowly and carefully. I'll go first, just in case. Listen for the second click. It'll be interesting to know how big this trigger really is."

Mallory gingerly rested his left foot on the hidden planks, waited for the click, and then stepped forward. He took four swift strides, and on the first three he could feel a very slight give below his feet, but on the fourth step it seemed that he was back on solid ground. Almost immediately Robin confirmed his guess.

"The second click came when you lifted your foot after your third step."

"That's what I thought."

Moments later, Robin stepped right beside him, and they both looked back at the end of the narrow passage.

"I wonder what it does," Robin mused.

"It's probably better that we never find out," Mallory said. "Now let's see what we have here."

He swung his flashlight, the beam fitfully illuminating different parts of the open space in which they were standing. He wasn't surprised, though he was definitely disappointed, when their quick visual search suggested that the large chamber was empty of everything except rocks and more rocks.

"Have we been beaten to it?" Robin asked.

"I hope not, after all this. Hang on. What's that, over there?"

He shone his flashlight beam across the cavern toward a large dark oblong. There were shadows all around them, but that looked like something else. Something different.

They walked briskly across the cave floor, shining their flashlight in front of them.

"It's a tunnel," Mallory said. "A wide tunnel. Let's see where it leads. Maybe there's another chamber beyond this one."

The start of the tunnel was easily wide enough for the two of them to walk side by side, and had a firm floor that sloped gradually upward.

"There's something at the far end," Robin said. "Something metallic, I think."

As they neared the end of the tunnel, perhaps fifty yards from the cavern, they found themselves facing a blank stone wall. And positioned in a neat line against that wall, on a patch of level ground, were half a dozen ironbound large wooden chests, three resting on the stone floor and the other three positioned on top of them. Beside the two right-hand chests was a much smaller box, again reinforced by bands of metal.

"Could that really be it? The long-lost Templar Archive?" Mallory asked. "If it is, it's a lot smaller than I was expecting, but we're still going to need a biggish van or a truck to haul it all away."

"There's only one way to find out," Robin said, and started walking over toward the chests. "Let's see what we've got here."

Toscanelli strode briskly across the cavern to where they had dropped their waterproofs, picked up one of the jackets, and slipped it on.

"Follow me," he said, and waited while the other men donned their protective clothing and prepared themselves. Then he walked back over to the vertical column of falling water and stepped straight through it, his pistol held ready for whatever he might be confronted with on the other side.

He switched on his flashlight the moment he stepped clear of the water.

He found himself in another chamber, noticeably larger than the one he had just left, and carved out of the same dark and damp rock, but equally as empty. Or at least, empty of their quarry and the treasure Toscanelli still believed he was close to recovering.

But there was one obvious difference. Whereas the outer chamber had no obvious exits, on the far side of this inner cavern was an arched opening. In front of it were several lengths of stout timber and a scattering of heavy stones.

As the first of his men stepped through the waterfall that concealed the archway between the two chambers, Toscanelli walked over to the opening. He shone his flashlight up the passageway that lay beyond, then turned back to look at the fallen timbers.

"They must have gone down that tunnel," Mario said, walking over to him.

"Obviously," Toscanelli snapped, then pointed at the stones and timbers. "I think these planks were probably used to hide this archway, the wood placed against the wall and then the stones used to cover up the timbers. It would probably have looked quite natural. I wonder how they knew it was here?" he mused.

"Does that matter?" Mario asked.

"No. Of course not. Let's go. What we seek must be at the end of this passage. Have your weapons ready," he instructed, raising his voice.

The four men began striding down the tunnel, Nico in the lead with Toscanelli virtually beside him, both men focusing their attention on what lay ahead of them, upon the possible danger posed by their quarry.

What they weren't focusing on was the floor of the tunnel they were hurrying down.

Nico reached the large pool of water in a few seconds

and stepped into it without hesitation. The instant he did so, the double layer of thin planks of old wood, which Robin Jessop had assumed was rock, the seams caulked to make them watertight and lying just below the surface, shattered and split apart. The water cascaded down into the pit that opened up beneath it, and Nico's body inexorably followed.

He screamed as he fell, but the sound was cut short almost immediately.

33

Canton of Schwyz, Switzerland

"The two English people have been in the cave system for over ninety minutes," the spotter said quietly into his mobile phone, "and the Italians followed them inside about fifteen minutes ago."

"All of them?"

"No. The last time we observed them, there were two Italians or Dominicans here, one watching the valley and the other waiting in a car. This time, six of them appeared, in two cars, and four of them are now inside the cavern. One's watching from the tree line below us, and the other man is waiting in one of the cars. Have you confirmed their identity yet?"

"That is not your direct concern," the deep-voiced man the spotter had called replied, "but according to the car hire company records the vehicle you obtained details of yesterday was rented at the airport by an Italian. Flight records show that he flew to Switzerland from France on the same aircraft as the principal targets. Interestingly he was one of four Italian citizens on that flight traveling on a diplomatic passport."

"So are you saying that they *are* diplomats or embassy officials or something?"

"No. Not everybody traveling on a diplomatic passport is a diplomat. Some are just people that their government or host organization wants to insert into another country without having them or their luggage searched. In this case, the passports weren't issued by the Italian government but by the *Supremus Ordo Militaris Hospitalis Sancti Ioannis Hierosolymitani Rhodius et Melitensis*, more commonly known as the Sovereign Military Order of Malta."

"Who the hell is that?" the spotter demanded.

The man he'd called chuckled before he replied, "It's a very ancient Roman Catholic religious order. It was originally headquartered in Malta, hence the name, but now it's based in Rome, in the Palazzo di Malta, the Magistral Palace, on the Via Condotti near the Spanish Steps. More important, it's the modern continuation of the even more ancient order of the Knights Hospitaller, which was of course contemporary with the Knights Templar."

The spotter shook his head, obviously confused.

"I thought they were supposed to be Dominicans," he said. "What have the Hospitallers got to do with all this?"

"Quite a lot, but only indirectly. Really briefly, the Hospitallers were supposed to be given all the recovered assets of the Knights Templar, but the Dominicans—who were the pope's personal torturers and tasked with interrogating the Templars—failed to find anything much. Nobody outside the two orders knows for certain, but the probability is that the Hospitallers have been helping the Dominicans track down every Templar asset that's been discovered over the last half a millennium simply because those assets actually belong to them. So providing diplomatic passports to a bunch of Dominican enforcers isn't really all that surprising."

"Okay, I see that, but the more obvious question is what you want us to do now. Keep watching, go home, or what?"

"We haven't decided yet. For the moment, stay where you are and maintain surveillance. Call me immediately if anything else happens, but be prepared to move quickly if necessary. We may decide to send you into the cave to finish this."

"Understood. But remember that there are just the two of us, and there are now six people inside the cave and two more outside. We can pick them off one by one with the rifle if they're in the open air—that wouldn't be a problem and that was what we were contracted to do—but we would need different weapons if you want us to go into the cavern. As I told you a few minutes ago, we're pretty certain that all of the Italians are armed with pistols because we've seen the four men who went to the cave carrying them. So at the very least we'll both need pistols and either combat shotguns or machine pistols before we go inside. That's nonnegotiable. And a couple of extra guys would be a help as well."

"That will take time to arrange."

"That's your problem, not ours. What I'm telling you is that there's no way we're going to walk into a confined space like that cave carrying a long-distance sniper rifle to face four men armed with pistols. That would just be an interesting and unusual way of committing suicide. Either you get us what we need to do the job or we stay right where we are. Your choice."

"What was that?" Robin said, turning to stare back the way they'd come.

"A scream," Mallory said, somewhat unnecessarily. "Wait here and I'll take a look."

He strode away from the row of chests that they'd been examining and walked back down the tunnel and into the cavern and crossed to the point where the entrance tunnel started. He stepped over the hidden planks and went a few yards down the passageway, feeling his way with his flashlight switched off, until he could clearly hear the sound of voices—loud and angry Italian voices—and see the fitful light of their flashlights reflected off the rock walls.

That was enough for him. For a couple of seconds he stood there, listening, but knew that his feeling had been right: they had been followed, presumably again by members of the Dominican Order, and they were again in immediate mortal danger. He had no doubt whatsoever that they would be killed out of hand by them if they were caught. He was going to have to do something about that, if he could.

Mallory turned and walked slowly back to the narrowest

part of the passage, using his flashlight as little as possible, though he guessed he was well out of sight of their pursuers. Then he reached up, plucked the crowbar out of the hole in the rock, and called out softly to Robin, who'd followed him across the floor of the cave.

"Shine your flashlight down here, please," he said. "I need light for this bit."

"You're not going to—"

"It's the best plan I've got," Mallory said, interrupting her. "I heard at least two voices back there in the tunnel, and we know what will happen if they catch us. This might slow them down a bit. I think whatever was under that puddle took one of them out—that was the reason for the scream we heard—and hopefully this will do the same."

As he'd been talking, Mallory was walking back a short distance down the tunnel. Now he turned and took a couple of deep breaths, getting ready.

"Aim the light at the ground," he said, "and try not to dazzle me, because that really would write me off."

Robin did as he asked, then held her breath as well, not that doing so actually helped either him or her.

Mallory sprinted the short distance down to the narrow section of the passage, and about a foot before the point where he knew the planks were situated he launched himself into the air, arms flailing as he tried to cover the maximum possible distance, his hands brushing the walls on either side as he jumped.

He landed hard and stumbled on the rocky ground a couple of feet from Robin, who grabbed his arm and pulled him to his feet as he did so.

They both looked back, fearful that he might have tripped the trigger to unleash whatever hideous anti-intruder device the Templars had constructed, but all was silent.

"You did it," Robin said flatly. "Were you an athletics star at school? House captain, that kind of thing?"

Mallory shook his head.

"Not so's you'd notice," he said. "I did all the usual stuff, but I was never much good at any of it. But it's amazing how the prospect of imminent death can improve your athletic performance. Now we have to try to find another way out of here, if there is one. And if there isn't, we'll have to find somewhere we can hide from these Italian killers."

Nico's body had slammed into the double row of sharpened stakes and rusty sword blades that projected from the bottom of the hole, each rooted firmly, wedged into holes chiseled into the bedrock.

Toscanelli barely managed to stop himself from following Nico into the eight-foot-deep pit, and stared down in horror at the carnage, Mario and Salvatori beside him, their flashlight beams coldly illuminating the dreadful sight.

The Italian's body, the limbs still twitching fitfully, had been pierced by at least five of the lethal stakes, one of which had been driven straight through his chest, killing him instantly. That was the only mercy—he would have been dead the second he landed at the bottom of the hole. There was surprisingly little blood, because once his heart had been penetrated it would have stopped pumping, but as they looked down they could hear the faint sound of dripping as Nico's lifeblood was released from his multiple wounds.

Mario crossed himself as he stared at the dead man, a gesture repeated by his two companions.

"Who did this?" he demanded, his voice hoarse with the rush of emotions he was feeling. "Was it the two we've been following?"

"Of course not," Toscanelli said. "This is old, really old. This trap was set for a very different group of intruders, many centuries ago. This was prepared by members of the Knights Templar order to protect their treasure. At least we now know for sure that we're on the right track. And that nobody else has been in here since this trap was set."

"So how come the English couple didn't end up like Nico? How did they get across the pit?"

Before he answered, Toscanelli moved his flashlight and stared all around him. Then he pointed farther down the tunnel, the beam of light illuminating part of a straight dark brown shape leaning against the wall.

"They used those," he said. "Two or three of the wooden planks from the other cave. They must have laid them over the puddle, walked over it, and then removed them."

"But that means they must have known about the booby trap," Mario said. "And known that we'd be following them."

"I don't know too much about those two, but they do seem to be lucky. And cautious. They've seen Templar engineering before, so maybe they were expecting something like this. Some kind of protection device to be concealed in the tunnel. They can't have known that we'd be coming along behind them, but they're probably paranoid and shifted the timbers just in case anyone was following them. But either way, it doesn't matter, because now we're here in the cave system with them. There's no way out, and we'll finish them in here."

The three men returned to the cavern they'd left minutes earlier and walked back into the tunnel, each carrying one of the heavy timbers they'd seen there. They maneuvered the wood into position to form a substantial bridge over the lethal booby trap. With a last glance down at the twisted and torn body of Nico, they stepped onto the wooden planks they'd placed over the pit and walked down the tunnel. They were moving much more slowly and cautiously than before, alert for any fresh sign of danger, their pistols held ready in their hands, their flashlights showing the way.

Mallory had hoped that the large open area in the cave would be penetrated by enough tunnels and passageways that they could lose themselves and take refuge from the men who were even then audibly getting closer. But although they had quickly searched all around the perimeter of the cavern, all they had found was that wide single tunnel on the opposite side to that by which they had entered. And there were no hiding places in that short passageway that either of them had spotted.

"We've got two choices, as far as I can see," Mallory said. "We can try to hide somewhere in this cavern, if we can find anywhere that offers some kind of cover, and hope like hell that they don't spot us. The problem with trying to hide is that we already know the tunnel is a dead end and there aren't a lot of options in this cave. The other option is that we confront them right here in this cavern and hope that we can take them out before they kill us."

Robin's face was a pale oval in the darkness as Mallory swept his flashlight beam around the cavern once more, just in case they'd missed anything.

"I'll say this for you," she said. "Life with you is never boring. Exciting, even terrifying, yes. And probably terminal. But boring, no. You seem to be offering a choice of different ways to die. Basically being hunted down like cornered rats somewhere in this cave system, or getting killed in hand-to-hand combat, but going down fighting. And if it's all the same to you, I've never been much of a rodent. Let's see if we can do these guys some serious harm."

Mallory wrapped his arms around her and kissed her firmly on the lips. Then he disengaged and took a step back.

"I thought you'd say that," he said. "The trick is going to be trying to find any weapons at all in here that we can use. I mean, we can lob rocks at them, and we might get lucky, but I wouldn't put much money on our chances."

The walls of the tunnel seemed to close in on the three Italians as they walked farther into the mountain. Their progress slowed as the opportunities for inadvertently tripping some ancient Templar booby trap became more obvious. In the narrowing passage, another hidden killing pit or something similar was a serious possibility.

Salvatori was in the lead, Mario directly behind him, and Toscanelli, as the senior man present, a slightly more distant third. The beams from the flashlights of the men were never still, the circles of light moving from the ground, up the wall, across the ceiling of the passageway, and back down the opposite wall to the ground again, pausing only when some object or mark attracted the attention of one of the men.

They had nearly reached the narrowest part of the tunnel when Mario tapped Salvatori on the shoulder to make him stop moving forward, and then turned to Toscanelli.

"Are these two people likely to be armed?" he asked. "Because walking down this narrow passage carrying flashlights would make us sitting ducks if they're waiting for us in the darkness up ahead with a couple of pistols."

"That's most unlikely," Toscanelli replied quietly. "They flew to France from England and then from France to Switzerland. It's not that much of a problem to get a disassembled pistol, especially something like a Glock, which is mainly plastic anyway, onto an aircraft in the hold luggage. But according to Vitale, these two only had carry-on bags, and that makes it much more difficult. And in order to smuggle a gun onto an aircraft, you have to have a gun to smuggle, and in Britain that's not easy."

"But not impossible. They could have bought one from a criminal contact."

"Yes, but unless I've misunderstood what's happened, you and your men picked them up in France and you've had them under virtually constant surveillance ever since, so if they had managed to source a weapon from somewhere you would almost certainly have to know about it."

Mario nodded, still not entirely satisfied with Toscanelli's answer, but recognizing the essential logic of what the other man had just said. He turned back and gestured for Salvatori to continue forward.

A couple of minutes later, Salvatori stopped, the light from his flashlight illuminating an even narrower section of the tunnel beyond which a vast expanse of blackness seemed to extend in all directions, the flashlight beam seemingly being absorbed by the dark, fading away into nothing.

"This last section of the tunnel is really narrow," the Italian said. "If the Templars constructed another booby trap, this is the most likely place for it."

The three men stopped about a dozen feet from the tunnel exit and began searching everywhere with the beams of light from their flashlights, looking for anything that seemed out of place or that could possibly function as a trigger.

"I don't see anything," Mario said. "Maybe that killing pit at the other end of the tunnel is the only one they built."

"Don't be so hasty," Toscanelli said. "The two targets aren't going anywhere. We've got plenty of time to check this thoroughly. I'm not stepping out into that next chamber until I'm certain it's safe to do so. We'll examine every centimeter of this tunnel before we move on."

But even after five minutes of searching, none of them had seen anything that suggested there might be any kind of hidden hazard.

"I think we're just wasting our time here," Mario said. "There's nothing to fear. Let's get the job done and finish this."

Mallory had crept closer to the entrance to the narrow tunnel, his flashlight in one hand and the crowbar in the other, Robin a few feet behind him. This was not so that he could hear what was being said, because he didn't speak or understand Italian, but so that he could hopefully ambush any of the men who survived the Templar booby trap when he or they stepped into the chamber. Assuming, of course, that the Italians tripped the device. And obviously also assuming that the device still worked.

After a couple of minutes, he realized that they were checking every part of the narrow section of the tunnel, and that meant they would probably find the same group of hidden planks on the ground that he had detected. If that were the case, then they'd also most likely find the hole into which the length of wood or metal needed to be inserted to disable the mechanism.

Once they'd done that, the three Italians—probably three armed and very angry Italians—would be able to walk into the cave and Mallory and Robin would be completely at their mercy. Even with the benefit of surprise, there really was no way that two basically unarmed people—because crowbars and rocks didn't really count—could tackle three men carrying pistols.

He was going to have to try to do something else.

"Wait," Salvatori said urgently.

He was on his hands and knees in the most constricted section of the tunnel, feeling the ground directly in front of him.

"There's something under the surface right here. Something that's not rock. It's more like wood, planks or timbers of some sort laid across the path." He leaned forward slightly and pressed gently on the wood with his hand. "There's some give in it. I think it's probably connected to something. Some mechanism."

Mario and Toscanelli peered over his shoulder at the area on the ground that Salvatori was investigating.

"Are you sure?" Toscanelli asked.

"Of course I'm sure. I'm not going to walk on this, but if you want to get in front of me and stamp all over it, you be my guest. I'll just stand back and watch."

Toscanelli took a couple of steps backward and looked around. "If there's a trap here, there must be a way of disabling it or bypassing it. Can either of you see a lever or anything? If we can't find it, we'll have to haul a couple of those planks up here from the other cavern and put them over whatever it is."

But although they all checked both sides of the tunnel, for some reason they either didn't see the hole drilled into the rock, or didn't associate it with the hidden device, and after a couple of minutes Toscanelli lost patience.

"It'll be quicker if we just get the wood," he said to Mario. "You stay here, just in case the two targets try to get out of that cavern. If they do, shoot them. In fact, shoot them if you see any sign of them. Salvatori and I will go back and collect a couple of planks."

Mallory stood silently in the utter blackness of the cavern watching the activity in the tunnel entrance about twenty yards away. When two of the shadowy figures abruptly left and headed back down the passageway, he whispered to Robin, who was standing right beside him, "I think they've spotted the trigger for the booby trap and they'll probably haul along a couple of lengths of wood to bridge it. And if they do that, we'll have nowhere to hide and nowhere to run."

"So that's it? They'll just walk in here, kill us, and take the boxes?" Her voice was calm but determined.

"If they can, yes, but we're not dead yet. We can try to ambush them when they come out into this cave."

"At the precise moment when they'll be expecting an attack, you mean?" Robin didn't sound encouraging. "Two of us and a couple of crowbars against three armed and irritated gunmen? Forget it. I think I've got a better idea."

"What?"

"You're standing right beside it. I spotted it when we first walked in here, but it didn't make any sense then. Now I think I've worked out what it is."

She took his hand and forced him down into a crouch, then pressed his hand down on the ground.

"Feel that?" she whispered.

Mallory's hand traced a smooth groove in the stone floor, like a very shallow dish or the bottom part of a wide tube or pipe. He ran his hand around the carved rock, trying to get a feel for the overall shape of whatever Robin had found.

"It's like a gully or a channel for water," he murmured.

"Shit hot, Sherlock. It *is* a channel, but not for water. There's a pretty big stone in the gully right where we're standing. It's almost completely round, like a big bowling ball, and there's a smaller wedge-shaped rock positioned right in front of it. Move that away, and the larger rock will roll all the way to the tunnel entrance."

"It's a second trigger, you mean?"

"That's what it looks like to me, yes."

Mallory paused for a moment, considering the implications.

"We don't know what will happen if it's triggered," he said. "We could be locking ourselves in here for eternity."

"I don't think so," Robin whispered. "As far as I know, the Knights Templar weren't big on suicide, so if this is a device to trigger the booby trap from inside the cavern, there has to be another way out. We just haven't found it yet."

Mallory stared ahead at the entrance to the tunnel, where they could both hear the sound of approaching footsteps.

"It's make-your-mind-up time," he muttered. "That

sounds like the other two coming back with the planks. They'll have the wood in position in a couple of minutes. So do we do this or not?"

"We do it," Robin replied quietly. "In my opinion, we really don't have a choice."

"Okay. I'll pull the round stone back a bit. See if you can shift that wedge."

He wrapped his arms around the stone and heaved. It was heavy—really heavy—and probably hadn't been moved in over five hundred years, but he felt it give slightly. But the movement wasn't quite enough to allow Robin to remove the wedging stone.

"It's not shifting," she whispered urgently, very conscious of the sounds of activity in the tunnel, where the other two men were just coming into view, dragging lengths of timber toward the narrow section.

"I'll use my legs," Mallory whispered.

He let go of the stone and stepped around it. He lay down flat on his back and placed his feet against the stone, braced himself, and then pushed as hard as he could with the soles of his feet against the heavy rock.

This time, he felt the stone move a fraction more than before, but still Robin couldn't shift the wedge. He relaxed again, took a couple of deep breaths, and then pushed with all the strength in his legs.

He heard the sound of stone moving against stone and then the rock shifted noticeably.

"Got it," Robin said, pulling the wedge-shaped rock out of position and moving it to one side.

For perhaps a second, Mallory kept his legs in position,

feeling the brutal weight of the rock pressing against his feet, then rolled sideways, away from the gully. And immediately the rock began to move, the rumbling sound as it gathered speed unmistakable in the silence of the cavern.

Then the beam of a flashlight speared out from the tunnel entrance and bathed Mallory in light, and a moment later two rapid shots rang out, the sounds echoing deafeningly from the walls of the cavern.

34

The mobile phone in a pocket on the spotter's ghillie suit vibrated—for obvious reasons the ringer was set to silent—and he answered the call by touching a button on his Bluetooth earpiece.

"Yes?"

"Your orders are unchanged. Until we know exactly what these intruders have discovered, we intend only to watch them. However, we will be supplying the additional weapons you requested so that you will be able to act immediately should the situation change. They will be delivered to you within the next half hour or so. I'll call again when I've heard from the courier."

"Understood."

"What is the situation now?"

"Also unchanged. The English pair are still inside the

cave, along with the four Italians. We've seen and heard nothing since they walked through the waterfall."

"Good. Keep me informed."

Mario stared ahead into the darkness, hearing sounds that he couldn't immediately identify.

He'd swung the flashlight beam around the cavern, and at the instant the light had passed over a crouching figure he swung the flashlight back, raised his pistol, and snapped off two quick shots toward the target. Both had obviously missed.

Then he saw the reason for the noise, the spherical rock rolling down the gully toward him, its speed increasing with every second, and for an instant he just stood there, trying to assess what he was seeing. It didn't look dangerous. It was just a big rock rolling, and actually rolling fairly slowly, down the slope toward him. He could easily dodge it, just step to one side, so why had the targets set it in motion? Or had they just knocked it as they moved around in the cave and that had started it moving?

And then he moved the flashlight beam to the area in front of the rock, and spotted the gully for the first time. Realization dawned.

The groove in the rock floor that the stone was following ran arrow-straight toward the end of the tunnel where he was standing. It was nowhere near big enough to block the passage, but there was absolutely no doubt in Mario's mind that the weight of the rock would be more than enough to trip the hidden trigger located at the end of the tunnel.

He took one final glance at the oncoming, and certainly unstoppable, rolling rock, then turned tail and ran back down the tunnel toward the other two men.

Mallory had dived into cover the moment Mario started shooting at him. Both bullets had missed him, one only barely, smashing into a rock less than three feet from him and ricocheting away into the darkness.

Then the Italian's attention had obviously switched to the oncoming rock, and Mallory had taken the chance to get out of his line of fire, ducking sideways and jogging across to where Robin was waiting. She'd moved as soon as the boulder started to travel down the gully, putting as much distance between herself and the end of the tunnel as she could, because they had no idea what would happen when the rolling rock triggered the device left there by the Templars.

"You okay?" she asked as Mallory appeared beside her. "Both shots missed?"

"One of them came pretty close, but that was all," Mallory replied.

"Are we safe here?"

"I've no idea. All we can do now is wait and hope, but we're a good distance clear of the tunnel entrance. My guess is the booby trap will be a pit or something like that, which will block the tunnel completely and keep those Italians out of this cavern."

Toscanelli and Salvatori heard two shots from just in front of them. Both men reacted instantly, dropping the lengths of timber they were dragging and pulling out their pistols as they stared ahead down the tunnel, their flashlights switched off so as not to make them easy targets.

Moments later, they saw and heard Mario heading toward them, the beam of his flashlight bouncing wildly as he ran.

"Get back!" he yelled.

"What is it?"

"They've triggered the booby trap. Used a heavy rock."

"Did you kill them?" Toscanelli demanded.

"No. I missed. Now we need to get clear."

A matter of just seconds later the rock, still slowly gathering speed, reached the tunnel entrance and rolled onto the hidden wooden platform. There was a cracking sound as the ancient planks gave under its weight, and then the rock dropped into a shallow cavity that had been dug underneath the floor of the tunnel.

But the boulder didn't disappear completely, just dropped about a foot below floor level on top of the shattered timbers, because this trap wasn't a killing pit and didn't contain spikes or blades to impale an intruder. This trap was something very different.

For roughly a second or two nothing else seemed to happen. Then the cavern filled with an ominous rumbling sound, a noise that quickly became deafening. And then the entire roof of the cave near the tunnel entrance seemed to come apart, rocks crashing and tumbling to the ground as a massive rockslide began.

The whole place seemed to shake with the repeated

impacts of the heavy stones and a tremendous, deafening roaring filled the entire space.

The boulders smashed into the floor of the cavern like a black waterfall of rocks and rubble. Most of them crashed into the area around the tunnel entrance, but the trap had obviously been designed so that some fell into the tunnel as well.

It probably took only a few seconds, but the utterly deafening rumbling and crashing sounds seemed to last for minutes. And when it finally stopped, the entire appearance of the interior of the cave had been irrevocably changed.

Where the tunnel entrance had been was now hidden somewhere under a rock pile, a heap of boulders that in some places reached almost as high as the roof of the cavern. The entire area was shrouded in a cloud of dust created by the falling rocks, giving it a surreal and almost filmic quality in the light from Mallory's flashlight.

"Bloody hell," Robin muttered.

"Did you hear that?" the sniper asked.

"I felt it more than heard it but yes, I certainly did. What the hell was it?"

"Could have been a distant explosion. If this was winter, it would most probably have been the sound of an avalanche. But in this valley, at this time of year, my guess is that something's happened inside that cave. Maybe there was a bit of unstable rock and one of them trod on it and that started a rockslide."

"Or perhaps it was man-made, an explosion. More than a grenade, obviously, but maybe one of them had some C-4 or Semtex with them and triggered it. That would do it. I'll call it in."

The spotter selected the contact number for their employer on his mobile and initiated the call.

"There might have been an explosion in the cave system. We both heard a sound like distant thunder, but we're pretty sure it came from the ground in front of us."

"Any visible indications on the surface? Is that Italian watcher still in place?"

"No and yes. The Italian was sitting down on a fallen tree, but now he's standing up and watching the waterfall through his binoculars, so I guess he felt or heard it as well."

"Keep watching and contact us as soon as anyone comes out of that cave. The courier with your close-quarter weapons will be with you in about twenty minutes. One of you needs to walk back down the valley to meet him. I'll text you the grid reference."

"Copied. I'll be there in fifteen."

"Beautifully put," Mallory said. "I certainly didn't expect anything like that."

"I'll tell you one thing. There's no way we're leaving this place the same way we came in. If we leave it at all, that is."

"Have faith, Robin," Mallory said, with a confidence that was built almost entirely on hope and faith rather than reason. "I don't believe for a moment that the Templars would have trapped themselves in here with no way out. That rock and the groove cut in the floor must mean that they intended to be able to trip the rockslide from within the cave, to protect their assets in the cave if it ever came under attack. So somewhere in this place they must have built an escape route."

"So all we have to do is find it. And that sounds easy if you say it quickly."

"Yes. Let's try to have a proper look around right now to make sure we can get out. Otherwise we'll have to try shifting those bloody rocks, and that's not something I want to even think about doing."

They walked all the way round the cavern, using their flashlights freely now that there was no danger of the Italians interrupting them. The perimeter was rocky and uneven, full of nooks and crannies that at first seemed to suggest the entrance to a narrow tunnel but none of which, as they'd already discovered on their first, hasty inspection just after they'd entered the cave, actually led anywhere.

"It must be somewhere in the tunnel," Mallory said, sounding uncharacteristically defeatist when they reached the edge of the pile of fallen rock, the farthest point they could search.

He led the way toward the comparatively wide entrance to the tunnel they'd briefly explored already, and where they'd found the wooden chests. They walked side by side along the tunnel, carefully examining every inch of the walls. The sides of the tunnel, although fairly straight, were deeply fissured and cracked, just like the walls of the cavern, but every opening they saw proved to be a disappointment, extending only a maximum of a few feet, and sometimes only a few inches, into the bedrock around them.

"The only thing I've seen," Mallory said, "is a length of old timber that seems to have been jammed into the rocks on that side of the tunnel about halfway along"—he aimed his flashlight at the object he was talking about—"but I really don't see what . . ."

He broke off as another thought struck him.

"What is it?" Robin asked.

"Why did they leave the chests here at the end of the tunnel instead of somewhere in the main part of the cavern? If they needed access to them, to get documents out or put others inside, it would make better sense to have them in the cave, where there's plenty of room. This tunnel is narrow. That's why they've had to pile them up on top of each other. Or at least, I think that's one reason they're stacked like that."

Robin looked at him.

"What are you driving at?" she asked.

"Just thinking out loud, and putting together the way those chests are positioned and that piece of timber on the side wall of the tunnel."

"You think there's a connection?" Robin asked.

"Maybe. Yes, maybe there is. Just think about the route we had to follow to get here. The entrance to the cave was invisible because it was behind the waterfall. Then there was the internal waterfall that led to the second chamber, and in there the other entrance was completely hidden by those heavy timbers and piled-up rocks. We saw one booby trap, and tripped another one, and now we're standing here at the end of a short tunnel that leads nowhere, looking at a collection of chests."

"So the cave was very well hidden and protected internally, but isn't that pretty much what you would have expected?"

"Yes, but it also reminds me of a kind of phased retreat, moving deeper into the mountain. I think that length of timber we saw could well be another—a final—trigger for a last line of defense. Probably another rockfall that would block this tunnel and stop any attackers reaching this end of it, and getting access to the chests."

"But that would trap the defending Templars at this end, in this tiny space. And we know they weren't suicidal."

"Exactly. So I think we're looking at the way out of here."

"We are?" Robin demanded. "Where?"

"Hidden in plain sight. We just move the chests and I think we'll find another tunnel behind them. That's why they're piled up like that. They're hiding the entrance."

35

Toscanelli and his two companions moved carefully forward through the clouds of dark dust that the rockfall had produced, heading toward the narrow entrance to the cavern. They had all tied handkerchiefs around the lower part of their faces in an attempt to keep the worst of the dust out of their mouths, but even with the cloth in place, they all seemed to be breathing as much dust as air.

"This is just a waste of time," Mario said. "That rockfall must have blocked the entrance completely, but at least it's saved us having to kill the two targets. They'll just die a long and painful death inside the chamber."

"We're going to check it anyway," Toscanelli snapped. "And those two seem to have the luck of the devil, so until I see their dead bodies we're going to assume that they're alive and that there is another way out of that cave. This job isn't finished until I say it is."

As they'd expected, the narrow part of the tunnel was now blocked with rocks, but because the entrance into the larger cavern was so narrow, they were all fairly small, apart from the large boulder that had been used to trigger the booby trap. But only about half of that rock projected above the floor, the remainder having sunk into the pit excavated by the Templars centuries earlier, and stepping around or over it was easy enough.

"Shift enough of the smaller rocks so we can move around here," Toscanelli ordered, and the three men set to work, lobbing or rolling rocks out of the narrow section of the tunnel and into the wider area down which they had just walked.

It was hot, hard, and dusty work, but within about twenty minutes they had cleared a path all the way to the end of the tunnel, and for the first time they could see the full extent, and the impressive effectiveness, of the trap the Templars had constructed.

Shifting the chests was heavy work, but the prospect of getting out of the cave added strength to their arms.

Mallory positioned his flashlight on one side of the tunnel, where the beam illuminated the pile of chests, and then he and Robin grabbed hold of the ends of the chest on the top left of the group. The wood was old— obviously—and the metal strengthening bands that ran around it were speckled and discolored by rust, but the structure itself was perfectly sound. Mallory maneuvered the end of the chest far enough for Robin to be able to grab the other end, and together they manhandled the heavy container out of position and lowered it to the ground.

Then they both turned to look back at the section of the tunnel wall they'd exposed, Robin taking out her flashlight to illuminate it.

There, now visible that the chest had been moved, was the upper part of a dark semicircular opening, very obviously the entrance to another, much lower and narrower tunnel that promised a potential escape route from the cave.

"Now, that is a beautiful sight," Robin said, altering the position of her flashlight to shine the beam into the exposed opening and deeper into the cavity. "It looks like it goes more or less straight, but we'll only be able to see properly once we shift the rest of these chests."

"No sign of daylight at the other end, I suppose?" Mallory said, hopefully peering into it.

"Not that I can see," Robin replied, briefly extinguishing her flashlight and also looking down the tunnel.

With the first chest removed, shifting the others took only a matter of minutes. They laid them along the sides of the tunnel and then they both shone their lights into the exposed opening. It was only about half the height of the tunnel they were standing in, so they would both have to crouch to walk along it, and it seemed to extend at least as far as their flashlight beams would shine.

"There's no guarantee that it is the way out of here," Mallory said, "but I can't think of any other reason for it being here. And the tunnel was obviously either constructed or modified by the Templars or by somebody else because I can see chisel marks on both sides of the opening."

"So, do we go down it right now, or do you want to look at the chests first?"

"The chests are the end of the trail we've been following, so I definitely want to see what's inside them. Then we can decide if whatever's in there is worth coming back for, once we've got ourselves out of here. And there's still that smaller chest to look at," he added, pointing at the one chest they hadn't shifted because it wasn't directly in front of the cave opening, but over to one side of it.

"We could probably take that one with us," Robin suggested. "It's small enough that we could carry it between us."

They walked over to the larger chests and stopped in front of one of them.

"What we don't do," Mallory said, looking at it, "is just open the lid. Remember what happened on Cyprus. There may well be a booby trap or something built into it."

They each took one end of the box and moved it clear of the wall so that they could walk all around it. It was about four feet long, three feet deep, and the same in height. Plain and undecorated iron bands reinforced both the lid and the base, and there did not appear to be a lock to secure it, only a kind of over-center catch held in place by a rusty bolt.

"No lock," Mallory said. "Maybe these chests were in constant use when the Templars were active, documents being removed, inspected, and replaced all the time, and having a lock worked by a key would just have slowed everything down."

"Perhaps their security was where the chests were stored," Robin suggested. "If they were in an inner chamber of the Templar preceptory or commandery, nobody except the Templars themselves would have had access to them, so they might have thought that a lock was simply superfluous."

Mallory bent down in front of the chest and carefully slid the bolt to one side, then freed the catch. While Robin moved a few feet away for safety, he moved behind the chest, reached over it to grasp the catch, and then lifted the lid.

Almost disappointingly nothing else happened. Unlike the chests they had already discovered in the cave on Cyprus, there was no brutal antitheft mechanism built into the lid. Mallory stepped back around to the front of the chest. Robin joined him and they both looked inside the box.

It was almost full of documents of various sorts. They could see parchments, some folded, others rolled and probably originally secured with leather ties, a couple of slim codices, a large number of papyrus scrolls, and even a handful of documents written on paper. Robin pointed them out to Mallory.

"They're made of paper?" he asked. "I thought that was a later invention and didn't reach Europe until about the fifteenth century. Gutenberg and the Bible and all that."

"No, paper is much, much older than that. It was probably invented in China in the early part of the third century and the discovery slowly migrated west along the Silk Road, but by the late twelfth century we know there was at least one paper mill working in France and another one in Spain. Obviously parchment was still the most popular medium for writing because it was so readily available, but the use of paper became more common once the industry was established because it was a lot cheaper to produce. Between the thirteenth and sixteenth centuries, paper mills started to appear all over the place, usually outside the larger towns. This was because they were so noisy and smelly—the water-powered trip-hammers beating the pulp created quite a din—that medieval law usually required them to be located outside the city limits."

"You know a lot about paper," Mallory pointed out.

"Old books, my dear. I buy them and I sell them and they're made of paper, so of course I know about it. It's the biggest part of my business. Now let's see what we've got in here."

While Mallory held his flashlight steady, Robin picked up a piece of folded parchment and opened it. The material was still quite supple, so presumably the conditions and environment in the cave were conducive to its preservation.

"It's written in Latin, obviously," Robin said, her eyes tracing the first few lines of the document.

Mallory leaned closer to her to see it better. The ink on the parchment was somewhat faded, but the text was still perfectly readable.

"It's part of a short-term loan arrangement, by the

looks of it," Robin said, studying the text. "This states that a man named Anselm of Paris deposited a quantity of jewelry and other assets at the Paris preceptory—there's a list of the various items here with their assessed values—in March 1275 and received a cash sum in return. He completed some kind of business transaction, which isn't specified in this document, presumably because the Templars weren't interested in what he did with the money because they had the assets to cover the loan. Anselm then reclaimed the assets just over two months later. The Templars charged him a fee, so he repaid more than he'd borrowed, and that was the end of the transaction."

"So it's basically a record of a completed transaction," Mallory said. "Just a document to keep their records straight."

"Pretty much, yes," Robin replied, picking up another piece of parchment. She looked at it for a few seconds, then nodded. "This is another one, another completed transaction that's quite similar, though the amount of money lent by the Templars to this man was a lot less."

A third and a fourth record revealed information that was very similar, assets being deposited in exchange for ready cash, sometimes for gold, and those assets then being recovered by the individual involved at a later date, with a fee charged for the loan. The documents were certainly interesting from a historical perspective, but as each referred to an ancient completed transaction, they had no other value and certainly no relevance to the present day.

"Interesting, but not valuable," Robin said, replacing

the last piece of parchment they'd looked at. "Unless you're a Templar researcher or medieval historian, of course."

They quickly examined the contents of the other five large chests, picking three or four documents from each of them for Robin to examine. But each piece of parchment, paper, or vellum she looked at contained broadly the same kind of information: the record of some kind of completed transaction, the deposition of assets in exchange for cash, followed sometime later by the recovery of those same assets, or the deposit of funds in one Templar preceptory or commandery and the issue of equivalent funds, less the Templars' equivalent of a bank charge, in another establishment, sometimes in a different country.

"Just like a bank draft or a bearer bond," Robin commented. "A way for a businessman to deposit the money he needed for some kind of deal in one place so that he could travel the roads in safety because he was carrying nothing of any value, and then draw out the funds at his destination."

"But these have no value today, obviously. I was hoping we'd find some of the records of the land grants and deeds that we know the Templars were given by new recruits and people who supported the order. But I think we should take some of them with us, just in case there's anything on them that we've missed. And they're interesting historical records in any case."

Mallory opened up his rucksack and stuffed as many of the ancient deeds into it as it would take.

"So that just leaves the smallest box," Robin said. "Maybe what's in that will be more interesting."

Mallory lifted up the final box—it was heavier than it looked, but not too weighty for him to manage—and placed it on top of one of the larger chests. For a few moments, he and Robin just looked at it; then Mallory stretched out his hand and attempted to lift the catch that held the lid shut. Unlike the other chests, this catch was slotted into a large and quite ornate lock on the front of the box, and as soon as he tried to free it, he knew it was locked.

"That's a bit of a bugger," he said, "but I have got a few tools in my bag that might shift it."

He fished around in his rucksack and pulled out a plastic box containing a number of slim black steel tools, each shaped somewhat like a flattened letter *S*.

"What are those?" Robin asked. "Lock picks?"

"No. They're double-ended Allen keys," Mallory replied, "but you're right: they do look like lock picks, and they work in a very similar fashion."

He shone his flashlight at the fairly large keyhole, selected one of the smaller Allen keys, and began probing the lock, trying to deduce which pieces of metal the tool was touching were the tumblers, and which were the wards.

"It feels like a fairly simple lock," he said, "and the key was probably a basic design." He put down the tool he'd been using and chose a larger key to insert into the keyhole. "Let's see if this does it."

He turned the Allen key around and slid the end into the lock, then rotated it gently. When the end made contact, he tried turning it, but it wouldn't move.

"Probably hitting one of the wards," he said, almost to himself.

He moved it very slightly, felt the end of the key slip off one piece of metal, and tried again. This time, he managed about a quarter of a turn before it stopped, and no matter what he did, it wouldn't turn any farther.

"I think it needs a smaller one," he said, selected an appropriate size, and inserted it into the ancient lock.

This time, the Allen key turned easily through a quarter turn and then, after a slight hesitation, continued to turn. There was a distinct click as the key completed the turn.

"It's open, I think," he said.

"Now be careful. I've got used to having you around."

With a glance at Robin, Mallory stepped back from the chest, took out his crowbar, placed the curved end of it under the catch, and twisted his wrist. The catch popped open with a complete absence of drama or unexpected events.

"Stand well back," Mallory said.

He moved around the chest until he was standing behind it. Then he changed his grip on the crowbar so that he was holding it by the point, reached over the chest and hooked the curved end under the front of the lid, and slowly lifted it. The lid moved slowly, the hinges protesting audibly at being disturbed after over half a millennium of stasis.

Then there was a sudden thump and the chest rocked backward.

On the other side of the rock pile, the mass of stones completely muffling the sound of their voices, the three

Italians were standing in a group and staring at the section of the rock pile that they could see.

It was obvious that the narrow entrance to the tunnel had stopped any of the bigger rocks from entering it, which in turn meant that the tunnel itself remained passable. All of the larger boulders had smashed into the walls of the cavern beside the entrance, forming an untidy pile.

"It's not completely blocked," Toscanelli said, sounding pleased. "There's a gap over to the right that I can see," he added, shining his flashlight beam that way. "If we can shift half a dozen of those rocks, we should be able to climb up the stones and get into the cavern that way."

Mario looked doubtful.

"They're big," he said, "and we have no tools with us."

"No, but we do have those planks of wood. We can use them as levers to move the stones. You and Salvatori go and grab a couple of them while I try to climb up that slope and see how high I can get."

Minutes later, they'd worked out a potential route over and through the rock pile, and had already started levering away at some of the stones that blocked their path.

Mallory released the lid and he and Robin walked around to the front of the chest to see what had happened.

What they saw was almost a repeat of the antitheft mechanism built into the chests they'd found on Cyprus. Except that this mechanism was a lot simpler, though identical in concept and operation.

Projecting from the gap below the partially open lid

were two double-edged steel blades, each well over a foot long. They had obviously been forced out of the chest by a powerful spring when the opening of the lid released whatever mechanism had held them in check over the centuries. The blades were long enough that if somebody had been standing at a normal distance in front of the chest when it was opened, he would have suffered two very serious, perhaps even fatal, stabbing wounds to the abdomen.

"Whatever you think of the Templars," Robin said, looking at the two blades, "you can't deny that their engineering was first-rate. Lethal, but first-rate."

Mallory extended the crowbar again, positioned the end of it under the edge of the lid, and lifted it to open the chest fully. The two blades and the mechanism that had driven them were clearly visible as he did so, attached to the underside of the lid of the box.

"Hopefully there aren't any other nasty surprises lurking inside," Robin said.

"Probably not. It's not that big a chest, and there really isn't room for another device like that one."

"I was thinking more about poison on the documents inside it, that kind of thing."

"I doubt it," Mallory said, looking at the collection of pieces of parchment revealed by opening the lid of the chest, "because whatever these papers are, they're records that would be handled by members of the order and perhaps by other people as well. I think poisoning them would have made that far too difficult. And, even if they had been, a medieval poison probably wouldn't be dangerous today. But maybe we should wear gloves, just in case."

He pulled a packet of latex gloves out of his rucksack, and they each pulled on a pair. Then he reached into the chest, pulled out the document that lay on top of the pile inside, and handed it to Robin.

"So, what have we got this time?" he asked, then turned round to stare back into the cavern, where he'd just heard the sound of a rock falling.

"What was that?" Robin demanded.

"Probably just a stone settling in the rock pile."

"As long as it's not those bloody Italians tunneling their way out."

"Look at the size of the pile," Mallory said. "I think it'll take days or weeks to get through that lot."

Robin stared back into the cavern for a few moments, then unfolded the parchment and looked at the first few lines of the Latin text.

"I'm not going to bother translating it," she said, "but I can tell you that this is a land grant made by a nobleman and it relates to a large piece of property in France. Obviously we would need to do a bit of research to find out exactly where the land is, but according to the first section of this grant, it was in the vicinity of the Templars' Paris preceptory. And that, as you told me the other day, was pretty much in the center of the city."

She unfolded the final section of the parchment and looked at the last few lines, mentally translating the Latin as she did so.

"So presumably this French noble gave the property

to the Templars when he joined the order?" Mallory asked.

"Yes, but there is a kind of caveat. In 1204 he handed over control and ownership of the property and the farms and buildings that were on it to the Knights Templar in perpetuity, but there's another sentence here that is interesting. He specifically gave the land also to the then grand master, Phillipe de Plessis, and to his descendants—I suppose the modern expression would be his 'heirs and assignees,' something like that—in the event that the Templar order ever ceased to exist. I suppose that was a kind of belt-and-braces provision, but what's really interesting is this short Latin phrase, *prout moris est*. That translates as 'according to custom' or 'as is usual,' something like that. That suggests that giving assets both to the Knights Templar and to a named individual within the order was the normal procedure. In this case, logically that provision should have been exercised when the Knights Templar were purged and the order dissolved. And that's very interesting."

"It is," Mallory agreed, "because if Phillipe de Plessis had any children—and a lot of the Templars were married and had families before they took their vows and joined the order—that could mean that some French family actually has a genuine legal title to a significant part of the French capital. That document you're holding could potentially be worth billions of euros."

"And that's just the first one," Robin agreed. "This stuff is explosive, if this document is any indication of what else is in that chest."

"Right," Mallory said. "That is what we were hoping to find, so let's find our way out of here."

He carefully reset the antitheft mechanism, because carrying the chest with the blades extended was far too dangerous in case either of them stumbled, and secured the lid and used his Allen keys to relock it.

The escape tunnel they had uncovered by removing the larger chests was too narrow and low to allow them to walk side by side, so Robin led the way, Mallory following a few feet behind her and carrying the chest.

The tunnel ran fairly straight for perhaps a hundred yards, the slope gradually increasing, then turned somewhat abruptly to the left and widened significantly.

"I think this is probably a natural fissure in the rock that the Templars just opened up," Robin suggested, taking hold of the handle on one side of the chest to help Mallory with the weight. "Cutting this tunnel out of the rock would have been far too much work otherwise."

"You're probably right. And there's something else. Have you noticed the air? It seems to be fresh, not musty, which is what you'd expect if this tunnel was sealed. There must be a way out of it somewhere ahead of us."

"I hope so," Robin said. "I have what I hope is a long life ahead of me that I have every intention of enjoying. Ending my days trapped in an underground tunnel in Switzerland was never a part of any of my long-term plans."

"Then let's hope that that blank wall I can now see in front of us doesn't mean that we're out of options."

Robin looked ahead, at where Mallory's flashlight

beam was illuminating a flat and largely featureless wall of rock, and muttered a curse.

"Oh, shit," she said.

The opening that Toscanelli and the other two men were trying to create was both very restricted and close to the roof of the cavern, but as far as he could see, it was the only way through the mass of fallen stones.

When he'd climbed up onto the tumbled rocks, he was able to see the solid and undisturbed roof of the cavern only in one place. And that was where they were now directing all their efforts. The stones they were trying to move were cumbersome and extremely heavy and the space around them severely restricted, meaning that using the lengths of timber as levers was much more difficult than any of them had expected. But they were making progress.

It was hot, sweaty, and exhausting, made that much more difficult by the extremely restricted space and having to work only by the light of their handheld flashlights. All three men were filthy, their clothes blackened by the dust and debris that coated the rocks, their hands bruised and bloody from their exertions. But they'd managed to shift more than half a dozen boulders already, painstakingly levering them far enough out of the way so that they could get past.

They still had perhaps another five or six stones to move before they could climb all the way to the top of the pile of rocks and then—hopefully—find a way down the other side to the floor of the cavern.

And when they got out, it would just be a matter of tracking down Mallory and Jessop, silencing them permanently, perhaps taking their time over the woman, and then recovering whatever the English couple had found.

They lowered the chest to the floor of the tunnel and looked around. The wall in front of them appeared to be depressingly solid, as were the side walls of the tunnel.

"I don't believe there isn't a way out," Mallory said bitterly. "What was the point of the Templars opening up this tunnel if all it does is lead to a solid wall?"

Robin didn't reply, just turned slowly through a complete circle, the beam of her flashlight covering the walls and floor. Then she shone the flashlight at the roof of the tunnel, which seemed just as solid and featureless as everything else around them. But then she stopped moving and glanced at Mallory.

"You mentioned the air," she said. "I think I can feel a very slight draft on my face. If I'm right, that means we must be fairly near the surface. If we can find out where the air is coming from, maybe we can open up whatever gap there is and get out that way."

"That could take a while," Mallory said, "if it was even possible." He looked around the end of the tunnel again, and pointed at the clear marks on the stone made by the chisels wielded by medieval masons. "But I can't believe they would just have opened up this tunnel and done nothing else. I mean, what would have been the point? There must be something here that we're not seeing."

They both stood in silence, shining their flashlights

back down the tunnel and around the blank wall facing them.

Then Mallory let out an exclamation and pointed.

"I missed that," he said, aiming his flashlight beam. "Or rather I saw it as we walked past it but I missed its significance."

"What? Oh, I see."

About twenty yards behind them a wooden arch had been constructed of ancient blackened wood, a length of heavy timber positioned vertically on each side of the tunnel with a horizontal crosspiece linking them at the top.

"This is solid rock, possibly granite or something, so why would they have needed to build a wooden archway? And we haven't seen any other timber structures like that since we walked into the tunnel."

They strode back to examine the wooden supports.

At first sight, the vertical timbers looked entirely normal, but when they aimed their flashlight beams at the very tops of them, where the horizontal length of wood had been positioned, they both realized something at the same moment.

"The crosspiece isn't resting on both ends of these uprights," Robin said, "only on one of them. The other end has been placed on a ledge cut into the rock. So at least one of these uprights must have another purpose. Another trap, maybe?"

Moving the last stones at the top of the pile didn't take as long as Toscanelli had feared, precisely because they were at the top of the pile, with no other rocks or boulders resting on them and holding them in place. Salvatori had moved the final two rocks by the simple expedient of lying on his back in the narrow opening and pushing the stones out of the way by using his feet, sending them tumbling down the outside of the rock wall to land on the floor of the cavern.

Moments later, he stuck his head out of the opening, his flashlight in one hand and his pistol in the other, and quickly scanned his surroundings.

"They're nowhere in sight," he reported, and climbed out onto the rocks and began making his way down the pile of stones.

He was followed within seconds by the other two men. They moved cautiously around the mass of fallen rock, using their flashlights as sparingly as they could and talking as little as possible.

The entrance to the tunnel that had been uncovered by moving the six chests was clearly visible, and it was immediately obvious to the three of them that that was the only way their quarry could have gone. There were no other possible exits, and they clearly weren't hiding somewhere in the cavern.

Toscanelli shone his flashlight at the wooden chests as they approached the tunnel entrance.

"Those are probably what Mallory and Jessop came for," he said. "We'll check out the contents once we've dealt with the two of them."

And then he began moving slowly and cautiously down the tunnel in front of them, his pistol ready.

*   *   *

Mallory and Robin shone their flashlight beams at the upright on one side of the tunnel. As far as they could see, it was completely solid, the base of the length of timber set into a cavity in the tunnel floor, and the top wedged behind a projecting piece of rock on the roof. When Mallory stuck the end of his crowbar in the narrow gap behind the timber and tried levering it, absolutely nothing happened.

"It's completely solid," he said.

Robin nodded, her eyes following the beam of the flashlight as she ran it up and down the wooden pillar.

"What about the other one?" she asked.

They crossed the few steps to the other side of the tunnel and repeated their inspection of the other length of timber.

"The bottom of this piece of wood is in a hollowed-out cavity," Mallory said, "just like the first one, but the top isn't locked in place as far as I can see."

He lifted up the crowbar and repeated the treatment on the second length of timber. This time, the heavy balk of wood moved very slightly as Mallory applied pressure to the end of the tool. He removed the crowbar and looked up thoughtfully toward the roof of the tunnel.

"I'm wondering," he said, "if this upright is acting as a kind of hinge, or maybe a release for the horizontal timber above us." He shone his flashlight at the roof of the tunnel again. "If you pulled that vertical timber out of place, then there'd be nothing supporting the end of the horizontal length of wood."

"You might be right," Robin said, "but what we don't know is what would happen if you did that, and I've got no intention of standing underneath this kind of wooden archway if you're going to experiment. Bearing in mind what happened in the other part of the cavern, that could just literally bring the whole roof down on top of us. This could just be another Templar trap."

"It could be," Mallory agreed, "but I don't think it is, because there's one very clear difference between what we're looking at here and what we saw in the cavern. Back there, the trigger was carefully hidden and positioned so that almost anyone entering the cavern from the narrow tunnel would trip it. This is completely different. In order to move that timber you have to actually lever it away from the wall, a very deliberate act. I don't think that this is a booby trap at all. I think this could be the location of the last hidden exit from the tunnel system that the Templars prepared in case they were ever trapped inside this cave."

"You might be right, but do you really think it would be a good idea to stand here, stick the crowbar into position, and shift that timber?"

"No, I don't. And I very much doubt if the Templars would do so, either. Think about it. There are three pieces of timber here, one supporting another one and the third one doing absolutely nothing apart from being waged firmly into position on the opposite side of the tunnel. That was done for a reason, and my guess is that it was to provide a fulcrum, a way of pulling the other upright out of position from a distance."

"But a lever wouldn't work," Robin objected, but then

she smiled in the darkness. "Right. Now I see what you mean. Not a lever, but a rope."

Mallory nodded and pointed at the fixed length of timber.

"When we were looking at that," he said, "I noticed that about two-thirds of the way up there's a gap between the wood and the rock behind it, and the back of the timber looks very smooth, almost as if it had been planed so as to provide a gentle curve. No rough edges or sharp bits sticking out." He shifted the beam of his flashlight to point at the other upright. "And in about the same position on this timber is another gap between it and the rock, where you could tie the end of a rope. And rope is something that we have."

Mallory opened up his rucksack and took out a coil of climbing rope, thin and tough but immensely strong.

"Before you do anything else," Robin said, "you need to work out where you're going to stand."

"What do you mean?"

"If you're right about using that upright as a fulcrum, or rather as a kind of rudimentary pulley, then obviously you could pull the rope from either side, either the cavern side of where we're standing or the dead end of the tunnel. So what you need to decide is what the Templars were thinking when they constructed it. Which side of the structure is going to be the safest."

"I think that's fairly obvious," Mallory replied. "This had to be a last-ditch location, somewhere they would only use if they'd been beaten back all the way through the cavern system. That means they'd trigger from the end of the tunnel, which is where they would make their last stand."

"Then let's hope that your logic is the same as the Templars'. Let's get on with it."

The locations that he had identified on both timbers were higher than he could comfortably reach, so he unraveled the end of the rope and passed it to Robin, then hoisted her up onto his shoulders so that she could thread it through the gap that he had identified. Then he simply walked across the tunnel to the other upright with her still on his shoulders so that she could tie the end of the rope around the timber.

"Make it a good knot," Mallory said.

"I did think of that," Robin snapped. "I tied a clove hitch. If it's strong enough to moor a boat, it should be strong enough for what we need."

She clambered down off his shoulders, and together they moved the chest all the way down the tunnel to the wall at the end. Then Mallory uncoiled the remainder of the climbing rope and walked with it to the tunnel end. He took a firm grip on the rope with both hands, winding some of it around his arm to ensure that it wouldn't slip out of his grasp.

"Are you sure about this?" Robin asked.

"Frankly no. But as far as I can see we're right out of other options."

And then they both heard the unmistakable sound of approaching footsteps and muffled voices from somewhere down the tunnel and knew that, against all the odds, somehow the Italians had managed to find their way around the rockfall.

"Kill the lights," Mallory said urgently as he and Robin extinguished their flashlights.

But then other flashlight beams speared toward them, the Italians looking for targets, confident that they had now finally trapped their quarry, unarmed and helpless at the end of the tunnel.

Mallory braced himself and started to heave on the rope, knowing that their only possible chance of survival lay in the hands of the medieval carpenters and masons employed by the Knights Templar.

Then the light from one of the flashlights picked him out and immediately the tunnel echoed to the sound of a shot, the bullet missing him by a matter of inches rather than feet before smashing into the solid rock wall behind him.

And as the other flashlight beams converged on Mallory, Robin ran to his side and grabbed hold of the rope that was already pulled taut, and then both began heaving as if their lives depended on it.

36

Canton of Schwyz, Switzerland

Time seemed almost to stand still.

For several long seconds—or at least that was what it felt like to Mallory and Robin—their frantic heaving on the rope produced no results whatsoever.

Another flashlight beam picked them out, and Mallory knew that behind the light one of the Italians was moving steadily forward and taking careful aim with his pistol, closing the distance to be sure of his shot.

And then, at the very instant when they both guessed that their lives were at an end, the rope moved slightly. They pulled even harder, exerting every ounce of strength that they possessed, their shoes scrabbling for grip on the rock floor beneath them.

They both heard a loud creak from the wooden structure and suddenly the rope went limp, causing them both to collapse backward onto the ground. A volley of shots rang out at the same moment, the bullets accurately tracing lethal paths through the spaces that their bodies had occupied just a split second before.

But then they all heard an ominous rumbling, the sound of stone striking stone, and the Italians switched their attention to the roof above them, their flashlights illuminating the dark rock.

As the vertical length of heavy timber moved out of position, pulled by the rope that Robin had attached to it, it freed the end of the horizontal beam running across the roof of the tunnel. And behind that, held in place behind a massive wooden platform, as dark and almost as solid as the rocks themselves, tons of stone had been carefully positioned ready for precisely this eventuality.

Freed from its vertical support, the end of the horizontal beam swung swiftly downward in an arc, pivoting about its other end. In the intermittent light of the flashlights, Mallory could see a black and ominous shape—the wooden platform itself—emerge from the rock ceiling. And behind it the first of a virtual torrent of stones and boulders tumbled into view, seeming to move almost in slow motion.

"We've got to move—now," he shouted, scrambling to his feet and reaching down to help Robin.

She was already moving, and the two of them fled deeper into the blackness of the tunnel, heading for the dead end where they'd left the wooden chest. They already knew that there was no escape that way, but at least they hoped to avoid being crushed by the falling rocks.

Behind them the roaring and crashing sounds increased

as yet more rock poured out of the roof of the tunnel. When they reached the end, they turned round and looked back, Mallory clicking on his flashlight as they did so.

"The light," Robin began. "We're targets. They'll see us."

Mallory shook his head. "It doesn't matter. We're too far away now for accurate pistol shooting. And they've got other things on their minds right now," he added.

The beam from Mallory's flashlight shone on swirling clouds of dust that almost filled the tunnel like a vast plume of black smoke. Beyond the dust, and as far as he could see completely blocking the tunnel, was a tumble of dark boulders, more stones falling from somewhere in the mountain above them.

As they watched, the noise died away as the last stones fell, to be replaced by complete and utter silence.

For a few seconds neither of them spoke. Then Robin coughed to try to clear some of the dust from her mouth and sighed deeply.

"Well, that certainly seems to have stopped the Italians," she said, a catch in her voice. "It's just a shame that we've buried ourselves alive in the process."

"I wish we knew what the hell is going on inside there," the sniper murmured. He was studying the forked waterfall at the end of the valley, a waterfall that appeared completely unchanged, despite the second unmistakable rumble of what sounded like an explosion from somewhere underground.

"I'll call it in," the spotter replied, "but I bet we'll just be told to keep watching. I just wish they'd make their mind up about what they want us to do."

He was right. Their anonymous employer listened with interest to his report and then rang off, apparently to consult with his colleagues.

He called back about five minutes later and instructed the two-man team to continue with their surveillance.

"What about these explosions, or whatever they are?" the spotter asked. "Do you know what's going on?"

"We're not certain," their employer replied, somewhat reluctantly. "Our best guess is that the people in there are opening up locked chambers, and possibly using explosives to do it. We have an interest in what those chambers might contain, so contact me again the moment you see any of the targets emerge, and take special note of anything they may be carrying. We may want you to act immediately if the targets bring out large boxes or anything of that sort. Confirm that you now have the weapons you requested."

"Confirmed," the spotter said, glancing at the dark green bag he'd collected a few minutes earlier from a man wearing camouflage clothing and waiting at the coordinates he'd been given. Then he ended the call.

On the opposite side of the rockfall, Toscanelli stared at the vast pile of boulders that completely blocked the tunnel and cursed fluently and lengthily in Italian.

As soon as they'd realized what was happening, he and his two companions had run back along the tunnel, retracing their steps to get as far away from the ancient Templar

trap as possible. Once they were satisfied that the last stone
had fallen, they stopped and walked back cautiously.

Unlike with the rockfall they'd managed to find a way
round in the main cavern, this time the tunnel was completely blocked, floor to ceiling, and without even trying
to move any of the stones, the three men knew that they
were just too heavy to shift without specialist equipment.

"So that's it," Mario said. "To get through that lot we'd
need winches and hydraulic jacks and ideally a forklift
truck, and you know as well as I do that there's no chance
of us getting anything like that down here. Let's go."

Toscanelli nodded slowly, his flashlight beam quarter-
ing the area in front of them, looking for any possible way
through the rockfall, and finding nothing.

"When we saw those two before the rocks fell," he
said, "did either of you notice if they were carrying anything? Or was there anything near them in the tunnel?"

"The man—Mallory—had a rucksack on his back,"
Salvatori said. "Was that what you meant?"

"No. I was thinking of a chest or a box, something of
that sort. Something that they might have recovered from
the cavern and were taking with them."

"I was trying to get a decent shot at them," Mario said,
"but I think I did see some kind of box behind them, right
up in the end wall of the tunnel. It could have been a chest,
I suppose, but I was looking at them, not at it. What I do
know is that it was nothing like the size of those chests we
saw back in the larger cave. They were probably too big
and heavy for those two to carry with them, so maybe
they'd just left them and were only looking for a way out."

"So there might have been a smaller chest as well," Toscanelli said. "That isn't what I was hoping to hear, but at least we know where it is, and if Vitale wants us to recover that as well, we'll just have to come back with the right sort of tools to get through that rockfall. And we'll check those other six chests before we leave."

"The targets might have opened them," Salvatori suggested, "and removed some documents from them. That is what you think is in them, isn't it? Old documents? The Templar Archive?"

"Probably." Toscanelli took another look at the impenetrable pile of rocks and shrugged. "If it were me," he said thoughtfully, "I'd rather take a couple of bullets than wait to die of hunger and thirst behind a rockfall in a cave. Still," he added, "knowing that they're rotting away behind those tons of stone is the best news I've had all day. At least we know they won't be bothering us again."

With a final look behind them, the three Italians turned away and again retraced their steps down the tunnel and into the larger cave, their flashlights lighting the way. They stopped beside one of the chests, and Mario tentatively eased open the catch.

"It's not locked," he said, "but I'm not opening it from the front. I know what happened with those chests you found in the cave on Cyprus."

"Stand on one side of it," Toscanelli instructed, and gestured for Salvatori to walk to the opposite end of the chest. "Don't use your hands," he added, "just in case. I gave you knives. Use them instead."

While Toscanelli stood in front of the chest, but a safe

distance away, and shone his flashlight at the ancient wooden object, Mario and Salvatori each produced a switchblade and clicked the button to open it. The single-edged five-inch blades sprang out and locked in place. Each man jammed the point of the blade into the side of the wooden lid of the chest and then slowly lifted it.

Nothing happened, except that the lid opened on its metal hinges to reveal a mass of documents placed haphazardly within the chest. Toscanelli strode forward, looked carefully inside the chests to ensure that there were no booby traps inside it, then picked up one of the folded sheets of parchment. He looked at it in the light from his flashlight, then shook his head.

"What?" Mario asked.

"I've no idea what it is," Toscenalli confessed. "I can only read the odd word or two, but I'm fairly sure that this is Latin."

He picked up another piece of parchment and looked at that as well.

"It's old, obviously," he continued, "but that's all I'm certain of. Check the other chests. Use the same method to open them, just in case."

Mario and Salvatori followed his instructions, and as each chest lid creaked harmlessly open to reveal another collection of ancient documents, he gave them a cursory glance and a brief inspection. But the contents of all the chests were remarkably similar: piles of old documents written in Latin.

"One of our experts is going to have to look at these

and see what we've got," Toscanelli said, a note almost of triumph in his voice, "but this looks to me as if it really is the Templar Archive. I mean, what else could it be?"

"So what do we do with it?" Mario asked.

"We get it out of here and back to Rome, obviously. That's not going to be easy, but we don't have any choice. We'll carry these chests over to the tunnel entrance, and then we'll just have to work at widening the path we made until we can fit the chests through it."

"Why can't we just empty the chests and carry the documents out of the cave?" Salvatori objected.

"Because the chests themselves might be important. There might be clues embedded in the pattern of the metalwork or inscribed inside them. The chests have to go with us. And the sooner we get started, the sooner we'll get out of here."

Grumbling under his breath, Salvatori grabbed the handle on one end of the chest and waited until Mario was ready to lift it. Then, with Toscanelli leading the way and illuminating the path with his flashlight, they carried the heavy object toward the place where they'd forced their way through the rockfall. Once all six chests were there, Toscanelli climbed up the slope and looked down at the passage they had forced, measuring heights and widths by eye.

"It's not too big a job," he announced, climbing back down into the cavern. "I reckon there are four rocks we'll definitely need to move, and two or three others that would make the job easier. We're probably only looking at a couple of hours' work."

*   *   *

Surveillance is one of the most boring tasks imaginable, but sitting in a car with nothing to read and nothing to look at, and with only a radio for company, is even worse.

Paolo had got fed up with just sitting there, trying to get comfortable, and walking around the small parking area was little better, so after he'd eaten his sandwich lunch—which he'd spun out as long as he could—he locked the vehicle, took a couple of candy bars from the trunk, and walked through the patch of woodland to where Carlo was watching the valley and waiting for Toscanelli and the other three men to return. At least he would have someone to talk to, if nothing else.

Once he got there, he and Carlo lounged on a fallen tree that offered them both a good view up into the blind end of the valley, ate the chocolate bars, and talked. It wasn't a scintillating conversation, but it did pass half an hour or so. Then, with not the slightest sign of the other men returning, he ambled back to the car, unlocked it, and climbed back inside.

He switched on the ignition and lowered all the windows far enough to provide a through breeze, but not so far that anyone could put their hand or arm inside and unlock the doors. Then he locked the doors, reclined the seat, and closed his eyes.

A few minutes later, he roused himself, his subconscious mind kicking him awake, and he sat up and looked around the parking area.

He hadn't checked the target vehicle, which was the main reason he had been told to stay there.

Grumbling under his breath, he got out of the car and walked over to the other side of the cleared area until he could see the other car.

"They're not going anywhere," he muttered to himself. "Don't know why I even bothered looking."

He walked back to his own car, climbed in, lay back again, and closed his eyes. Within five minutes, the interior of the car reverberated to the sound of his snoring.

37

The two-hour estimate suggested by Toscanelli to open up the route through and over the rock pile proved to be somewhat optimistic.

The problem, predictably enough, was the rocks. Their weight was brutal, and just lifting one far enough to get one of the lengths of timber underneath it to act as a lever sometimes took the combined strength of all three men. Add to that the extremely restricted space within which they were working and the absence of proper light, and it was perhaps not surprising that they had struggled for almost three hours before they managed to open up a big enough space to move one of the chests through.

In fact, the three of them only worked at it for about half an hour before Toscanelli realized that they needed help, and sent Mario back out of the cave to summon Paolo and Carlo to assist them. Even then, the space in

which they were working was so tight that they couldn't
all fit in it at the same time. But at least having the extra
two men meant that they could spell each other when
they got tired, and also meant that one of them could
hold a flashlight, and that greatly helped to illuminate the
area where they were working.

The other problem that hadn't been immediately
apparent was that on several occasions they had to move
a number of rocks before they could shift the one that
was actually blocking their path. And every rock that they
freed then had to be rolled and tumbled out of the way,
to keep the widened passage clear.

But eventually Mario and Salvatori picked up one of
the chests by the metal handles at either end and slowly
managed, with a great deal of inventive cursing and considerable effort, to get the first of the chests through the
opened-up rock pile and into the narrow end of the tunnel. That, in fact, was the most difficult part of the whole
maneuver, because they had to work the chest around a
virtual right-angle bend, which necessitated standing the
object on its end to make the turn. The sheer bulk and
weight of the chest made this impossible until they had
shifted another three rocks from that location.

The first chest, inevitably, was the most difficult of the
six to shift, and moving the remaining five proved to be
substantially easier. Working in relays, they carried each chest
down the tunnel, into the cavern, and through the internal
waterfall and then left it before going back to collect another
one. When all six chests had been positioned there, they took
a breather while Toscanelli decided what to do next.

"We can't lug these chests around," he said. "The Swiss are an observant nation, and if we're seen with an obviously medieval wooden chest in the back of a car—and that's assuming it would fit—I'm quite certain the police or some other official would stop us and start asking awkward questions. So what we need to do is hire a closed van or truck big enough to hold all six chests and keep them out of sight. Then we can simply drive over the border into Italy and deliver them to our headquarters in Rome."

"So you think this is the Templar Archive?" Mario asked. "The second most important part of the assets of the order that our ancestral brothers were looking for seven hundred years ago? But we still have no idea where to find the lost treasure of the Templars itself? Or their wealth?"

Toscanelli lifted the lid of one of the chests and picked a document—a folded piece of parchment—at random, then opened it.

"I don't read Latin," he said, by way of answer, "but even I can see that the seal at the bottom of this piece of parchment is Templar in origin. So yes, I do think we've found the archive. As for the rest of it, I have no idea where that trail will lead us."

He tossed the parchment back inside the chest and closed the lid. "Salvatori and I will go and hire a van right now. The rest of you, stay here until we get back. We'll be as quick as we can, but it's bound to take us at least a couple of hours."

"What about Nico?" Mario asked.

"What about him?"

"Do you want to just leave him there? Or should we try to bury him?"

"He's already buried," Toscanelli replied, with a wintry smile. "He just needs covering up, and there are plenty of stones and rocks in this place that you can use. You can say a prayer for him as well. But before you do," he added, "one of you needs to climb down into that pit and recover his pistol and spare ammunition, and anything else he has in his pockets. It might be a hundred years before anyone else comes in here and stumbles on his remains, but it's not worth taking a chance."

Minutes later, Toscanelli and Salvatori stepped out of the cave and through the waterfall.

It was late afternoon, but the sun was still high in the sky as the two men walked briskly down the valley toward the stand of trees that led to the car park.

On the hillside above them, the spotter watched their progress while talking to their anonymous employer on his mobile.

"They're definitely not carrying anything?" he asked.

"Not unless it's small enough to fit into a pocket of their trousers or jackets," he replied. "I think," he added, "that these two are a part of the original group of four men who went into the cave after the British couple, but I can't be certain of that."

"Right. Keep watching."

"I'm getting fed up with this," the spotter murmured as the call ended. "I've no idea what the hell is happening inside that cave or who these men are. Or even who the voice at the end of the phone belongs to."

"You talk too much," the sniper said equably, well used to his colleague's grumbling and complaining. "Just remember we're being paid well for this, and so far we've not even had to kill anyone."

Salvatori backed the car out of the parking space as Toscanelli clicked the buckle of his seat belt into place.

"Head back to Schwyz," he instructed. "There should be a vehicle hire company somewhere there."

On the way down the hill toward the town, Toscanelli pulled out his smartphone and switched on the tracker.

Pulsing steadily on the screen was a single return, confirmation—not that any was needed—that the target's car was still where it should be, tucked in among the trees at the end of the road.

After a couple of false starts, the two Italians stopped outside a small commercial vehicle hire company on the outskirts of the town. Toscanelli went inside and a little over a quarter of an hour later he drove out of the yard that abutted the office building at the wheel of a medium-sized white closed van. The logo on the back said that it was called a "Jumper."

He stopped the vehicle by the curb and waited for Salvatori to walk over to him.

"There's no need for us to take both of these back up to the valley," he said. "Lock the car and come with me. We'll pick it up later."

About twenty minutes later, Toscanelli pulled the van

off the road and parked it so that the rear of the vehicle would be easily accessible. Then he and Salvatori walked through the patch of woodland and headed toward the forked waterfall at the end of the valley.

When the two secondary targets had left, the spotter had left the sniper in place, covering the entrance to the cave behind the waterfall, while he himself had retraced his steps, walking back along the hillside until he reached a position from which he could see the rudimentary parking area beside the woodland. And there he had remained until he saw the white van approaching. He waited until he was sure of the identity of the two occupants—they were the same two Italians who had earlier driven away in one of the hire cars—and then reported in.

"Two of them drove away in a car," he told their employer, "and they've just driven back in a white van, probably another hire job. My guess is that they found something bulky inside the cave, something too big to fit in a car, and they're about to bring it out and put it in the back of that van."

"Excellent news," the anonymous man replied, his voice tinged with excitement. "We're on our way. Whatever happens, do not let those men put anything in the back of that vehicle. How far is it between the waterfall and the parking area?"

"Probably a couple of hundred meters, and it's very secluded."

"Good. Try to intercept them somewhere in that valley. We'll be with you within the hour. Use whatever force is necessary, but try not to damage the van. We may need to use that ourselves."

Once Toscanelli and Salvatori stepped back through the waterfall and into the cave, they quickly organized the removal of the chests. The most awkward part of the operation was clearly going to be lifting them through the waterfall itself, because the weight of the water falling onto the chests would effectively increase their mass significantly, meaning that it would be impossible for only two men to carry one.

"We'll use those timbers," Toscanelli said. "We'll take a couple of the shorter ones and use them as a kind of stretcher for each of the chests. The wood is heavy, but doing that means we can have four people doing the lifting, and we can bring the chests out sideways, so that they'll be under the waterfall for the shortest possible period of time."

"Hang on a minute," Mario said. "I've got a better idea, or rather a variation on that. If we take two of the longer pieces of timber, we can extend them through the waterfall and into the pond and then slide the chests along them. Use the wood as a kind of ramp. Two people in here to lift the chests onto the timber, and two people standing in the pool outside to lift them off once they're clear of the falling water."

"That's good thinking," Toscanelli conceded, "and doing that should be a lot faster as well."

They selected two of the timbers that were roughly

equal in length and the same thickness and pushed them forward, through the curtain of water and down into the pool, making sure that they were lying parallel to each other, and about one meter apart.

Then Mario and Salvatori pulled on their waterproof clothing and stepped down into the pool. Inside the cave, Paolo and Carlo lifted up the first of the chests and rested it on the ends of the lengths of timber. While they held it in position, Toscanelli wrapped a piece of waterproof tarpaulin over the top of it, to protect it and its precious contents from the falling water.

When everything was ready, they pushed the old wooden chest forward, through the waterfall, and into the waiting arms of the other two men.

It was a lot easier than any of them had expected, the force of the waterfall actually helping to move the chests along the timbers, and it took less than fifteen minutes to complete the operation. They pulled the lengths of wood back into the cave, because leaving them exposed would obviously attract attention, and they knew they might still have to go back inside again, with the right kind of tools, if Vitale decided that they did need to recover the small chest that Mario had seen—or that he thought he might have seen, to be absolutely accurate—just before the Englishman triggered the final Templar booby trap.

With all six chests resting on the ground beside the waterfall, the Italians stripped off their waterproof garments and replaced them in the bag. Then four of them set off down the valley toward the hired van, each pair carrying one chest between them, and leaving Mario by the waterfall with the remaining four boxes, just in case some wandering stranger appeared.

But they were only about halfway down the valley when a figure seemed to almost literally materialize in front of them. One moment that part of the valley appeared to be completely empty apart from the four of them, and the next second a nightmarish shape, the outline blurred and distended by the ghillie suit it was wearing, seemed to erupt from the ground just yards away.

But it wasn't the shape of the figure that stopped the Italians in their tracks. It was the sight of the SPAS-12 combat shotgun it was holding, the muzzle pointed directly toward them, and the unmistakable sound as the stranger worked the action to chamber a round.

Mallory hadn't replied to Robin's remark, because there really didn't seem anything useful that he could say.

Instead he'd switched off his flashlight and waited for his eyes to become accustomed to the dark, hoping against hope that he would see some glimmer of light that might suggest there was a way out of their new prison. But the blackness was total, and after a couple of minutes he switched his flashlight on again.

"I was just—" he began, but Robin interrupted him.

"I know what you were trying to do."

Robin switched on her flashlight as well, shone it all around the space they had found themselves in, then switched it off.

"The Templars did a pretty good job of that, didn't

they?" she asked. "It could take days, maybe even weeks, to shift enough of those stones to get through to the other side, and we'd be dead long before we were even halfway there. In fact, it's even possible that that rockfall is airtight, in which case we'll suffocate long before we die of thirst or starve. There's a kind of rule of three somebody told me ages ago: three minutes without oxygen, three days without water, or three weeks without food. They're all death sentences. And not a single one of them is an attractive option."

Mallory nodded, because again he couldn't think of a useful response. His mind was racing, figuring the angles, wondering if there was any possible way out, anything they could do. But they already knew the tunnel had been hacked out of the solid rock, and Robin was right about the tumble of rocks and boulders in front of them: there were just too many, and most or all of them would be too heavy to move.

But they still had to try to find a way out. And so, doing their best to conserve the life of the batteries in their flashlights, they examined almost every inch of their rocky prison, tapping the walls and checking the floor and ceiling for any crack or crevice that might possibly provide an escape route. After about half an hour, they ended up back again against the blank end wall of the tunnel, at the spot where they'd started, their patience exhausted and their last hopes dashed.

"So that's it, then," Robin said. "We've looked everywhere, and there's definitely no handy escape tunnel. There's no way out of this place. We've escaped getting shot, but we've managed to imprison ourselves in a stone tomb instead. I think, on the whole, I would have preferred to get shot."

"Yes," Mallory said shortly. "And I know it's too late now, but I'm really sorry I got you into this."

"Hang on a minute." Robin sounded more irritated than anything. "You didn't get me into anything. I walked into this with my eyes open, just like you did. And I still think triggering that Templar trap was the right thing to do. If we hadn't, right now we'd be lying dead on the floor of this cave. At least we're still alive. Deep in the shit, I grant you, but still alive."

Mallory wrapped his arms around her and squeezed her tight, tucking her head under his chin.

"Sorry," he said again, staring into the utter blackness that surrounded and enveloped them.

Then he released her because against all the odds he'd just seen something. And just thought of something else.

Toscanelli reacted first. Maintaining his grip on the metal handle of the chest, he spoke in Italian to his companions. "He can't kill us all. On my command, drop the chests, split, and then take him down."

"*I* can't kill you all," the figure said, in equally fluent Italian, his words relayed through his mobile to the sniper on the hillside above, "but my friend can. Look at your chest."

Toscanelli glanced down and there, right in the middle of his torso, was a tiny but fiercely bright red dot. And even as he looked, the dot skipped sideways, settling on each of his companions in turn before returning to Toscanelli.

"You have some things that don't belong to you, inside those chests you're carrying, and the people we work for want them back. So what I want you to do is lower those two chests to the ground, because your arms must be aching by now. Then you can step back and then, one at a time, each of you take out your pistol with your left hand and put it on the ground. Don't even think about doing anything stupid, because if I don't kill you, my friend on the hillside with his long rifle certainly will. This is an open valley, so you've got nowhere to hide and you can't outrun a bullet."

The spotter gestured with the end of the barrel of the SPAS-12 and the Italians lowered both the chests, then followed his instructions and removed their pistols as well. Once all five weapons—Toscanelli had been carrying Nico's pistol in his pocket as well as his own—were on the ground, the spotter ordered the men to step back and sit down cross-legged, because that would make it impossible for any of them to get up quickly. Then he collected the weapons and placed them on the ground behind him and well away from the Italians.

"Now what?" Toscanelli demanded, his voice grating.

"Now we wait."

"What for?"

"For some other people to arrive. When they do, they'll decide what to do with you."

Toscanelli didn't like the sound of that, but he—and the others—knew there was nothing they could do about it. Right then, they were outgunned and vulnerable. Their only ace in the hole was Mario, still armed and no doubt watching what was happening from beside the waterfall. But Toscanelli also knew that the sniper, hidden somewhere on the neighboring hillside, would undoubtedly be watching him as well as them, and at the first hostile move could kill him as easily as swatting a fly.

The only sound in the valley, apart from the occasional snatch of birdsong and the noise of insects, was the continuous and unvarying roar of the waterfall, but then a new sound began to intrude. At first, it seemed little more than a subtle alteration in the noise of the tumbling water, but after a few moments it was obvious to all of them that the direction the sound was coming from was entirely different—from down the valley rather than from its end—and that the noise was mechanical in origin. It was the sound of a big diesel engine, probably turbocharged, and within seconds it was also clear that there was more than one vehicle.

Out of sight of all of the participants, about a minute later three Mercedes four-by-four G-Wagens drove up to the end of the road and parked in a line across the center of the open area. Six men, all wearing dark suits, emerged from them, stood together in a group for a few moments, then set off through the patch of woodland toward the end of the valley.

"Company," the sniper said softly into his Bluetooth earpiece. "Six men, no visible weapons, approaching from behind you."

"Understood."

The spotter glanced quickly over his shoulder, then looked back at the Italians. He moved over to one side, away from the hillside where his partner was located so as not to get in his line of fire—you could never be too careful in his game—and clear of the path the six new-comers were taking.

Nobody spoke. Toscanelli and his companions were switching their attention between the approaching men and the spotter, just in case any opportunity to escape or turn the tables presented itself, though the ever-present unwinking red eye of the sniper's laser target designator, roaming among them, ensured that they didn't dare move.

The six men came to a halt just a few feet away.

Toscanelli stared at them. They looked like successful middle-aged businessmen, which was not at all what he had expected. Their dark suits and highly polished shoes sug-gested they would be far more at home in a boardroom or office somewhere than in an anonymous valley deep in the Swiss countryside. They didn't look like criminals, and that at least suggested that he could try to negotiate with them.

"Six men went inside the cave," the spotter reported in German as the new arrivals stopped and looked at him, "but only these five came out. The principal targets, the English man and woman, are still in there. I stopped these four carrying these two chests down the valley. The fifth man is still up there near the waterfall, with another four chests. He hasn't moved since I showed myself."

"And your colleague?" one of the men asked. "Where is he?"

"On the hillside, covering all of us."

"Can you ask him to join us?" the man asked, glancing toward the side of the hill.

The spotter shook his head firmly. "He'll stay where he is. He's my insurance policy against any possible problems."

The man's smile slipped slightly.

"Do you think we intend to betray you?" he asked. "Try to shoot you, or something?"

"I have no idea what you intend to do," the spotter said. "But I've been betrayed before. So he stays where he is, watching everything that happens, until this is over. If I go down, he'll kill every one of you. And we're linked through our mobiles as well, so he can hear everything that I say."

"There'll be no deception on our part; of that I can assure you."

"So you say." The spotter sounded entirely unconvinced. "Anyway, this is your show, and we've done our bit in stopping these guys, so over to you."

Toscanelli had watched, but not understood, the exchange in German between the two men, but he had formed the opinion that they were not on the best of terms. Perhaps working together out of necessity, but coming from very different molds: probably principal and mercenary. So as the man in the suit turned in his direction, he spoke up.

"Before you do anything," he said in English, hoping it might be a common language, "you need to know that we all hold diplomatic passports, and that our whereabouts is known to our government."

The man stared at him for a moment, then nodded.

"I already knew that," he replied. "I presume you're either Marco Toscanelli or Salvatori Vitolli, as those two were the last of the group to arrive in Switzerland, presumably only traveling here after your minions had identified the target. But I doubt very much if your government has the slightest idea where any of you are, because no government actually issued your passports. That was the Sovereign Military Order of Malta, though I've no doubt you've been keeping your Dominican masters in the Via di Sant'Alessio fully briefed with your progress."

That was absolutely the last thing that Toscanelli had expected the man to say, and he immediately revised his opinion of the new arrivals. They might look like businessmen, but the level of knowledge that that man had just displayed meant that either he was a senior member of the Swiss government or alternatively he had access to somebody who was. And that altered the game, and the odds.

"What are you going to do with us?" Mario asked.

"Anything we want," the man in the suit said coldly. "It all depends on what we find inside those chests."

38

Canton of Schwyz, Switzerland

"We're not dead yet," Mallory said, "and something's just dawned on me."

"What? And this had better be good."

"Two things. First of all, I can see just the faintest glimmer of light down there. It must have taken all this time for my eyes to adjust to the darkness."

"You mean there is a way out? You can see it?"

"Not exactly. Or not yet, anyway. But think about it," he went on, taking Robin's hand and leading her down the cavern toward the rockfall. "We've just triggered the Templars' last booby trap in this cave system. When they constructed it, they would have known that releasing that timber was going to completely block the tunnel—which it has—but as we said before, they weren't suicidal. And they would also have known that if they were being attacked by a large force, that rockfall wouldn't have been enough. A hundred men, equipped with picks and shovels and ropes, would be able to get through it in a few days, and if they did, then whatever assets the Templars had dragged in here to this end of the tunnel and were trying to protect would be captured."

"Which means what, exactly?"

"Which means that the rockfall trap could only ever have been intended to be a delaying tactic, just something to hold up their enemies long enough for the Templars to escape and to take their assets with them. There *has* to be another way out of here."

"Are you just saying that to keep my spirits up?" Robin asked, more than a hint of weariness in her voice.

"No. Definitely not. Look, we know the walls and floor here are solid, and the Templars would have known roughly how big an area those rocks would occupy once they were released, so the only possible way out of here is straight up. In fact, straight up the hole that those rocks have just come out of. It's the only possible escape route."

Robin grabbed his arm.

"Now, *that* is bloody good thinking," she said. "Let's get to it."

The height of the tunnel was around twelve feet, and as they approached the edge of the fallen rocks they shone their flashlights upward, into the dark cavity out of which the boulders had tumbled.

It was roughly circular, almost like the bottom of a funnel down which the stones had tumbled. That was not unexpected, given what they had witnessed, but Mallory realized it posed a very obvious problem: how were they going to be able to climb up it?

"I'll clamber up these rocks and take a look," he said, switching off his flashlight as Robin turned hers on to guide his footsteps.

The boulders were heavy enough that he had no doubt they would provide a firm foothold, and in a few seconds he was able to look up into the open space above him. And as he did so, he began to laugh.

"What is it?"

"I'll do better than tell you," Mallory said. "If you come up here I'll show you."

He shone the beam of his flashlight so that Robin could see the best route to climb, and in seconds she was standing beside him.

"So show me."

Mallory shone his flashlight up, the beam revealing the smooth walls above them.

"There's no way we're going to be able to climb that," Robin said, "so I hope that wasn't what you were laughing at."

"It wasn't. You know we can't climb that, and I know we can't climb that. But there's something else."

With a gesture to his colleagues to follow him, the man strode across to the first of the chests and lifted the lid. He and the other men peered inside, and then one of them reached into the chest and took out a handful of documents. He selected one of them, a folded sheet of parchment, opened it up, and then handed it to the man who was clearly the oldest member of the group.

He studied it carefully, his eyes and his right forefinger tracing the lines of faded Latin text, while the other men watched.

After a few moments, he shook his head, folded the parchment again, and handed it back, taking a second document from the other man. This time, his inspection was even quicker, and at the end of it he again shook his head. He issued a brief instruction in German, handed back the document, and stepped over to the open chest. There, he thrust his hands down into the pile of documents, reaching deep into the chest. He seized something, held it out, and looked at it. And, again, he shook his head, tossing the piece of folded parchment back into the chest.

He strode over to the other chest, opened it, and began scrabbling through the documents that it contained. He selected three from different levels in the contents and inspected each in turn, with the same result.

He called out the name Marcel, and the man who appeared to be the leader of the small group, the one who had spoken to Toscanelli, walked over to him and they had a brief conversation. Marcel then stepped in front of the seated Italians and issued a series of simple instructions.

"You will go back to the waterfall and bring the remaining four chests here," he ordered. "I presume the other member of your group waiting there is armed, so just in case you get any ideas about indulging in some heroics, let me remind you that the sniper will be watching everything you do. So when you get about twenty meters from that man, you are to tell him to take out his pistol, hold it up so that the sniper can clearly identify it as his weapon, and he is then to throw it into the pool below the waterfall. If he fails to do this or there is any doubt that he has actually disposed of it, I will instruct the sniper to kill one of you. The remaining four, or five if you've behaved, can carry the chests. If any of you do anything other than follow those instructions, the sniper will kill you. Now go."

Hardly taking their eyes off the spotter and the muzzle of his combat shotgun, the Italians clambered to their feet and headed up the valley toward the waterfall.

"Is there anything we can do?" Mario asked, once they were out of earshot.

"Nothing," Toscanelli replied bitterly. "At the moment, they hold all the cards. But all of you, keep your eyes open and if you see an opportunity, take it."

"More important," Mallory went on, "the Templars also knew that they couldn't climb it." He shifted slightly to one side and pointed. "So they helpfully built a staircase."

He pointed his flashlight over to one side so that Robin could see what he had found. A matter of about three feet above them, just above the bottom of what Mallory had mentally termed "the funnel," and in an oval opening on one side, was the start of a rough-hewn staircase that led upward, curving gently out of sight.

"That was their escape route, the way out of here that they would use as a last resort," he said. "I've no idea where it goes, but I can't believe it won't lead somewhere that will get us out of this cave system."

They climbed down from the rock pile and Mallory retrieved most of the length of the climbing rope, cutting it off where it vanished underneath the fallen stones. He knew they wouldn't need the rope to reach the stone staircase, but he thought it might well prove useful later.

The presence of the staircase also meant that they could take the small chest with them. It was heavy, but Mallory could lift and carry it unaided if necessary, and in the narrow confines of the staircase they would be able to manage it between them.

"You know," Mallory said as they reached the top of the rock pile again and prepared to start their ascent, "this is a really clever piece of design. And it must've been bloody hard work to construct it. There was probably a natural cleft in the rock already that connected the end of the tunnel to the mountainside above. I guess they opened it up to create the funnel, and hacked the staircase into the rock alongside it to provide their escape route. They would then have had to build that massive wooden platform down in the tunnel to seal the base and erect the heavy timbers to hold it in place before they filled the funnel with stones from the top."

"And of course the rockslide did two separate things," Robin agreed. "It blocked the tunnel to keep their enemies at bay, and would also have provided the Templars with a way of climbing up to reach the bottom step of the staircase, just as we're doing now. You're right: it's a very clever idea that, as it's turned out, has worked exactly as they'd intended, just about seven hundred years later than they would probably have expected."

The staircase was twisting and narrow, the builders obviously having taken advantage of the natural fissures and cracks in the rock to make their work easier, and it changed direction fairly frequently, though always keeping close to the side of the funnel, as they saw at intervals.

Neither of them was counting steps, but Mallory guessed they'd probably climbed at least fifty or sixty before they finally saw daylight in front of them. A few seconds later, they reached the end of the stone staircase and stepped out of a more or less oblong opening and onto a flat stone at the bottom of a pit about eight feet deep. Set into the sides of it were flat stones, clearly intended as steps to allow someone to leave the pit.

Carrying the chest up them was clearly not practical, because they were far too narrow, so Mallory took out his climbing rope, lashed it carefully around the chest, and then climbed out of the pit, carrying the remainder of the rope. Once he was standing on level ground, he pulled on the rope as Robin lifted the chest from the stone below, and in a couple of minutes they were both out of the pit and looking around, the chest lying on the ground in front of them.

Robin looked back down into the pit with a thoughtful expression on her face.

"I know what you're thinking," Mallory said. "These hills are probably full of hikers during the summer months, and the top of that staircase is clearly visible, so why didn't somebody spot it?"

"Got it in one," Robin said. "So what's the answer?"

Mallory grinned at her. "I think it's really very simple. Nobody spotted the staircase because it wasn't there. Look, the sides of the pit are bare earth. If they'd been exposed for any length of time, there'd be grass and plants growing all over them. I think that stone we stood on to climb out was originally at ground level, just another rock sticking out of the grass on the hillside. But unlike every other stone, it was resting on the top of that pile of rocks that tumbled down into the tunnel. When those rocks were freed, it fell down about eight feet and jammed itself, probably into a narrow cleft in the bedrock below, exactly as the Templars intended, and in doing so it exposed the staircase and at the same time provided a stable platform that they could have used to get out."

Robin looked at him. "I know I wasn't entirely convinced you were doing the right thing down there, but I'm really glad you spotted that release device and decided to activate it. Talk about a clean getaway. Do you think the Italians are at the bottom of that rock pile, or on the other side of it?"

Mallory shrugged. "We were able to get out of the way easily enough, so I don't see any reason why they couldn't have done the same. And that means they're not out of the game. They can get out of the cave system the same way we came in, so we'll probably run into them again."

"That's what I thought, so what do we do now?"

Mallory pointed at the chest. "What we can't do is run around Switzerland carrying that between us. So we need to walk down this mountain and work our way around the hills and back to where we left the car. And because we know that the Italians have been following us, we need to find another hotel and another car as soon as possible."

"And then?"

"And then we see exactly what we've got in that chest. Once we know that, we'll be able to decide what to do about it."

When the Italians reached the waterfall, they did precisely what they had been told to do, and about ten minutes later they'd walked back to where the other men waited and lowered both chests to the ground beside the first two. Then they repeated the journey, and recovered the final two chests.

Once again, the older man selected a random sample of documents from each of these chests as well, and examined them carefully. But none of the documents appeared to be what he was looking for.

Again, he had a brief conversation in German with Marcel, who then walked over and stood directly in front of Toscanelli.

"What do *you* think is in those chests?" Marcel asked.

The Italian knew there was no point in prevaricating. In his view, the identity of the documents—what they were—was self-evident.

"I believe we've found the Archive of the Knights Templar," he said simply.

Marcel clapped his hands in a manner that could only be described as ironic. "Bravo. Well done. And that's exactly what you have found. Unfortunately we know from our research that the order maintained two separate archives. The one that's contained in these chests is certainly one of them, but not the one we're looking for. What you've stumbled upon are the day-to-day records of the transactions that the Templars conducted, the loans, deposits, and payments and so on that they made as a part of their normal business. What we're looking for is the other archive, the records of major capital acquisitions, grants of land and property, and the like. That would fit in a box that would be, most probably, much smaller than even one of these chests, and it would almost certainly be locked."

Marcel looked appraisingly at Toscanelli.

"Now," he said, "despite your diplomatic passports and the illegal weapons you were all carrying, I'm quite sure that your interest in the Templar Archive is purely academic. No doubt you intend to take these chests and the documents that they contain back to Rome with you where they can be properly studied and eventually a few selected items might be placed on display in some of the better European museums. And the good news from your point of view is that we are perfectly prepared to let you do this. I noticed that you came here in a large van, easily capable of accommodating these six chests, and I might even be prepared to provide you with a document that will avoid the vehicle being inspected at the border, just in case your passports don't do the trick."

Toscanelli nodded, the man's comments reinforcing

his belief that Marcel was most likely a senior figure in the Swiss government.

"I have a feeling," he said, "that there's a large 'but' coming at the start of your next sentence."

"There is, and I'm glad we understand each other," Marcel said, with a brief and insincere smile. "All this is contingent upon you answering a couple of questions completely truthfully, and to my satisfaction. If you don't do that, we may just decide to dump your bodies in the cave behind the waterfall. Where, if I'm not mistaken, one member of your group has already lost his life, because he certainly hasn't walked out of the entrance. We'd rather not do that, because it would be messy and take time that we really haven't got, but just remember that it's still an option."

He again smiled bleakly at the Italian, and in that moment Toscanelli saw himself in the other man's eyes. He was a stone-cold killer as well, polished and urbane, but underneath the veneer of culture and civilization Toscanelli knew Marcel could be just as brutal and vicious as anyone he had ever met. Cooperating with him was the only way he and his men were ever going to walk out of that valley, and right then Toscanelli knew it.

"Now," Marcel continued, "have you also recovered a smaller chest or box?"

Toscanelli shook his head. "No. When we got inside the cavern, all we found were the six boxes you see here. But we weren't the first to get in there."

"I know. Mallory and Jessop were ahead of you."

"You know about them?" Toscanelli's surprise was obvious from the tone of his voice.

"We know almost everything. Our sources are both impeccable and reliable. Did you catch up with them in the tunnels or caves? They got inside sometime before you and your men did."

"We almost caught up with them in the final cavern, but they triggered an ancient Templar booby trap that nearly caught us. But what it did do was imprison them behind a wall of rock."

"Tell me what happened. From the time you entered the cave system."

Toscanelli briefly described how they'd followed the English couple, the booby trap that had killed Nico, and the trigger that had released the first rockfall.

"How did you get around it?" Marcel asked.

"The rocks didn't reach the roof of the cave, and we managed to shift enough of them to work our way up to the top."

"Carry on."

"When we got into the larger cavern, the chests weren't piled up, just standing on the floor of the cave, but I think when they'd been abandoned they'd probably been stacked one on top of the other, covering the entrance to the final tunnel. There were marks in the debris on the floor of the cave that suggested that."

"So presumably Mallory and Jessop had moved them," Marcel suggested.

"That's what I thought. We carried on along the

tunnel, and we'd almost reached the two of them at the very end of it when they used a rope to release another rockfall. It all happened so quickly that we couldn't see how they'd done it, but I suppose they'd identified another of the Templars' booby traps and decided to trigger it rather than face us."

"Presumably they knew you were going to kill them— that was your intention, obviously—so that might have seemed their only option at the time. They'd hope to find another way out rather than face a bullet."

"Maybe," Toscanelli agreed, "but it didn't do them any good. That last rockfall was even bigger than the first, and they were standing in a dead-end tunnel with no way out. They're going to die behind that rock pile."

"At least we know where they are," Marcel said, "and there's an obvious question I need to ask."

"I know," Toscanelli replied. "Did they have a smaller box or chest with them? And I can't give you an answer. I didn't see anything, but Mario"—he pointed at him—"thinks he might have seen something like that in the tunnel before the roof fell in."

"I can't be certain what it was," Mario said when Marcel turned his gaze to look at him, "but I think there was what looked like a box near the end of the tunnel. We only had flashlights, and we were trying to find the English couple, so that's what we were looking for. But my flashlight did pick out something. I'm sure of that."

"How big? Like a suitcase? Or something bigger?"

Mario paused before he replied, doing his best to replay the event in his mind. "Bigger, I think. What I really noticed was that it seemed out of place—I do remember that. Straight edges and square corners where everything else was rounded. The rocks, I mean."

Marcel nodded. "That could be what we're looking for. And at least we now know where it is." He paused for a few moments, considering, then continued. "That final rockfall—you said it blocked the tunnel completely, but presumably it would be possible to move enough of the stones to get through to the other side?"

"Yes," Toscanelli agreed, "but it wouldn't be easy, and you'd probably need special equipment, hydraulic jacks, hoists, and that kind of thing, because some of the stones are definitely too big to be moved by muscle power alone. But a properly equipped team of men could probably get through it in a couple of days."

"We'll think about that," Marcel said. "But I think we'll leave it for two or three weeks to make sure that Mallory and Jessop are dead. That will save us having to shoot them if they're still alive when we break through, and means we can explain away their deaths as a potholing expedition that went disastrously wrong."

He glanced at Toscanelli, then swept his gaze along the line of seated men, considering his options.

"I think you'd all better leave," he said. "Leave this valley, and get out of Switzerland. As soon as possible. Take the chests with you because we don't want them. I'm sure you'll be able to talk your way across the border into Italy with them. Leave the weapons. We'll take care of them. If I see any of you again, I'll have you killed. Now go."

Twenty minutes later, Toscanelli watched Salvatori and

Mario lift the final chest up and into the back of the closed van.

"That's it," he said as Mario closed and locked the rear doors of the vehicle. "We're out of here."

"Where are we going?" Mario asked. "And what are we going to do about the English couple?"

"We're going to do exactly what that Swiss guy told us to do, because we don't have any other choice. We've got the lost Archive of the Templars in the back of that van, and our first priority is to get it back to Rome. Don't forget that that Swiss expert—I suppose that's what he was—only looked at a handful of the documents they contain, and I think there's a good chance that the other deeds and stuff might well be somewhere in those chests, despite what he said. And as for Mallory and Jessop, they're as good as dead already, and they know it."

"And the smaller chest I saw?"

"I know we talked it up, but you aren't certain you saw a chest, Mario. But even if you did, there's nothing we can do about it. You can bet that the Swiss will keep that cave entrance under surveillance from now on until they move in and shift those rocks, and if we try to get involved they'll just blow us away. I know Marcel's type: he's a killer and if he said he was going to shoot us, that's exactly what he'd do. We're lucky we're walking away from this right now."

Toscanelli looked at the men standing in a rough half circle around him. "This is the end of it as far as we're concerned. Mario—you and Carlo can go in the van. Get back to the hotel, pick up your stuff, and then drive the van to Rome. I'll go in the car with Salvatori and Paolo. We'll collect the other hire car, hand them both back, and then fly out of here."

The three men watched as the van reversed out of the parking space, maneuvered around the three Mercedes G-Wagens that partially obstructed the road, and headed off down the valley. Then they walked over to their hire car. Paolo reversed out and then swung the steering wheel to follow the white van. As they started driving down the road, Salvatori glanced out of the side window by the backseat.

"Stop," he said urgently.

Paolo hit the brakes hard, and the car slewed to a stop.

"What?" Toscanelli demanded.

"Over there," Salvatori said, pointing to the opposite side of the rough parking area.

"I don't see anything."

"Exactly. That's the point. The car that Mallory and Jessop were driving has gone. Somebody's driven it away."

Toscanelli pushed open the passenger door and stood beside the vehicle, his keen eyes checking every possible parking spot at the end of the road. But Salvatori was right. There was no sign of the car that he knew the English couple had been using.

He sat down again in the front passenger seat and motioned for Paolo to drive on. At the same time, he took out his smartphone, swiped his fingertip across the screen to wake it up, and then navigated to the tracker app. He studied the screen for a few moments, then started laughing.

"The tracker is on the move," he said.

"They must be in front of us," Paolo said. "How far ahead?"

"They aren't ahead of us, according to this," Toscanelli replied, "and nor are they behind us. In fact, they're exactly matching pace with us."

Both Paolo and Salvatori instinctively glanced out of the windows, despite already knowing that they were in the only vehicle on the road.

"I don't know—" Paolo began, but Toscanelli immediately interrupted him.

"I know you don't. That's why I do your thinking for you. It means that Mallory must have found the tracker we placed on his car, and he's returned the favor. Somewhere on this vehicle the tracker is working perfectly, sending a signal to the three of us, sitting inside it."

"And that also means," Salvatori said, "that the English couple must have somehow managed to find a way out of that cavern after the rockslide."

"Exactly. And that means we know something that the Swiss don't, because they'll be looking in the wrong place, digging their way through a massive rockfall into an empty chamber. So now we're back in the game."

39

Switzerland

"What made you think there was a tracking device on the car?" Robin asked.

"Just because of the way they knew where we were. On these roads, up here in the mountains, there isn't that much traffic, and I was taking particular note of any cars that seemed to be following us. Which was easy, because there really weren't any. But despite that, when we went into that cave system, the Italians turned up right after us, and that more or less meant that they already knew where we were going. So there really had to be a tracker somewhere on the car. It was the only thing that made sense."

Robin's face clouded slightly. "And you still think it was a good idea to attach the tracker to that car, the one the Italians must have been using?"

"I don't think it'll make any difference. They would have seen that our car had gone when they left the parking area at the end of the valley, and that would have told them that we must have found a way out of the cave. And I think attaching the tracker to their car would have sent them a clear message that we know they're watching us and that we'll be on our guard."

"What about the second tracking device?"

"Yes. That was a bit unexpected. I can only assume that it was a kind of belt-and-braces precaution on their behalf, having a second tracker already in place in case the first one failed. It was odd that they were two different types, though. I would have expected them both to be the same model."

When they'd returned to their car, they put the small chest in the trunk. Mallory hadn't started the engine, just let the car roll slowly backward down the slight slope before turning it around, again using the vehicle's momentum, and coasting down the hill and away from the valley. He'd switched on the ignition so that the steering wheel was unlocked, and waited until they were some distance away from the patch of woodland before starting the engine by slipping the gear lever into third and releasing the clutch pedal as they coasted down the hill. Hopefully the sound of the engine starting wouldn't have been heard by the Italians, or by the unidentified owners of the three black Mercedes G-Wagens. And there'd been no sign of pursuit, so Mallory reckoned it had worked.

They'd driven straight back to their hotel, collected their bags, and checked out. They'd talked about surrendering the hire car, just to muddy the waters somewhat. But eventually they decided that doing so wouldn't really help, because it would take time that they hadn't got. And they would also have had to take a taxi to the new car rental company, and even the most unobservant cabdriver might well notice and remember an English couple hauling around an obviously medieval chest.

Speed, Mallory believed, was far more important, and trying to track down their rental vehicle without relying on a tracker would be difficult, perhaps even impossible. They needed to get out of Schwyz so that the Italians would have no idea where to even start looking for them. He flipped a mental coin and steered the car north out of the town.

"Where are we going?" Robin asked.

"I don't know exactly, but we're heading northish up toward Lake Zürich. There are good fast roads up there, plus railway stations, and the border with Liechtenstein isn't that far away if we need to get out of the country. There are several towns along the southern shore of the lake, so we should find somewhere to stay there fairly easily."

"And then?"

"And then we go to ground and try to work out what to do next. I don't want to try to cross the border until we know for sure what's in that chest."

They ended up in Richterswil, very close to the lake-shore, but didn't go near any of the hotels, because Mallory was worried. Instead he steered the car into a public parking area near a large group of shops, chose a spot at the far side, well out of the way, and switched off the engine.

"I've been thinking about that second tracking device," he said, an apparent non sequitur to their previous conversation. "There really wouldn't be any need for the Italians to have put two of them on the car—one would have been quite enough."

"And your point is?"

"I'm wondering if we've come to the attention of somebody else here in Switzerland. Or rather if what we've been doing has raised a red flag or two. Basically were our movements being monitored by some branch of the Swiss authorities, *as well as* those Italians? Hence the two trackers. One under each rear wheel arch."

"I see what you mean," Robin said. "If they are interested in us, renting a hotel room would be a really good way of letting them know where we are. They could track us by our passport numbers or credit cards, and we'd definitely have to use a card to take a hotel room."

Mallory shook his head. "We could try to find some accommodation that's off the books—a guesthouse or bed-and-breakfast place—but we could try something else first."

"What?"

He explained what he had in mind, and Robin nodded.

"That might work," she agreed, "and the worst-case scenario is that they'd turn us away, so let's give it a try. And if we can swing it, that would give us some breathing space and keep us below the radar at the same time."

"Right. Now there's something else I want to do first."

Mallory and Robin climbed out of the car, opened the lid of the trunk, and spent a few minutes examining the wooden chest. Then Robin sat down in the driver's seat and settled down to wait while Mallory headed off to the group of shops they'd seen when they approached the car park.

One was a kind of general and hardware store, where he found a good selection of ironmongery. He wandered the aisles, picking up and discarding packets, and eventually selected an assortment of nails, bolts, and screws of different diameters, but all between four and six inches in length. About three doors down was a shop selling travel accessories, including cases and bags. There, he bought a capacious soft suitcase that looked as if it would be easily big enough to hold the wooden chest, and then he carried his purchases back to the hire car.

With Robin helping him, he lifted the chest and maneuvered it inside the soft bag and zipped it up, so that it looked just like a piece of regular travel luggage rather than an obviously medieval wooden chest.

"That's a good fit," Robin said approvingly. "What about the other stuff?"

"In my pocket," Mallory said, pulling out a small paper bag and putting it in one of their other cases.

They drove out of the car park and headed east, toward the Swiss border with Liechtenstein, staying off the main roads and concentrating on the back streets where they would be more likely, Mallory hoped, to find a small hotel where the staff wouldn't ask too many awkward questions.

Robin was using the mapping application on her smartphone to guide him toward the few hotels she'd found listed in the database. They rejected two for different reasons, but when the third came into view they decided it was worth trying.

"Let me do the talking," Robin said. "I speak a bit of German, but I can also do the damsel-in-distress routine fairly convincingly. All you have to do is stand behind me looking worried and pissed off."

"I can handle that," Mallory said.

It was a small hotel, probably no more than a couple of dozen rooms, and with a small bar cum lounge on one side of the reception hall. The entrance was paneled in dark wood to about waist height and with somewhat faded wallpaper in a kind of floral pattern above this. It gave the appearance of a hotel that had left its best days behind it, but that still tried to cling to the values and traditions of the past. All this Mallory noted as he followed Robin over to the reception desk.

The girl standing behind it was wearing a dark green jacket with some kind of logo emblazoned on the left side of the chest, and greeted them with a warm smile and a couple of sentences in high-speed German that washed completely over Mallory's head.

Robin moved her right hand up and down as if she were patting the head of an invisible child, the universal signal from one person to another to speak more slowly. Then she launched into a halting explanation in the same language to explain why neither of them had either a credit card or a passport about their person. But she'd barely even got started when the receptionist interrupted her.

"If you prefer," she said, "we can speak English."

They did prefer, very definitely.

"We have a problem," Robin began. "Our car was broken into earlier today and my handbag and my husband's travel bag were both taken. We lost our passports and all our credit cards, but fortunately we were shopping at the time and so we still had cash in our pockets. We've contacted the Swiss police and we have been told to make a written report to them here in town tomorrow morning, but for now we just need a hotel room for a couple of nights."

The receptionist's smile had died away to a frown as Robin spoke.

"That is very unlike Switzerland," she said briskly when Robin had finished. "It was probably an illegal immigrant or someone of that sort who robbed you. But you obviously should not have left the car unattended, or at least taken your bags with you. But," she added, injecting a note of enthusiasm into her voice, "we can certainly let you have a room provided you have money to pay for it. We can process the registration information later, when you have had emergency travel documents issued to you."

She passed over a sheet of paper with room rates printed on it.

"These are our current rates," she said, "and in the circumstances we will obviously require payment in advance for both nights, and I'm afraid I'll have to ask you for a security deposit as well to cover the cost of any meals or drinks."

She took out a calculator, entered the figures that she needed, and then turned it around so that Mallory and Robin could see the final sum.

"Would that be all right?" she asked.

Mallory nodded and pulled out a wad of Swiss

francs—he'd drawn a decent sum at the airport when they arrived in Switzerland—counted out the required amount, and handed it over.

Ten minutes later, having registered as Mr. and Mrs. Devonshire, the first name that sprang into his head, Mallory carried the last of their bags—the soft suitcase containing the medieval chest—into the double room they'd booked on the second floor of the building. As Robin closed the door behind him, he unzipped the suitcase, lifted out the chest, and placed it on a small table against one wall of the room, a table that doubled as a desk. He looked carefully at the lid of the chest while Robin shone a flashlight at the old wood, supported by lightly rusted metal.

"There are quite a few holes in the wood," he said. "Might be a bit of trial and error."

"Try to keep the errors to a minimum," Robin said. "Trials I don't mind."

Mallory opened the paper bag, took out the nails, and began gently inserting them into the holes they'd seen on the lid of the chest.

"They should go quite a long way in," he said. "Some of these holes are only about half an inch deep, so they can't have anything to do with the mechanism."

Eventually he had identified three holes into which the five-inch nails sank virtually the whole way. He slid them home, then glanced at Robin.

"I think that's it," he said, "but there's only one way to find out."

He used the double-ended Allen keys to unlock the

chest, but took no chances when he lifted the lid. He placed the chest on the floor, made sure Robin was well clear, then stood behind it and lifted the lid. The lethal blades that had been triggered the first time he did that remained harmlessly in place, which was almost an anticlimax. Clearly he'd identified the correct locking positions and the nails he'd inserted had jammed the mechanism.

The logic was simple enough. Whoever had designed the antitheft device built into the lid of the chest must have also incorporated some means of deactivating the mechanism. Otherwise it would have been triggered every single time the chest was opened. They had spotted several holes driven through the metal scrollwork that adorned the lid, and it seemed obvious that some of these had to have been where the locking bars would have been inserted.

"Let's see what we've got," Robin said. She stepped forward and took half a dozen documents from the top of the pile inside the chest.

Toscanelli drummed his fingers impatiently on the steering wheel of the hire car, his gaze flicking between the rearview mirror and the entrance to the hotel where Mallory and Jessop had been staying. Paolo was checking the hotel's parking area while Salvatori had gone inside to inquire at the reception desk about his "English friends."

Both men returned to the car at almost the same time and reported the inevitable: the hire car had vanished from the car park, and the targets had both checked out about two hours earlier.

"I asked the receptionist if she knew where they'd gone," Salvatori elaborated, "and she told me they were heading to Zürich to fly back to England."

Toscanelli snorted in disgust.

"The only reason they would have told her that," he said, "was if they were doing something entirely different. My guess is that they're still in this area, somewhere. The trick is going to be finding them."

Realistically he had only one option. The Dominican Order consisted of a fairly small number of active members, no more than about six thousand, the vast majority employed on pastoral or religious duties in various locations around the world, but almost from the start the order had made a determined effort to recruit anonymous helpers, known within the order as tertiaries. These were lay or secular members of the Ordo Praedicatorum, meaning the Order of Preachers, because preaching the Gospel and combating heresy were two of the most important tasks for which the Dominicans were created. Tertiaries subscribed to the aims and beliefs of the order but were unable because of their employment, personal circumstances, or other reasons to become Dominican friars or priests. Tertiaries performed vital duties for the order behind the scenes, obtaining information, supplying documents and equipment, and generally assisting members as much as they could within the constraints of their employment.

Toscanelli had no idea whether there were any tertiaries in Switzerland who could help him track down Mallory and Jessop. That information was closely guarded, but obviously Silvio Vitale, as the head of the section, would have access to the classified database that would provide the answer.

Toscanelli rang the direct line number, and seconds later he was talking to Vitale himself.

"We know what Mallory and Jessop were looking for," he began. "They were following clues that led them to the Templar Archive, though we still don't know exactly what those clues were."

"And did they find it?" Vitale demanded.

"Yes and no."

"Don't talk in riddles, Toscanelli. I'm not in the mood for it."

"Right. They did find it, but there isn't just one archive, but two of them. Most of the documents seem to refer to their daily transactions, and those were stored in six large wooden chests, which Mallory and Jessop led us to."

"Where were they hidden?"

"In a complex cave system underneath a Swiss mountain, the entrance concealed behind a waterfall. We followed them inside, and we now have possession of this archive. Mario and Carlo are transporting those chests to Rome by road right now."

"That's good news." Vitale sounded both surprised and pleased, an unusual combination for him. "So, what are you and the other three men doing right now?"

The question wasn't unexpected, and Toscanelli knew there was no point in trying to duck it. He'd delivered one piece of good news: now it was time to pass on the bad.

"We lost Nico," he said. "The cave system had three booby traps in it at least. Three that we know of, I mean. We managed to avoid two of them, but when we went in Nico was in the lead, and he fell into a well-concealed killing pit. He was dead the moment he hit the bottom. There was nothing any of us could do for him."

There was a heavy silence as Vitale digested this unwelcome information.

"You'd better hope that that is as high as the body count gets, Toscanelli. I suppose it goes without saying that Mallory and Jessop somehow managed to miss being killed by these ancient traps?"

"Yes. They avoided the killing pit by putting wooden planks over it, and they actually triggered the other two booby traps themselves because they knew we were getting closer to them. They've been very lucky."

"With those two," Vitale said, "I don't think luck has much to do with it. They've shown themselves to be particularly astute and very competent. So are you telling me that they beat you to the punch and that they have the other part of the Templar Archive? And is that part the more important of the two?"

"We can't be completely certain, but we think they did get out of the cave system carrying a small chest, and that most probably contains the most valuable part of the archive, yes. The problem we have now is that because we encountered them in the cave system, they obviously know we've been following them. We had their hotel under surveillance, and fitted a tracker in their hire car, but now they've checked out and removed the tracker, we've got no idea where to find them. Do we have a tertiary in the Swiss police force or some other organization over here who could help track them down?"

"Possibly. I'd need to check. What exactly do you want?"

"Ideally the location of whatever hotel they've moved to. Switzerland is highly regulated, so I don't think they could get into a hotel here without showing their passports or using a credit card. If their details don't turn up, it might be worth trying Liechtenstein and the other neighboring countries, just in case they've decided to cross a border. And if they've hired another car—which I think they could well have done, just to move the chest they found, unless they're still using their original vehicle—then the same sort of regulations will apply. So I'd like the make, model, color, and registration details of whatever vehicle they're now using."

"I'll see what I can do," Vitale said. "Try not to get any other members of your team killed in the meantime."

Toscanelli and his men weren't the only people interested in locating David Mallory and Robin Jessop.

The Mercedes sedan that had been parked near the hotel to monitor the conversations recorded by the voice-activated bug in their room had been replaced by a small and anonymous dark blue van, the rear section of which contained an impressive array of surveillance equipment of one sort or another.

When the technician climbed into the vehicle to check the recordings that afternoon, a task that he expected to be a mere formality bearing in mind the known movements of the two targets, he was slightly surprised to note that there were three bursts of activity in the room that day. The first two were predictable enough: the two targets chatting together as they prepared to leave the room after breakfast, and the sound of the chambermaid singing softly to herself when she arrived to make up the room about two hours later.

The third recording was very short, the bug obviously having been triggered by the sound of the door to the room opening. What followed was apparently the sound of hasty packing, interspersed by a number of brief comments and remarks exchanged between the targets.

The technician played it twice to ensure that he hadn't missed anything. Then he locked the van, walked into the hotel, and showed his identification to the receptionist. Faced with his official credentials, she had no trouble in confirming that Mallory and Jessop had checked out earlier that afternoon. She also passed on one other piece of information that was somewhat unexpected.

The bug was now obviously redundant, so the technician returned to the room, accompanied by the duty manager, who used his passkey to open the door, and removed it. He returned to the van, stowed both the bug and the handful of tools he'd used to remove it, and then called his superior.

The substance of that call was passed quickly up the chain until it reached Marcel, who was sufficiently perturbed by what he had heard to insist on speaking to the technician directly. "You're certain about the time they checked out?"

"Yes, sir. The receptionist showed me the hotel documentation, but also the credit card receipt for the final payment. That slip included the time that the card was swiped, so there's absolutely no doubt."

"And she also told you that somebody else had been asking when they left and where they'd gone?"

"An Italian, she thought," the technician replied, "but she couldn't be completely sure of his nationality."

"Right. Thank you."

Marcel turned to his colleagues, who had assembled in his office as soon as they had been told about the information obtained by the technician.

"We have a problem," he said. "The birds have flown the coop. Mallory and Jessop are definitely alive and definitely checked out of their hotel two or three hours after those Italians claim the rockfall imprisoned them in the tunnel."

"Do you think they were lying to us?"

Marcel shook his head. "No, I don't. I think it's much simpler than that. I think that last Templar booby trap did more than just block the tunnel so that the Italians couldn't get to them and kill them. It most probably opened up another tunnel or route that they used to escape. It was almost certainly a deliberate construction, intended to delay an attacking force and give the Templars time to get away."

"So, what do we do about it?"

"Three things," Marcel said crisply. "First, we'll send up a chopper to try to find whatever exit those two people used to get out of the cave system. Once we've done that, we'll send a team inside the mountain to check the situation. But the very first thing we do is find these two people. I want details of all registrations from every hotel in Switzerland checked, along with every car hire company. We are looking for either the name Mallory or Jessop. And the other thing we do is find those Italians, because it looks like they're still sniffing about. Oh," he added, "contact the sniper team and get those men back here. I don't think we've finished with them yet."

40

Switzerland

Almost three hours after she'd started, Robin leaned back in her seat and stretched her arms above her head.

"Coffee?" Mallory asked, pointing at the fairly limited hospitality tray on the other side of the room. "Or we can go down to the bar if you'd like something stronger."

"Coffee for now," Robin said, "but definitely something stronger later on."

Mallory filled the kettle from the tap in the bathroom sink and switched it on.

"So, what have we got?" he asked, ripping the tops off the sachets of coffee and pouring the powder into two cups.

"Documents," Robin replied. "Lots of old documents, all written in Latin. I've no doubt at all that they're genuine. And, basically, they're explosive. Every single one is some kind of deed or transfer, some just relating to a

single farm or a small tract of land, while others are con-
veyances relating to hundreds or even thousands of acres.
It's impossible to be sure of all the sizes because many of
them refer to landmarks that were around in the medieval
period but that have probably long since vanished. But
what they all do is state clearly and unequivocally that
these deeds are in perpetuity and are irrevocable, presumably because that was the way the Templars wanted the
transfers done. And almost every one hands the property
over not just to the Knights Templar order, but also to
the then grand master or some other named high official,
and on from him to his heirs and assignees should the
order cease to exist."

The kettle boiled and Mallory handed her the cup.

"What we're looking at here," she added, "is undeni-
able proof that potentially huge tracts of what is now
prime real estate throughout Europe don't actually belong
to the people who think they own them. There are deeds
relating to most of northern Paris, large sections of southern France in the old Languedoc region, parts of Germany and Austria, a large chunk of Switzerland, a lot of
Portugal, and huge tracts of land in Spain. And those are
just the bits I remember."

Mallory nodded and took a sip of his drink.

"That isn't exactly what I was expecting to find when
we set off on this quest," he said, "but in fact what we
recovered is potentially more valuable than the bullion
and other stuff that formed the main part of the Templar
treasury. At the time, these documents were obviously of
value because if the Templars owned a particular estate,

they could employ farmers to work the land on their behalf to generate an income, or simply sit back and collect the rents if that was more appropriate. What they couldn't possibly have known was the way that land values would increase after the Middle Ages."

"In fact," Robin pointed out, "it's not just an extraordinarily valuable resource. It's also extremely dangerous. Almost every country in Europe has one or more pieces of land mentioned in these documents. If it became common knowledge that the land on which a city like Toulouse, for example, has been built actually belonged to some descendant of a Templar grand master, the potential legal battles that could result might drag on for years, and with a very real probability that the courts would decide in favor of that descendant. The financial implications are immense. More to the point, I can absolutely see why somebody who found out about that and was facing financial ruin as a result would feel entirely justified in doing their best to destroy the original deed or transfer document."

"And to probably kill anyone who stood in their way," Mallory agreed. "Which creates the obvious question: what the hell do we do with it? With all these documents?"

"We're right in the firing line," Robin said, "and in this case, that isn't just a figure of speech." She paused for a few seconds, then nodded. "As I see it," she continued, "there are really only two options. First, we can destroy all the documents. Soak them in petrol and set fire to them, or something like that. I really don't want to do that, because every one of these documents is of vital historical importance, and that would just be archae-ological vandalism. And the other obvious problem with doing that would be convincing anybody else that the documents really had been destroyed. Just reducing them to ashes might not be enough to stop those Italians—and quite possibly forces sent out later by most of the govern-ments of Europe if news of the archive gets around—from trying to kill us.

"The second option is to somehow deliver the relevant documents to the nations that are affected by them, so that the government of the day can decide what to do. As far as I can see, that's just as fraught with problems as destroying the deeds, and probably would be no more successful in getting us out of the target zone. So I think the expression that pretty much covers our present situ-ation is 'screwed.' I wish we'd never found that bloody chest. What the hell are we going to do?"

"There is another option," Mallory said, after a few moments, "but the trick is going to be pulling it off."

Robin looked at him hopefully.

"Right now I'll consider anything," she said.

Mallory collected his thoughts and began outlining the glimmerings of a plan that had struck him while Robin was talking.

"I've been trying to do a bit of lateral thinking," he said, "trying to approach the problem from the other end, as it were."

"That sounds good, but what do you actually mean? What, exactly, is lateral thinking?"

"Have you ever heard the story of the merchant's daughter?"

"If this turns out to be a dodgy story full of sexual innuendo," Robin stated firmly, "then I'm quite likely to hit you over the head with that chest."

Mallory shook his head.

"There's no sex in it," he protested, "and it's not dodgy, whatever you mean by that. What it does is illustrate the art of lateral thinking quite neatly. Briefly, a merchant had a beautiful daughter, but business was bad and he was falling further and further behind with the rent. Eventually the landlord approached him and told him they had to sort it out. The merchant couldn't pay, and the landlord knew that, so he proposed an exchange. If the merchant would let him sleep with his daughter, then the landlord would wipe out the backlog of rent owing."

"I knew there was going to be sex in it," Robin protested.

"There isn't. Just wait. The merchant told his daughter what the landlord said, and explained their dire financial situation. The daughter was unhappy, obviously, about it, but because of her love for her father she agreed, with one caveat. And that was that they should leave it to chance. The landlord agreed to a change in the conditions. The element of chance was to be decided by the daughter picking a pebble out of a closed bag. If she picked the white pebble, then the backlog of rent would be written off, but she wouldn't have sleep with the landlord. If she picked the black pebble, then again the rent would be forgotten about but she would have to sleep with the man. When the three of them met outside the house to perform the wager, for want of a better expression, the daughter noticed that the landlord had actually put two black pebbles into the bag."

Mallory paused in his recitation and glanced at Robin.

"So the obvious question," he said, "is what she does next. If she accuses the landlord of cheating, then he'll probably foreclose on the rent and evict her and her father. If she picks a black pebble out of the bag, then she knows she'll have to sleep with the landlord. Looked at in conventional, straight-line linear thinking, that is her only option. She has to bite the bullet, take out the black pebble, and lie back and think of England or wherever she came from. But there is one thing she can do that will guarantee that the rent arrears will be forgotten about, and without her having to sleep with anybody."

He paused and looked at Robin quizzically. "Any ideas?"

Robin shook her head. "No, actually. I haven't. So what's the answer?"

"She uses lateral thinking. What she actually wants out of this is one of two things. Either a white pebble in her hand, or a black pebble in the bag. So she sticks her hand in, picks out one of the black pebbles, and immediately drops it on the ground. Then she turns to the landlord and smiles sweetly, apologizes for dropping the pebble, but simply tells him that if he looks in the bag he will see the color of the pebble that is left and that will confirm the color of the one that she had picked out. So instead of thinking in a linear fashion from the beginning of the problem to the end, what she did was start at the end with the result that she wanted and then work out how she could obtain that result."

"It's easy enough," Robin said, "when you explain it. But I think our problem is a bit more complicated than picking out a pebble from a closed bag."

"But we can use the same technique. What we want is to walk away from here, ideally with that chest and the documents intact and undamaged. So what we have to do is work out a way of achieving that, while at the same time letting the Italians and anybody else who's chasing us think that they've achieved their objective. Which is probably destroying the archive and killing us in the process."

"I did have one idea," Robin said tentatively. "It's a little complicated, and we need to start right now if it's going to work. And it is," she added, "a bit of lateral thinking, I suppose."

Five minutes later, the two of them walked out of the hotel, Mallory carrying the soft bag containing the chest of documents.

The crew of the military helicopter had been quickly but comprehensively briefed. The aircraft was to be flown by one of the two pilots while the other man concentrated his entire attention on the landscape beneath them. Behind the pilots, four men wearing military camouflage clothing studied the view out of the side windows of the aircraft. Their instructions were simple enough: they were to start from the forked waterfall at the end of the valley and cover the entire area around that position, looking for any kind of entrance into the cave system that the Swiss authorities now knew was located inside the mountain.

The search didn't take long. Almost as soon as the helicopter flew over the top of the waterfall, the brown-and-white scar on the otherwise green hillside immediately attracted the attention of the crew. Landing the aircraft on the slope was not practical, so the pilot brought it to a low hover and held it there while the four men in the passenger compartment climbed out, each carrying a bulky rucksack and wearing a sidearm. Once they had deplaned, the pilot lifted off and flew the aircraft to a level patch of ground about five hundred yards away, landed the helicopter, and shut down the engines. While finding what looked like the entrance to the caves hadn't taken very long at all, exploring them might be a very long job indeed.

The rucksacks they were carrying contained climbing equipment, including ropes, belaying pins, pitons, and all the rest of it, but almost as soon as the men reached the feature that had caught their eye, they realized that most of it was probably superfluous. The upper end of an ancient stone staircase was clearly visible, as were the stepping-stones that led down to it.

The leader of the group quickly assessed the situation and then issued his orders.

"You two stay here," he said. "Jacob and I will go down and check it out. If one of us is not back in thirty minutes, radio the pilot and update him on the situation, and then one of you—and only one—is to follow us down."

The two men removed powerful flashlights from their rucksacks, checked that their SIG P226 pistols were loaded and cocked, with the safety catches on, and then made their way cautiously down into the almost circular hole and from there began descending the stone staircase.

They were both back at the surface less than twenty minutes later. As soon as they'd climbed out of the hole, the leader used his short-range transceiver to summon the helicopter, and ten minutes after that the chopper rose high enough into the air to allow reliable mobile phone communication, and he called a mobile number that he had been given during the briefing.

"Yes?"

"It's Erich Weiss," he began. "We've located the entrance to the cave and two of us have been down to investigate it. As you instructed, we've taken a large number of photographs."

"And?"

"It's a fairly small cavern, more like a tunnel, really. The walls and end are solid rock, and the other part of it is completely blocked by a huge rockfall. Getting into it was easy because whoever built it—you said it might have been a Templar construction—cut a stone staircase into the roof of the tunnel that led all the way up. The rockfall itself provided access to the bottom of the staircase, which meant that—"

"Never mind that. Was there anything in the cavern? Anybody or anything?"

"Nothing at all, though clearly somebody had been there, because we saw the end of a new climbing rope sticking out from underneath the rocks."

"That's all we need to know. You can return to base and stand down, but stay at five minutes' notice. Draw assault rifles and ammunition. I've detailed a sniper team to join you, so expect them to reach you within the hour. We may need you to stop a vehicle leaving the country."

For a couple of seconds, Weiss didn't realize that the other man had ended the call. He removed the earphones—essential for making a telephone call in the noisy confines of the helicopter—and put the phone in his pocket. Then he moved the boom mike on his headset in front of his mouth, switched on the intercom, and told the pilot what he wanted him to do.

"Back to base," he instructed. "Make sure the aircraft is fully fueled, and stand down to alert five. We may need to get airborne again at really short notice, and I've been told to draw more weapons. And we'll have a couple of passengers as well. A sniper team will be flying with us as a precaution."

"As a precaution against what?" Jacob asked.

"Right now I don't really know."

When Silvio Vitale rang Toscanelli's mobile about three hours later, he had no concrete news to impart.

"Basically," he said, "they seem to have dropped off the radar. The last credit card transaction that Mallory undertook was settlement of his hotel bill in Schwyz. Since then, there have been no charges placed on his card of any sort. No cash withdrawals, no hotel booking, no hire car deposit, not even a tank of petrol. It's possible that they've already left Switzerland, and we're also running checks on the neighboring countries, but so far with no results. Don't forget," he added, "that these transactions sometimes take a while to filter through the system, so it is possible that they have booked a hotel room but we just haven't heard about it yet. We have two tertiaries looking into this now. We're also checking traffic cameras for any sightings of their original hire car, just in case they're still driving it."

That definitely wasn't what the Italian wanted to hear.

"We need something, anything," he replied. "At the moment, we're stuck here in Schwyz because there's no point in moving unless we have a definite indication of where these two are."

Toscanelli fell silent for a couple of seconds, wondering if he should mention the other matter that he had so far not discussed with Vitale.

"There's something else," he said. "We weren't the only ones looking for Mallory and Jessop in that cave system. When we came out we were stopped by a sniper team, the man with the long rifle hidden somewhere on the hillside and completely out of our reach, while his spotter turned up at the bottom of the valley with a combat shotgun. There was nothing we could do about either of them, and they held us there waiting for some other people to appear."

"Go on." Vitale's voice sounded dangerously calm.

"A group of six men appeared, and from their appearance and conduct, and what they obviously knew, my guess is that their leader was a senior member of the Swiss government. They were after the chests as well, and they looked at the contents of the six that we had recovered, but decided that they weren't whatever they were looking for. They told us to leave Switzerland immediately, and threatened to kill us if we didn't. Have your contacts heard anything about this?"

"It was mentioned, yes," Vitale replied, "by one of the men I have spoken to. I wondered when you were going to bother telling me about it. If you're expecting me or the order to intervene, you're wasting your breath. We have long arms, but the upper echelons of the Swiss government are out of our reach. That's a problem that you're going to have to sort out on your own."

"Anything?" Mario asked as Toscanelli ended the call.

"Nothing so far. There's no point in moving from here, so we'll just check out of the hotel and find somewhere else to stay. That will at least make it look as if we're obeying that Swiss official. But until Vitale comes up with something definite, we're stuck here and there's nothing else we can do."

But a few minutes later, sitting in their hire car having collected their bags from the hotel and paid the bill, he changed his mind.

"No, we can't just sit here," Toscanelli said. "This is the first place that Swiss guy will look for us, which is bad enough, but I'm also pretty certain that Mallory and Jessop are long gone."

"I agree," Mario said. "Getting out of here is a really good idea. The problem is that we don't even know which direction to head."

"We don't know, but I think we can make a guess." Toscanelli opened up a relief map of central Switzerland and pointed at their present location. "We're here, and while we don't know what the English pair have in mind, it makes sense that they would want freedom of movement, and that really means they must have headed north. If you look the map, down to the south of the town there are basically only two roads, one heading east and the other one going south along the shore of that lake. We know these two are cautious, and so I don't believe they'd have taken either of these routes, just because they'd have a huge lack of options if they did. One roadblock could trap them and that would be that. I think they've gone north. There are several roads up to the north of this place and if you go a bit farther there's a railway station and an autoroute as well. They're somewhere up there."

Mario and Salvatori both stared at the map, following Toscanelli's reasoning.

"That makes sense," Salvatori said, "but how far do you want to go?"

"Not far, and we need to stay close enough to the main roads so that when Vitale does come through with a sighting, we can move quickly." He looked at the map for a few moments, then pointed. "We'll go there," he decided. "Rothenthurm. It's got a railway station and Route 8 runs pretty much through the middle of it."

It was late evening when Mallory and Robin returned to the hotel. Implementing her plan had taken longer than they had expected, because it was immediately clear that

Richterswil was too small to provide what they needed, and so the very first thing they'd done was to drive the twenty miles or so northwest, following the shoreline of the lake up to Zürich. There, they'd separated, Mallory searching for a very particular kind of shop and an even more specific type of purchase while Robin headed in a completely different direction with a different aim in view.

The first two places Mallory tried had nothing suitable, but in the third one he found almost exactly what Robin had told him to look for. It was more expensive than he had anticipated, and the shopkeeper was notably inflexible about the price, but he did have sufficient cash to cover it. Robin had had a slightly easier time of it, because the very first shop she went into was exactly suited to her needs. She made a number of purchases, and then insisted that the shopkeeper comply with two other requests before she handed over the money.

They met up back at the car, with two more tasks to achieve. The first took less than five minutes at a garage, while the second took very little longer. Although that was a crucial part of Robin's scheme, it proved to be almost the easiest job of the lot, the company they selected having both the materials they needed and a complete lack of curiosity about their objective. The staff there also expressed no doubts at all about the description Mallory inserted in the appropriate field on one of the forms that had to be completed.

They'd celebrated with a hasty meal in a backstreet restaurant before driving back to their hotel.

"I do rather wonder if all that lot was overkill," Robin

mused when they walked back into the bedroom. "I mean, we could have just gone for it. We're quite close to the border with Liechtenstein. We could have stuck everything in the back of the car and driven out of here."

"The only problem with that idea is that Switzerland isn't part of the Schengen group—which seems to be falling apart anyway—but if we'd crossed the Swiss border in the car, there's a pretty good chance that we would have been stopped and perhaps the vehicle might even be searched. I have no idea what Swiss laws are about the removal of ancient relics from the country, but I'm reasonably certain they wouldn't just say that it was all okay and wave us through. This way is definitely safer. A lot more complicated, but a whole lot safer."

"So we'll cross the border tomorrow, in daylight?"

Mallory nodded. "Crossing at night is probably a bad idea, simply because the crossing points will be much quieter. But tomorrow morning there should be a good flow of vehicles in both directions and we should be able to slip through unnoticed in the traffic."

"Nothing?" Marcel sounded incredulous. "Two people can't just vanish like that, not in a country like Switzerland."

"We have no record of any credit card transactions," his assistant said, "and no indication that they have taken a hotel anywhere or hired another car. In fact, according to the company from which they hired the original vehicle, they're still driving around in it. The only positive indication that they are still in the country is that their passports haven't been scanned at any of the airports or border crossing posts. But as you know, that isn't entirely foolproof."

"And there's nothing else?"

"Just one unconfirmed and inconclusive report. A vehicle that might have been the one they hired when they arrived in Switzerland was recorded by a traffic camera in Zürich a couple of hours ago. The car was the right make, model, and color, but it was in fairly heavy traffic and the camera did not record a clear image of its registration plate. The officer I spoke to was only prepared to say that it might been the car we're looking for. According to the registration database, there are just over thirty cars in Switzerland that could be a match, vehicles that have the right partial registration and are the correct model and color."

Marcel nodded. It wasn't much, but it was better than nothing.

"Which direction was it heading?" he asked.

The assistant looked at the printed report in his hand. "It was on the southern outskirts of the city and it was heading north, toward the center."

"That would also take it toward the airport," Marcel said. "Increase surveillance there and around Zürich itself. If they try to board an aircraft, arrest them on suspicion of stealing valuable archaeological material. And the moment there any other sightings of the car, call me."

He pulled up a detailed map of Switzerland on the screen of his desktop computer and studied it for a few moments. Then he appeared to come to a decision.

"There are too many places for these two people to hide," he said. "We need to find them and flush them out as quickly as possible. Implement the second phase of the search immediately. If you have any problems with the media, refer them directly to me."

41

Switzerland

They had an early breakfast in the hotel and then returned to their room to pack their few possessions. They were almost ready to leave when Mallory's attention was drawn to the television screen on the opposite side of the room. They'd put it on more or less as a reflex action when they woke up that morning, and while Robin had been taking a shower Mallory had flicked through the channels hoping to find something in English that wasn't a news program.

He had left the set tuned to one of the local Swiss channels with the sound muted, and even as he watched the moving images a sense of cold and compelling familiarity washed over him, because what the screen was displaying at that precise moment was quite definitely the valley at the end of which the forked waterfall tumbled into the pool at the base of the cliff.

He grabbed the remote control, aimed it at the television, and increased the volume.

The newscaster or reporter was speaking in German and Mallory glanced across at Robin to see if she was listening, which she was. But then any doubt about the substance of the report was immediately removed when two photographs, undeniably showing both Mallory and Robin, appeared on the screen behind a newscaster sitting in a studio. And then a strapline appeared at the bottom of the screen giving a number for people to call. And, again, there was no doubt about the organization that was interested in them, because beside the number was a single word: *polizei*. As the newscaster moved on to a different story, Mallory turned to Robin.

"What was all that about?" he asked.

"Nothing good," Robin replied. "I didn't follow everything in that report, because my German's not that good, but apparently we're wanted by the police, and not for stealing antiquities or anything as mundane as that. According to that reporter, we're wanted for murder."

"The Italian in the tunnel," Mallory said as realization dawned. "We need to get out of here, right now."

As if to emphasize his words, at that very moment they heard the distant sound of a police siren, steadily getting closer.

"I hope that's nothing to do with us," Robin said, standing up and picking up her computer case. Mallory had already placed all the deeds in the chest, which was in the soft bag they'd bought to conceal it.

As they walked to the door of the bedroom, they both realized that the noise of the siren had stopped abruptly.

"We'll take the fire escape," Mallory said. "I don't know much about the Swiss police, but that car could well be coming for us, using the siren to cut through the traffic, and then killing it close to their destination so as not to spook the targets. Maybe the receptionist saw the same news report that we did, or perhaps an earlier version, and made the call."

The fire escape was at the end of the corridor opposite the main staircase. Mallory walked briskly over to it and gave the horizontal bar a hard shove to open it. From somewhere behind him he heard the sound of an alarm. Obviously there was a trip on the emergency exit that indicated when it had been opened. He ignored it and headed down the metal staircase outside the building, carrying the soft bag containing the chest, the heaviest single item, and with his computer bag slung over his shoulder. Robin was close behind him lugging everything else—they were traveling light, and apart from the chest they had only an overnight bag and their two computer cases.

The hotel had no dedicated parking area, only a drop-off zone in front of the main door, and Mallory had left their hire car on a side street behind the building. At the bottom of the fire escape, he turned left and began to walk as quickly as he could along the pavement toward their vehicle, Robin easily keeping pace with him.

When he was a few yards away from the vehicle, he used the remote control to unlock the doors, and the moment he reached it he lifted the lid of the trunk and swung the soft case inside, followed by his computer bag. The two items Robin was carrying followed immediately. Then Mallory headed for the passenger-side door, handing the keys to Robin as he did so.

"Just in case," he said. "You're better at this than I am."

In a series of economical and fluid movements, Robin sat down in the driver's seat of the hire car, depressed the clutch pedal, started the engine, engaged first gear, and altered the position of the rearview mirror. Then she pulled out from the side of the road, buckling her seat belt as she did so. She accelerated gently, knowing that squealing tires and aggressive driving would just make it more likely that somebody, and especially a police officer, would see them.

Because she was constantly checking her mirrors, Robin very clearly saw two uniformed figures appear behind the hotel to stare up and down the street, just as she made a left turn.

"Good call on the siren," she said. "Two members of the Swiss thin blue line have just appeared at the back of the hotel. I don't think there's any doubt who they were looking for."

"Did they spot the car?"

"No idea, because I turned off the street at pretty much the same time, but they probably did. So where to?" she asked.

"That's a bloody good question," Mallory said.

"And have you got a bloody good answer? Because we're coming up to a main road and I need to go either left or right."

"Because they plastered our faces all over the Swiss television network," Mallory said, "trying to cross the border probably isn't going to work. They're bound to have our mug shots there as well. Maybe we should have tried to do that last night after all. I think we should just try to get out of this town and head south or west while we try to figure out what to do next."

"Got it," Robin said, and swung the car to the right at the T-junction. She increased speed only to the legal limit, again to avoid attracting attention, and then took the next westbound road she saw, the 388 signposted to Gruenfeld.

Once again, Mallory was quietly impressed by Robin's skill behind the wheel. The hire car was fitted with a diesel engine, and she used the gearbox the way the conductor of an orchestra uses his baton to keep the engine revolutions at the optimum level, the band where the motor would generate the most power and torque. The changes were so slick it was almost like being driven in a car with an automatic gearbox. The moment she cleared the town limits and drove onto the open road, she really wound it up, using the whole of the road where appropriate and safe to do so.

"I think it was the racing driver Graham Hill who said that his job was basically straightening out corners," Mallory said, "and for the first time I can see exactly what he meant."

Robin nodded, and a slight smile crossed her face, but she didn't respond, her concentration absolute.

A couple of minutes later, Robin saw the unmistakable

flashing of the lights on a roof bar of a police vehicle some distance behind them, as the road swung around in a wide curve to the south.

"We've got company," she said, "but quite a long way back. Maybe half a mile or so."

Mallory turned round in his seat to look through the rear window of the car.

"Can you lose them?" he asked.

"That depends on the driver and what car he's sitting in. This rental isn't exactly the fastest thing on the road, and if he's in a big-engined BMW sedan or something like that, he's going to reel us in no matter what I do. But if he's in an SUV, I'll leave him eating my dust. But," she added, "that's not what I'm worried about. It doesn't matter how good a driver you are or how fast a car you've got, the solid fact is that you can't outrun the police. They can set up roadblocks, vector other vehicles to join the chase, and ultimately stick a chopper in the air and track you that way. We can't outrun him, and I'm not sure we can outdrive him, so what we really have to do is lose him."

"And that," Mallory responded, "means we have to opt for plan B. It's sooner than I was expecting to have to do it, but we both know what's involved. And right now I don't see we have any other options."

"Got it. Let's hope it works."

"We're just coming up to the junction with the A3 autoroute," Mallory said, just moments later. "Do you want to try losing him on that?"

Robin shook her head. "Definitely not. Too few exits

and it's too easy to block that kind of road. We're better off sticking to the back doubles."

Toscanelli's mobile rang, and when he snatched it up he saw that the caller was Silvio Vitale.

"I hope he's finally found something," he said, swiping his finger across the screen to answer the call.

"If you're not in the car, get in it and start driving," Vitale instructed. "One of our tertiaries working for the local police force has just reported that the targets have been seen driving away from a town named Richterswil near Lake Zürich and are heading south more or less toward you. The Swiss police are in pursuit, but they haven't caught them yet. Keep this line open, and I'll relay the position information as soon as I get it."

"We'll be mobile in two minutes," Toscanelli promised.

Salvatori was the fastest driver of the three of them, so he took the wheel and steered the car out of Rothenthurm and took the main road heading north. And until Vitale came through with any further information, that was all they could do, and Toscanelli knew it.

"The targets are southbound on the 388," Vitale reported. "According to my contact, if they stay on that they'll join Route 8 at a place called Schindellegi, and that road runs south direct to Schwyz, so if you start heading north there's a good chance you'll be able to intercept them, hopefully before the Swiss police do."

"We're on that road right now. We weren't at Schwyz. We moved north to Rothenthurm last night, and we're just leaving the town. That puts us only about ten kilometers south of Schindellegi."

"Are you armed?" Vitale asked.

"We were," Toscanelli responded, sounding irritated, "but the Swiss group that intercepted us by the waterfall took our pistols. We haven't had time to do anything about that yet."

"Well, the good news is that the targets probably aren't armed, either, so it'll be a level playing field. You'll just have to improvise. Don't forget you can use the car as a weapon. Force them off the road somewhere."

"And if the Swiss police are right behind them?"

"Then that's your problem. You'll just have to work it out. But I can give you a name that will help. Another of our sympathizers is a minister in the Swiss government. He would rather his name wasn't mentioned in this incident, but if there is no other way to obtain the chest, you are authorized to state that you are acting on behalf of Gunther Kleinmann, and he will confirm this if the police contact him. They will have access to a confidential directory that will list his telephone number. But whatever happens, don't come back without that chest and the documents inside it."

"He's still there," Robin said, "but I don't think he's any closer."

Mallory didn't respond immediately because he was using the GPS and mapping facility built into his smartphone to try to work out a way of losing the police car.

"At the end of this straight piece of road," he said, "there's a gentle right-hand bend, looks quite fast. Then the road straightens up and there's a gentle left-hand bend. Maybe a hundred yards after the first bend there's a turning on the right. If the cops aren't in sight, take that. The road gets narrower and ends up winding its way into the hills, and there are lots of turnings up there where we can lose ourselves."

"Understood."

As they reached the first bend, Robin checked the mirror, but the police car was not in sight. She braked firmly but gently so as not to leave obvious skid marks on the road, then made the turn onto a much narrower road and accelerated hard. After a couple of hundred yards, the road bent quite sharply around to the left, and once they made that turn they were completely out of sight of the other road.

"Now that we've got some breathing space," Robin said, slowing down slightly, "what do we do next?"

"Keep going," Mallory said. "It won't take the Swiss plods long to realize that we must have turned off somewhere. They'll start backtracking and punch a chopper into the air, and sooner or later they'll find us. So we need to make sure that when they do reach us, it's at a place of our choosing, where we still have some control."

Mallory studied the map on his phone for a minute or so while Robin concentrated on keeping the car moving as quickly as possible along the road he had told her to take.

"This area is a warren of roads following the valleys and leading up into the mountains," he said. "We've got two choices, as I see it. We can keep dodging the police, getting ourselves deeper and deeper into the Swiss countryside and eventually being cornered, or we can pick our own spot to end this and just wait for them to find us. Hopefully we'll be able to walk away if we do it right."

"We talked about it," Robin said, "and I still think it's the only option we have. Let's do this on our terms."

Mallory nodded.

"Right," he said. "In a minute or two you'll come to a Y-junction. Take the left fork. It might be signposted to a place called Hütten. When we get to that village, we'll turn left and start climbing. That'll take us over a river and up into the hills. Then we can pick a spot and just wait."

A few minutes later, they saw a scattering of houses that marked the beginning of the village. Robin slowed down and they both started looking for the junction Mallory had described.

"There," he said, pointing to the left-hand side of the street, where a narrow road angled off toward the higher ground.

Robin indicated and took the turning. This road followed the contours of the land, meaning that it was rarely straight. After about a quarter of a mile, and just after a sharp bend to the right, they saw a bridge over the river Sihl right in front of them. They crossed it and immediately the road turned back on itself, and then swung the other way again almost immediately. There was a left-hand junction on that bend, but Mallory pointed to the right and they followed the road around the side of the hill.

From this vantage point, significantly higher than the

land they had just left; they could see some distance behind them.

"I can see flashing lights again," Mallory said, looking back over the valley. "I didn't think it would take them long to find us."

He leaned forward and peered through the windscreen, looking up into the sky.

"There's a helicopter," he said, pointing. "Probably two or three thousand feet above us. That'll be relaying information to the local control room and probably direct to the cars on the ground as well."

"This road's a dead end," Robin said. "I just saw a sign. Where do you want me to stop?"

"Somewhere open, where we can see anybody approaching us, so ideally above the tree line."

A couple of minutes later, Robin steered the car off the road and onto a rough track that petered out after only a few yards. Beyond it, the ground climbed gently toward the nearest peak.

"Will this do?" Robin asked.

"It's pretty nearly perfect," Mallory said. "Let's get moving."

He opened the trunk of the car, lifted out the bulky soft bag, and strode away with it up the slope. Robin followed a few feet behind him carrying the other purchase they had made the previous evening.

When they got about a hundred yards clear of the car, they stopped on a slight rise that offered them a clear view of their surroundings. Mallory lowered the soft bag to the ground, released the zip, and lifted out the contents, the ancient wood of the chest glowing in the sunlight.

Then they just stood there, waiting.

"They've stopped," Vitale said. "I'm getting the feed through our tertiary at the same time as the police on the ground. Stand by for a location. Right, it's a dead-end road above a village called Hütten."

He passed Toscanelli the correct grid reference.

"We're less than two minutes away," the Italian said, checking the map, and urged Salvatori to drive even more quickly.

"According to the crew in the helicopter," Vitale added, "the two targets have left the vehicle and have walked up the hill where it's parked. Mallory is carrying some kind of box."

"That must be the chest with the deeds. But what the hell is he doing? He can't get away."

"No doubt you'll find out in a few minutes," Vitale said. "And according to my source, the helicopter is carrying a sniper team, and they'll be dropping them off anytime now."

Mallory watched intently as the helicopter came to a low hover a couple of hundred yards away to their right. A single figure disembarked from the aircraft and immediately vanished from sight.

"The Swiss are playing for keeps," he said. "I think that chopper's just dropped off a sniper."

"Are you sure?"

"No, but I can't think of anybody else likely to be wearing a ghillie suit, carrying a rifle, and being ferried around in a Swiss military helicopter."

Robin shivered involuntarily.

"I hope to hell this works," she said.

They could now both see and hear the approaching police car winding its way up the hill road, siren blaring and lights on the roof bar flashing a sporadic accompaniment. Just before it turned up the short path that Robin had taken, the helicopter swooped low over the limited area of level ground by the road and then landed.

The sound of the twin jet engines died away to a whine as the rotor disk visibly slowed its rotation. As soon as the rotors came to a stop, the rear doors opened and three men appeared. One was also wearing a ghillie suit, but he was carrying what looked to Mallory like a combat shotgun rather than a sniper rifle, and he guessed that it was a two-man team—a sniper and a spotter—but because of the close range and open terrain the sniper was able to work alone. The spotter, he assumed, would probably be in radio communication with his partner, and would be there to quite literally call the shots.

Somewhat incongruously, the other two men were both wearing dark suits. All three stared up the hill to where Mallory and Robin were standing, the ancient wooden chest in front of them. The crew of the police car stepped out of their vehicle at that moment, and one of the men wearing a suit walked over to them, appeared to show some form of identification, and then issued instructions to them.

"I can see a helicopter," Salvatori said, "just around the next corner. It looks like a military bird. And there's a police car parked a few meters off the road as well. What do you want me to do?"

Toscanelli hesitated for a few moments, then nodded.

"I'd hoped to beat them to it," he said, "but now we really have no choice. Drive up and park next to the police car and we'll try to talk our way into getting the chest."

Salvatori swung the car off the road and braked it to a stop. The three men climbed out and strode briskly toward the two waiting police officers. But they never got there.

"I thought I told you to get out of Switzerland," an unpleasantly familiar voice said, and Marcel moved into view from the other side of the helicopter. "What are you doing here? And how did you find out what was going on?"

"We have contacts," Toscanelli said. "High-level contacts in your government. We're working on behalf of Gunther Kleinmann. If you check with him, he will confirm that. He has authorized us to take possession of the chest that the English couple found in the cavern."

"Has he, now? The bad news for you is that I outrank Kleinmann and, more important, I'm here on the spot, so it'll be my decision. But you'd better get used to the idea that you won't be taking possession of that relic. And I'll be talking to Gunther about this."

Marcel shook his head, then motioned one of the

policemen forward. He spoke to him in rapid German, then turned back to Toscanelli.

"You will stay here while we resolve this situation. If you move from this spot, I've instructed this officer to shoot you. Do not make the mistake of thinking that he will not do so. Here, I am the law, and he will obey me."

Then Marcel turned away and walked back to where his companion and the spotter were waiting.

"This looks like the reception committee," Mallory said, looking down the hill to where the two men dressed in suits were walking steadily toward him, the spotter in the ghillie suit a few paces behind, his combat shotgun held ready for any trouble.

He bent down and, out of sight of the approaching three men, released the cap on the metal container that they had purchased in the garage in Zürich the previous evening.

"Are you doing it now?" Robin asked.

"No, not yet. I'm just getting ready. We'll stick with what we planned."

When the men were about fifty yards away, Robin leaned over and gave Mallory a brief kiss full on the lips.

"Wish me luck," she said, then turned and walked down the hill to meet the approaching trio.

The moment she started moving, the three men stopped and just watched her. The spotter murmured something into the earpiece he was wearing, and immediately the bright red dot of a laser designator appeared on Robin's back and held steady as she walked down the slope.

"You must be Robin Jessop," one of the men wearing a suit said. "My real name is unimportant, but you may call me Marcel."

"I don't think we're going to have a long enough acquaintance to get to know each other on Christian name terms," Robin replied sharply.

"Perhaps not. First, let me congratulate you on locating the Templar Archive. We've been searching for it, off and on, for about the last five hundred years. I presume you found some clue that everybody else had missed?"

"More like a series of clues, really, but how we found it isn't nearly as important as what we should do with it. I'm a bookseller. I specialize in antiquarian works, and what I've read in those deeds has convinced me that the entire archive is of immense international importance."

"Maybe, but I—" Marcel said, but Robin immediately interrupted him.

"Please, let me finish. As I said, it's a hugely important archaeological find, one that would add enormously to our understanding of the medieval period and specifically clarify the way that the Knights Templar conducted their financial business. On the other hand, and I hate saying this with every fiber of my being, it's an incredibly dangerous collection of records. In the wrong hands, it could create havoc throughout Europe."

She paused briefly and pointed down the hill at where Toscanelli and his two companions stood, glowering up at her. "I can see that you've already encountered some of the Italians who've been dogging our footsteps. When I mentioned the 'wrong hands,' those were exactly the kind of people that I had in mind. I don't know what they would do with the archive if they got possession of it, but I'm quite sure that studying it properly and scientifically would come quite a long way down the list."

Marcel nodded.

"A remarkably accurate analysis, if I may say so," he said. "So what are you suggesting?"

"I'm not suggesting anything," Robin replied. "We've already decided, my partner and I, that the only safe thing to do with the archive is to utterly destroy it."

She turned back toward Mallory and gave a brief nod. "We're not prepared to hand it over to anybody, here or in any other country, simply because we can't trust anyone else's motives. So we're going to destroy it ourselves right now to make sure."

Behind her, Mallory opened the lid of the chest and then upended the red can of petrol that they'd bought in the garage, splashing the highly volatile liquid over both the ancient wood and the paper and parchment documents that were inside it. Once the can was empty, he replaced the cap, took a step back, fished in his pocket for a box of matches, struck one, and dropped it straight into the chest.

There was an audible *whump* as the fuel ignited, and a sheet of flame leaped some three or four feet into the air as the fire immediately took hold.

For a moment, Robin wondered if Marcel—or whatever his real name was—was going to try to intervene. The police car would almost certainly carry a fire extinguisher as part of its standard equipment. But he just stood there, apparently quite relaxed, watching the conflagration as both the ancient documents and the wooden chest were steadily consumed by the flames.

"I think," Marcel murmured, as the flames began to die away, "that that is what you English call a fait accompli. I don't disagree with your motives, but I would have very much liked to get the documents studied before they were destroyed. But rest assured, if we had taken possession of them, ultimately we, too, would have consigned them to the flames. They were just too dangerous, and potentially too destabilizing, to be allowed to exist."

"So what now?" Robin asked. "We saw the television news report that said we were wanted for murder."

Marcel nodded. "Once we realized that you had found a way out of the cave system, most probably with the Templar Archive, we initiated an immediate search for both of you. But somehow you managed to evade all of our normal surveillance procedures, and so the only recourse we had left was to get your faces out there so that the ordinary citizens of Switzerland could help us find you. And there was, after all, a dead man lying somewhere in the cave. Somebody was responsible for that, and it was a convenient hook to use in the police report."

"But you do know, I hope, that we had nothing to do with it. We have no idea how he died, but we assume that he was probably caught by one of the Templar booby traps hidden in the cavern."

"I do know that. The police report was my idea, and I will ensure that the appropriate steps are taken to sanitize the record and eliminate your details from it."

"Thank you. I've recorded what you just said on my phone, just in case there's a problem in the future. And so I ask you again, what now?"

Marcel looked behind her, up the slope to where the last few bits of the wooden chest were still burning fitfully.

"I think we're done here," he said, "and as far as I'm concerned you're free to go. I'll ensure that you experience no problems at any of our airports if you fly home or at our border crossings if you decide to drive out of the country. Thank you for locating the archive, and thank you again for doing the right thing with it."

As Marcel turned away, the red laser designator on Robin's back snapped off. Mallory walked down the hill to join her, and together they made their way back to their hire car.

"You haven't heard the last of this, Mallory," Toscanelli spat as they walked past him. "If it's the last thing I do I'm going to kill you. Both of you."

"Are you?" Mallory said. "You've tried before a few times, as I recall, but you really don't seem very good at it."

"I don't know if it's of any interest to you, Marcel," Robin said, "but this man is wanted for murder in England."

Toscanelli's face paled as he realized the implications of what she had just said.

"Is he, now?" The Swiss government official sounded interested. "In that case," he said, "it might be as well if I made a couple of phone calls as soon as I get back to the office."

The Italian glared at Mallory and Robin, then turned

tail and strode back to his car with his two companions. Seconds later, it drove off down the road at speed.

"You've obviously met him before."

"Yes. He nearly killed us in Britain and later on tried again in Cyprus," Robin said.

"It might help you to know his name. His passport was copied when he entered the country. A routine precaution. He's Marco Toscanelli, or at least that's the name in his passport. Perhaps the British police could create an international arrest warrant for him. Obviously we can't hold him here in Switzerland, because he's committed no crime here that we're aware of, and we have received no request from any other country to arrest or extradite him."

Marcel nodded to Robin, briefly shook hands with Mallory, then climbed back into his helicopter with his companions. The jet engines on the aircraft started up with a whine that grew into a roar. The rotors began turning and it lifted up into the air. The pilot flew just a short distance to pick up the sniper from the hillside, and then it climbed into the air and quickly vanished out of sight behind the mountain.

Without a word, two police officers climbed back into their vehicle, reversed it onto the road, and drove away.

Robin stepped over to Mallory, wrapped her arms around him, and squeezed him tight.

"For a moment," she said, "I thought we weren't going to get away with it."

"O ye of little faith," Mallory replied. "Let's get out of here."

42

Dartmouth, Devon

Three days later, Mallory walked into Robin's antiquarian bookshop in Dartmouth and nodded to Betty, who was making coffee behind the counter. He sat down at one of the small round tables Robin had positioned in the shop, and accepted both a cup of coffee and a slice of Betty's excellent homemade carrot cake.

The bell on the door rang and a few moments later Robin sat down in the seat opposite him.

"Feeding your face already, I see," she said.

"It's only one slice," Mallory said.

"It's very difficult to have only one slice of any of Betty's cakes, and I'd like you to remember that. Did you contact that irritating man Wilson?"

Mallory nodded. "I even spoke to him in person. I gave him Toscanelli's full name, but he said there wasn't much the police could do unless he came back to Britain.

I told him that Marcel had suggested issuing an international arrest warrant, and he just muttered something about there being better uses for a few sheets of paper. Anyway, at least he knows, so now it's up to him."

"Let's just hope we don't see those Italians again," Robin said. "By the way, I've had a delivery. While you're here, you can give me a hand unpacking it. Once you've finished your coffee, I mean."

Ten minutes later, Robin released the two fabric bands securing the lid on a heavy-duty black plastic box, the outside covered in canceled shipping labels, courier information, and details of the sending company. Inside the box, underneath the packing material, were several obviously old books, the musty smell of old leather quite unmistakable.

"You found a couple in English," Mallory said, picking out two of the books and looking at the titles. "The rest are all in German."

Robin nodded.

"I had to take what they had in the shop in Zürich," she said. "I was lucky that I could talk them into letting me take the box to the post office, because that gave us time to put the other things inside it."

She lifted off the last few of the old books. Below them, arranged in neat layers, were all the deeds of gift and irrevocable transfers that had composed the most secret and most important part of the Templar Archive. She lifted out the pieces of parchment and vellum almost reverently and placed them on an empty shelf in the bookcase beside her.

"What will you do with them?" Mallory asked.

"Right now I don't know. They need to be properly studied and analyzed, so I'm thinking maybe I'll hand over one or two to the British Museum, but I really haven't decided yet. It was a shame that we had to burn the other documents you took from the larger chests in the cave. But they really were of no particular value compared to these, so I guess it was a good trade-off. And you were lucky finding that late medieval chest in the Zürich antique shop."

Mallory nodded. "I was gambling on the fact that none of them, not even the Italians, had actually seen the small chest, so as long as I've found something that was more or less the same size as they were expecting, I guessed that we could fool them. Which we did. And has the real one arrived yet?"

"Yesterday," Robin said, pointing at a heavy-duty cardboard box tucked in one corner of the shop.

Mallory picked it up and walked over to where Robin was sitting. Taking a knife from his pocket, he sliced through the fabric tapes holding it together, noting as he did so the prominent label affixed to the top of the box, which described the contents, in German, as "reproduction medieval chest, quantity one," accompanied by details of the shop where he'd apparently bought the item and labels affixed by the Zürich branch of an international courier company.

He reached inside the box and lifted out the ancient chest, the lid closed and locked and the lethal blades secured by the nails he'd inserted to lock the mechanism.

"It's still bloody impressive," he said, "bearing in mind

how old it is. Another genuine medieval antitheft device in perfect working order."

He checked that all three of his locking nails were in position, then took a double-ended Allen key from his pocket and unlocked the chest. He lifted the lid and looked inside.

"We'd never have got it through customs with all the documents inside it," Robin said. "Splitting them was the only way it was ever going to work, just in case any customs officer along the route insisted on opening the box and looking inside."

"True enough. So, what are you going to do with it? You can't really flog it on eBay, can you?"

"Definitely not. Either it'll have to go to a proper auction house in London, which might be awkward if they ask any questions about provenance, or it'll end up as a gift to a decent museum. Or maybe I'll just keep it around as a kind of unusual souvenir from Switzerland."

"Personally I think I'd keep it."

He sounded a little preoccupied, and Robin looked closely at him.

"What is it?" she asked.

"I've just seen something that's a bit odd," he said. "Have you got a ruler?"

"A ruler?"

"Yes. Measuring stick, that kind of thing."

"I do know what a ruler is, thank you."

She walked over to the counter. Betty saw her coming, opened one of the drawers, and gave her a plastic ruler about eighteen inches long.

Mallory took it and placed it vertically against the outside of the chest.

"Seventeen and a half inches, near enough," he said.

"So?"

Then he put the ruler inside the chest and measured the internal depth.

"Fifteen inches," he announced. "But the wood on the sides of the chest is only about an inch thick. So why is the base about two and a half inches thick?"

"Good question. Does it feel like it's solid wood?"

Mallory picked up the chest again and hefted it in his hands.

"No," he said. "I don't think so. It's not heavy enough. There must be a hidden compartment that we never spotted earlier."

"The circumstances weren't ideal, if you remember. So stop messing around and get it open."

There were no obvious catches or ways to release a secret door, and in the end Mallory realized there wasn't anything like that built into it: it was just a false bottom. He used a thin knife blade to slide down the inside of the chest, eased the tip between the side and the wood on the bottom, and levered it up. The panel that emerged was about half an inch thick, quite heavy, made of old wood, and so precisely cut that it was invisible to a visual inspection.

"What's in there?" Robin demanded, leaning over to peer inside. "No, wait," she added. "Use gloves. It might be fragile."

She stepped behind the counter again and returned with a pack of thin latex gloves. She handed a pair to

Mallory, who pulled them on and then reached down into the chest. He lifted out a folded sheet of vellum, brown with age, but apparently unmarked and still supple.

Robin and Betty cleared away the plates and cups from the table they'd used and spread a cloth over it. Mallory placed the vellum on it and slowly and with infinite care unfolded it.

The inner surfaces of the vellum were much lighter in color, presumably because they'd been protected both by being internally folded and placed in a closed space.

The letters on the inner surface were solid black and clearly legible, and both Robin and Mallory bent over the vellum eagerly, trying to read the text.

"Do you need me to transcribe it?" Betty asked.

Mallory looked at her in surprise.

"I've told Betty what we've been up to," Robin said in explanation. "Or most of it, anyway."

"So, do you?" Betty asked again. "Want me to transcribe it?"

Robin stared at the handwritten text on the vellum, her gloved finger tracing the course of the top line.

"It looks like Latin," she said, "but I can't read it, so I'm pretty sure it's another piece of encrypted text. Honestly this is like one of those nests of bloody Russian dolls. What do they call them? *Matryoshka* or something like that. Every time you get to a point where you think you've reached the last one, you find that it opens as well to reveal yet another doll inside it."

She shook her head in irritation, but Mallory could tell she was excited about what they'd just found.

"I suppose we could run Atbash on it," he suggested. "See if that makes any sense of it."

Robin nodded.

"Yes. I won't be able to sleep until we've found out what this is all about," she said, "so yes, please, Betty. Start on a clean sheet of paper, please. I'll call out the letters to you one at a time. If the letter isn't clear, I'll give you whatever the possible alternatives are, and you should write those in a vertical line below my first guess at the letter. I'll tell you when I see a break in the text, and you should start a new line each time I do that. Okay?"

"I'm ready when you are," Betty said, picking up a pencil and checking the point.

Mallory looked at Robin, at the fierce concentration on her face as she stared down at the lines of text on the vellum, and smiled as she read out the first letter of the text.

"Here we go again," he said.

Author's Note

Total Surveillance

Mention has been made in this novel and in the first book of this trilogy—*The Lost Treasure of the Templars*—of various surveillance systems, and the truth of the matter is that Big Brother really is watching you, using a myriad of devices and systems.

Echelon is by far the oldest global surveillance system, and that was started back in the 1960s by the Americans during the Cold War, but today it's operated by what are known as the Five Eyes: Australia, Canada, New Zealand, the United Kingdom, and the United States. The system can monitor and intercept all telephone calls, faxes, and e-mails sent by landline, broadband, or satellite that originate or terminate in or are routed through any of the five member nations, as well as other friendly territories like Germany and the Netherlands. In practice, that means Echelon sees just about everything, because most of the

Internet servers are based in America and Western Europe. It's about as near to a global surveillance network as it's possible to get, and "Echelon" is just one of several names for the system, and that's the name which is most commonly used by the American National Security Agency, who kind of run it. But Lockheed calls it "P415," and a couple of the software programs that run on it are called Silkworth and Sire.

Carnivore is different. That was run by the FBI and started in the late 1990s, but was a lot more specific, intended to be aimed at an individual target, one particular suspect or group. It was later called DCS1000, and was replaced in about 2005 by more sophisticated commercial programs like NarusInsight, but although the software and the name are now different, the system is still out there and still listening.

PRISM is an official code name for a data-mining and collection program called US-984XN that began in 2007 and ran in the States with the legal backing of the American Foreign Intelligence Surveillance Act. It was designed to tap in to data from the principal network companies, like Google, Yahoo, Microsoft, and Apple, as well as social networking sites including Facebook and YouTube. There was a leak in mid-2013 by a man named Edward Snowden, who was a contractor for the NSA, and then the protests started, because American citizens were being illegally spied upon by their own government, and because of the information he made public, they knew it. He also leaked that GCHQ at Cheltenham in Britain was a part of the system, and that meant that the same thing was happening in the U.K. The reality is that we were and we still are—all of us—being watched.

PROMIS was by far the most shameful. That program—its full name was the Prosecutor's Management Information System, hence PROMIS—was developed in the mid-1970s for the United States Department of Justice by a small American company called Inslaw. It was a very effective piece of software, designed to track individuals and identify links between them and other people, and the American government basically stole it.

They refused to pay for the enhanced version of the software, did their very best to drive Inslaw into bankruptcy so that the company couldn't take legal action against the government, and then even sold versions of the software on the black market. There were several legal actions, and almost every finding supported Inslaw's contention that the software had been stolen, but despite this the company received no compensation. The government actually replaced judges who agreed with the findings with other judges who did not, or who had been told not to support the conclusions.

One attorney general was implicated in the theft, and another one simply ignored all the recommendations of the House Judiciary Committee and reneged on every relevant agreement he had made with that committee. To say it was a corrupt administration barely even hints at the lengths the American government went to in order to avoid paying for the software program that they'd ordered, and then stolen and were using.

The final kick in the teeth for Inslaw was when the

U.S. Court of Federal Claims ruled that all versions of the PROMIS program were in the public domain, so the government could do what they liked with them. The female judge presumably had no idea what the word *copyright* actually meant, or, far more likely, she'd been told exactly what her finding should be before the hearing even started.

But the final irony is that some of the copies of the program that various American officials sold on the black market for their own personal gain almost certainly ended up in the hands of Osama bin Laden's al-Qaeda and other terrorist groups, so the software that the American government had stolen was actually used against America by terrorists, the very people whom the program had been designed to identify and locate. Now, is that ironic or what?

In short, modern electronic surveillance systems are all-pervasive. The CIA and NSA and all other three-letter agencies in America and Britain—they're often referred to collectively as "Alphabet Soup"—extract an enormous amount of data from Internet traffic. Of course, what they claim to be doing is watching out for terrorists communicating with one another by e-mail as they plan some new atrocity, and there's a thing called the Echelon Dictionary, which allows any intelligence service to choose words and phrases that they believe to be important, and that that particular surveillance software will look out for. Some of the obvious words include *bomb, explosion, weapon, assassination,* and so on.

The problem, fairly obviously, is that today's terrorists

are certainly not stupid. Fanatical and misguided, definitely, but stupid, no. Absolutely the last thing any terrorist is going to put in an e-mail is something like: "We plan to position the bomb at the United Nations building next Saturday evening at eleven o'clock." They're far more likely to say: "We will be at the farm with the donkey on Saturday evening at eleven."

Of course, some of the code words used by terrorists are quite well-known. Al-Qaeda, for example, uses the word *wedding* to refer to a planned attack or other atrocity, but the trick is to identify an al-Qaeda "wedding" from within all the tens of millions of real marriage ceremonies that might be referred to on the Internet at any one time, an almost impossible task.

And even when a potential terrorist is known about, and his communications are being monitored, clues can still get overlooked. Back in 1999 the American government started a program called "Able Danger," which was intended to source intelligence about potential terrorists and possible targets of international terrorism. According to one of the senior officers involved in the program, Able Danger identified a man named Mohammed Atta as a possible suspect. He, of course, later steered American Airlines Flight 11 into the north tower of the World Trade Center in New York on September 11, 2001. There was a lot of controversy about the quality—and even the existence—of this information, and the officer who had revealed it had his security clearance revoked and was essentially sacked, probably just to shut him up.

But whatever the truth of that, it's certain that in the

summer of 2001 Mohammed Atta was in contact with a terrorist cell in Germany, disguising his e-mail correspondence as messages to a fictitious girlfriend named Jenny. In one of them he used a rather curious phrase: "two sticks, a dash, and a cake with a stick down," which obviously meant nothing to anyone who saw it. But if you draw something like that on paper, what you end up with is the number eleven and the number nine, and that was essential information for Atta's masters in al-Qaeda, because it told them the date the attack on America would be launched. That would have enabled them to work the financial markets and make a real killing when the planes slammed into the World Trade Center, because they knew absolutely that the American stock market would tumble.

It's never been proved, though it's widely believed, that al-Qaeda bought a whole load of put options, well out of the money, on the market index and on the two airlines whose planes were hijacked. If that did happen, the al-Qaeda traders would have purchased the options through a whole flock of proxies, so tracing the ultimate investor would be almost impossible. But it would have made sense if they'd done that, because it really wouldn't be a gamble. Once those planes hit the Twin Towers, the only direction American stocks, and especially airline stocks, were heading was down.

This also highlights the near impossibility of using electronic surveillance to discover terrorist plots, because unless you know what code words the particular terrorist group is using, or the terrorists are monumentally and terminally stupid, there's almost no chance of gleaning any useful intelligence through this kind of monitoring. In fact, the Americans have admitted this in various confidential reports. Mostly it's a complete waste of time, effort, and resources.

Undeciphered Letter Code

Mention has also been made of various cipher systems, and particularly Atbash, the simplest possible single substitution code. But some early ciphers have so far refused to yield to decryption. One of the most interesting codes that has never been solved is the line of initials on the eighteenth-century Shepherd's Monument at Shugborough Hall in Staffordshire in Great Britain. The inscription is underneath a carving that is a mirror image of a painting by Nicolas Poussin, the *Shepherds of Arcadia*, a painting that is itself full of symbolism and unanswered questions. The inscription has two letters placed slightly below the line, *D* on the left and *M* on the right, and between them is inscribed "O U O S V A V V." There have been a lot of interesting theories about that, but the truth is that nobody has ever come up with a convincing explanation of what the letters mean.

The Dominicans and Roberto Calvi

In Britain the Dominicans were known as the Black Friars, as in the bridge over the Thames. That was the bridge under which the body of a man named Roberto Calvi was found hanging in 1982. He was known as "God's Banker" because he headed the Banco Ambrosiano, which collapsed spectacularly in June of that year owing something like one billion American dollars, most of which had been transferred to it from the Vatican Bank, which ultimately meant that the money came out of the Vatican's resources.

It could almost be said that Roberto Calvi had stolen the money from the pope, and if you take a somewhat jaundiced view of what happened, the result was virtually a kind of joke. Calvi had stolen the pope's money and offended the Vatican, and even if his murder wasn't actually engineered by members of the Dominican Order the "Black Friars," and nobody knows for sure whether it was or not, it's probable that the site chosen to kill him, underneath Blackfriars Bridge, was meant as a definite warning to others. It showed metaphorically that the pope's torturers and enforcers were still around and still able to take whatever action was needed to protect the pontiff.

At first his death was ruled to be a suicide, until it became quite obvious to everyone that it was simply impossible. The construction of Blackfriars Bridge means that a man of his age and physical condition simply could not have climbed up to the spot where his body was found, tied a noose around his neck, and jumped off. In short, he didn't jump. He was definitely pushed, and it had to involve more than one other person.

It seems clear that his killers chose that location deliberately, to send a definite and unmistakable message to somebody. Otherwise why would they decide to kill a man in such a public place, in the middle of one of the busiest cities in the world, with all the risks that that would entail? If they just wanted to murder him in revenge for the collapse of the bank, they could just have driven him out into the countryside somewhere, shot him or knifed him or something, and then dumped the body. The event only makes sense if it was intended as a reminder that nobody gets away with messing with the Vatican, even today.

Chartres Cathedral

Without any doubt, the Gothic Cathedral of Chartres, located in the town of the same name about fifty miles southwest of Paris, is one of the biggest and most impressive structures of any sort on earth. Roughly four hundred and twenty-five feet long, a hundred and fifty feet wide, and crowned by a tower that rises over three hundred and seventy feet, it contains over a hundred and seventy windows that basically tell the story of the Bible in stained glass. Almost as famous as the cathedral itself is the pavement labyrinth located on the west side of the nave.

Unlike a maze, which is deliberately intended to be confusing, the labyrinth has a single entrance, which is also its exit, and was probably designed to be a meditative tool, allowing worshippers to walk the path while praying or reflecting on their religious beliefs. The labyrinth is forty-two feet in diameter and contains eleven lunations or circular paths divided into four quadrants, and the total distance from the entrance to the center and back again, following those paths, is about one-third of a mile.

The present cathedral is at least the fifth, possibly the eighth, religious building erected on this site, each being destroyed in succession by fire or war or some other calamity. The existing cathedral dates from the first half of the thirteenth century, at a time when the Knights Templar were at the height of their power, and was one of about eighty cathedrals built in France during this period. It cannot now be definitely established, for obvious reasons, but it is at least possible that the construction of this great building was financed wholly or in part by the Templars.

The cathedral broke new ground in a number of different ways, including using flying buttresses to support the massive weight of the walls, which in turn allowed larger windows to be fitted, and there is some evidence to suggest that the architect was familiar with what is known as the golden ratio. This is a mathematical relationship (approximately 1:1.618) that can be found in nature, in mathematical constructs such as the Fibonacci number, and in geometric shapes such as the pentagram. It can also be applied to architecture, and can be found in both the Parthenon in Greece and in Chartres Cathedral. It produces visually satisfactory and pleasing proportions.

According to one authority, most of the major dimensions of the cathedral are unequivocally based upon this ratio and this is the principal reason for the feeling of calm and serenity that many visitors experience. And this is despite an expensive and extremely ill-conceived renova-

tion project nearing completion in the cathedral. Widely
condemned, this attempt to re-create the interior as it
would have looked just after the building had been completed has been described as a "scandalous desecration of
a cultural holy place" and an "unfolding cultural disaster."

The carvings depicting the Arc of the Covenant and
the carved inscriptions are exactly as described in this
novel.

About the Author

James Becker spent more than twenty years in the Royal Navy's Fleet Air Arm. Throughout his career he has been involved in covert operations in many of the world's hot spots, including Yemen, Russia, and Northern Ireland. He is the author of *The Lost Treasure of the Templars* as well as the Chris Bronson novels, including *The Lost Testament* and *Echo of the Reich*. He has also written action-adventure novels under the name James Barrington, military novels as Max Adams, and novels exploring conspiracy theories as Jack Steel in the U.K.